The Hunted

PETER CARTER

The Hunted

Farrar Straus Giroux   New York

*For those brave Italian soldiers who, in World War II,
helped the helpless and defended the defenseless.*

Peter Carter

Copyright © 1993 by Peter Carter
All rights reserved
Printed in the United States of America
First published in Great Britain by Oxford University Press, 1993
First American edition, 1994

Library of Congress Cataloging-in-Publication Data
Carter, Peter.
The hunted / Peter Carter. — 1st American ed.
p.   cm.
1. World War, 1939–1945—Jews—Juvenile fiction. [1. World War,
1939–1945—Jews—Fiction. 2. France—Fiction.] I. Title.
PZ7.C2478Hu 1994 [Fic]—dc20 93-34211 CIP AC

PREFACE

In 1939 Britain and France declared war on Nazi Germany. In 1940 Italy, or, rather, its Fascist dictator, Mussolini, entered the war on Germany's side.

In 1940 France surrendered. Germany occupied the north of France, leaving the south to continue a tenuous existence under a semi-puppet government headed by Marshal Pétain. This government had its offices in the town of Vichy; hence the name Vichy France.

In November 1942 British and American forces invaded North Africa. Germany took full control of Vichy France, allowing Italy to occupy a strip of French territory along the Swiss and Italian borders—roughly speaking, the old Dukedom of Savoy.

Escaping Nazi terror, many refugees moved into the

Italian zone, where all, including Jews, were protected by the Italian Army.

In July 1943 Mussolini was deposed and in September Italy surrendered. The Italian forces in France immediately, and sensibly, dashed for the mountain passes to their homeland, taking with them as many refugees as they could.

To their eternal honor, more shining than any brutal victories, Italian infantrymen, burdened enough, carried Jewish children over the mountains.

If you wish to know more about this little-known episode, read *The Italians and the Holocaust* by Susan Zuccotti (Basic Books, 1987).

My thanks to the Musée Des Alpes Chamonix, to Monsieur Gerrard Simmond, also of Chamonix, and particularly to Monsieur and Madame Martin of St.-Nicholas-la-Chapelle.

Peter Carter
St.-Nicholas-la-Chapelle
France
1992

BOOK
1

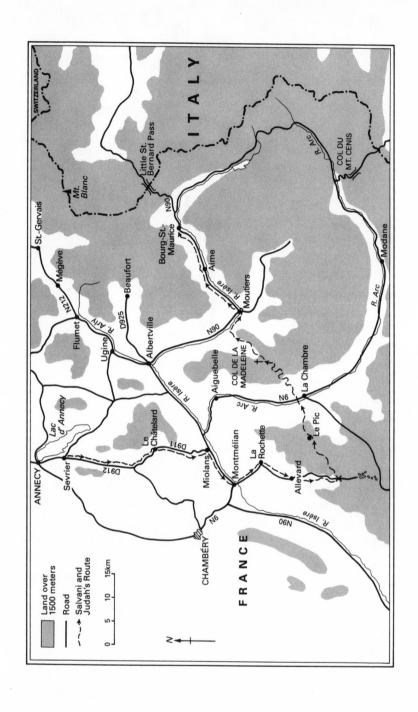

Legend

Land over 1500 meters

— Road

- - ▲ Salvani and Judah's Route

N ←

0   5   10   15km

Places and Features

SWITZERLAND

ITALY

FRANCE

Mt. Blanc

St-Gervais

Mégève

Flumet

N212

Ugine

R. Arly

Beaufort

D925

Albertville

Little St. Bernard Pass

Bourg-St-Maurice

N90

Aime

R. Isère

Moûtiers

N90

Aiguebelle

COL DE LA MADELEINE

La Chambre

N6

R. Arc

COL DU MT. CENIS

R. Arc

Modane

R. Arc

Le Pic

Le Châtelard

D911

Lac d'Annecy

ANNECY

Sevrier

D912

Miolans

Montmélian

La Rochette

Allevard

R. Isère

N6

CHAMBÉRY

N90

R. Isère

1

In the steady heat of a French September afternoon, at the ornate gateway of a château in Savoie, not far from Annecy, home of a company of the Italian Army of Occupation, Corporal of the Guard Vito Salvani slouched in a creaking wicker chair, half listening to the other men of the Guard, Privates Rosseti and Modesta, peasants both, bicker over the best way to destroy some mysterious agricultural pest—Modesta, not much more than seventeen, getting the worst of the argument from Rosseti, middle-aged, gnarled, and bitter-tongued.

"Corporal," a suspicion of tears in his youthful eyes, Modesta appealed to Salvani. "Fredo just called me a . . . a bad name."

A good-natured man, and with the bulk and muscle to

be good-natured—or the opposite if he felt like it—Salvani would normally have told Rosseti to leave the fellow alone. But it wasn't a normal sort of day, or week, or month, come to that, if anything could ever be said to be normal in wartime. And besides, for the first time that afternoon, someone was coming along the dusty road, a man in a heavy black suit and a stiff black hat, like an undertaker, leading a child by the hand.

Salvani knew the man: a French Jew, one of many scattered around the local towns and villages, refugees from German-occupied France sheltering under the benign cloak of the Italian Army. Salvani groped for the man's name . . . Fleur, a perfume manufacturer, something of a spokesman for the other Jews, rather chummy with Major Balbo, Salvani's commander, and a signore—a gentleman, ready not only to buy the impoverished Italian soldiers a drink but to sit with them in a café, turning charity into hospitality; but bearing a tragedy, his wife, Italian by birth but French by marriage, being missing in that other France where the swastika and the torture chamber ruled.

"Signor Fleur." Salvani heaved himself up. "Good afternoon, and to you, little one." He stooped over the child, who promptly hid behind his father. "Ah! What's his name?"

Fleur screwed his head around. "Tell the corporal." He turned back. "He's been told not to give his name," he said apologetically. "These days . . . these times . . ."

"Yes." Salvani felt a deep sadness at the thought that a child had to have his parent's permission to give his name, especially if the child was Jewish, and especially to a man in uniform. "I'm sorry," he began, when the boy popped out from behind the fence of his father's legs.

"I'm Judah," he shouted. "I'm strong!"—vanishing again.

"He speaks Italian!" Salvani beamed.

"His mother." Fleur's voice was troubled. "Of course, she wanted him to speak Italian as well as French."

4

"Sure." Salvani was understanding, it being perfectly natural that anyone would want to speak Italian, the language of the angels. "And so, signore, what can we do for you?"

"Ah." Fleur looked at Judah, who was creeping from his father's protective presence. "I was hoping to see Major Balbo."

"Sorry." Salvani shook his rugged head regretfully. "Can't be done. No one is allowed in without a special pass. Or out, either."

"Oh?" Fleur frowned. "And why is that?"

Salvani took Fleur by the elbow, led him a few paces away from the gateway, and peered into Fleur's sallow, refined face—which looked as if it knew how to keep secrets. "Signore, you know a thing or two."

"Know?" Fleur glanced anxiously at Judah, who was taking tentative steps toward Modesta—like, as it were, attracting like, innocence innocence. "Know about what?"

Salvani rubbed his unshaven chin. "Signor Fleur, there's something going on back home we've not been told about. We're stuck here—" He waved a hand like a shovel at the pastures and mountains. "There's been no mail for weeks, and now we're all confined to barracks. Come on, signore. You must have heard something on the British radio— yes"—as Fleur raised his slender hand—"I know it's forbidden but we'd listen if we had a set. Come on now, you owe us that favor."

"Yes." Fleur looked again at Judah, who, gleefully, was climbing on to the shoulders of an equally gleeful Modesta. "Well, there's heavy bombing, food riots, a big strike at Fiat, and they say that there is fighting in the north— between Partisans and the Fascists. But surely you know this?"

Salvani nodded. Since the Allies had invaded Italy in July—in fact, since Italy had entered the war—it had been a familiar litany—of disaster.

"But"—Fleur dropped his voice to a whisper—"there is something else going on."

5

"And what's that?" Salvani turned his bulky shoulders away from Rosseti and Modesta, who, Judah on his back, was prancing down the road making neighing noises.

Fleur opened his hands. "There were to be ships, in Nice, for us. To take us to Africa—"

"What!" Salvani raised his voice but was hushed by Fleur.

"Yes. Your government was sending them, to save us. But . . ." Fleur's eyes were pools of anxiety. "We've heard that the ships have been stopped. That's why I wanted to see Major Balbo. All we have is rumor. It's very important, Corporal."

I'll bet, Salvani thought. Ships to Africa, to safety . . . but—he sucked his chipped teeth. "I'm not sure that you'd want to go in just now. The cops are here. Plainclothesmen."

"Police!" The anxiety in Fleur's eyes turned into alarm.

"Ah, don't worry about them." Salvani was dismissive. "They're never away, complaining about chickens being stolen and what have you. But listen, I'll send Fredo up to the château and—what the devil!"

A car was coming to the château, a huge open gray car with a vast hood like a battleship's bow, an immaculate driver in field gray, and behind him two officers—one, also in gray, ramrod-straight, the other black-uniformed, sunglasses hiding his eyes, leaning back indolently, one arm bearing a bloody swastika, and with the malevolent badge of a silver skull grinning from his cap.

The huge car swung across the road, its hood pointing at the château gates. Acutely conscious of his undone tunic, of Rosseti in his frayed uniform, of Modesta, bootlaces untied and galloping down the road with a child, but also of the two stripes on his sleeve, Salvani raised an uncertain arm.

"Er . . ." he said, uncertainly, "er, what do you want—" adding, with bitter reluctance "—sir?"

The army officer looked Salvani up and down, with the

6

dispassionate stare of a vivisectionist, although his black-clad companion had swung his dark glasses on to a white-faced Fleur.

"You need a pass," Salvani said.

"Pass?" The officer said in polished Italian. "Move away, dolt." He tapped his driver on the shoulder with a swagger stick. *"Weg!"* Drive on.

The car moved forward, forcing Salvani to jump aside, the officer staring ahead.

"You . . . !" Salvani glared after the car, longing for one savage moment to grab his antiquated rifle and blast the German into eternity. "Hear what he called me?" He turned around. Rosseti was scowling, Modesta open-mouthed, but Fleur, his son in his arms, was backing away down the lane.

"Hey, signore." Salvani walked after him. "Don't worry about those pigs. They're probably just going to see the major about something."

"Something!" Fleur's voice was trembling. "You saw the man in black, the SS officer? Murderers, assassins—Jew hunters. But excuse me, please, I must go, I must." Clutching his son, who raised beseeching arms to Modesta, he hurried down the white lane toward the village.

"Look, Corporal, what's going on?" Rosseti, a cigarette dangling from his lips, scowled at Salvani.

"Search me." Salvani jammed his fists into his pockets, thinking of how the German officer had looked at him, as if he was an animal, and of what he had said. He looked at his men—Rosseti dressed as if ready to plod behind a mule in the Abruzzi, which is where he ought to have been, and Modesta, who should have been playing top and whip with the village children instead of playing at soldiers. Despite himself, he grinned. Bravo the men of the Eighth Reserve Regiment—and Christ alone knew what the Ninth looked like—trundling about in wheelchairs and baby carriages most likely.

7

But their turn would come, the turn of the supermen and their pathetic Italian mimics. In fact, Mussolini's turn had already come, although even that thought didn't wipe away the bitterness he felt, and he was still sour when, after a couple of hours, the guard was changed in a desultory way, and with his comrades he slouched to the château.

The château had been built when that part of France had been under an Italian duke, and had spires, turrets, a dome, and a line of stables, now the men's quarters and the cookhouse.

Salvani walked to the cookhouse then, with a bowl of pasta and a bottle of wine. He went to a weird addition to the château, a huge statue erected by an eccentric English millionaire which, from a distance, looked like a bulky Moor threatening the village with a club and a bomb but which was a statue of Queen Victoria holding her Imperial orb and scepter.

The French, to show their bitterness at what they regarded as the British betrayal at Dunkirk, had made a halfhearted attempt to deface the statue but it remained largely whole, battered but still formidable—rather like Britain itself—and it was regarded with some affection by the Italian troops, the more simple of whom actually thought it was a statue of the Virgin Mary and occasionally put flowers at its feet.

The plinth of the statue was marble, always cool, and Salvani strolled to it and sat down next to a Sergeant Gulli, a cynical elderly crook who was in various quasi-criminal activities with Private Agostini, the major's servant.

"Luigi." Salvani sucked up his pasta and waved his fork at the grounds. Usually the overgrown lawns were full of sprawling soldiers in their vests, or their more industrious peasant comrades hoeing private vegetable plots or clucking over their stolen chickens, but today, in the late-afternoon sun, the men were huddled in uneasy, gossiping groups, the tomatoes untended, and the chickens. "Luigi—"

Salvani pointed at the huge German car and a tiny Renault. "What's happening? Come on, you hear everything."

Gulli, immune to anything except bribes, nonetheless unbent a little. "The cops who came, in that little car, they're not local. They're Vichy. The secret police—what do you call them?"

"The Milice!" Salvani was astounded. "What are they doing here? They're not even allowed in our zone."

Gulli shrugged. "Neither are the Germans. But listen, Agostini, he says there was a big row—the major and the French. Something to do with the refugees."

"The . . ." Salvani put his plate down.

"Right." Gulli picked up the plate and began eating the pasta. "All about arresting them. Then the Germans came."

Salvani remembered Fleur's look of terror. "But," he said slowly, "if they're talking about rounding up those poor devils it means . . ."

"Means what?" Gulli looked sideways through crafty eyes.

Salvani shook his head, not knowing what it meant except that for the seven months the company had dawdled away their time in France, despised but harmless enough, he had never so much as seen a German soldier, let alone a French Milice, and now—"Why don't they tell us?" he growled.

"Tell us what?"

"What's happening." Salvani was fierce. "We've a right to know, haven't we?"

Gulli licked the plate and finished the bottle of wine. "They'll tell us when it suits them or"—more realistically—"they won't." He yawned, showing blackened teeth. "I'm going to get my head down. Never know what's going to happen. Know what I mean?"

Salvani did. Two years in the army had taught him to eat, drink, and sleep whenever he got the chance, but he didn't take Gulli's advice. Instead, he stayed on the plinth, brooding as the day slipped away. The mountains glittered red in the setting sun, and night stole in.

The dark brought its own disquiet. Although someone put a record on the enormous gramophone looted from the Englishman and Beniamino Gigli warbled of doves and broken hearts, and the tiny owls which haunted the buildings called *ting, ting, ting,* like harmonious alarm clocks, the men sprawled on the grass weren't talking, as usual, of the relative merits of Inter Milan and Turin F.C. before the war, or of their sweethearts and wives, but, in the night, where rumors sprouted like mushrooms, that they might, just conceivably might, be going home, to the land of milk and honey and never failing song, to the very heart and soul of civilization—to Italy.

Lying back against Queen Victoria's ample skirts, Salvani listened to the speculations. Like prisons or dictatorships, the army was rife with rumors, all of which in his experience turned out to be false, but this . . . With Italy falling to bits it might, just, be true. On the other hand—he looked at the ominous car outside the château and his throat constricted—they might all be about to be rounded up like cattle, stuck on a train, and herded off to the slaughterhouse of Russia. And sod that, he thought. I'll desert first, get over the Alps and home—can't be more than a three or four days' walk . . .

Deep into the velvet night, the bugler sounded Lights Out, adding, as he always did, a few unmilitary Verdi-like flourishes. The call was a mere formality, sounded because the bugler enjoyed playing rather than because he, or anyone else, expected the order to be taken seriously, but tonight, to their indignation, the men found themselves being harried to their quarters by the company sergeant major and his sergeants.

"Inside," he barked. "No, nothing has happened"—flying in the face of reason—"and nothing is going to happen.

10

Turn in!" Giving the corporals strict orders that *no one* was to be allowed as much as a peep through the windows.

He stamped away, but none of the men made the slightest pretense of going to bed. They peered through the windows and moved restlessly from room to room, rumor and counterrumor flitting through the darkness like bats.

At midnight, car doors slammed. The men crowded to the windows and saw the Milice and the Germans leave, the tiny Renault leading the huge Mercedes like a pilot fish before a shark, both driving away to a chorus of boos and catcalls.

"Well, that's over," Rosseti said. "Whatever it was."

"Yes," Salvani agreed, although thinking that *it*, whatever *it* might be, was only just beginning, driving the men to their sagging cots although he himself stayed by a window, looking at the lawns, white in the moonlight, thinking of the whiter wastes of Russia, and of his home and family, as the owls called and bats flickered against the vacant face of the moon, until he, too, lay on his bed and let sleep take him into that dark world where rumors were the truth.

2

His years of service had habituated Salvani to waking just before the bugler blasted out Reveille, but the next morning he was rousted out by Sergeant Gulli saying roughly, and concerned, "Come on, Vito, get the men turned out *quick*. Early parade. Jump to it."

Salvani and his men jumped and within minutes, blinking, unkempt, and unshaven, were on parade on the gravel drive, their rifles rattling an uncertain salute as the bugler

11

gave a blast, the Italian flag jerked unsteadily up its pole, and Major Balbo, flanked by his officers, came from the château and mounted a platform made of old wine crates.

"Men!" Balbo stared at his command with none of the semi-humorous despair which marked his usual inspections. "Fellow Italians!"

Fellow Italians! There was a murmur of surprise from the soldiers, who were more used to being castigated as a crowd of ragamuffins.

Balbo took a deep breath. "Fellow Italians, we have served here for seven months, doing our duty, behaving toward each other in a sincere, comradely Italian manner—" He paused and gazed at the flag as the incredulous soldiers stared at him, until some wag said, sotto voce, "Christ, he's going to take up a collection!"

There were muffled sniggers, some not so muffled, until the sergeant major, mustachioed whiskers bristling, roared "Silence!"

Balbo waited until the men fell silent, then, "Comrades," he said, "I have grave news for you."

The soldiers were, at once, not merely silent but attentive—and Salvani's heart sank. Grave news! That could mean only one thing; they *were* going to be sent to Russia—which was why the goddamned Germans had been at the château, arranging for a battalion of storm troopers to arrive and make sure that they did go, and he saw, not the friendly, comical château, swallows swooping across the clear pale blue sky, but a vast, icy plain littered with burned-out tanks, frozen corpses, and a few maimed, frostbitten men hobbling toward a horizon they would never reach . . .

"Grave news," Balbo said again, every man now straining to hear. "Last night"—he visibly gulped—"last night, our commander-in-chief, Marshal Badoglio, with the full consent of our King, announced that after a noble struggle, but faced by overwhelming odds, Italy has unconditionally

12

surrendered to the Allies. The war"—his voice broke—"the war is over."

There was a roar of unrestrained joy. The war over! No more danger of death or mutilation or spending years rotting in some godforsaken prisoner-of-war camp, but instead home, family, safety. Surrounded by jubilant men, Salvani stood dazed, his back pounded, thinking: I've done it! By sweet Jesus, I've come through safely. Yes!

The major, grim-faced, waited until his command had temporarily calmed down. "The war is over," he rasped, "but military discipline will be strictly enforced. All officers and noncommissioned officers to join me in my office now. Long live Italy! Long live the King!"

He stepped off his boxes and then a cry came from the ranks, a defiant voice ignoring military discipline, strict or otherwise, yelling, *"Viva la Repubblica! Viva il socialismo!"* Long live the Republic! Long live socialism!

The major half turned, his face bitter, then with a resigned shrug went into the château, followed by his officers, sergeants and corporals—the sergeant major, knowing all, staying behind to keep his mastiff's eye on the men.

In his office, a palatial, mirrored salon, Balbo waved to the men to sit and sank into a gilded chair behind a vast desk, all eyes on him—paunchy, thinning, dyed hair, pompous, not a good man, but not a bad man either, easy-going, within limits, not above a little black-marketeering, and now, despite all his braid and trimmings, shrunken, deflated, defeated. But still the commanding officer, and as the only man present who knew what was going on, a man to be listened to.

"I'll be frank with you," he said. "Communications are difficult and everything is a . . . well, a mess. But my orders are to be ready to move at a minute's notice—to Italy, of course. Via Modane and Mont Cenis Pass. That's easy enough, just a few hours' drive, so let's pack up and be ready to go. But there is one thing I want to add."

13

He drummed his fingers on the marble desk, sweating and casting a longing eye on a bottle of brandy. "I heard that shout, long live socialism. Well, maybe we're moving into a different world, I don't deny it. But let's keep politics out of this until we get home—or maybe we won't get home at all."

He sighed, the last puff of air from the balloon. "That's about it, except for the civilians."

"Civilians?" Corporal Valchi leaned forward.

"Yes." Balbo stood up, strode to the window, and frowned out at the privates, who, despite the sergeant major and the orders to maintain strict military discipline, were already opening bottles of looted wine. "The refugees. That's why the Germans are here, and the Milice. They were claiming that the Jews weren't to leave with us. But our orders are absolutely clear. *Anyone* who wants to come with us may do so, and under our protection. Understood?"

It was understood, but there was an unease, voiced by Sergeant Gulli, not a man noted for sympathy for his fellow human beings.

"Foreigners," he said. "Why should we bother with them?"

"Bother?" Balbo strutted back to his desk and without false modesty looked at himself in the mirror, smoothing his mustache and pulling in his paunch. "These people, families, came to our zone for protection. Now that we are leaving, are we to withdraw it?" He stood a little straighter, acting a part, but at least a decent one. "We may be defeated, but we have some honor left. So, get packed, and try and keep the men sober. Dismiss."

The men shuffled uneasily from the room, but Balbo called Salvani back. "I've a job for you, Corporal," he said.

"Sir?" Salvani was as wary as a fox.

"Yes." Balbo finally gave in to temptation and poured himself a glass of wine, and one for Salvani. "You speak French, don't you?"

Salvani shrugged. "A bit"—he alone among the men of the entire company having taken the trouble to come to grips with the language.

"Well, I want you to take your section and go to the village, to 12 rue Annecy, and find a man called Fleur—"

"I know him, sir," Salvani said.

"Oh?" Balbo raised an eyebrow. "All the better. Get him and bring him here, and his little boy."

"Yes, sir." Salvani downed his drink. "Er, there are other Jews in the village . . ."

"Bring them, too, of course." Balbo nodded. "All you can find. Fleur will help you. And don't let anyone obstruct you."

"No, sir." Salvani stuck out his jaw. "But can I ask you a question? I mean, back home there are laws—against Jews"—he shrugged—"not that anyone I ever knew paid any attention to them. But this—this rounding them up by the Germans and French . . . I mean . . . what do they want them *for*?" But he got no answer to that question.

Salvani gathered together his section. In his youthful, gamboling way, Modesta was eager to go to the village again, but the rest of the men, led by Rosseti, flatly refused to leave the grounds of the château.

"But it's an order!" Salvani was exasperated. "We've *got* to go."

"What do you mean, *we've* got to go?" Rosseti said. "*You've* got to go, but you can count me out," adding something extremely unpleasant about orders and what Salvani, the major, and Marshal Badoglio could do with them. "The war's over, isn't it?"

"Look," Salvani said, "we're only going to pick up a few Jews. We'll be back in half an hour."

"Sure." Rosseti screwed up his face. "And when we get back, this lot will have cleared off."

"That's ridiculous," Salvani said, but with a shadow of doubt crossing his mind.

"Is it?" Rosseti said. "You don't know much about the

army, then. Anyway, if it's so easy, why don't you go on your own?"

"I will if it comes to that," Salvani shouted. "For Christ's sake, it's just to see the Jews get here. And the kids."

"*I've* got kids," Rosseti said. "And I want to make sure I get back to them."

"And *I've* got kids," Salvani said. "And I want to see mine, too. But all right"—helpless, knowing that he was not going to hand over Rosseti to whatever authority might be left in the company, and knowing Rosseti knew that, too. "I'll go on my own. Still"—with an edge of bitterness—"you were always ready to take a drink off him, weren't you?"

"Off who?" Rosseti asked.

"The Jew, yesterday," Salvani said, feeling as if he was talking about a different century. "That Signor Fleur and the kid."

"Him!" Rosseti threw up his hands. "Why didn't you say so?"—a real person, Jew or not, with a lost Italian wife and a nice little boy, being quite a different kettle of fish from some anonymous stranger who didn't care any more for you than you did for him. "What are we waiting for? Let's go and get him."

"But—" Private Mori, an ex-unemployed and virtually unemployable laborer, none too bright, turned on Rosseti. "You said we'd be left behind. You just said that. Didn't he?" appealing to the other men.

"Ah!" Rosseti screwed up his wrinkled face. "This lot," he said, with a supreme lack of consistency, "they'll be lucky if they're ready by Christmas. Come on."

Rosseti having crumbled, the rest of the men, if not enthusiastic, were willing to go, although, to Salvani's further exasperation, they flatly refused to take live ammunition, making it absolutely clear that they were not prepared to get into anything remotely resembling a firefight, and anyway, and probably rightly, believing, as Rosseti said, *their* ammunition was likely either not to go off at all or, if it did, to explode in their pouches. Then, with an air of great reasonableness, and as a personal favor to Salvani—and once they made it clear they expected to be repaid in free drinks—they were ready to take their rifles and to fix bayonets, too.

Exhausted by the prospect of another debate, Salvani settled for that, and not less than an hour after being ordered to do so, he led his section from the château and down into the village.

3

The soldiers marched to the village at an amazingly fast pace, the thought at the back of every man's mind being that by the time they returned to the château it would be deserted.

Breathless and sweaty they arrived in the village, but, although he was out of breath, Salvani was aware of change: there were no old men under the lime trees playing *boules*, no postman dawdling on his yellow bicycle, no priest in his black *soutane* hurrying from the church for his breakfast; even the pestiferous, snarling dogs were absent. The windows of the houses were shuttered, blank and blind; the two cafés were closed; and there were none of the usual gibes: "Ice cream, spaghetti, organ grinders," from closed shutters. The word has got around, Salvani thought. They know we are out and that the Germans are coming in, so black looks now for the defeated and, no doubt, cheers and flowers for the coming conquerors—until they found out what it was like to live under the heel of the jackboot. That idea mildly cheered him as they came to the rue Annecy, which, belying its resonant name, was a narrow alley, and to number 12, a house sealed and shuttered, too.

Salvani hammered on the door with his rifle butt. There was no answer and he hammered again, the sound of the blows echoing off the walls of the alley and rousing a dog, which yammered frantically, somewhere behind the blind walls.

"No one here," Rosseti said flatly. "Right, that's it"— already on his way.

"Hang on," Salvani said. "Wait a minute. Just one minute." He opened the letter box and shouted through it. "Monsieur Fleur. Signore. It's us, the Italians—from the château. *Signor Fleur!*"

Rosseti scowled at Salvani. "I tell you, there's nobody in. Anyway"—in a tone of voice that didn't invite any argument—"I'm off."

Salvani sighed, resigned. Probably Rosseti was right. The Jews had gone, run off to find another hiding place . . . But as he turned from the door he had a disturbing vision of Fleur cowering in a darkened room clutching his child . . . listening to the hammering on the door, knowing that whoever did hammer, hammer on his door, came for one purpose only—and Salvani remembered how, in Italy, when Mussolini came to power, men in black shirts had come, hammer, hammer, hammering on doors . . .

"One more time," he pleaded.

Rosseti glared at him and he glared back. Then Rosseti threw up his hands. "Two minutes," he said. "Just two and then we're going. Right?"

"Right," Salvani said, and then, as if a signal had been given, the shutter of a window creaked open above them and a voice whispered, "Corporal?"

"For Christ's sake!" Salvani stared upward, furious. "Fleur? Get down here. Quick! Come on. *Move!*"—his rage boiling over as, seconds later, the door was cautiously opened and Fleur stood in the dark rectangle.

"What are you playing at?" Salvani shouted. "We've been banging at the door for —— hours! We're here to help you!"

"Sorry. So sorry." Fleur held out his hands in apology. "We didn't know, couldn't be sure—"

Salvani cut the apologies short. "Get the kid—what the . . . !" as, following Fleur from the house, carrying suitcases, bags, rucksacks, came one, two, three, six men and four women, followed by Judah, squeaking with delight as he wriggled past them and clasped an equally delighted Modesta by the legs.

"We heard the news on the radio," Fleur said, "and gathered together. Thank you, thank you for coming. We didn't know whether we could get to the château."

"Yes, yes." Salvani brushed the thanks aside. "Come on. Now!"

The men formed an untidy escort, Modesta holding Judah by the hand, the Jews, two ancient and bearded, one of the women fat, elderly, hobbling, inside the fence of soldiers, all of them, soldiers and refugees, fragments of a Europe shaken together by the kaleidoscope of war, and terror, and insane hatreds.

Led by Salvani, they went up the alleyway, across the deserted square, past the church and café, and saw, parked across the road to the château, a long, dark blue van with tiny barred windows, and, leaning against it, cigarettes dangling from their mouths, revolvers on their hips, four men in blue uniforms and berets, and, lurking behind them, a man in civilian clothes, his face masked by a dark slouch hat.

"Keep moving," Salvani barked. "Left," he shouted. "Left, right, left—" groaning as from the corner of his eye he saw Modesta skipping to get into step and failing, and Judah cheerfully skipping with him; like children in a playground.

"Left," Salvani shouted. "Left," drawing nearer to the police van, nearer, swallowing hard as the uniformed men spat out their cigarettes and stood up, menacingly. From behind him, from one of the Jews, he heard a muted, despairing moan, like the cry of all the persecuted and defenseless victims who had ever existed, and he saw, or thought he saw, on the faces of the Frenchmen contemptuous grins—the mark of bullies who have found easy prey. All right, he thought. Sod it. Just plain sod it. And full of inarticulate compassion and rage, he strode to the van and as the plainclothesman stepped forward, one hand menacingly inside his jacket, Salvani hit him, shoulder to shoulder, driving him sideways, in that one, deeply satisfying blow paying back the sniggering insults he had endured for seven months.

The man reeled back against the van, and led by Rosseti, the soldiers brought their rifles to the ready, showing a very serious-looking fence of bayonets, and Salvani led his charges around the van, out of the village, and on to the dusky sweet-smelling lane.

We did it! Salvani thought. Sweet Mary and all the saints, we did it!—grinning with relief as he turned and saw the Jews, white-faced, and his men, grinning too, and Rosseti, who gave a totally uncharacteristic wink—all of them light-hearted and light-footed as they made their way back to the château.

Inside the château, the grounds had lost their usual air of languor. The lawns were littered with the company's possessions: kit bags, stacked rifles, the machine gun with so little ammunition that it had never been fired, even if it was capable of firing, bedding, guitars, an accordion or two, birds in wicker cages, baskets of bread and salami, crates of wine, the gramophone with its vast horn, and packing cases containing glass and china—the officers' perks, not actually being looted but, as was understood, not being left behind for the Germans.

Salvani dismissed his men, who made a beeline for the cookhouse, profuse thanks from the Jews following them—and squeals of anger from Judah enraged at being separated again from Modesta—and led his charges to the château itself.

"Wait here," he said to Fleur, and went inside the company office, where Major Balbo and Agostini were stuffing documents into a stove.

"Sir." Salvani saluted as Balbo raised a red and sooty face. "They're here. The Jews. We've brought them."

"Jews?" Balbo frowned and then nodded. "Oh yes. Good. You have Signor Fleur?"

"Yes. And some others."

Balbo mopped his forehead. "Did you see any Germans? No? Well, they probably won't even bother with a place like this—not for a while, anyway. But did you have any trouble?"

Salvani rubbed his chin. "Some sort of police were there, with blue berets—"

"Milice," Balbo said.

"Maybe," Salvani said. "Them and a man in plainclothes, sort of in charge. They didn't like it—us and the Jews, I mean. The plainclothesman tried to stop us."

Balbo scowled. "And what did you do?"

"Just . . . well, just barged him out of the way." Salvani was diffident but nonetheless felt a slight prickle of pride.

"Did you, now?" Balbo gave Salvani a rather calculating look, as if seeing him for the first time. "That's the way. So, get some food, and see that the Jews eat, too, and tell Signor Fleur I would like to see him, now. You report to me when you've eaten."

Wondering just what the last order entailed, Salvani wandered out, directed the Jews to the cookhouse, but held Fleur back as he delivered Balbo's message.

Less elegant than the previous day, Fleur held out his hand. "I don't know how we can thank you."

Salvani scuffed the gravel of the drive with an unpolished boot. "Nothing," he said. "Nothing at all."

21

"Nothing?" Fleur looked at Salvani through skeptical eyes. "Corporal, you saved us from . . ." His voice died away for a moment. "And the way you dealt with the Milice."

"Oh, they *were* Milice, were they?" Salvani asked.

"Yes." There was bitterness in Fleur's voice. "We will never forget it, Corporal. Never."

Salvani gave an embarrassed grin. "Well, if we can't handle a few cops, we—" about to say: We might as well all go home; and then as he remembered that they *were* going home, the grin turning into one of pure delight. "But forget it, really. Just look after yourself, and"—he ruffled Judah's hair, receiving in return a glare of intense irritation—"and the little one here."

Salvani walked to where he had spotted Sergeant Gulli. Joking soldiers were loading the ramshackle truck, which, with the equally ramshackle bus, a car confiscated from the French, and a dubious motorcycle, made up the company's transport. But Salvani had no intention of joining in, thinking, virtuously, that he had done his duty and more that day. Instead, he sprawled next to Gulli, who was clearly of the same opinion and was sitting comfortably in a wicker armchair, food spread around him, and bottles of good wine, that being another commodity not to be left for the Germans when they came.

"If they come," Gulli said.

"If?" Salvani took a hunk of bread and salami.

"Ah!" Gulli waved a bottle contemptuously. "Remember the Rule. The golden rule of the army." He swigged some wine and wiped his mouth with the back of his hand. "Whatever they say *isn't* going to happen *does* happen, and whatever they say *is* going to happen won't."

But with all the cynical cunning Gulli had acquired during his long period of swindling the Italian Army, he was wrong, because as the sun began to slip toward the west, the sergeant major appeared.

"Fall in!" he roared. "Fall in!"

The men fell in, some of them who had been too anxious to prevent the Germans from tasting the wine literally so, and one, emboldened, shouted, "What's up, then? Got any news?"

The sergeant major glowered at the heckler but, surprisingly, answered. "Yes. Oh yes. I've got news. The phone has been cut off."

The cheerful babble in the ranks died away. The announcement sounded sinister, ominous. For most of the men the telephone was almost a magical instrument. And now it was cut off! It was as if some malevolent enemy, the more malevolent because invisible, was marking them down and stealing up on them as silently as a spider in its web.

"Right." The sergeant major nodded, as if to say: Now you know what it's all about. Now the summer jaunt is over. Now it's back to school, but one where the teachers wore gray uniforms and jackboots and could, and would, blow you to pieces without blinking an eye. "Salvani report to the major. On the double."

Salvani broke away and, on what passed for the double, that is to say, he took his hands out of his pockets, went into the château, passing the lieutenants and orderlies, who were still busy packing pictures and ornaments, and, to his surprise, Fleur and Judah patiently sitting in a corner, and went into the salon.

"Corporal!" Balbo beamed. "Come in, come in. Close the door. And have a drink—" He motioned toward a table. "Corporal, you will not be leaving with the men. Don't be alarmed—" as Salvani gulped on his wine. "You *will* be leaving, of course, but with me!"

Salvani stared into his glass as if it had been given to him by Lucrezia Borgia. "And why is that?"

"Ah!" Balbo stood up. "Corporal, I noted what you said this morning, about the Milice, and Signor Fleur has told me how you dealt with them. Like one of Caesar's legion-naires! A true Roman, upright, fearless—"

"You mean you want a bodyguard," Salvani said and put his glass down on the marble top with a sharp *clack*.

"A bodyguard? I, a Balbo?" The major stood up and stuck out his chin, a hand on his holster, the elbow bent outward, like a pocket Mussolini. "Not I, Corporal. No, no. I have no fears for myself. But—" He dropped his chin and his hand and stood like a normal human being. "But I am taking—personally—Signor Fleur, and his child, of course, with me in my car."

Salvani gulped again. It's a day for gulps, he thought. "With you?"

"Yes." Balbo began to pace about the salon, peering occasionally through the window to where the men were sorting themselves into groups: those chosen by the sergeant major to travel in what passed for comfort standing smugly by the bus; those cast from his favor standing sullenly by the truck.

"And the other Jews?" Salvani said.

Balbo picked up the phone, stared into it, and put it down, shaking his head. "They're coming with us, of course. But the child, the *bambino*—" He patted the air about two feet from the ground. "A drive in a car, a little comfort . . ."

"The women need comfort, too," Salvani said.

"Certainly." Balbo peered through the window again to where the men, once separated into buses and trucks, as it were, had now mingled and were engaged in a vigorous debate, obviously about who in fact was going to travel by bus or on a swaying and uncertain truck. Balbo shook his head sadly, as if he was a sympathetic outsider. "They will go by bus—the women. But the child . . ."

He's acting, Salvani thought. Putting on a show. He didn't really doubt that Balbo was concerned for Judah's comfort—who wouldn't care for a child, especially a moth-

24

erless one? But there was something exaggerated about the major's manner that suggested playacting. Salvani did not regard himself as a clever man, and he was no more cynical than anyone else who had spent half his life under a ramshackle dictatorship, but perhaps, he wondered, perhaps Balbo had been bribed by Fleur—paid to be given a comfortable, safe ride to Italy, with an armed man to look after his back. He flushed with anger at the thought of being used, and suddenly even the wine tasted sour.

"I thank the honorable major," he said, with heavy sarcasm. "I thank him for his generous offer of a ride in a motorcar, but I think it is my duty to stay with my men. It's a question of honor, sir. As you said, we have some left."

He gave a mock heroic salute and, feeling rather proud of that flourish, turned about-face and walked out of the room, where a lieutenant and Agostini were admiring a painting before packing it, and saw Fleur.

4

Fleur was in his corner, still, with his patient, impassive face, and lying across his knees, his face blurred by sleep, cradled in his father's arm, was Judah. Change father for mother and it was an image as familiar to Salvani, and any other Italian, as the back of his hand. It was a Pietà. Mary holding her crucified son.

Salvani hesitated and as he did so Fleur looked him in the face, then stared down at the sleeping child, as if to say, Look. Look at a child, not crucified—yet.

What the hell, thought Salvani. What the hell did it matter if Fleur *had* bribed Balbo? Who wouldn't bribe if it came to saving the life of his son. Anyway, the whole of Italy had lived on bribes of one sort or another for the last twenty years. And what did it matter how he himself got there, as long as he *did* get back. A few hours' drive and the entire company would be home; *and* searching for reasons, knowing Balbo, it wouldn't hurt to have another man along; thinking which, he turned on his heels and went back into the salon.

Balbo was standing at his desk, drinking brandy and calling into the telephone, "Hello? Hello? Anyone there?" But at the sight of Salvani he let the receiver drop.

"All right." Salvani didn't bother saying "Sir." "I'll go. For the kid's sake."

Balbo nodded absently, like a man with his mind on other things. "I'm glad you changed your mind. Can you drive?" he asked, as politely as a man addressing a stranger.

"A car?" Salvani grinned. "I can handle a motorbike, just about, but a car . . ."

"No, of course you wouldn't have one. What did you do, before the war?"

"A plasterer," Salvani said. "Just rough work. Nothing like this." He gestured at the elaborate swags and cornices which festooned the room.

Balbo tapped the phone, as if that might make it ring. "You are a socialist, aren't you? Oh yes—you've been heard whistling socialist songs." He smiled wryly, as if the falling of the barbed wire of rank and discipline allowed him to speak freely, like a human being. "Lieutenant Menotti wanted to have you court-martialed for that. A serious offense, you know. Or was. But I stopped it."

"Oh? And why was that?" Salvani said, thinking he might just have a little word with Menotti before he left.

Balbo shrugged. "You're a good soldier, and I wouldn't put a man in prison for a daydream. And that is what these—visions—are. Daydreams. But we'll see, won't we? When we get back to Italy."

"Yes," Salvani said. "We'll see, then."

"So." Balbo tapped the phone again. "There is just one more thing."

"And what's that?" Salvani looked through the window. The row between the men was still going on and the lawn was littered with bottles—most of them empty.

"I'm sending the men away as soon as they are ready," Balbo said. "But we are going later."

"Why so?" Salvani said.

Balbo poured himself another drink, his hand trembling.

"There might be a message, from the colonel. The phone might come back on. Orders."

"Then why send the men away?" Salvani asked.

"Did I say send? I should have said not try to stop them." Balbo stared at where, in the long shadows, the men were actually climbing on the transport.

"If they go, there's no point in us staying," Salvani said.

Balbo sipped his drink, then swigged at it. "We've had a wonderful war. Wonderful! Defeated by everyone we've fought. The Germans despise us, the enemy laughs at us, the French hate us. There have been times when I have thought of shooting myself. Do you know that?"

"No, I don't," Salvani said, wondering if Balbo was off his head.

"It's a mortal sin, though," Balbo said. "Even that way out is barred to us. But I thought that . . . that at least I could wait, here. Not be the first to run. Do you understand that, Corporal?"

"No," Salvani said.

"Well, you don't have to," Balbo said. "But I thought that if there was no news by eight I'd leave."

"All right," Salvani said.

"You don't have to wait."

"I know that. Major, you'll be doing the driving?"

"Yes."

"Then go easy on that brandy. And we *leave* at eight."

27

Salvani went back into the hall, deserted now save for Fleur and Judah, who was still sleeping. Salvani gave Fleur an encouraging nod. "Soon," he said. "Not long," and strode through the doorway and on to the drive.

"Corporal!" Rosseti stumbled toward him. "Where have you been?" He screwed up his wrinkled face. "They're telling us we've got to go on the truck! Why should they go on the bus and us on the back of that wreck? It's not right. Go and tell them. Tell the sergeant major—"

"Just get on it," Salvani said. "Or you might get left behind," going for his kit as Rosseti, struck by that appalling thought, scrambled on to the truck and wedged himself between an ormolu writing desk and a vast oil painting of Diana at the Hunt.

In his quarters, Salvani gathered his few belongings: badly darned socks, patched shirts, ragged vests, much-creased letters, a minuscule photograph of his wife and family, then sat down on a creaking cot and looked at the battered room—a row of sagging cots like his own, a pair of trousers left behind, a boot looking lonely, a half-eaten bowl of pasta, wine bottles with dregs in them, a picture of the King of Italy, his nose colored red by some joker; various scribbles on the walls: *Viva Italia!* Love from Marco. *Viva il socialismo.* Long live Stalin. Marie at the café will give you a good time! Vulgar and unpleasant suggestions as to what the incoming Germans could do to themselves—and the French. A remark by some optimist that an obscure village in Sicily was the best place on earth—to which some wag had added, "For lunatics." A political message again: "Shoot all landlords and officers"—and what would Balbo make of that, Salvani wondered—and the usual hodge-podge of obscene drawings.

Salvani lit a cigarette, sitting on the edge of the squeaking cot, a big burly man, smoking quietly in the hot, still evening. Not much to leave behind, he thought: misspelled messages and weirdly incorrect anatomical drawings. He had a hazy knowledge that other Italians, the Romans, had invaded foreign countries—and evacuated them, too—but they, at least, had left behind buildings, roads, bridges, aqueducts, temples, laws, even their own language. Now this . . . He finished his cigarette, ground the butt under his heel, stood up, took out a stub of pencil, and added his own scrawl: "At least we didn't hurt anyone." Signing it with a flourish before leaving.

Although at its best the company had shown only a slight, almost humorous resemblance to a military unit, even that façade, which had been cracking all day, had now virtually disintegrated. Half the men were drunk, some incapably so, stretched out snoring on the grass, and the other half were clearly doing their best to catch up. The men in the bus were singing a raucous medley of ribald songs, the din punctuated by the crashing and splintering of crates and packing cases, broken glass and china, as the unfortunates on the truck heaved off the loot, demonstrating their wrath, making more room for themselves, and, drunk though they might be, striking a blow at the assumption of privileges by their officers, none of whom, wisely enough, was present—the real figure of authority, the sergeant major, standing a grim observer, scowling as Salvani joined him.

"Can't do anything with them," he growled. "A rabble. It's what happens."

"Happens?" Salvani was amused.

"Yes, happens!" the sergeant major barked. "See? No order. No discipline! I'd . . ." He waved his stick, with which, in some remote, golden era, he struck miscreants and laggards. "Yes," he growled, a toothless dog, "I'd like to—"

The rest of his words were lost as the men on the truck, having chucked out several million lire worth of *objets d'art*, democratically joined in singing with the elite on the bus.

"*Goory ooory, gobberri O*
Orroby orey orroby O."

29

They bellowed—or something like it—singing lustily, laughing, whooping, the bugler blasting discordantly, the men tearfully, sentimentally, alcoholically embracing each other—

"Gobbelly Obbelly, Obelly O
Obelly Gobelly, Gobelly O."

—every man having his own words, tune, and message, a mixture of "We're going home," "Ave Maria," operatic arias, football songs, "The Internationale," insulting references to various Italian districts, comical references to comparisons between officers, sergeant majors, and chimpanzees . . .

"Something or other!" the sergeant major roared, red-faced.

"What?" Salvani cupped his ear.

"It's . . ." The sergeant major groped for words in the soggy layers of his myth-haunted brain. "It's *bolshevismo!*"

For a moment Salvani was tempted, truly tempted, to smash the sergeant major in the ear, to give him one huge, ox-felling blow, but, to the sergeant major's amazement, and somewhat to his own surprise, he burst out laughing.

"Bolshevism," he chortled, waving at the company, which now appeared to be settling in for an all-night party—a fancy-dress party at that, Rosseti of all people wearing a top hat three times too big for him, the bugler in a moth-eaten tailcoat, an amiable, half-witted gorilla from another section in a frothy ball gown . . .

"I'll do it," Salvani said, and with a mixture of cheery cajolery and beefy brute force getting all the men in the bus and on the truck—some of them protesting, as they actually believed that they had *arrived* in Italy—and finally getting the Jews on the bus and noticing that, drunk though the soldiers were, they were not so far gone as not to willingly give up seats to the women and the old men, and, highly embarrassed, having his hand kissed by them, until finally, with the sergeant major blocking the door of the bus, and a highly nervous lieutenant and sergeant guarding the truck, he was able to give a sigh of relief and walk to the château door, where he found Balbo, Fleur, and Judah waiting on the steps.

"All ready to go," Salvani said.

"Ready?" Balbo stared unbelievingly at the transports, where the men, vigor undiminished, were bawling and singing.

"They're just enjoying themselves," Salvani said. "Having a last fling."

"I ought to speak to them," Balbo said. "A last word."

"I wouldn't," Salvani said.

"No?" Balbo sounded like a man anxious to do his duty, but relieved not to have to do it.

"No." Salvani smiled sardonically. Jesus, he thought, the war ended yesterday and I'm giving orders to an officer already. The Revolution has begun! "No," he said again firmly, thinking of the menacing scribble in the barracks: *Kill all officers.* "I'll send them off. Just give me the command"—adding, with a touch of mercy—"Major."

"Perhaps that might be best." Balbo made a pretense of bracing himself and staggered backward. "Yes. Yes, I suppose they might as well leave. There's been no word, you know, but I'll take the responsibility. Please order the men to go, Corporal."

"May I come, Corporal?" Fleur's voice drifted from the shadow behind Balbo. "To say goodbye to my . . . my friends?"

"Sure," Salvani said. "Come on." He walked back with Fleur and Judah. Fleur climbed into the bus, making fervent gestures to the other Jews, while Salvani stood by the truck, stoically enduring good-natured abuse, the cacophony of the brazen-lunged and indefatigable chorus as it bawled away—Oogley oogley oogley ooo—and the roar of exhausted engines revving up, the belching of petrol fumes, and shouting, "Yes, I'm coming along—later—see you soon and the same to *you*—" laughing in answer to someone's comment on his ancestry. "Now move. *Now!*" Grabbing Judah, who, as the transports screeched into gear, had realized that Modesta was leaving and who had dashed to the truck with piercing squeals of anguish.

He held the wriggling Judah firmly by the collar as the two ancient vehicles, spraying gravel from under their worn tires and swaying precariously, lurched down the drive, the men singing lustily and lustfully, cheerfully throwing out empty wine bottles and, with a gratifying crash, the machine gun.

"And so we leave." Balbo's voice, bitter with defeat, came from the gloom.

"So we do." Salvani, watching the vehicles scrape through the gates, songs echoing from them as if the company was a cheerful factory outing, resisted the temptation to say: And better than the way we came, swaggering with guns; watching as the first owls called, and the first bats came out to flitter through the night—and the telephone rang.

"The phone!" Balbo shouted, as if to reassure himself that the ringing was not in his ears, and dashed inside.

Salvani, Fleur, and Judah followed him and found him at his desk, the phone clamped to his ears, and shouting down it at intervals, "*Si, si, no. Si, no,*" yes, no . . . until finally he put down the phone and, despite Salvani's open disapproval, poured a tumblerful of brandy. "The colonel," Balbo said. "It was the colonel." He gulped more brandy and mopped his face with a handkerchief. "The French allowed the call to come through. The colonel says that the Germans are moving into our zone now. They don't take long, do they?" He laughed and stared aimlessly around the room.

"And?" Salvani said.

"And? Oh yes." Balbo drank again and laughed without humor. "We have permission to leave."

"Then let's get going," Salvani said.

"Now?" Balbo sat down. "I thought tomorrow. Get a night's sleep, make up a lunch, drive down through Modane—" sounding as if he was contemplating a pleasant picnic.

"No." Salvani had given up any pretense at officer-man relationship. "We get out now while the going is good. Who knows what the hell might happen tomorrow. Anyway, we can catch up with the company. Are you ready, signore?" He turned to Fleur.

"Yes." There was relief in Fleur's voice, and anxiety, too. "I do think it best that we leave as soon as possible. The French will be here soon, if not the Germans."

"Right." Salvani snapped his fingers. "I'd forgotten about them. Major, get the car ready. I'll rustle up some grub."

"I'll help," Fleur said. "Please allow me."

Salvani nodded an assent, and with Judah in tow, they went to the cookhouse, where Salvani shoved loaves, salami, cheese, wine, and—thinking why not?—cooking oil into a knapsack. "That's enough to keep us going," he said. "Not that we've far to go. We'll be there before dawn, easy. How's the *bambino*?"

Fleur gazed down on his son. "Judah? All right. He *is* strong, you know."

"Sure." Salvani fished a cigarette from his pocket and leaned forward to take a light from Fleur. "He means a lot, hey? The kid—to you."

"Everything," Fleur said.

" 'Course." Salvani made a rueful face. "Stupid question."

Fleur raised his hand and spoke in his odd, confessional, forgiving way. "He is all I have left."

"Yes. Er . . ." Salvani cursed himself for a blundering

33

idiot. "But never mind. I mean—*listen*. We'll be in Italy tomorrow at the latest. I don't know what's going on there . . . could be anything, I suppose. But I'll get you there. As God is my judge, I'll get you there, you and the kid." He cleared his throat with a hoarse cough. "Can you drive a motorcar?"

Fleur raised his eyebrows. "Yes."

"It's the major," Salvani said. "He's been drinking like a fish all day. I can't drive a car myself . . ."

"I understand," Fleur said. "Of course I'll drive, but it might be a little awkward. Perhaps if you tactfully suggest that I'm used to driving in France."

"Right," Salvani agreed, but in the event neither tact, which might have been Fleur's strong suit, nor strength, which was certainly Salvani's, was of any avail, for Balbo, gripping the steering wheel of the car, an ancient, rusting Bugatti, made it absolutely clear that no one, no one at all, was going to drive but himself—gripping also, as it were, on to the last vestige of his authority—and short of knocking him senseless, Salvani could see no way of getting him from the driving seat.

"Then drive," he said. He shoved Fleur, Judah, and the provisions into the back seat and climbed next to Balbo, his rifle jammed by his leg. "But take it easy. You hear me?"

"I'm perfectly competent." Balbo yawned unnervingly, and, even more so, hiccuped. "But I'm not sure . . ." He tapped the gear lever. "We could stay the night."

For a moment Salvani was tempted to agree. It would get Balbo out of the car and then Fleur could drive. In fact, they could leave Balbo, dump him among the splendors of the salon, the mirrors, and the brandy bottles; but he shrugged the thought away. It wouldn't really be right to leave an Italian, for all his faults, to be made a prisoner of war while he himself, and two French Jews, jaunted away.

"No," he said. "We're going. Now."

Reluctantly Balbo fiddled with the starter, and equally reluctantly the engine coughed into life. The gears screeched and the car bumped forward, and bumped again, and despite himself Salvani laughed. Christ, he thought, we're going to hop back home, laughing as they left the château, the vegetable plots, and Queen Victoria frowning into the darkness.

Two hours later they were in trouble. Balbo had coped well enough driving through the twisting roads which led to the town of Miolans, where a competent sergeant in the military police had directed them to the main road to Modane.

"Further orders there," he said—and no, he hadn't seen Balbo's company, there was a lot of traffic milling around, but if Balbo didn't get moving and stop blocking the road he, the sergeant, and his two ugly-looking men, would be perfectly happy to pull him, Balbo, out of the car and place him under arrest, and give him something to think about while they were doing it, as he, the sergeant, had no intention of hanging around until the Germans arrived. *"So get moving!"*

Which they did; edging on to the tail of a convoy of banged-up trucks and buses, motorcycles, cars, the red light of the last truck glowing in a friendly way, showing that they were with friends, and on the way home, until suddenly, as they swung into a village and the road curved right, the red light went out and they were alone, and not only solitary but on a road which certainly did not seem as if it might lead to an important town.

Fleur pointed that out. "Excuse me," he said diffidently. "But surely this isn't the road."

"What!" Salvani, who had been half dozing, started awake.

"Surely," Fleur said. "I know the road to Modane and this—" He grabbed Judah as the car jolted over a pothole.

"Major." Salvani turned to Balbo. "Do you hear that?"

Balbo gripped the steering wheel more tightly. "It's all right," he said with the stubbornness of a drunk who knows that he is all wrong. "Right way. Think I don't know what I'm doing?"

"No, Major." Fleur was soothing. "Of course not. Easy to make an error but—" The car bounced again and Balbo swung the car around a hair-raising curve.

"For Christ's sake!" Salvani put his hand on the steering wheel but Balbo elbowed him away.

" 'S all right," he shouted, his voice blurred with drink. "Turn off soon—*Cristo!*" Shouting as a dark animal shape loomed from the night, and swinging the steering wheel left, then, catching Salvani's elbow in his face, swinging it wildly right, shouting *Cristo* again as the car, with a life of its own, left the road, hurtled through the air and, to the splintering of glass and the squeal of gouged metal, crashed down a slope and came to a shattering halt—jagged litter among a litter of jagged limestone boulders.

5

The limestone crags and boulders gleamed coldly in the moonlight. The scrub in the gorge grew blacker in the shadows. The stars shone, the moon rose higher. Owls hooted and a small animal, a creature of the night, snuffling after blood, scampered away as, groaning, Salvani moved.

He moved, then lay inert. Moved again and coughed, a cough which brought with it savage, racking pains. He gasped and cried aloud, lay still, and then, like a man bearing the weight of the world upon his shoulders, dragged himself to his hands and knees, panting, bloody saliva dripping from his mouth.

He coughed again and groaned, swinging his head. "What?" he mumbled. "What?" as one arm buckled and he fell, face down, into dewy grass. The moon shone, the stars wheeled slowly against infinity. Salvani opened his eyes and, fighting against the pouncing pain, heaved himself back to all fours and stayed there for a minute, or a month, a year, then opened his eyes—one of them, rather; the other seemed stuck. "Silly sods," he grunted. "Sticking a man's eyes together. Just wait. Just you wait."

Feeling as if he was tearing himself in half, he raised his head. In front of him was a white shape—a man! He stretched out his arm and touched it. "Give us a hand," he whispered throatily. "Come on, be a pal—" feeling something solid and grasping it. "Thanks. Won't forget it." Muttering as he heaved himself upright, clutching the rock as the moon and the stars and mountain peaks, blacker than the sky, swung around him and a private firework display went off behind his eyes.

"Stop it!" he called to the moon and the stars. "Stop it! Do you hear? Put you on a charge! That's better," as the heavens and the earth slowly settled into their proper places. He wiped his bloody face with a bloody hand. In the gorge a bird shrieked. "You, too," he said menacingly. "Shut up. Let's have a bit of peace. Settle down."

He lay against the rock, sinking into a drowsy half sleep, deeper, deeper, and then, deeper than the sleep, in the deepest darkness of his mind a thought began to flicker, flashing on-off, on-off, like a far-distant lighthouse. On-off, on-off, on—

"Jesus!" Salvani heaved himself upright. "Jesus Maria!" Wincing with pain, he lurched away from the rock. "Major!" he shouted. "Fleur!" scraping scraped hands and gashing gashed flesh as, spitting blood and cursing, he plunged through scrub with thorns as fanged as barbed wire, until, raked and slashed, he found the car.

It was on its side, tilted against a huge boulder, the hood ripped off and the engine mashed metal. Halfway through the windshield was Balbo, and sprawled across his shoulders was Fleur. Salvani shoved away what was left of Balbo. "Fleur," he shouted, through the blood in his throat, "Signor Fleur!" But there was no answer from the shape that had been the suave perfume seller. "Judah!" Salvani called. *"Bambino!"* But there was no answer from the child, either.

"Mother of God!" Salvani edged to the side of the car, scrambled onto the boulder, and heaved on the door. It was buckled and jammed. He hauled again and the handle came off in his hands, sending him sprawling. But between the door and the car body there was a gap. Ignoring the pains in his chest and his lacerated hands, Salvani stuck his fingers in the gap and pulled. "Come *on,*" he muttered. "Come away, you . . . !" Straining with every last ounce of his massive strength, a trip-hammer pounding inside his head—until, grinding and squealing, the door came away.

Salvani kicked the door aside and, not far from collapse, shoved his head past the dead Balbo, and the dead Fleur, and found no Judah.

Salvani couldn't believe it. He shoved farther into the car and rummaged around. "Come out!" he barked, as if Judah was playing a childish practical joke, and then he understood. He himself had been thrown clear, and Judah had been sitting behind him on the same side of the car and so—

"Mary and Joseph!" Salvani dragged himself from the wreckage of the car and leaned back against the rock, feeling drained to the last, torn fiber of his being. Got to find him, he said to himself, got to do it; while another voice, sly, insinuating, whispered: Why bother? The kid's dead, got to be. He's not like you. He couldn't survive. Anyway, he's not your kid . . . Just lie down. Down.

"Stop it!" he croaked. "Do you hear? Stop it," as he had ordered the stars and the moon, and began to scrape his way up the gorge. "Judah," he muttered. "Judah. Come on, now, be good. Stop hiding." Staggering backward as a bird exploded from a bush, stones clattering down behind his lunging feet, and wanting, as he had never wanted anything before in his life, to fall down and sleep; and then, as he almost did, almost simply lay down, blindly groping, he touched a hand, an arm, a face—a warm face or, at least, a face still warm.

Well—Salvani sank to the ground. Well. Found you, anyway—while that dark other voice whispered: Wish you hadn't, eh? Make life easier—"Got to do something," he said to the night. From the depth of his memory he dredged up recollections of a rudimentary first-aid course he had done in the army. He knelt over Judah, testing for broken bones: none, so far as he could tell; pulse, beating. He sank back on his heels. Keep him warm, he thought. Cover him. Don't move him—internal injuries—spine. Then get help. Right. Do that.

He looked into the night and the shadowed gorge, and slowly the shrubs and trees and mountains began to move, swinging a circle. He jerked his head in the opposite direction, the landscape swung more quickly, and he was violently sick.

"God Almighty." He spat out fragments of pasta and cheese, but at least the scenery had stopped its horrible swinging. He dragged himself to his feet. "Come on," he said, "come on and stop talking to yourself," before slithering back down to the car.

"Sorry," he said, as he moved Fleur's legs, groping for the sack of provisions and the blankets. "Excuse me—" thinking: I've stopped talking to myself, now I'm talking to a dead man. He felt inside the knapsack. By a small, bitter miracle, the bottles were intact. After a moment's hesitation he pressed Fleur's eyelids shut, although there

39

was no need to do the same last service for Balbo. But he took the major's revolver and holster, and his own rifle.

Medicine, now, he thought, yanking the brandy bottle out and taking a swig. He stood, letting the drink take effect, staring at the car and the two broken bodies, and then, with great reluctance, muttering more apologies, he slid his hand inside Fleur's jacket and, after poking around a little, found what he was looking for: Fleur's wallet. "For the kid, signore," he said. "Not for me. Not stealing. Honestly." For a moment he did think of going through Balbo's pockets, but he shook that temptation aside.

He took another sip of brandy, then, step by heavy, lunging step, dragging the knapsack, his rifle, and the revolver and belt, he climbed back to Judah. The child was still breathing, and as Salvani draped the blanket over him, he twitched and whimpered.

"All right, *bambino*," Salvani said. "I'll get help. I will. In just one minute. One minute," as his legs gave way beneath him.

Sprawling beside Judah, the breath rasping in his throat, he stared around. Beneath him the gorge plunged down: stunted trees, scrub, boulders, rocks, scree; far below them an invisible stream gurgled and splashed, and across the cleft rose a line of crags, spectral in the moonlight. But in the whole eerie valley there was not one light, no spark or glimmer, not even the howling of a dog, which might mean a house, a farm, help.

Salvani stared vacantly, then shook his head, rousing himself and trying to think sensibly. The road, or path, they had come along, had there been a house there? Nothing that he could remember, only darkness and the drunken Balbo driving like a madman. Still, it came from the main road. So that was the place to go to. But battling through pain and fatigue, and shock, too, he had another problem to solve. He was afraid to move Judah, but he couldn't leave him alone. There were foxes, and maybe, in this wilderness, wolves—bears even, for all he knew. Groaning, this time as much with bafflement as with pain, he leaned over the child.

"*Bambino. Bambino!*" he shouted. He patted Judah's face, and then again harder, sickened by the thought of slapping too hard. "Come on, wake up, kid—wake—" and almost dropped with a heart attack as Judah suddenly sat up straight, opened his eyes, and gave a piercing wail. "Papa!" he screamed. "Papa!"

"All right. It's all right." Salvani clutched him. "Can you move? Move your arms—and your legs. Remember me? I'm your friend." He grinned into Judah's face but winced and cursed as Judah struck him a surprisingly hard blow on his closed eye.

"I want my papa," Judah screamed. "I'm *hurting*."

"Yes. I know. I'll make it better in a minute," Salvani said.

"Papa!" Judah lashed out again with his amazingly hard fist.

"He's . . . he's just gone. Only for a little while. He'll be back before you know it." Salvani stood up. A stinging eye and nose assured him that there was nothing seriously wrong with Judah. "In fact"—it came to him that whatever happened he had to get Judah away from the sight of the car and his father's dead body—"in fact, we'll go and find him. Now!"

He pulled the knapsack over his abraded shoulders, and his rifle, buckled on the revolver, picked up a squirming and wailing Judah, and began to scramble up the mountainside.

He knew that an Italian had climbed a giant mountain in Africa, and that some crazy Englishmen kept trying to climb Mount Everest, and that even crazier people went climbing in the Alps for *fun*, but he doubted if anyone, anywhere, had ever made as hard a climb as the one he was undertaking. He felt as if every bone in his body had

41

been broken and every square centimeter of skin had been flayed as, sliding back a pace for three he made upward, he hauled himself, and his burdens, up through dangerously shifting rocks and across maddeningly crumbly bare earth. And even then his burden increased. He kicked something, not a stone or a broken branch, but Fleur's suitcase. Hardly knowing what he was doing, he stopped and grabbed it. "Tidying up," he said, to no one, and burst out laughing, and he was still laughing like a lunatic as a hundred meters farther, which took him half an hour to climb, he came upon the path. And down the path another hundred meters or so, set back, clinging to a meadow, clearly visible in the bright moonlight, was a shed.

Salvani half dropped Judah. "Can you walk?" he asked.

"I want my papa!" Judah opened his mouth as a prelude to another wail, but Salvani had heard enough wailing for one night.

"I know you do," he said, torn between wrath and pity, and speaking roughly. "But can you walk?"

"I *can*," Judah said, almost testily, "but I'm *hurting*."

"I'll make that better," Salvani said. "Promise. But first we've got to sit down. Come on." He didn't bother to persuade, or cajole, but took Judah's hand and pulled him along the path and across the meadow to the shed. And there Judah stopped dead.

"Is Papa in there?" he asked.

"No." Salvani realized that if he were a child he would be more than dubious about being led into a sinister-looking shed by a large and battered man, but deciding that honesty was best, and thinking that in any case they *were* going in, he was honest. "No. He's not actually in there, but we've got to rest for a bit—before we go to him."

Salvani didn't wait to see if his explanation had any effect but bustled Judah into the shed. It wasn't a very successful shed. Part of its roof was missing and moonlight shone on a pile of moldy hay. Salvani made Judah sit down and, with

42

a fit of inspiration, took out the cooking oil and rubbed it into Judah's wounds. "Have a mouthful of this, too," he said, and coaxed a drop of brandy down the boy's mouth.

"There," he said. "This will make you better. Soon be better now"—talking as much for his own comfort as for Judah's, murmuring assurances as the brandy, and exhaustion, mastered pain and terror, and the boy drifted into a battered and fretful unconsciousness.

"And I don't blame you," Salvani said. "You've had enough for one day, and so have I. Christ, what a day." He spread the blanket over Judah and sat by the door, smoking and sipping brandy. Ought to go and get help, he thought. Ought to. Once he made an effort to get up, but sleep claimed him, too, and he fell into a nightmarish half world of shattered rocks and jagged metal, where dead men wandered and called for lost children, and lost children wandered and called for their dead fathers.

Orion climbed in the sky, the Dog Star at his heels, and, sword belt glittering, chased the stars across the pastures of the night. The child and the soldier slept; but other soldiers were awake and moving. Soldiers in field gray and jackboots; crossing the river Var in the moonlight, trucks rumbling through silent villages and sleeping fields—like a tide on a rocky coast, gray fingers poking at this village, that town, that city; and behind them came other men in black with silver skulls on their caps, and with them were still other men, in plainclothes or blue uniforms, pointing now at this apartment building, now at this villa, this hotel, that cottage, that last, remote refuge, hammering down doors, snuffling in terror-stricken streets, as from the perfumed coast of the Mediterranean to the farthest gaunt valley of the High Alps, the *rafle*, the great Jew hunt began.

6

Judah woke first, crying with pain and a terrifying sense of loss, the more poignant because he had no words to express it or experience in which to frame it. But as he opened his smeared eyes in the sickly light of dawn, he stopped crying. Young as he was, hard lessons had been driven into him: if father wasn't there or a guardian, be still; don't make a noise, be as inconspicuous as a mouse in a meadow when a hawk hovers over it or that hawk will pounce and bear you off in its talons. So, after the first cry, he lay silent, motionless, but staring at the man sprawled by the door; vaguely recalling a sun-lit street, his father shaking hands with the man, and himself playing with a soldier—and then, as the man by the door gave a huge snort and jerked upright, Judah closed his eyes tightly, hoping that if he did not see the hawk, the hawk would not see him, the mouse, lying still in the moldy hay.

Salvani, snorting awake, grunted with pain. He stared through one eye at his bloodied hands and torn uniform. God Almighty, he thought, I look as if I've been in a car crash—then remembered that he *had* been in one. His head pounded as he remembered the crumpled car, the bodies of Balbo and Fleur ... He fingered his gummy, sealed eye and swollen cheekbone and prodded his elbow, which felt as if an elephant had whiled away an idle hour stomping on it. "That goddamned Balbo," he spat—and then remembered something else.

Disregarding the wrenching pains, he jumped up. "Kid," he called. ". . . Judah! Where the hell—oh, there you are."

44

He limped toward the hay, and Judah, peering upward through slitted eyelids, saw looming over him a huge figure, its whiskery face, bruised and swollen, set in a snarl, bloody fists reaching toward him, and, hard lessons about silence forgotten, gave an appalling ear-splitting scream.

"No, no." Salvani held up his hands. "It's all right. I brought you here—" wincing as another amazingly powerful scream rattled his eardrums. He rummaged in the knapsack. "Look, food!" As Judah opened his mouth to scream again, Salvani stuck a chunk of salami into it. "Eat," he said—and then, inspired, added, "Eat and then we'll find your papa. Very soon. I'm eating, too. Look!"

Judah looked but wasn't comforted. He saw a man tearing at a lump of meat with blackened teeth, one bloodshot eye glaring . . . Judah had seen pictures of a man like that, a monster, Cyclops, lurking in its cave; and Judah knew what Cyclops did in his den of moldering bones. He opened his mouth to scream again, but then the man, man-monster or monster-man, stood up and brushed crumbs from his clothes, and that, although he hardly knew why, Judah found reassuring. After all, it wasn't exactly the sort of thing monsters did, nor did they pat their victim's head, or smile, even through bloodied lips, or pick one up and say, with soothing, easing words, that now they would go and find one's papa.

And so, when Salvani had packed up, walked to the door, and beckoned to him, Judah, raw and sore as he was, followed him, although less from any real trust than because, young as he was, he saw no alternative. And at least following the man meant that he would be outside. Although even then he knew that he might be walking out to meet those *others*, men worse than any Cyclops, who only devoured people one by one; but men; Goyim, who for some reasons known to none, not even God, devoured whole families of Jews, whole villages even; and he knew that the soldier was a Goyim, a non-Jew, a Gentile, the sort of man who could fawn on you one day and the next turn and rend you with talons more merciless than any hawk. And, Judah, hawk-eyed himself, saw that the man had taken his father's suitcase.

"Mine!" he yelled, grabbing at the case. "Papa's!"

"What?" Salvani, who wasn't sure why he had the suitcase, was startled by this sudden renewal of normal behavior in Judah.

"That's my papa's," Judah said fiercely.

"Yes," Salvani said. "I'm not going to steal it." He forced a smile at the mistrustful face scowling up at him. "We're taking it *to* Papa." He limped on, slowly, followed by Judah, who was also limping badly, both of them at a snail's pace.

But, in fact, it was true that Salvani was feeling better than he had the night before. His left eye was a giant blister, his left shoulder was wrenched, and he had the impression of having been skinned alive, but he was a man used to hardship, an Italian workman for whom a few more knocks and blows were no more than to be expected in life. Bearing up, he thought, slogging along—the kid, too. He looked over his shoulder at Judah, scraped and bruised also, but steadily plodding behind him. Take a lot, kids, he mused. Take things that would lay out a man for a month, and as long as Judah believed he was going to meet his father he would keep moving. Although what was going to happen when the kid found out he didn't have a father anymore he *didn't* care to think about. Leave that problem to someone else to sort out, he said to himself. Get to Italy first. Yes. In the meantime, he had other things on his mind and the first was: where the devil were they? The previous night, with Balbo driving like a lunatic, they must have covered a good few kilometers, and here, wherever they were, was a wild country. Low clouds, or fog, hung upon limestone crags which plunged down and down, into a gorge. There was no sign of life at all. So which way to go?

46

He hesitated, Judah by his side. Flip a coin, he thought. Heads, left; tails, right. But as he fumbled in his pocket for a coin, under the growing heat of the sun the sullen line of clouds rose, slowly at first, and then with surprising speed, dissipated, and like a frown clearing revealed in the remote distance, as if in another world, the vast, snowy brows of a range of mountains.

Salvani slapped his thigh. Those glittering peaks, rising above all others and dwarfing the world, could only be the Alps, the real Alps, and behind that ice-bound barrier was Italy, was home, and the path led toward them.

"Come on," he said, taking Judah by the hand.

"To Papa?" Judah asked.

"To Papa."

They walked along the path, Salvani shaking his head, baffled at how Balbo had actually got a car up here, and went through a grove of pines where a woodpecker rattled away from them in a splash of scarlet and lemon. On the other side of the grove the trail turned into something approaching a narrow road, which snaked down the side of the mountain, and then with butterflies dancing around them, and as the cooking oil daubed on their faces melted in the heat of the sun and trickled down their collars, and as the thought of water, or cooling wine, was beginning to raise itself in their minds, they passed through another sparse grove of scrubby oak, and a few hundred meters beneath them saw a road, a real road, coming from some-where and, presumably, going somewhere, and where their trail met the road, there was a cluster of houses.

It was a hamlet, if that. A few hens fluttered away as Salvani and Judah walked down the dusty road. A huge dog barked and bared its teeth at them, a donkey swished its tail, and there was a strong, sour-sweet odor of manure; but there was no police station, no butcher's, no baker's, no church even, and, it seemed, no people either, but over a blistered green door there was a sign saying *Poste* and behind the door a café, of sorts; at least there were a couple of tables, a few cane chairs, a tiny bar with bottles behind it, and looming over the bottles a large picture of Marshal Pétain.

"Hello?" Salvani called. "Hello. Service!"

Somewhere at the back of the house a door creaked, there were footsteps, and a man, unshaven, in a vest, a cigarette dangling from his lips, shuffled into the bar. "Yes?" he said. Then his jaw dropped, the cigarette fell from his mouth, and he took a step backward. "What the— who the hell are you?" he demanded.

"*Signore.*" Salvani held out his hand. "Excuse me. We, I and this little one, we've had an accid—" He realized what he was doing. "Sorry." He used his rough, workable French. "Do you speak Italian?"

"No." The man shook his head. "No Italian," he growled.

"Monsieur." Salvani groped for words. "Accident. We've had an accident. I need medicine—for the child."

"I don't understand," the man said, but his eyes shifted from Salvani to Judah.

You understand, Salvani thought. You understand but you're not letting on, you crafty swine. And another notion flicked across his mind: that the man knew Italy was out of the war and that the Germans, and the French authorities too, come to that, might not look too kindly on anyone helping an Italian soldier and a Jewish kid. "All right," he said. "You don't understand me. Right." He tapped Judah on the shoulder. "Tell him we need medicine and food." Judah looked up with questioning eyes and Salvani nudged him. "Tell him," he said with a growl in his voice.

"Monsieur." Judah broke into rapid, fluent French, then stopped as suddenly as he had begun.

The man rubbed out the smoldering cigarette with his boot, grinding it into the floor. "*Pas de médecine,*" he said.

"He says—" Judah began, but Salvani understood. "Don't give me that," he rumbled, his face dark with anger.

48

"You've got *some* medicine here—ointment and stuff." He stepped forward, his bulk blocking out what light crept in through the dusty window. "*Get* it."

The man looked sideways at Salvani—and his weapons—then shrugged, sullenly. "Hélène," he called over his shoulder.

A woman appeared, her eyes widening at the sight of Salvani and Judah and, as the man spoke to her in a clattering dialect, darkening with suspicion. "Italian?" she asked, then pointed at Judah. "What are you doing with him?" Salvani hesitated. With Judah present he could hardly say that the boy's father was lying dead in a smashed car on the mountainside. In any case, looking at the two hostile faces before him, he decided that he had better keep that bit of information up his sleeve, at least for the time being. "He's lost, the kid. I'm looking after him for a bit. Now get that medicine."

Deeply unwilling, the couple backed through the door, and Salvani and Judah followed them into a rough kitchen. The woman poured hot water into a bowl and, without enthusiasm, began dabbing at Judah's scratches, while the man, his face sour, poured wine into a cracked mug and shoved it at Salvani, deliberately slopping it. Salvani gulped the wine, a thin, sour wine at that, and peered carefully at the man and woman through his one good eye.

The surly couple weren't simply being suspicious; anyone seeing a battered foreign soldier wandering about with an equally battered kid might be that; and they weren't just resentful, as anyone having their kitchen invaded by an armed soldier would be. They were hostile. Maybe they were pro-German, Fascist, in which case the sooner he and Judah got out of the dump the better.

"Where's your telephone?" he asked.

"No telephone." The woman's voice was shrill.

"Map," Salvani said.

"No map."

"No?" Salvani walked into the front room. As he expected there was a Michelin tire map on the wall. Every café in France had one. He took out his bayonet, yanked the map off the wall, took it back into the kitchen, and ripped it from its frame. He laid it on the table and squinted at it. It was, he was pleased to see, quite a large-scale map—not of the whole of France but of the region, Savoie, with gratifyingly clear blue lines, which meant good roads, leading into Italy. He stabbed a blunt finger onto the map. "Where?" he asked. "Where are we?"

The man stared across the table and waved his hand contemptuously. "France," he jeered. "We're in France."

Salvani stared back and took a deep breath, and then another. "Now listen to me, mister," he said slowly, but not really caring whether the man understood fully or not. "You see me? Me, standing right here? Right. I'm a soldier. That's all. Just an Italian soldier, and I should be in Italy right now. At home. Instead of which—" He moved around the table and grabbed hold of the man's vest. "Instead of which I'm here, in a pigsty of a café, knocked to bits and with a kid who's hurt, and I come looking for a bit of help, and what do I get? I get you. *You* son-of-a-bitch. Now—" He pulled the man forward. "I'm going to spell this out for you and you'd better listen. And listen carefully. That hag there"—he pointed to the woman—"she can start looking after the kid properly. And you"— he loomed over the man—"you answer a civil question properly or I'll break your —— neck. Got that? Got it?"

He shook the man like a dog with a rat, full of genuine wrath, but at the same time he was amazed at himself: what was he doing, in the middle of nowhere, cursing, swearing, making venomous threats? But still, trying *not* to be enraged, feeling more so. "So," he said, his voice thick, "where are we?"

He gestured to Judah to repeat what he had said in clearer French, but there was no need for that, any more

50

than a dog would need its growls of menace to be translated. The woman, her face a bitter mask of resentment, laved Judah as if he was made of porcelain, and dabbed him with ointments, violet-blue and yellow, as the man, resentment creasing his blue jowls, pointed carefully at the map.

Salvani leaned forward, staring, and sucked his teeth thoughtfully. It wasn't as bad as he had thought it might be. Somewhere Balbo had cut off the main road and now they were here, at the head of a long valley. But—he measured the distance with his thumb—about thirty kilometers at the most. Well, they could walk that if they had to, not that he intended to walk. Anyway, they could get back to the main road and pick up a lift from some Italian truck, and with any luck at all they would be over the Mont Cenis Pass and in Italy that night.

"Right." He slammed his hand down. "Soup, bread, and wine. And make that decent wine, and boil some eggs. *Pronto. Vite!*"

Twenty minutes later they were ready to go. Salvani stuffed bread and hard-boiled eggs into the crammed knapsack. "Right, kid?" he said, and was ready to go when the woman burst into a tirade. Salvani, baffled by the dialect, stared at her, bewildered, until Judah, sharper than he was, tugged at his sleeve.

"Money," Judah said. "She wants money. *Payment.*"

"Does she?" Salvani said. "Does she, now?" For a moment he was tempted to tell the woman what she could do with her demand, but instead shoved a few crumpled notes on the table. The woman saw the money and her face contorted with anger and she burst out into another passionate torrent of language.

"No good cursing," Salvani said. "It's all I've got"—lying—"and it's all you're going to get," shoving the worthless Italian occupation lire at her.

The map in his pocket, armed to the teeth, knapsack over his shoulder and Judah at his heels, he strode from the café on to the road and got a small surprise. The road was no longer empty. Outside the café there was a little crowd, old men and women, stepping back in alarm as Salvani, big and scarred, weapons rattling, stepped out into the sunlight. Salvani half grinned; a flock of old crows; amazing where they came from: but across the road there was a man he didn't feel inclined to grin about.

The man, maybe in his forties, was dressed in brown corduroy breeches and jacket and wearing a slouch hat. He had a thin, tanned, sour face with a slit of a mouth. He was leaning on a bicycle, and over his shoulder he had a hunting rifle.

Salvani stared hard at the man, and the man stared back, Salvani calculatingly, the other man too, but with a kind of snuffling alertness which sent a tingle of apprehension down Salvani's spine as he walked down the road, towing Judah with him.

"My—" Judah began, but Salvani cut him off.

"Later," he said.

"But we've—"

"I said later." Salvani was brutally abrupt, not liking the atmosphere in the hamlet at all, not liking the café owner or his wife, but most of all, not liking the look of the sour-faced man with the rifle.

They walked on, out of the hamlet, past a small wooden cross, a scummy water trough where dragonflies hovered, past small vegetable plots hemmed in by greasy rock, and into a cleft, dank and shadowed by scrubby trees, and there Salvani stopped and, yanking Judah with him, stepped behind a boulder and, putting his finger to his lips as a warning, he waited.

Insects droned about their ears, the heavy, rank odor of ferns filled the air, buzzards mewed high above them; and then, gliding slowly, silently, on his bicycle, swinging his head this way and that, came the man with the rifle, skidding sideways as Salvani pounced.

"What's your little game?" Salvani demanded, one meaty hand on the handlebars of the bicycle, the other holding the man by the scruff of the neck.

"Game?" The man's foxy eyes met Salvani's. "It's no game. Not for you it isn't, nor for me. But that pair in the café—" He jerked his head. "*They're* waiting to play a little game."

"And what game is that?" Salvani asked.

The man gave a dry, cynical smile. "To turn you over to the police. You know that, don't you? You and the kid."

"Is that so," Salvani said.

"Yes. Not nice people, those two. Informers."

"And you," Salvani said. "What about you, mister?"

"Oh—" The man wriggled his shoulders. "Do you mind?" he asked politely. "Thanks," as Salvani released his grip. He swung off the bicycle and leaned against it. "Oh, we're not all like them. But what about you—and him?" He pointed at Judah, who, amazingly spotted yellow and purple, playing with a fern, looked more like a pantomime elf than like a child. "Just what are you doing here?" He held up his hand as Salvani glowered suspiciously. "Nothing to me, nothing at all. But you need advice. Advice and help. You know that, don't you? And you've got to trust someone, sooner or later. So . . ."

"So why should I trust you?" Salvani said.

The man stroked his chin. "No reason. None at all. But there's no one else, is there? Still—" He shrugged. "If you don't mind—" He eased the bicycle from Salvani's grasp. "Best of luck."

"Wait," Salvani said. "All right," accepting the inevitable. He walked the man up the road a little, out of Judah's earshot. "It's—" He looked back up the road, but the man was calming.

"This is the only way out of that place," he said. "And no one's going to come down the road with you hanging about."

"Well . . ." Salvani told his tale, the man staring at him through shrewd eyes.

"Some story, too," he said, when Salvani had finished. "But you won't make it down this road."

"No?"

"No." The man shook his head emphatically. "You come to Allevard. There's a police post there." He bared his teeth. "The café owner—nice man, heh? Let me tell you something. He *wants* the Germans to get here. And his brother is a sergeant of police at Allevard. And *he* wants the Germans to get here, too. So they can have a nice little roundup."

"Roundup?" Salvani asked.

"People they don't like," the man said. "People like me. And he's not going to let you walk through Allevard with the kid."

"Well, that's fine," Salvani said sardonically. "Just fine. Thanks." He looked around at where on both sides of the road the huge sides of the valley swept upward. "So what do we do, fly?"

"No, no." The man waved the badinage away, a little impatiently. "It's not as bad as it looks. You can go over there"— he pointed to the northeast—"and come to the Mont Cenis road. You think that your troops will still be moving out?"

"I'm sure of it," Salvani said with grim humor.

"Yes . . ." The man looked intently at Salvani, taking in his battered appearance. "You can make it? Walking across the mountains?"

"All the way!" Salvani said.

"And the child?" The man jerked his thumb to where Judah was still playing with the fern, muttering a childish chant to himself. "One, two, three, four, someone's knocking at my door . . ."

"He'll do it, too," Salvani said. "And if he can't I'll carry him."

"Right." The man rubbed the handlebars of his bicycle with his sleeve. "You know, we're not all like him—in the café."

"I know that," Salvani said.

"Yes . . . and there are places . . . in the mountains, where the kid could be looked after . . ."

"No," Salvani said. "I'm taking him home. It's . . ." He thought of Judah's father, that subtle, smiling man, trusting because there was nothing left to him but to trust. "It was a promise."

"Well, a promise." The man shrugged as if that resolved all argument. "We'll get going, then."

Salvani called Judah, who came toward them, walking a little more unsteadily than earlier, but able to cry with pleasure as the man swung him onto the saddle of the bicycle, and the three of them set off down the road, through the dank, insect-haunted chasm, into sunlight, the road dropping steadily, the sun hotter, a stream on their right murmuring, the short, sweet grass a dazzling green and the limestone crags a blinding white, until they came to a rough trail leading off the road to the right.

"This is where we part company," the man said. "Cross the stream and follow the trail. Up there."

He pointed and Salvani lifted his head. "All the way up?"

"All the way," the man said. "That's not a big hill."

"It isn't?" Salvani said.

"Not around here," the man said. "Still think you can make it?"

"We'll make it," Salvani said.

The man spat out his cigarette and lit another. "The path gets you to a farm—sort of. Le Pic. They'll feed you and show you the way."

"Who do I say sent me?" Salvani asked.

"Say . . ." The man hesitated, then said, "Le Chasseur. Tell them the Chasseur from the Seven Lakes."

"Chass—hunter. That's your name?"

The Hunter tapped his nose. "I've got no name. So if you get caught you can't tell, see?"

"I wouldn't tell," Salvani said.

"No?" The man looked at Salvani through cynical eyes.

"No," Salvani said, but under that gaze less certainly. "Anyway, we'll be in Italy by tonight—tomorrow, anyway."

"Sure," the Chasseur said. "But there's just one more thing." He took Salvani by the elbow, turning him and speaking from the corner of his mouth.

"The people up there, in the mountains, they're poor, you know?"

"So?" Salvani opened his hands as if to say, who isn't.

"Le Pic's all right, but there might be others who . . . they're good enough, but—" He peered at Salvani. "You don't know what I'm talking about, do you? In Vichy France they *paid* for Jews, and now the Germans are here, maybe the same thing will happen. Nice, hey? Still, that's the way it is. Not that it should bother you. Like you say, you can be home and dry tomorrow. But just watch out." He pointed at Judah's multicolored head. "He's not exactly inconspicuous, is he?"

He fished out another cigarette, lit it, and blew out smoke. The stream gurgled, crystal-clear, butterflies fluttered. Swallows dipped and swooped, and above them the ever present buzzards circled, giving their curious cat-like cries. "You wouldn't think that there was a war on, would you?" An unexpectedly charming smile illumined his sour, foxy face. "So." He shook Salvani's hand. "Good luck."

"And to you," Salvani said. "Judah—"

"Find another name for him," the man said. "Non-Jewish."

He walked away, pushing his bicycle. Salvani raised a hand in farewell and, with Judah, walked down the rough trail and crossed the glinting waters of the stream.

The beneficent sun shone on the peaks and mountains of the Alps, and on the broad valleys and rivers of France, and on its cities, towns, villages, echoing to the sound of rifle butts crashing down doors, and to the whimpering of children, and the shuffling of despairing feet as men and women and children were goaded onto trucks, each man, woman, and child meticulously ticked off by the men in black with their silver skulls grinning mercilessly—as did the men who bore, entirely appropriately, that emblem; they themselves, for all their well-tailored uniforms, polished jackboots, blue eyes, and sleek blond hair framing handsome faces, being no more than ghouls haunting the Europe of Dante, Beethoven, Goethe, Tolstoy, Einstein, Michelangelo, which they were turning into a reeking boneyard.

One by one, ten by ten, hundred by hundred, thousand by thousand, the Jews were dragged from their last refuges; and meticulously and efficiently the names were numbered, indexed, and filed. So many plucked from Nice, from Grasse, Grenoble . . .

And as Salvani and Judah paused to rest under a pine tree with ravens croaking at them, other men, quite ordinary, normal men who liked football, a cigar now and then, a glass of wine or beer, a stroll in the park, worked out timetables: so many trains to go here, so many to go there; this station to be cleared, that signal box warned—unaware or indifferent to what the trains were carrying, or if they were aware, knowing that the slightest objection on their part and they might find themselves and *their* families crammed into a cattle truck on one of the trains which rattled so efficiently to the charnel houses of the East. But all of them, whether unaware, indifferent, or gloating, working with the obsessive diligence of psychopaths let loose in a gigantic lunatic asylum where it was the wardens who were insane.

"It's going well, Major."

"Is it?" Major Barbie SS walked to the window of his stuffy office and stared out into a gloomy courtyard surrounded by a high wall spiked with broken glass and barbed wire. Beyond the wall, the city of Lyons baked in the sun, but its light didn't touch the courtyard, the walls casting long shadows, as if anything normal or natural was debarred from entering the prison. In the yard a few policemen lounged by a black van with barred windows. One of the men was gesticulating and the other men laughed, one slapping his thigh, doubled up with mirth.

"It's only been twenty-four hours." The other man, a civilian, French, was nervously apologetic.

The major didn't answer, staring through the window at the courtyard. The policemen were still laughing heartily. One of them called to another, waving him over to share the joke.

"The trouble is," the Frenchman said. "Er . . . Major . . . the trouble is, we don't have a register for the Italian zone. In fact, we don't even know how many Jews were there. The Italians wouldn't cooperate. They simply wouldn't."

The major turned from the window and sat behind his desk, not speaking, his silence unnerving.

The Frenchman mopped the back of his neck with a handkerchief. "In fact, we hear that the Italians are actually taking Jews with them—to Italy. And anyway, there were Jews everywhere. You know, here and there, in the mountains, and with the Resistance—"

The major stared balefully. "There is no Resistance," he said. "Only traitors."

"Of course, of course. Traitors. Traitors to France. Excuse me, a slip of the tongue." The Frenchman wiped his neck again. "But the traitors, and the Italians, they've made life difficult—"

The telephone rang and the major picked it up. "Barbie," he said, and listened for a moment. "No," he said impatiently. "Not veal. Lamb cutlets? Yes, with salad." He listened again, considering carefully, a man making a serious decision. "The mousse. Yes, with caramel. And Beaujolais—and that light Rhône wine." He put down the telephone and spoke to the civilian. "The veal isn't good. Not good at all."

"I'm sorry to hear that," the Frenchman said, sticky with sweat, not all of which was due to the heat. "Very sorry indeed. But about the Jews—"

"All!" Barbie slammed the desk with his fist, his ascetic features suddenly, terrifyingly contorted with rage. "*All!* Every last one. Man, woman, and child. That is an order from the highest authority. Do you understand that? The *highest* authority!"

"Of course, Major. Of course." The Frenchman backed away. "Immediately. At once. Every last . . ." Sweating, he bowed himself from the office, tripping over his feet, trembling.

He stumbled through the dark corridors and down dark stairways which led to darker places, crossed the courtyard, where the lounging men still laughed, got into his car, and was driven through the bleak gates and along the streets of the city, where men and women looked down and away as he sped past, to the Préfecture.

In his office he kicked off his shoes and gulped white wine, and then snapped out his orders.

"And at once!" he shouted. "All. Every man, woman, and child. Orders from the highest authority."

The orders went out across the enchanting sliver of France: phones burred, telegrams were clacked out, postmen, toiling on their bicycles, delivered imperative messages, the police snapped awake, and, like dogs snuffling the objects of their desire, the men of the Milice raised their unsavory muzzles and went on the hunt—so that none would escape. None.

7

From behind the shelter of a clump of stunted thorn bushes, Salvani was looking at Le Pic.

The farmhouse was half a kilometer away in a hollow on a bare, forbidding shelf of mountain. The house looked less like a house than like a pile of boulders jumbled together with a stump of chimney jutting out. It had an air of foreboding, its blank windows staring across a few dilapidated wooden outbuildings, and the bare fields.

Jesus Maria, Salvani thought. Who'd live up here? I hope they're not loonies. There was no sign of human life, only the ominous house, crows pecking in the fields, and the ever present buzzards circling overhead in heavy, dreamy circles. Salvani began to wonder if anyone did live in the house, but then a donkey wandered from behind one of the sheds.

"Someone there, then," Salvani said to himself. "A donkey . . . but wait a bit, anyway. Be careful. Watch out." And for the first time since leaving the château, thinking that they really had better watch out, that they weren't just two poor devils trying as best as they could to get home, but that maybe they were fugitives, on the run—and if what the Chasseur had said was true, one of them was worth money.

He lay on his side and looked at Judah, with his amazing purple and yellow head—a good kid, bravely bearing his cuts and bruises and tramping up the long hill with never a murmur of complaint. Christ alone knew what he was going through—his head bashed to bits, his father missing, and wandering about these God-awful mountains with a ragged hulk who was armed to the teeth. Salvani felt a surge of pity.

"Here." He rummaged in his knapsack, pulled out a piece of bread, and stuck it into Judah's mouth.

Judah chewed for a moment, although, Salvani noticed with some irritation, with the air of one who has known better things, swallowed, and then spoke.

"Signore," he said.

"Yes?" Salvani was delighted. "Yes, what is it? Do you want some more bread, some salami, wine?"

Judah shook his head. "Signore," he began again.

"Uncle!" Salvani had a brainstorm. "Call me Uncle Vito." He said it with, and from, affection, but it also occurred to him that that might make some sense of them being together—although whether he could explain how an Italian soldier and his nephew came to be roaming around France he had no idea. Anyway, he would cross that bridge when he came to it. "What do you want?"

"My case," Judah said. "My papa's suitcase."

"Oh." Salvani clicked his teeth. Of course, they had left it at that café—clean forgotten it. "I don't have it," he said. "Sorry. Left it behind. But don't worry. I'll get you another one. Just as good. Better!"

Judah rugged at a clump of grass. "Will Papa be angry?"

"No!" Salvani struck up an exaggerated vein of joviality. "No, no. In fact, those people will keep it for us. Don't you worry about the suitcase, ha! ha!" He grinned and rolled his eyes in a simulation of mirth, then, after a moment's thoughtful reflection, said, "Er, the case . . . what was in it?"

"Clothes," Judah said.

"Oh." Salvani shrugged. "We can get more of those." He turned to look at the house again, but Judah hadn't finished.

He looked at Salvani through huge, lustrous, and disbelieving eyes. "Are you really my uncle?" he asked.

"Am I . . . well, not *exactly*. No, not exactly . . ." Salvani was beginning to think that his brainstorm wasn't so brilliant after all. "But I'm *sort* of an uncle!" He grinned at Judah, who looked back, showing if not disbelief then something very like it. "Just *think* of me as your uncle. Like"—affection turning into irritation—"like—who's your favorite uncle?"

Judah thought for a moment, then said, "Uncle Benjamin."

"Good," Salvani said. "I'm like your Uncle Benjamin."

"Uncle Benjamin is dead," Judah said.

"Christ!" Knowing that he shouldn't be, and feeling ashamed of himself, Salvani *was* irritated.

"And Aunt Rebecca," Judah said. "And cousin Aaron, and cousin Rachel. Papa said the Germans took them away. Papa said I mustn't speak to Germans. If I see any, I've got to run away and hide."

Salvani had heard of people seeing red but had thought it was just an expression, a manner of speaking, but as Judah finished, Salvani felt that his head was exploding as a red glare filled his eyes, and with a pulse in his temple hammering and his hands trembling, he looked at Judah and was enraged again.

The child was staring at him, knuckles to his mouth, cringing away from Salvani's wrath, and as Salvani shook his head to clear it, Judah raised an arm to ward off a splintering blow.

"No!" Salvani cried. "No! It's all right. Don't be afraid. Don't. I'll look after you. I will." He threw a huge, rough-clad arm around Judah. "And I'll get you some nice hot soup soon. You'll like that. And a nice bed . . ."

"And Papa?"

"Ah—Papa. Maybe not just tonight. But we're going to him. Yes. And don't be afraid. I will look after you, by Christ. I will! That's better." He stroked Judah's head and the boy slowly relaxed, although even then his face had a disturbing watchfulness, unfitting for a child.

"Good," Salvani said. "No one will ever hurt you. Not

while I'm here." And then, from the corner of his eyes, something caught his attention.

He peered through the thorn. The farmhouse was still silent, blank-windowed, bare on the melancholy plateau, casting long shadows as the sun dipped, but now there was something different. A plume of smoke was rising from the chimney.

"All right," Salvani said. "All right." Somebody home, and not a trap, either; they wouldn't be lighting fires if it was. Smoke, fire, food, a bed—and for the first time he realized that it was getting chilly. The height, he supposed; and there was a breeze, feather-light but bringing with it an icy breath from the fastnesses of the Alps.

"Come on, chico." He stood up, heaving Judah with him, noticing again that Judah had a sickly look about him. "Come on. Time to get you to bed."

He took Judah by the hand and left the shelter of the bushes and had not walked three paces when two shapes came from the farm, arrow-straight, howling and baying: two huge dogs, mouths agape and dripping fangs bared, dogs big enough to pull down a deer—or a man.

"Jesus!" Salvani swung Judah on his shoulders and lashed out with his rifle. "Get off!" he roared. "Off!"— thinking what a way to end up, being eaten alive by giant dogs; little ones, too, as a terrier joined in, snapping at his ankles until Salvani caught it with his boot and sent it flying through the air.

"Get off!" Salvani bellowed, and "Get off" Judah echoed, showing courage from the safety of his perch, and shouting defiance at the fangs and baleful rolling eyeballs of the hounds. "And sod this," Salvani said and was about to pull out Balbo's revolver and inflict some serious damage on the dog population of Le Pic when the dogs suddenly backed away, still snarling and showing teeth like man-traps, as a woman appeared in the doorway of the farm-house. A woman holding a shotgun.

"Madame!" A wary eye on the circling dogs, Salvani

walked forward, and it seemed a long walk too, with the coarse growls erupting at his every step, but then too short as the shotgun swung up and he found himself looking down two menacing barrels which seemed as big and black as railway tunnels, and above them two eyes as menacing as the gun barrels.

"Who are you?" the woman said, her voice as welcoming as the dogs' howls. "What do you want?"

"Madame." The hounds at his heels and the shotgun leveled unwaveringly, his French escaped him. He gave a sickly, strained smile which he feared looked more like the menacing leer of a maniac. "Judah." He joggled the boy on his shoulder. *"Bambino.* You've got to help out here. Tell her, in French. Tell her that the Chasseur in the village told us to come. Can you do that?"

"Si," Judah said. *"Si,"* with surprising confidence, as though being on Salvani's shoulders, for once looking down on adults instead of peering up at them from somewhere around knee level, had raised him, instantly, to maturity, although when he spoke his voice had enough of the shrill penetration of healthy childish lungs to make Salvani wince.

"Madame," he cried. *"Mon compagnon est un soldat Italien. Dans le village un homme, le Chasseur, nous a dit . . ."*

His clear voice rang out, and as if he was Pan playing his pipes, the dogs stopped their terrifying snarling and growling, and even more reassuringly, the shotgun was slowly lowered, but slowly and not very low, and the woman's finger was still on the trigger and her eyes were, if not implacable, still wary. She spoke again, in her harsh, unyielding voice, and Judah tugged at Salvani's hair.

"She says—"

"Yes." Salvani nodded. "I understand her. But call me uncle, remember." He lowered Judah, then carefully put down the rifle and the revolver. *"Ça va?"* he asked. All right?

64

"*Ça va*," the woman said. "*Entrez*," waving the shotgun at the door.

Treading nervously, the dogs still snuffling at their heels, Salvani and Judah went into the farmhouse. It was more like entering a cave than a house. The walls, made of rock, were unplastered, the ceiling low, with flitches of bacon hanging from a vast beam, a smoldering fire with a pan rammed on it, bits and pieces of plank furniture, a cupboard bed in one alcove, one padded chair, as out-of-place as a burglar at a policeman's ball, and, nailed to a wall, four photographs, three of them in somber frames with black crepe bows stuck on them.

The woman pointed at the photographs. "*Mon père, mon frère, mon fils. Tous morts!*" She jabbed at the fourth picture. "*Mon fils, prisonnier de guerre en Allemagne. Sales Boches.*" She spat, literally, not figuratively.

Salvani nodded—in fact, he wagged his head vigorously to make sure the woman understood that *he* understood, sighed sadly and spread out sympathetic hands: father, brother, son, killed by the Germans, and a son still a prisoner of war. That meant he had been away two years at least . . . He felt a prickle of unease at the thought; and no wonder the woman was bitter, spitting out her curse, *sales Boches*, filthy animals, or something like it, but perhaps it was her bitterness toward the Germans that had made the Chasseur think they could find shelter here. "I'm sorry," he said, feeling stupid for saying it but feeling sorry, too, looking at the long-dead faces, and the gaunt woman in a room one step up from an animal's den.

"Ah." The woman waved a lean arm, bent over the fire, and stirred the pot, her hard cheekbones picked out by the flames, muttering to herself in the dense patois. Still mumbling, she left the fire and the room, and Salvani raised an eyebrow at Judah, who shrugged back. "I don't understand," he began, but stopped as the woman came back with mugs of sour-smelling milk.

65

"*Reposez-vous,*" she said, handing over the mugs. "*Reposez-vous*"—sit—ordering rather than inviting, and went back to the fire and the pan, muttering and stirring as the fire glowed, and glowed brighter still as the daylight faded, and faded further, ebbing away, to violet to purple dusk. Judah sat by Salvani, his milk undrunk, and Salvani sat, longing for wine. Mice skittered up and down the walls and things sounding more ominous scratched in the walls, and still the woman muttered and stirred and the fire glowed and the pot bubbled as if, like the woman, it was mumbling to itself.

"*Madame.*" Salvani coughed. "*Madame, vous êtes mariée?*" You have a husband?

"*Oui.*" The woman turned her lined face to him. "*Oui. Avec les chèvres—*"

With the goats! That sounds about right, Salvani thought. And if he was anything like his missus, he was probably trying to teach them to play cards, because she looked, sounded, and for all he knew was, a genuine one hundred percent crackpot—and who wouldn't be, living up here in a cave, with pictures of dead men staring down on you.

"Soon," the woman croaked. "Soon. He comes soon."

Salvani bared his teeth in a grin, intended to be friendly, half inclined to say that it couldn't be soon enough for him, and turned to Judah. "Drink," he said. He raised a mug to Judah's lips. Judah obediently opened his mouth, but there was something disturbing about the way he was sitting, rather stiffly, like a wooden puppet, and some of the bluish milk spilled down from his lips.

"All right, *bambino?*" Salvani asked, a trace of doubt in his voice. "Just tired, hey?" Hoping that was the case, but troubled by the fact that Judah's eyes were wide open and had a glassy brightness. "Madame"—he turned to the woman, wanting to say—quite what he did not know, but something like, "Do you think that the kid is okay?" But the woman was on her feet, and outside the dogs were *woofing*—not the ferocious baying with which Salvani had been greeted or warned off, but more a respectable coughing, which made unnecessary the woman's remark that her husband was here, which she said as she strode with her long, ungainly stride out of the house.

"And I hope to Christ he isn't like her," Salvani said, not at all relishing the prospect of another mutterer joining them, especially as, he realized with alarm, he had left his rifle and revolver outside; but he was more alarmed when, after a moment or two, the weapons came in, held by a man.

"Monsieur." Salvani made to stand up but thought better of it, not wishing with his bulk to seem intimidating.

Not that the man looked as if he would be easily intimidated. He was short and slightly built, but he had hard, weather-beaten features, sharp eyes, and he was handling the weapons with an unnerving familiarity.

"Monsieur," Salvani began again. "Excuse me . . . my French . . . er, I . . . we . . . were told—"

"My wife explained outside," the man said. He sat down on the amazing easy chair and spoke to his wife, who poured him wine into a cracked glass, then stepped back into the shadows.

The man drank and held out his glass to be refilled. "You met the Chasseur?"

"Yes." Salvani looked longingly at the wine and told the story: a crash, the café, the Chasseur. "And we're just trying to get home. To Italy. If you can help us . . . well, what can I say?"

The man sipped his wine instead of gulping it, lowered his glass and, his face as bleak and chipped as a sliver of rock, looked at Judah. "Him?" he asked.

"My nephew," Salvani said. "He was staying with me. On holiday," thinking that if you believe that, then you're as crazy as your wife.

The man nodded. "Le Pic," he said. "Me." He spoke to his wife over his shoulder. She shuffled in the darkness and opened the door and the dogs came in, fawning by Le Pic, their tails drooping, their baleful eyes still on Salvani, the corners of their mouths dragged back, showing yellow and white fangs, long enough to slash an elephant to pieces.

"They won't hurt you." Le Pic scuffed the head of the nearest dog.

"Sure," Salvani said. "Pets like," vague memories of someone in the Bible in a lion's den stirring in his mind.

"Well . . ." Le Pic waved his hand ambiguously. "You have papers? *Documenti—*" breaking into Italian.

"You speak Italian?" Salvani said.

Le Pic swished the wine in his glass. "Who doesn't speak some—around here? But—" He snapped his fingers. "The papers."

"Right, no problem." Salvani fumbled in his pocket and handed over his paybook.

Le Pic held the book to the lamp and peered at it, then lowered his hand.

"That seems to be in order," he said. "Yes. Excuse me for asking, but you know . . . we have to be careful . . ."

"Sure. Exactly." Salvani was eager, anxious, to be friendly. "Absolutely. I'd be the same. Believe me."

"Bon," Le Pic said. "Now his—the kid's."

"Ah!" Salvani coughed and made vague gurgling sounds, playing for time while cursing himself for not having made up a story to explain *that*. "The . . . the thing is . . . er . . . he—I mean we, lost them, his papers, in the crash. You know I told you—we had a crash . . ."

"Yes," Le Pic said. "You did. You did tell me. *Oui. Si.*" He flicked the paybook back, throwing it rather low so that Salvani had to stoop to grab it. And when he raised himself he saw that the revolver was pointing at him.

"Oh," he said. "Like that, is it?"

68

"Yes," Le Pic said. "Just like that. I don't like your tale, Corporal. I don't like it at all. Who is the child?"

"I've told you," Salvani said, a little desperately. "He—"

"Don't give me that." Le Pic's voice was as hard as his face. "Soldiers don't have their nephews visiting them in wartime. Right, Mama?"

"Right," answered the woman, and she didn't seem crazy at all as she came from the shadows with the shotgun in her hands.

"So," Le Pic said. "The truth. *Vite*." Quick.

Salvani licked his lips, wondering for a brief moment if he could jump the man, then thought better of it as the dogs rolled their eyes at him. "All right," he said. "There's something more to it. But look, can the kid go out for a bit?"

Le Pic pondered, then nodded. "The kitchen," he said to his wife.

"Go on," Salvani said. "Go with the nice lady. I'll be here."

With that strange doll-like stiffness, Judah slid off the bench and went with the woman to the kitchen. Salvani frowned after him. "I think he's sick," he said.

"I'm not surprised." Le Pic settled himself in his chair. "Now, what's this something?" his tone of voice making it clear that the something had to be good.

"It's—" Salvani leaned forward, saw Le Pic's thumb on the hammer of the revolver and leaned back again. "The crash, that's true. But the thing is, the kid, his father was killed in it, see, but I don't want him to know. He thinks his old man has had to go somewhere and that we're going to meet him. I don't want him to find out. Not yet, anyway."

"And you're taking him to Italy?" There was a sneering disbelief in Le Pic's manner, and Salvani felt a growing anger and exasperation in himself.

"What do you expect? You think I should have left him in a gorge with his father smashed to bits? Or with those

69

pigs down in the café? 'Course I'm taking him. He's got relatives in Italy."

"He's French," Le Pic said flatly. He shouted to his wife and got a spate of words back in impenetrable idiom. "She says he speaks French like a native."

"His father was French," Salvani admitted. "But his mother was Italian."

"Then why not leave him in France?" Le Pic said. "He must have relatives here."

"Because . . ." Salvani closed his mouth, trapped by his lies and his decency.

"Because he's a Jew." Le Pic grinned and licked his lips. "And Jews are worth money, even little ones. Money." And he rubbed his fingers together.

The fire crackled and spat, the pan plopped and bubbled, and Salvani swung his head like a tethered bull. What a mug, he thought. What a mug. What an idiot. The biggest idiot in the world. Pointed by that smooth-talking bastard of a Chasseur up to this godforsaken hole, his weapons taken from him, double-talked into staying by a crazy woman who wasn't crazy at all, and now caught helpless under the gun by a crafty, venomous swine who, he had no doubt at all, was going to hand them over to the Germans and get a nice little wad for his trouble . . . He tried to swallow, swallow, as it were, his self-disgust at his stupidity, and then from the kitchen came a thin keening: Judah whimpering.

Salvani swung his head around. "You hear that?" he cried. "Doesn't it worry you?"

He turned back, his one good eye glaring, and saw Le Pic, *his* face suffused with anger, standing, and the revolver, cocked, not a hand's breadth away.

"Worry?" Le Pic said. "Worry about the child? No. He doesn't worry me." He jabbed the revolver against Salvani's forehead, jabbing again, and again. "You do—" Another probing jab. "You."

Salvani gaped. "Me?"

"Oui," Le Pic hissed. *"Oui,"* and jabbed again. "You weren't taking the kid to Italy. You were going to the Germans. Jew seller!"

It's a nightmare, Salvani thought. I'm having a nightmare, the shadows flickering, the ominous bubbling of the pot, the dogs on their feet, hackles raised, the gun against his head, and the man cursing him, the woman too, her harsh voice crackling from the kitchen—*"Cochon; chien; bête humaine"*: pig, dog, human beast; and to cap it all Judah, whose whimpers were now full-blown wails.

"Jesus Christ!" Salvani shouted. "I'm saving the kid. *Saving* him! Ask him. Ask about how we saved him and his father, and the other Jews. *Ask him!"*

"All right," Le Pic said. "All right. I'll do that. But you're very close, *Italien.* You know that."

Salvani did, and he didn't need to ask close to what, either. Le Pic nodded, then called to his wife, who brought in Judah, who took one look and changed his wails into ear-splitting screams.

"It's all right," Salvani said, thinking that it must be the most improbable remark ever made to a child, or anyone else, come to that. *"Bambino,* tell them about the château."

"Uncle," Judah wailed.

"Uncle?" said Le Pic. "Uncle?"

"I told him to say that," Salvani said. "And put that pistol down. Can't you see you're frightening him. And back away. Your wife has got the bloody shotgun. Just speak to the kid quietly."

Le Pic stared down over the barrel of the revolver, stared for a long moment, then backed away a pace, two, three. "One move," he said. "Just one. Understand?" sitting as Salvani wagged his head to show that he did understand. He understood only too well.

"Child," Le Pic said. "Come here."

"Do it, Judah," Salvani said. "Just tell the truth. The man won't hurt you."

"Of course not," Le Pic said. "Just come here a moment,

71

child," coaxing Judah to him and then speaking in a clear, fluent French, too quick and too good for Salvani to fully comprehend, and after a while Judah began to answer, "Yes, no, yes," although in an odd, mechanical way, as if someone else was speaking through his mouth, until Le Pic gently patted him on the head and said, "Thank you. Thank you, little one. You understood that?" he asked.

"Some," Salvani said.

"He says that you have told him to tell lies," Le Pic said. "He says that you told him he had to tell everyone that you were his uncle but that you aren't." Carefully he eased Judah back into the arms of his wife, and he was still holding the revolver, and it was pointing straight at Salvani's belly.

Salvani felt heavily languorous, the slow ponderous exhaustion of extreme fatigue. You learned too well, Judah, he thought. "Not your fault," he said aloud.

"Fault?" Le Pic frowned and then glanced down. "Oh, the revolver. Excuse me. I'd forgotten! Strange, hey, to forget such a thing."

"You mean it's all right?" Salvani's voice seemed to be coming from a long way off and, like Judah's, to be spoken by someone else.

"Oh yes," Le Pic said. "Quite all right. Sorry, for not trusting you. But these times . . ."

"These times . . ." Salvani stretched out his bruised hands to the fire. "So, what now?"

"Now we eat," Le Pic said.

The woman lit a guttering oil lamp, rattling out plates, spoons, soup, hunks of bread, hard goat cheese, wine. Salvani gulped the wine down and attacked the soup while the woman, transformed from a muttering hag into a caring, maternal figure, and with a name, Jeanne, spoon-fed Judah, urging him to swallow soup and chew bread dipped in wine. "Eat," she said. "Eat, little one," with a concern on her face that Salvani didn't want to see.

Le Pic finished his soup and reached for the cheese. "We have to talk," he said. But the talk was postponed as Judah was suddenly, violently sick, and fell face forward into his bowl of soup.

"Ah!" Jeanne clutched Judah, saving him from drowning, and held him in her arms. "Ill," she said. "The infant is ill," mopping his face and looking accusingly at Salvani.

It didn't need Jeanne to tell them that Judah was ill. He lay limp in Jeanne's arms, his eyes half open and the pupils rolled upward.

"Yes." Salvani lurched to his feet and made a futile gesture with his arms. "He's had a hard time . . ." He looked helplessly at Le Pic, who didn't seem to be concerned.

"Shock probably," Le Pic said. "I've seen it happen before, when I was in the army. It can take time to catch up with you. He's been all right, hasn't he? Walking, knew who he was?"

"Yes." Salvani stooped over Judah. "Yes, but suppose . . . I mean, suppose it's something worse. I mean, really bad. Shouldn't we get a doctor?"

Jeanne started back and Le Pic stared across the table sardonically. "A doctor? *Italien*, where would we get a doctor?"

"We could take him . . ." Salvani spoke uncertainly.

"Yes, we could do that," Le Pic said. "Fifteen kilometers to Allevard. And what then?"

"Oh." Salvani hadn't thought of that little difficulty. "But even so . . ."

Le Pic finished his wine in a mouthful, stood up, and walked around the table to where Jeanne was holding Judah. Then, incongruously, he roughly tickled Judah's ribs. Judah jerked, arms and legs twitching, and made a strange, almost animal noise. Le Pic stood back. "It's a thing we do with young animals, lambs and kids. If they twitch like that, they're usually all right. Wash him in hot water," he said to Jeanne. "Then wrap him up and sleep with him in the bed, keep him warm that way." He felt Judah's face. "He's got a fever, but I think he'll be all right. We'll see tomorrow."

"And if he isn't?" Salvani said.

Le Pic didn't answer for a moment or two, but when he did he wasn't encouraging. "That's up to you," he said. "But I think we ought to have our little talk. Come on."

With a stub of candle he led the way into the kitchen, if that is what it was: a rickety line of shelves, littered with pots and pans and a few rusting tins of food, a battered unlit iron stove, a tub stuffed with clothes, a rough table, two hard chairs, and mice and cockroaches scuttling away as they entered. Le Pic produced two glasses and a bottle of what looked like brandy. He sat down, gesturing to Salvani to do the same, and poured out two drinks. "*Santé*," he said, raising his glass—Good health—then paused as Jeanne bustled in and took a pan, speaking rapidly in the dense dialect.

"For the hot water," Le Pic said. "For the child. He needs cleaning up." He placed his glass down on the table, rippled with generations of scrubbing. "We have tomorrow to think about."

"Yes." The kitchen was bitterly cold, although Le Pic seemed immune to it, and Salvani downed his glass, glad of its fiery warmth. "Yes. We do," he said, but, in fact, he didn't want to think about the next day, or even the next hour.

"The child," Le Pic said, across the guttering light of the candle.

"The child." Salvani felt an obscure sense of grievance. He was ill, too: battered, bruised, cut, torn, wrenched, aching from the top of his head to the sore tips of his toes; and all he wanted was to drink himself into oblivion and then also be washed in hot water and to lie down, to lie down in a warm bed and drift into a deep dreamless slumber. But—he braced himself, forcing himself upright as

Le Pic poured another drink and shoved the glass over the table. "Yes," he said, "the kid—and tomorrow."

"Well." A plume of cigarette smoke came drifting across the penumbra of the candlelight. "I was thinking that tomorrow I would take you over the mountain to La Chambre. That's on the Mont Cenis road. You ought to be able to pick up Italian transport there."

Salvani forced himself upright. "That sounds fine," he said. "Fine. Is it far?"

"No." Le Pic poured out some more of the brandy. "Not far at all. Not for you or me—" He held out a hand as if to suggest that a bone-shaking tramp over twenty kilometers of mountain, rising to over two thousand meters, was a mere stroll. Which no doubt it was, to him. "But the child . . ."

"I'll carry him," Salvani said.

"Sure." Le Pic turned his hand out as if to say: who couldn't. "But he's sick, you know?" He put his hand down on the scrubbed tabletop, next to Salvani's massive fist. *"Italien—"* He tapped Salvani's knuckles with a thin finger. "I would take you to La Chambre tonight, but"—the slender finger tapped again, like a bird's beak hacking at a tree trunk—"but maybe a night's sleep, hey? Hey?"

"Hey." Salvani dragged himself upright again, fighting through a drowsy fog of fatigue and alcohol. "A night's sleep. Yes. That sounds all right. A good sleep."

"Now," Le Pic said.

"Now?" Salvani gave a mighty yawn.

"Now. Sleep."

"The child." Salvani shoved himself up.

"He'll be all right," Le Pic said. "Don't disturb him. You'll have to shake down in here. Will that do you?"

"I could sleep on broken glass," Salvani said.

"I guess you could." Le Pic left the room and came back with a couple of rough woolen blankets. "It's not a grand hotel," he said.

"Better than ten of them," Salvani said, lying down. "Not that I've ever been in one . . ." already drifting off, sleep and brandy taking away the day and all its cares.

Night fell over the farm of Le Pic, where the mice came scuttling out and the rats, and the cats hunted in the moonlight and, if they wandered too far, were themselves hunted by foxes and the huge mountain owls, hunters and hunted in the clear night, squeaks and squeals and snuffles of satisfaction and agony on the plateau, and the mountains, and in the tumbling gorges; and in the villages and towns, too, cries and screams and uglier squeals of satisfaction—laughter and jeers—as other victims were seized by other hunters as, curled in the arms of Madame Le Pic, Judah slept the unfathomable sleep of a child, and Salvani, sprawled on the floor by the restless dogs, slept his drugged sleep, but with the images of dead men pursuing him into his dreams.

8

Salvani dreamed his haunted dreams, and away from the plateau of Le Pic, and away from the murmur of the waters of the streams flowing from the Seven Lakes, a worse nightmare, dreamed by a warped, evil, and darkened mind far away, was being turned into reality as the *rafle* gathered momentum. Trucks, crammed with Jews, roared to railway stations, and trains belched their way to Drancy, Paris, and from Drancy other trains clanked to the east, to the drab plains and brooding, secret forests of Poland, taking the Jews to the reeking chimneys of new factories; but not to factories which made useful things for people but which made people into things, useless things; corpses.

The jackboots echoed down cobbled streets, the huge dogs barked and bared their fangs, the clerks meticulously noted down names, nationality, sex, date of birth, and already, within twenty-four hours, the denunciations began, furtive anonymous notes and telephone calls: Pierre X gave food to a Jew; Marie Y gave a room to a Jewish family; Louis Z has helped Jews to hide in the hills; old scores and ancient grudges being paid off; Marcel K is a Communist; Hector T said he wanted Germany to lose the war; Martin S has listened to the English radio broadcasts . . . and the dogs and rifles came for them also, and took them to foul cells and dungeons where men waited for them with rubber truncheons—and worse.

Major Barbie sat in his shadowy castle in Lyons, and, between fussing over his veal cutlets and torturing people, sent out his imperative messages: letters, telephone calls, telegrams. All Jews to be taken. *All.* None to escape— *none*—savoring his pâté and wine and sending his cancerous messages, like a malignant tumor invading a brain, as, in the night, the remnants of the Italian Army straggled over the mountain passes to their homeland, taking with them *their* Jews: all of them, Italian, French, Dutch, man, woman, and child; all to be saved. All.

The messages went out from Lyons to the largest towns, and the smallest villages, and to Allevard, where a sergeant of the uniformed police, the Gendarmerie, was talking on the telephone to his inspector in Chambéry.

"Yes," he was saying. "An Italian corporal and a kid. Badly knocked about. The café owner up there is a cousin of mine. This corporal burst in and threatened to shoot them. Robbed them, too. Well, I've only just found out, that's why. The postman came down with the news."

At the other end of the line the inspector scowled at the phone. "So what do you expect me to do about it? Send in

77

a report and keep your eyes open for this Italian. And make sure you get the paperwork right." He was about to slam down the phone when a curious gargling sound from the sergeant made him hold on. "What was that?"

"There's a bit more to it," the sergeant said.

"Well, what is it?" the inspector said. "Get on with it."

"It's like this." The sergeant spoke slowly, picking his words thoughtfully, and when he had finished speaking, the inspector was thoughtful, too.

"Yes," he said, "I see what you mean. Get up there tomorrow, first thing, and see what you can find out. Do that lot up there good to be rousted out, anyway. And *make sure* that you explain why you were so late in reporting this."

He slammed down the phone and walked to the window and peered out. Chambéry was a handsome town, important too, with a railway station, at the head of a network of main roads which led to the south and to Switzerland and Italy. It had handsome streets, cafés, hotels, and a cathedral, but the inspector was looking at none of these. Instead, he was peering across the road where, imposing even in the darkness, loomed the town hall, the Hôtel de Ville, and in particular at its ornate entrance, where two soldiers stood, two soldiers in steel helmets, bearing rifles, and dressed in field gray and jackboots.

The inspector didn't actually like Germans but he did admire them: their efficiency, smartness, and, at least in public, their politeness. In fact, you had to hand it to them; it was only thirty-six hours since they had invaded this part of France and already they were well established in the town, with their company headquarters, signals, transport—and police. And that thought made the inspector hesitate.

He drummed his fingers on the window. Unlike their blue-clad allies of the Milice, the German police were also polite—in public—but like their gray-clad comrades, they were also extremely efficient, and, he thought, probably

78

very unforgiving, and if they suspected that a Frenchman, even one as important and imposing as himself, was not cooperating wholeheartedly, then they might take him across the road into the Hôtel de Ville, draw the curtains, as it were, and commence, efficiently, to do extremely un-polite things to *him*.

And so, instead of going home to his buxom wife, he took his hat and walked down a gloomy corridor to a room marked Detectives, where, behind a scarred desk, a detec-tive sergeant was drinking vermouth and talking to an-other man, also in plainclothes, also drinking, his chair tilted back, his feet on the desk, a hat pulled over his eyes and a cigarette dangling from the corner of his mouth.

The inspector took him to be a cheap criminal, an in-former, and was about to kick the chair from under him to teach him manners, when the detective raised his hand.

"This is Monsieur Palet. He's . . ."

"Milice," the man said. "Special agent."

"Monsieur is from Lyons." The detective stressed the name slightly with a hint of a warning behind it. Not that the inspector needed the stress; the name alone was warn-ing enough. Every policeman knew of the prison of Sant-erre, and what was going on in that stony subworld.

"Understood." The inspector, crisp in his uniform and white shirt, held out his hand. "Anything we can do to help, of course."

Palet, in a creased, expensive suit and grimy linen, didn't bother to shake hands. "Get on with it," he said.

"What?" The inspector frowned then, realizing to whom he was speaking, unfrowned as it were. The faceless loung-ing figure and his masters, the men in black and silver, like beings from some alien, arid world, had inconceivable powers, and at a mere nod of the head even an inspector of police could find himself . . .

"Aaagh." His mouth had become, suddenly, dry. "It's this"—glad to go back to the mundane affairs of catching people. "My sergeant at Allevard—" He told the story of the brutal Italian soldier robbing cafés and assaulting people, and of the child he had with him.

"So?" The detective shrugged. "It's a job for your people, isn't it? You'll pick him up or the buzzards will get them. Who cares, anyway?"

The inspector sat down on a heavy, battered chair which had seen people on it more battered, by the detective. "We all might care," he said. "Especially Monsieur Palet."

"What does that mean?" Palet said.

"It's like this." The inspector hunched forward. "It's amazing, really, I suppose it's because the café owner is a relative of my sergeant—well, I mean it's amazing they handed it over, because they're all a pack of thieves up there. But this Italian left something behind. A small suitcase with some funny things in it, see. A shawl and funny little hat and a book in some sort of foreign language— like gibberish."

The detective cocked a sardonic eyebrow. "Are you kidding us?"

"Not at all." The inspector turned to Palet. "I'll bet Monsieur knows what I'm getting at."

Palet turned his head away and spat. "No, I don't," he said, snarled. "What the —— are you talking about?"

Even in a police station which had heard enough curses and blasphemies to burn the ears of a sergeant major, the oath was shocking, like a deliberate act of vandalism: the oath and the spitting both, a calculated insult. The inspector would like to have picked Palet up in his expensive suit and given him a few minutes of the treatment normally handed out to uncooperative criminals—that is, those who didn't immediately confess to their crimes and any the police hadn't been able to solve. Instead, he swallowed his wrath.

"They're *Jewish* clothes. Jewish. What they wear in their synagogues, aren't they? And the book in that gibberish.

It sounds like it's Jewish. So this Italian, or the kid, one of them—maybe both—they're Jews. Stands to reason, doesn't it?" He stood up and rammed on his kepi—smart, trim, efficient, a guardian of the state whose motto had been Liberty, Equality, and Fraternity.

"I'll let the Préfet know in Grenoble and I've told my sergeant to get up to this village and do what he can. I'm just letting you know, *officially*. Although all we can do is ask around."

"Oh?" Palet raised his head, for the first time showing his face. And he was, the inspector saw with some surprise, not a criminal type at all; if anything, he was rather good-looking, youthful and handsome with a clear olive skin and confiding brown eyes.

"Yes . . ." The inspector suddenly wanted to get away. He was unnerved by Palet, who, handsome though he was, wore his well-cut suit as though it didn't belong to him, and who made even the chair he was sitting on seem ugly, an instrument of torture rather than something to relax in. But behind him, the inspector knew, were other men, men who could break you, strip you of your smart uniform and the authority that went with it, and put you in a place where you looked at the world through iron bars. "Of course," he said. "Of course. All cooperation. Just ask. So I'll be off, then."

"All right," Palet said.

"Good." The inspector walked to the door feeling unprotected, as if an assassin was about to stick a dagger in his broad, blue-clad back, then turned. "You must come and have a meal with us one night," he blurted out. "My wife . . . an excellent cook . . . excellent. Well . . . good night."

Palet didn't deign to answer, unless a flick of a dirty finger, more a gesture of dismissal, was an answer, and the inspector went home to his wife and supper, which he ate without relish, and after a while the detective went home to his wife and his supper, and a little later, after finishing the detective's vermouth, Palet slouched to his hotel, where he had a room.

His room had the bare minimum for living. A table, a chair, a cracked wardrobe, a dusty bed, illumined by a naked, low-wattage, flyspecked light bulb. But the room was perfectly adequate for him. Indeed, any room anywhere would have been. He was as indifferent to his surroundings as a spider, except that the room had two advantages: it could only be approached up one flight of stairs, and down them, in an equally bleak room, there were two of his uniformed Milice, one of whom was always in.

He drank a glass of water, then filled it with brandy, and sprawled awkwardly on the bed, thinking about the Italian soldier and the kid with him, and the suitcase with Jew clothes in it.

Palet detested Jews anyway, believing, quite wrongly, that his father, who had run a bicycle shop in Grenoble before the war, had been ruined by Jewish competition, and he was genuinely pleased to arrest them, and their allies the socialists and Communists and sickly do-gooders. In fact, he was happy to arrest anyone, the richer the better—sleek, well fed, well dressed—although he enjoyed arresting poor people too, seeing the terror on their faces as he showed his identification. Sometimes he pretended to arrest people just to amuse himself, like a bully making an ugly face, or a boy pulling wings off flies.

But this Italian and Jew kid . . . He kicked off his shoes and sipped his brandy and thought about them. An Italian and a kid . . . He could think of many reasons why a man should abduct a child, most of them sickeningly unpleasant, but they didn't make sense in this case. No—he poured out more brandy—there was only one conceivable reason why this Italian was wandering over the mountains dragging a kid with him, and that was money.

Some people walked past the hotel, laughing. Palet scowled. That sort of laughter displeased him—the sound of people enjoying themselves; all his life, he had believed that when he heard laughter it was directed at himself. The footsteps clacked away as a dog barked. Palet sipped his brandy and hoped the dog was biting the passersby.

He slumped back on the bed and thought about the two wanderers. Probably the kid had rich relatives somewhere who would pay for him, and almost certainly he had money on him, although not money as such, but jewels—diamonds, most likely. Of course, the Italian wouldn't know that or he would simply have taken them, killed the kid, and sloped off on his own, which was what he, Palet, would have done. So he was taking the kid for ransom.

He brooded over that, sweat trickling down his neck, his socks soggy, and lit a cigarette with a silver lighter he had taken from an arrestee, one of the many agreeable perks his job offered. He knew perfectly well what the inspector and the detective thought: why bother about one soldier and one kid? Oh, they would go through the motions, send a cop or two up to the village, bang a few heads together, cover themselves, although it was crystal-clear that they didn't think they would find anybody out there in the tangled wilderness. But Palet had his own views on that, his own views and the power to see that what he wanted done *was* done.

He licked his lips and leaned back, staring at the cracks in the ceiling. It could work out neatly. Get the kid—a dirty Jew—that would be a feather in his cap—and get the diamonds. No need to mention those, of course, and the Italian . . . He pulled out his pistol and squinted down the sights. *Pow*, he whispered, *pow*, seeing the man crumple before him. *Ça va*, he said, it's okay, sweating brandy, listening to the clock of the Hôtel de Ville clank out midnight, and really looking forward to the morning, when his manhunt could begin.

The dawn came and Salvani awoke from his dreams and the specters which had haunted them, to find Jeanne leaning over him.

"Coffee," she said, and shoved a mug at him containing a murky fluid. "We make it ourselves, from acorns. Or you can have wine."

"Wine." Salvani struggled to his feet. "The child?"

"Sleeping," the woman said. "But he is better, I think. No fever."

"That's something." Salvani drank the weak wine and rubbed his eyes. "Wash?"

"Yes." Jeanne beckoned. Salvani followed her out of the house, past two pigs and a donkey, to a water trough. Might have guessed, Salvani thought, but the kid is going to have a proper bath, with hot water. When he had finished and rubbed himself down with his shirt, he found that Judah was already washed and was sitting eating, although now his head and cuts and bruises were painted bright green.

"Medicine," Jeanne said. "Special."

"Very," Salvani said and laughed. "Very special." He took a piece of bread and dunked it in wine, then looked up sharply. "Where is your man?"

"The village." Jeanne waved her arms.

"What?" Salvani was immediately suspicious.

"Every week," Jeanne said. "Every week on this day. If he doesn't go, perhaps someone comes to find him. Not good for you, hey?"

"No," Salvani said. "Not good at all. Nor for you," he added.

"Eh!" Jeanne waved that away.

Salvani chewed his bread. "He was talking about taking us to La Chambre today, if the child was up to it."

"We'll see, we'll see," Jeanne said. "But come now. Come. A hiding place until Le Pic comes back," snapping out the words that did mean *now*, and not after some vast delay— such as two minutes—making sure that Salvani got the message by shoving the guns and knapsack at him, and swinging Judah onto her hip.

"Hiding?" Salvani said, more feebly than he would have liked as he was swept through the door.

"A bas!" Jeanne elbowed him aside and with long, swinging strides loped across the bare field. *"Vite,"* she cried, *"vite"*—quick, quick—as the sun began to suck up the mountain mists, striding on until they came to a limestone ledge jutting from the fields like a set of jagged teeth.

"There." She pointed to a crack in the rock which looked hardly big enough to take a rabbit, let alone a man.

"There?" Salvani said dubiously.

"Yes." Jeanne lowered Judah and tugged away at a flake of rock, showing a more sizable hole. "In. *In. Vite!*" shoving Salvani forward.

"All right." Salvani was irritated by the shoving and barging, and by no means happy at the prospect of getting into the hole, which looked ominously like the entrance to a tomb, but giving way to the inevitable, and somewhat daunted by Jeanne, feet first he wriggled into the rock and found himself in a sizable cave, big enough to stretch out and even crouch in.

"Here." The rifle and revolver banged about his ears, and the knapsack, followed by Judah. "In the bag," Jeanne said. "Wine, water, food," and then the daylight was blotted out as the flake of rock was shoved back.

And the hell with that, Salvani thought. He shoved his head out. "No. Leave it." The cave was bad enough without having a gravestone sealing it. "Leave it. Tell her, Judah. Tell her to leave it."

Jeanne rattled off some acrid words and Judah poked his head under Salvani's arm. "She says this way no one can see us," he explained.

"No, and we won't be able to see them, either." He looked around and could see the whole of the plateau, the farm, and the trail leading to the valley. "This is all right. Tell her that if we can see anyone coming we'll pull the rock back."

Sourly enough, and not without reason, Jeanne accepted that, but as she strode away, she shouted stridently over her shoulder.

"What was that?" Salvani asked.

"We've got to stay in here," Judah said. "Stay in all the time. And watch. Keep watching." He stared at Salvani, his face anxious. "She's angry."

"No!" Salvani affected a jovial, lying manner. "No, she isn't. Not at all. Why, she likes you."

"Honest?" Judah said.

"Double honest." Salvani touched Judah's cheek tenderly. "Double, double honest. She's a nice woman. Really nice."

"She said you're an idiot," Judah said.

"What!"

"An idiot," Judah repeated, adding, with what seemed to Salvani quite unnecessary accuracy, "A great big idiot." He scrambled over Salvani and peered intently in his face. "Are you?"

"Am I?" Salvani took a deep breath, the sort he might normally have taken before thumping someone on the ear. Then, bumping his head on the roof of the cave, he laughed. "Maybe," he said. "Maybe I am—" and thinking that there was no maybe about it; lurking in a hole like a frightened rabbit, with a kid whose head changed color from day to day, when he could have been back home; maybe he was. Maybe he was a genuine idiot at that.

But, idiot or not, it was too late to do anything about it now, although, as he peered through the crevice, he wondered about that. To the east, not a hundred kilometers away, still veiled in cloud, were the High Alps, with passes through them, and not twenty kilometers away was a road which led to one of the passes . . . In fact, if he were simply to get up and go now, just get up and amble off, instead of waiting for someone else like Le Pic to deal the cards . . . Ah! he sucked his blackened teeth and thought of the last time he had played cards with Rosseti and Modesta—and where were they now? Lolling in some trattoria, knocking back drinks in Italy. He dragged his thoughts away from that desirable image and, screwing his neck around at an awkward angle, stared into the gloom of their hiding place. "A nice cave, isn't it?"—sounding improbable even to his own ears.

"Nice?" Judah's question echoed the improbability as he, too, looked into the gloom.

"Oh yes." Salvani forced a smile, the cuts on his face smarting as he did so. "Nice. Dry! It's dry, isn't it?"

"Yes." Judah admitted that indisputable fact. "But, Uncle—" He tugged at Salvani's collar. "Uncle, will Papa—"

"Of course. Certainly! Don't worry. Soon. Very soon!" Salvani gabbled, and anxious—desperate—to keep off that topic, he rolled his eyes and bared his teeth. "Listen, this cave . . . I'll bet . . . I'll bet bandits lived here!"

"Bandits!" Judah's eyes filled with tears and his mouth opened wide, but before he could scream Salvani grabbed him and held him reassuringly to his breast, wincing as Judah's amazingly hard head struck his bruised ribs.

"No," he said. "No . . . not *bad* bandits! Good bandits! Good ones, who helped poor people! Yes, ha! ha! yes, helped the poor. And listen!" He had a spurt of inspiration. "Maybe they buried treasure here! They did that, you know. Yes, they buried treasure all over the place—" And thinking for a moment, Well you never know your luck, maybe they *had* buried treasure in the cave, "Why not look? Why, there were bandits all over—*good* ones. Just see— wriggle down there and see. Anyway," he added, more for his own sake than for Judah's, "we could do with some."

"Some what?" Judah asked.

"Money."

"Money?"

"Yes. But—" Salvani chopped his words off. "But, hey! Don't worry about anything at all."

"Are you poor?" Judah asked.

"I'm not rich," Salvani said ruefully.

"Do we need money? Need it to see Papa?"

"It wouldn't hurt." Salvani turned and looked out and then his arm was lightly punched and Judah whispered to him.

Salvani looked over his shoulder. For a child, Judah had a curious expression—earnest and calculating and something else, perhaps: the shadow of experience, as if a ghost was peering through innocent eyes. "What is it?" he asked. "You're not feeling ill, are you?"

Judah shook his head slowly. "I've got something," he said.

"That's nice," Salvani said. He looked around again. All was still peaceful, Jeanne was feeding the hens and a few goats had joined the donkey, one of them with a bell around its neck which clanked in a melancholy way.

"Uncle," Judah's persistent whisper echoed around the cave. "Uncle, I've got diamonds!"

Salvani swung around, his eyes popping. "You've—Jesus, you *have* found treasure!" Not only were his eyes popping, but it felt his brain was, too. On the run, and to actually find buried treasure! Of course, it stood to reason, in a weird way. The entire country was overrun by smugglers and they had to dump their loot somewhere. And they'd found it! Lucky, lucky day!

"Where did you find them. *Where?*"

"It's a secret," Judah said. "You mustn't tell. Promise."

"Promise, yes, *promise*. Cross my heart, see!" Salvani could actually feel himself salivating.

"I didn't *find* them," Judah said. "Papa gave them to me."

"Aaaah . . ." Salvani saw the light, and in more ways than one. Of course, a man like Fleur, forever on the run, dodging this way and that—what better than to carry diamonds, small, light, easily hidden, and worth hard cash anywhere in the world—and good luck to him. And he'd been right in the first place, thinking that Balbo was after something when he'd taken Fleur with him. He'd been bribed. Fleur had got what he wanted: an officer as escort, a car, and as a bodyguard that mug Salvani. Well, that little plan hadn't worked. They were dead and here he was, alive and kicking, and with a hatful of diamonds and a life of luxury ahead, although—and the warm, sugary taste of saliva turned into bile—it was the last time he was ever going to do a good turn.

"It's a secret, is it?" he said, echoing Judah's words. "Well—" He scowled down at Judah, as if he was responsible for the setup. "Well, it's not a secret now. Hand them over."

"Uncle . . ." There was a quaver in Judah's voice, but he held out his hand, tiny beside Salvani's calloused palm, opened it, and revealed, not shimmering fire, but a dull pebble.

"A diamond! A . . . *diamond!*" Salvani's fist shook with rage, and for one appalling moment he almost struck Judah, as if the child had made him the victim of a malevolent practical joke, but as he looked into the child's grave eyes he sighed. What the hell, kids hoarded things, rubbish to anyone else but invested with magic by themselves, a stick becoming a wizard's wand, an old box an airplane, and a pebble turning into a diamond . . .

"Sure, kid," he said. "Sure. A diamond. A nice diamond. But you keep it. Keep it safe, mind. Safe. Yes, we might need it. You know? Need it. But you look after it, that's a good boy." He turned away, resigned again to poverty, with the harsh tongue of a lifetime of hardship and oppression saying to him: So what did you expect, mug? What did you really expect? Diamonds for Salvani? Despite himself, he grinned, it sounded like the title of a ridiculous film, and although a part of him, some deep, murky part of his mind, bitterly regretted that there were no diamonds, another part wasn't that displeased. Fleur, that dapper, courteous, civilized man, had not, after all, been playing him for a fool. Fleur had been, after all, a *signore*, a gentleman, *un uomo*—a human being. And that was worth something. Worth a lot, really—although he still wished the pebble was a diamond.

He leaned back, on a grindingly aching shoulder, and ruffled Judah's green tufts of hair. "Keep it safe," he said. "Tuck it away and don't tell anyone else . . ." longing for a cigarette, and longing for Le Pic to return, and longing for Italy, and his own family, and his own children, closing his vast hand over Judah's hand, then releasing it, turning away to look, watchfully, at the farm of Le Pic, and the snaking path which ran down to the dark valley.

"*Si*," Judah murmured. "*Si*, Uncle." He slid the pebble back into the secret pocket in his jacket, where five more pebbles nestled. He was puzzled by the rejection. The big soldier had said that they were poor, and anyone knew that money was a good thing to have—and if the soldier took the diamond, why, they could probably buy an airplane and fly to wherever his father was. Certainly they could get a taxi.

Still, if the soldier didn't want them, there was nothing he could do about it. In fact, there wasn't much he could do about anything except to keep quiet and make himself very small. So he let the matter pass, it never occurring to him that a grown man would never have seen an uncut, unpolished diamond.

The morning crept away. Salvani gave Judah an egg, bread, water, drank wine himself, ate bread and cheese, and watched the path. But no one came. Jeanne vanished inside the house. Only the crows cawed and the melancholy goat bell clanked dismally. Judah slept, murmuring in his sleep. The sun slipped over its meridian and high fleecy clouds drifted across the pale blue sky. Salvani's eyes began to close and he started to drift away, drift from the cave, and the plateau, and the farm, and his aches and pains and cares, drifting into that hazy half state where dreams come stealing into the mind, transfiguring all they touch, like a fog on a familiar landscape. And then he jerked awake. A man was calling.

90

It was Le Pic, giving a long, high yell, almost a yodel. He walked to the farmhouse and met Jeanne at the door. They stood talking for a moment, then went inside.

And what now? Salvani wondered. What were they up to? Sitting in their ghastly room while police and soldiers sneaked up to the cave; drinking; gloating and smacking their lips in anticipation of a nice little reward. He hitched up his rifle and fingered the safety catch, wondering if he would use it.

And then Le Pic reappeared. He seemed in no hurry, looking at the sky, lighting a cigarette, and then he walked slowly across the plateau, driving a goat forward, moving rather aimlessly, merely a peasant finding a decent patch of grazing for his animal; but behind the aimlessness was a purpose as he led the goat to the outcrop of limestone, and the cave. He squatted, his back to the rock, and puffed casually at his cigarette, but there was nothing casual in the way he spoke.

"Italien," he said. "Can you hear me?"

"Yes," Salvani whispered.

"You can speak up," Le Pic said, somewhat testily. "How's the child?"

"Sleeping," Salvani said.

"Is he sick?" Le Pic asked.

"Er, no, I don't think so. Not too bad, anyway. Why?"

"Listen, Italian. They know about you. The cops. That pig in the café let them know. And they know the child is a Jew. You left a case behind with Jewish clothes. And they've found the car with bodies. They've put two and two together, you know?"

"Christ!" Salvani bit his lip. "So what now?"

"Now?" Le Pic was grim. "That's not all of it. If it was just the Gendarmerie, it wouldn't be so bad. But I spoke to a cop down there. He said the Milice are coming up. You know about the Milice? They're bad news, *Italien.* They'll come up with dogs."

"But why are they coming?" Salvani said.

"Who knows?" Le Pic spat out his cigarette end. "The child's father, maybe he was a big shot . . . Anyway, the cop says they're going insane about Jews. Insane. But the thing is . . . Look, we want to help you, you know that?"

And here it comes, thought Salvani. We want to help you, *but*; but move on, friend. Beat it, wander about the mountains until you die of starvation or get rounded up. "You'll point us the right way, won't you?" he said.

"What do you mean?" Le Pic was indignant. "Point you! I'm taking you. But we have to start now."

"In daylight?" Salvani asked.

"We'll have to chance it." Le Pic stood up. "It won't be long before the Milice come knocking on this door. I'll go to the house and look around. If it's all clear, I'll whistle. Then come quick. Quick, you hear?"

The whistle came and Salvani, dragging Judah, ran, doubled up, to the farmhouse, where Jeanne packed the knapsack with iron-hard bread and iron-hard cheese, and handed over a virulently green bottle. "For the child," she said, rubbing Judah's head.

"Madame," Salvani said, awkwardly. "I thank you," but his thanks were brushed aside.

"Go," Jeanne said, anxious, Salvani guessed, as much for herself and Le Pic as for him and Judah. "Go. Quick. Quick," bustling them through the door where Le Pic was keeping watch and saying *"Vite"* too, and even on that flinty little man's face there was fear.

"Come," he said, and as they left the farmhouse, Jeanne stood, shadowed in the doorway, and cried, "God be with you, *pauvre enfant, pauvre soldat,*" poor infant, poor soldier, as they hastened across the meadow, heading east, to where, in the light of the westering sun, the Alps glittered, blood red.

At a half run they crossed the plateau, went through a jumble of boulders, and, for a perilous half hour, cut across a bare, slanting hillside, open to the world, but then they were threading their way through more boulders, scrub oak and juniper, climbing to a bare, scraped ridge, and there Judah demanded a rest.

"My *legs* are hurting me," he said, as if they were somehow independent of the rest of his body. "I want to sit *down*."

"We'll have a little rest, then," Salvani said, not averse to a sit-down himself. "All right?" he asked Le Pic—and was taken aback when Le Pic said, sharply, that it was absolutely not all right.

"Move," he said. *"Move!"* He grabbed Salvani's arm and pointed to a vast range of savage rock. "We have to go far. *Far!* And tonight."

"Far," Salvani said glumly, "and tonight. Okay."

"Maybe in one hour," Le Pic said. "Then a rest. *Short.* You can do that?" mildly taunting.

"I can do it," Salvani said.

"And him?" Le Pic gestured at Judah sprawled on the grass.

"I'll carry him," Salvani said.

Le Pic glanced sideways at Salvani as if to say: If you believe that, you're crazy, friend; but when he forced Salvani to his feet he took the pack and rifle while Salvani heaved Judah over his shoulder.

"Twenty kilometers," Le Pic said.

"Right," Salvani said.

"But we rest in an hour." Le Pic grinned. "Now, *vite.*"

They moved along the ridge, into another gorge, and another, but always climbing, losing height now and again to edge around the ax-like cliffs, but creeping back up again, up to where no trees grew and no grass—Le Pic as nimble as a goat, Salvani plunging and stumbling, every joint in his body creaking, but thinking: All right, scamper as much as you like, pal, but I'll be with you at the end—right slap-bang behind you—shifting Judah from shoulder to shoulder as they crossed another ridge and another gorge, Le Pic allowing a break now and then, but always, before it seemed to Salvani five seconds had passed, springing to his feet and moving on.

Darkness came and the valleys filled with mist. The men climbed up through the shrouded, ghostly mountains and crags, black and white under the cold light, like travelers in a dream dreamed by some silent, haunted sleeper—and then Salvani realized that they were going downhill, really downhill, not merely skirting cliffs or precipices, and that the dark shape before him was not Le Pic waiting, but a tree. Le Pic was standing by it, a shadow as black as the tree itself. "Rest," he said.

Although he felt like falling down on the spot, Salvani braced himself, straightening his creaking shoulders and his head. "Rest?" he croaked. "Is it worth it?"

"Worth what?" Le Pic was puzzled.

"Putting the kid down," Salvani said. "Like we are going to *rest*, are we?"

"Oh yes," Le Pic said. "We're going to rest. We're over the range."

"We are?"

"Yes. A long way over." Le Pic tapped the tree. "Where these start to grow again."

"Right," Salvani croaked. "Trees." He let Judah slip down his chest. "So we're safe here?"

"Safe?" Le Pic tilted his head. "You're not safe, *Italien*. Not until you are in Italy. But safe enough for now."

Salvani let Judah slide to the ground, then slid down after him. They were on rough grass wet with dew. He hauled off his overcoat and spread it under Judah. "All right, *bambino*?" he asked.

Judah's head lolled, but he opened wide, enigmatic eyes. "Papa?" he whispered.

Salvani stifled a groan. "No, it's me. Uncle, you know? Uncle? It's all right. We're . . . we're—" Despite himself he laughed. "We're on a mountain. But don't you worry. It's

94

a . . . well, just don't worry. Would you like some—" As he spoke, Judah's head tilted sideways and his eyes closed. "Judah?" Salvani patted Judah's lolling face. "Just tired," he said. "Isn't he?"

"I don't know." Le Pic left the shadow of the tree and knelt by Salvani in the moonlight. "Tired, maybe. Sick . . . He was all right today? In the cave?"

"Yes, I guess so. Sleeping a lot."

"It's a good sign."

"You think so?" Salvani looked up hopefully.

"Surely." Le Pic put his hand on Judah's brow. "He's cool. That's good, too. You have children, *Italien?*"

"Yes," Salvani said. "I've got kids. Five."

"Five!" Le Pic grinned. "You should know about children, then. One minute sick, the next running around playing games. And he's had a hard time, hey?"

"He has that," Salvani said. "It would knock a horse down. But what if he is. Sick?"

Le Pic fished out a crumpled packet of cigarettes and handed one over, then drew from the never failing knapsack a bottle of brandy. "Take," he said. "Drink. Go on, you've earned it."

They sat for a little while, sipping from the bottle companionably, Salvani stretching aching legs, arms, shoulders, neck—and wishing he could stretch his brains while he was about it.

Le Pic pulled a corner of the overcoat over Judah. "*Italien*, if he is sick"—he tapped his head—"the concussion, I don't know what you do. But down there"—he jabbed a finger at the blackness below them—"a long way yet but down, down, there is the road to Mont Cenis, to Italy, hey? So, you get a lift from your soldiers. And maybe that's all right. But there's a town, La Chambre. There's a doctor there. But what then? Maybe he hands the child over to the police and they hand him over—"

"To the Germans," Salvani said.

95

"Maybe not," Le Pic said. "Who knows?" He puffed on his cigarette, the red end glowing in the night. "Maybe he's a decent man. There's some around. More than you might think."

"Yes," Salvani said. "There are, at that. Trouble is, there's lots of the others, too."

Le Pic laughed. "That's so. But wait and see. See how the kid gets on. Rest!"

"We're staying here, then?" Salvani asked.

"Not we." Le Pic stood up. "You."

"You're not leaving us?" Salvani, alarmed, aches and pains notwithstanding, scrambled to his feet.

"No, no." Le Pic raised a calming hand. "I'm coming back. Only down there, *là*. I know someone. He can help you."

"Can or will?" Salvani asked.

"Eh?" Le Pic shrugged. "Ah, both. Or maybe neither. How can I tell? But I'll go and find out. You stay here, *Italien*. You understand?"

"I understand," Salvani said as Le Pic moved away, a shadow among shadows, and then was gone.

Salvani leaned back, looking at the stars swing across the silent sky. But, with Le Pic gone, he realized that the valley they were in wasn't silent. An owl, maybe two, or ten, was screeching; something, a goat or a cow, and not, Salvani sincerely hoped, a wolf or bear, was making furtive sounds. Not too far away, there was the steady, muted mutter of a waterfall, a rather unnerving clicking of stones, and then a really unnerving, huge crash, a rockfall, the aged mountain answering, at last, the call of gravity, the sound echoing and reechoing around the valley as the rocks ricocheted down a thousand meters.

"What?" Judah started awake. "What's that?"

"Nothing, nothing." Salvani was instantly assuring, or thought he was, because the instant he said that it was merely rocks falling, Judah gave a healthy scream of terror.

"Not on us," Salvani said, although he looked upward just to make sure that they weren't.

"Why are they falling?" Judah asked, or rather, in the somewhat irritating manner he sometimes showed, *demanded* to know.

"Well." Salvani rubbed his chin. "Because they're old, I suppose. Old and falling to bits. Like me," he added ruefully.

Judah sat up and peered at Salvani. "Are you falling to bits?"

Salvani sighed. "Not exactly, though I feel it right now. I've lost a few teeth." He bared his gums. "See?"

Judah looked into Salvani's mouth with interest. "My grandmama's teeth fell out," he said. "All of them! She had false teeth. She used to put them in a glass at night."

"That's what some people do," Salvani agreed, pondering for a moment on that section of the world where people could afford false teeth.

"I tried them once," Judah said.

"What!"

"Yes!" Judah gave a gurgling chuckle. "But they were too big for me."

Salvani chuckled, too. "Good thing she didn't catch you."

"Mmm . . ." Judah's attention wandered from his grandmother's teeth. He scrambled onto Salvani's lap. "Are you very old?" he asked.

"Not *very* old." Salvani was rather offended.

"You *look* old," Judah said.

"Do I?" Judah had a rather unnerving trick of becoming, in the tick of a second, annoying, and although he knew it was ridiculous, Salvani *was* annoyed, and quite unconsciously, he raised his chin and pulled in his stomach. "Lots of people don't think so."

"I do," Judah said emphatically. He rubbed his hand slowly over Salvani's face. "You've got whiskers. All over your face."

Salvani's irritation went as quickly as it had come. "Get away with you, and leave my whiskers alone. But listen, chico—I want to ask you something and I want you to tell me the truth. And don't pretend anything. Will you do that?"

"Do it?" His hand still on Salvani's scrubby face, Judah slowly began to push himself away. His father had told him something about the big soldier. What it was, exactly, or even vaguely, he couldn't remember—in fact, he was living in a phantasmagoria, a jumbled dream world of caves, old women muttering over fires like witches, huge crags white as old bones in the moonlight, and valleys black as pitch in the shadows, men as strange as giants carrying him over mountains as if he were a child in a fairy tale, and he seemed to be moving from one world to another, from a world he understood, a simple one of cuts and bruises, bread and cheese, being washed, daylight, to that other world of incomprehensible images flickering in the night. There was nothing he could do about that but allow himself to be picked up, carried, put down, have food stuffed into his mouth, be daubed with stinging ointments; but from beyond this dream world, and he did think, insofar as he thought at all, that he was dreaming, he could hear, as clearly as if he was awake, his father's voice, telling him over and over, and again and again, don't answer questions. And suddenly he could see his father, leaning over the big soldier's shoulder, raising a finger to pale lips. And so, slowly, slowly, he pushed himself away, as if moving away would make himself dwindle, grow smaller, dwindle away until he became invisible.

Salvani, his stained, chipped teeth showing in his battered face, one eye a mere slit, a gash under the other, felt Judah sliding away from his bruised fingers and, like a man holding a bird in clasped hands and feeling the silent terror in its frail body, slowly and gently released his hold on the child, sensing that he had said something deeply disturbing, that he had crossed an invisible border, taking with him not a gift of human charity, no matter how roughly expressed, but something appalling, the more so because it was unknown and unseen, like the bearer of a plague.

And so, although he, big, strong, adult, father, soldier, had, no more than Judah, small, weak, child, orphan, words in which to express what he felt, he opened his hands, and his arms, and allowed Judah to back away a little, and a little more, and farther, until, as it were, there was a zone of safety between them, one such as allows a deer to graze and browse while, in the hot grass, a leopard raises its mottled head. And then his natural common sense butted in. "Kid," he said. "I just want to ask how you are? I mean how do you feel?"

Judah turned away his dappled head. That wasn't a bad question, the sort he shouldn't ever answer, like who are you, where are you from, are you a Jew? It was a question he could answer, if he knew how. "My head feels funny," he said. "Sometimes."

"Sometimes?" Salvani cautiously leaned forward. "When sometimes?"

"I don't know." Judah frowned. "Just sometimes. I can't remember."

"Can't remember when your head hurts?"

"No." Judah shook his head. "I can't remember some *things*. I forget. Was my papa here?"

"Your—" Salvani leaned forward a little. "Your papa?"

"Yes. I saw him." Judah pointed. "There, behind you."

Salvani's neck prickled, and despite himself, he turned, looking at the pallid hillside, littered with boulders. "Er, no," he said. "I don't think that your papa was here, but"— bracing himself for a lie—"he's not far away. Not far away now. Do you hear?"

He leaned forward anxiously, but Judah didn't move or flinch away, or even look at him. He was staring into the night, his head cocked. "Uncle," he said. "That tree is moving."

9

Salvani batted Judah away as if he were a fly and was on one knee with his rifle in his hand, rattling its bolt, when, not a tree moving, but Le Pic, calling *Italien*, came forward, followed by another man.

"Careful with the rifle, *Italien*," Le Pic said. "This"—he gestured to the man with him—"this is . . . someone. He's going to help you."

Someone, Salvani thought. That figures. Someone is someone, and anyone is no one—and all the better if the cops pick you up. He held out his hand, and Someone took it. "Call me Maurice," he said.

"How's the child?" Le Pic said.

Salvani thought that Judah wasn't well, not well at all, what with him saying that his head felt funny, and forgetting things and one moment laughing about his grandmother's false teeth and the next seeing ghosts, but he didn't intend to say so. He might have told Le Pic, but with the mysterious Someone Maurice, or Maurice Someone at his elbow, he thought it better to keep those disturbing thoughts to himself for a while—after all, Maurice might be ready to help a battering great man but draw the line at a sick child. So—"Fine," he said. "Just fine."

"I'm glad to hear that," Le Pic said. "Er, *Italien* . . ."

"Yes?" Salvani said.

"A word," Le Pic said. He plucked at Salvani's elbow and led him away a few paces. "*Italien*—" He glanced over his shoulder at Maurice. "I don't like saying this, believe me. But . . ."

"But what?" Salvani asked, actually knowing the answer in advance.

"It's Maurice—" Le Pic's voice had lost its habitual whip-crack air of command. "He . . . well . . . he's a good man . . . straight, you know? But—"

"Don't tell me," Salvani said. "He wants paying."

"Yes." Le Pic sighed and opened his hands. "You know, for him it's a risk, taking you down there. Maybe he's seen with you . . ."

Salvani jammed his fists in his pockets, hunched up a burly shoulder and, conscious of Fleur's wallet inside his breast pocket, said—*growled*, "I've got no money," saying that as a sort of gamble—testing the opposition, as it were.

"Aaah." Le Pic cocked a skeptical eyebrow.

"A-haa," Salvani echoed Le Pic's sigh. "So what's the problem? It's all downhill, isn't it? You said so yourself."

Le Pic shook his head. "*Italien!* Down. Yes, down, down but up, too. Up and down, this way, that way. But—" He stopped as if struck. "*Italien.* Go. Go if you wish. No one will tell. And I?" His voice sharpened. "I want nothing. You understand?" He prodded Salvani with a stiff forefinger, somewhere in the region of Salvani's stomach.

Salvani glanced down, half smiled, and gently brushed Le Pic's hand away. "I didn't mean that," he said. "Not for a minute. You know?"

"I know, *Italien.* I know that." Le Pic nodded. "But"— he raised his finger again and smiled ruefully—"you need help. Let me talk to him. Yes?" He called Maurice over and they spoke together in the rapid local patois, as impenetrable as a thorn hedge, until, finally, Le Pic turned to Salvani.

"All right," he said. "He doesn't want money but . . .

but he will take that," tapping Salvani's side where Balbo's revolver was slung in its holster.

"Will he, now?" Salvani took a step back, as if making room to draw the gun. "Oh, will he?"

"*Si.*" Maurice spoke, in surprisingly good Italian, "I'll take the pistol—instead of money." He held out his hand as Salvani, every nerve in his body tingling, took another step back, and another, not thinking, or even dreaming, of drawing his revolver, but definitely wondering whether to give Monsieur Maurice a bang in the jaw hard enough to knock him all the way over Mont Blanc.

"*Italien,*" Le Pic broke in. "You have a problem? About the gun?"

"Yes." Salvani took another step back. "I've got a problem."

"Ah!" Maurice clicked his fingers. "You think that you and Maurice will go for a little walk in the woods, hey?"

"A what?"

"Go for a walk but you don't come back."

"Maybe something like that," Salvani said.

"That's all right," Le Pic said, in an even, reassuring voice. "Give me the gun. I'll hand it over to Maurice when he gets back." He shrugged. "You won't need the pistol in Italy."

"If I get to Italy," Salvani said.

"You'll get there," Le Pic said. "Why not? But you have to make up your mind. Dawn's coming."

Salvani looked up. The stars still shone, but there was a subtle change to the east, a barely perceptible lightening of the sky, and in the woods in a valley a bird cheeped feebly, as if uncertain whether to wake or not.

"Don't worry," Le Pic said. "I wouldn't buy a goat from Maurice, not without looking at it three times, but he'll get you to the road."

"All right." Salvani unbuckled the revolver and handed it over to Le Pic. "I'm sorry, but you know how it is."

"Sure," Le Pic said. He grinned at Maurice. "Right?"

"Right." Maurice grinned back. He picked up the knap-sack. "I'll carry it. No extra charge."

Salvani nodded his thanks and scooped up Judah. "Come on, kid," he said. "Won't be long now." He turned to Le Pic. "Thanks," he said. "Maybe after the war . . . ?"

"Maybe," Le Pic said. "Who knows?"

"Surely." Salvani shook hands. "Er, where are you going now?"

Le Pic looked mildly surprised. "Back home, where else?"

"It's a long haul," Salvani said, thinking that it was, at that, back over the mountain range, across the gorges and ravines and unforgiving crags. A long way to here, and a long way to there, for nothing, for no reason except to give a poor devil a helping hand.

"Not so long," Le Pic said. "Without you, hey?" And then he was gone, moving up the mountainside with the light-footed agility of a deer.

"And us?" Salvani said.

"A cabin," Maurice said. "A little shelter, not far. We eat, rest a little, and then . . ." He shrugged. "We take a look at the road."

"The road to Italy?" Salvani asked.

"That's the one," Maurice said. "But we won't get there by talking. Come."

He swung on his heel and led Salvani and Judah down, down into the dark woods where the birds were beginning to peep and cheep, restlessly preparing for a new day's struggle for survival.

They went along a track which slanted diagonally through the wood, mere scrub clinging to the mountain like drowning men struggling to maintain their grasp on life, climbed another ridge where huge slabs of granite jabbed through the limestone, as if some elemental being was struggling from a pallid grave; over the ridge; and descended again through another wood, a bigger one with taller trees, by waterfalls drizzling down a hundred feet of cliff; and as the sun struck at the sky with gold and red lances, they came to a grove of trees, not stunted pine but dense chestnut, and beyond that, across a clear stream, a meadow of odorous grass, and a wooden hut.

"*Là!*" Maurice turned. "There."

"*Là.*" Salvani nodded. "Let's get to it," and without waiting to be led, trudged, heavy-footed, across the meadow.

The cabin wasn't much—a chair, a table, a crude stone fireplace, a few pots and pans, and a rough bed which Salvani eyed with a deep heartfelt longing, but on which he laid Judah.

"It's just for the summer." Maurice followed him in as Salvani laid Judah down. "In winter, the snow—" He fluttered his hands.

"It's fine," Salvani said, and in fact it was better than Le Pic's farmhouse and his own hovel in Italy, come to that. He stooped over Judah, who lay inert, his eyes closed. "I'm worried about him," he said. "He sort of comes and goes. Last night—well, this morning I suppose, while we were waiting for you, he was as right as rain, joking, and now . . . ?"

"Sure." Maurice put a hand on Judah's brow. "He's been hurt, what do you expect?"

"It's not the cuts." Salvani lit a cigarette. "It's his head, I mean inside. His brain . . . I don't know."

"I don't know either," Maurice said. "The brain!" He tapped his head as if to make clear to Salvani just where the brain was. "Who does know? But the child, maybe he needs a good rest, food."

"Maybe he needs a doctor," Salvani said, with more than a touch of grimness. "There is one, right? Somewhere around here?"

"In La Chambre," Maurice said.

"You'll take me there?"

"Take—" Maurice looked, and sounded, alarmed. "No, *Italien*." He held out his hand as if to ward off a blow. "Listen, if you want to go into La Chambre, that's fine with me, and what I will do, I'll take you down to the road, outside La Chambre. Now if you want. But why not wait? Give the kid time to sleep properly. And yourself."

"Me?" Salvani rubbed his eyes with the heel of his palm, and, the word *sleep* bringing its own sly reflex, yawned deeply. And he did need some sleep. In fact, he felt as if he could sleep until the cows came home, and he was tired, tired down to the bottom of his boots . . . actually swaying with fatigue.

"And what can the doctor do?" Maurice said. "I'll tell you. Nothing. Rest. Let the child rest."

"Medicine," Salvani said, mumbled, rather.

"Medicine." Maurice was contemptuous.

"It's just that . . ." Salvani sighed. "If I don't take him he might . . . you know—" unable to utter the word.

"And if you do—" Maurice made a chopping gesture. "The cops! Wait, *Italien*. Let the kid rest, go down the road, pick up your comrades, maybe they have a doctor, or maybe they'll take you to one—then no cops, hey?"

Salvani hesitated, and hesitated again, and was lost. "An hour," he said.

"An hour." Maurice nodded. "Now eat."

They ate, cheese and smoked ham, then Salvani slept, and Judah, too. The sun rose in its full splendor; the birds, their chorus of praise over, flitted about the grove and meadow; marmosets scuttled among the rocks; and the hawks and buzzards rose on languid wings and floated in their effortless circles; and Le Pic heaved weary legs over a last rocky edge and onto the plateau.

His goats browsed on the spare pasture; rooks foraged at their heels; marmosets popped up and down from their holes. All as it should be, but he hesitated. Where were the dogs? Not a sign of them or their clamor. There was something wrong and a shadow of doubt and fear clouded his mind, but then, distinctive in her long black dress and headscarf, his wife came from the farmhouse, scattering grain for the hens.

"Jeanne! Jeanne!" Le Pic called in the high, long cry which carried kilometers.

Jeanne turned, putting one hand over her eyes and raising the other in salute before turning back to the hens.

"The dogs—" Le Pic began but let his voice fall. Time to ask about them soon enough, and so he strode forward, the goats scattering and the crows, drawing nearer to his home, nearer, closer, close, saying, "Jeanne, where are the dogs?" and then his heart stopping as Jeanne turned, a pistol in one hand and grinning, tobacco-stained teeth showing in a pale, handsome face, while Le Pic heard the clicking of safety catches and glancing behind him, he saw two men in blue uniforms and blue berets carrying rifles.

"Oh, oh," he said as he felt his heart beating, pounding inside his chest like a sledgehammer. "What—" He tried defiance. "What the hell's going on here. Who are you?"

The man grinned again and pulled off the headscarf, with his head bare looking bizarre, disgusting really in the long black dress. "You'll find out," he said. "The revolver— hand it over. Slowly, that's the way. We don't want any little accidents. Good. Now inside."

Jabbed and prodded by the men's rifles, Le Pic stepped through the clucking hens and past his dogs lying sprawled with open eyes, fangs showing through bloody froth, and into his house.

His wife was there, in a patched chemise, her arms crossed over her bony chest, crouched by the flickering fire, and in a blood-splashed corner, wrists bound, his face battered, was the Chasseur, who, as Le Pic was shoved forward, shook his head and mumbled, through broken teeth, "Not me," before he was booted into silence.

"Now." The man in Jeanne's dress stood with his back

to the fire and briskly rubbed his hands. "Palet. Agence de Milice." He produced an identity card and held it before Le Pic. "Just so you know this is all legal."

"Legal?" Le Pic looked at his wife and at the Chasseur.

"Legal." Palet stuffed his card away. "In defense of the state," savoring the words as if merely pronouncing them made him judge and jury, prosecutor and defense counsel. "Now. Where are they?"

"Where's who?" Le Pic asked, and got a sickening blow from a rifle butt on his shoulder blades which drove him to his knees.

"Wrong answer," Palet said. "Try again."

"I don't know what you're talking about," Le Pic said and felt another shattering smash which drove him onto all fours.

Palet lit a cigarette, taking his time about it, then put his foot on Le Pic's hand. "Wrong again." He shook his head ruefully, like a kind schoolmaster with a slow pupil. "Look, Le Pic. We know they came here, the Italian and the Jew kid—"

"The pigs in the café," Madame Le Pic shouted.

Quite casually, Palet hit her back-handed across the mouth. "Shut up," he said. "*Shut up!* Now, Le Pic—" He leaned forward, grinding his heel on Le Pic's hand. "We *know* they met him—" He jabbed a contemptuous thumb at the Chasseur, semiconscious, in the corner— "So it's even money he brought them here. Now, I'm a busy man. In fact, I could be reprimanded for taking all this trouble over one Jew kid. And these men"—he gestured at the lounging Milice—"they've got lots of things to do as well, and we all want to get home before dark. So, where's the Jew?"

Le Pic coughed, as if he was coughing out his soul, and felt his shoulder blade grind. Broken, he thought. Shattered. No more farming for me. No more striding lithely over the mountain with his dark-eyed goats and calm, benign cows. No more, probably, of anything. With infinite care he raised his head: the firelight flickered on the crude walls, and on his wife, and the Chasseur, the nonchalant, blue-clad Milice, and on the photographs of the dead, and on Palet. Le Pic coughed again and spat out a long string of dribbling saliva. "Take that dress off," he said. "You obscene dog. Take it off."

"This?" Palet pulled the skirt up. He opened his eyes in mock surprise. "I thought that it suited me!"

The Milice laughed. "Paris model," one said, to more laughter.

"Ah, well," Palet said, "if that's what you want." The men still laughing, he pulled off the dress, his heel grinding into the back of Le Pic's hand. "There," he said. "Better? Better, Pic? Now. Last time. Positively the last time. Where are they?" He crouched and grabbed Le Pic's hair and yanked his head back. "This—" He jabbed Salvani's revolver at Le Pic's eye. "It's an Italian pistol. So where . . . are . . . they?"

"Don't know," Le Pic said.

"*Tss, tss.*" Palet rose to his feet, his heel grinding the subtle bones in Le Pic's hand. "The woman," he snapped.

With horrible, practiced speed, the Milice pounced on Madame Le Pic and, with equally horrible, practiced skill, doubled her arms behind her back and dragged her to Palet, who grabbed her by the scruff of the neck and, unbelievably, began to shove her head down to the flames.

"You can't do that," Le Pic said, less speaking to Palet than appealing to a moral code he could not precisely articulate but which he believed existed, somewhere, a code which made it impossible to push people's heads into a fire.

"I can't?" Palet said.

"No." Le Pic swung his head sideways. "It's not allowed."

Palet laughed, a strange snigger. "You don't understand," he said. "I can do anything. *Anything!*" He sniggered again and there was a sickening smell of singed hair, and Le Pic believed him and told him.

*　*　*

Something was pursuing Salvani. He was in a tangled wood, trying to wrestle his way through thorns and clinging vines. He was swearing terribly and not making any progress, while behind him he could hear his pursuer drawing nearer—slow footsteps, more frightening simply because of their deliberateness, as if the pursuer knew that it had all the time on earth to catch its prey.

Salvani fought with the vines and thorns and fought himself awake, sweating with his greatcoat over his face. He flung it aside and lay for a moment fighting off the dream, staring at the rough timber of the roof, until he realized that, although he had left the nightmare behind, the steady clumping was continuing.

He swung off the bed and listened, his head cocked, then leaned sideways and, with satisfaction and relief, found his rifle. He picked it up and padded across the room to where Judah, wrapped in blankets, lay sleeping soundly.

He brooded over the child for a moment, then walked softly to the door of the cabin, slid back the safety catch of the rifle, swung the door open, and jumped out.

His back to the cabin, chopping wood, the clunk of his ax echoing from the hillside, was a man, and the man was not Maurice.

"You," Salvani said, and brought up his rifle.

The man turned, the ax head buried in a block of wood, his hand on the shaft, casual, unafraid, youthful.

"Who the hell are you?" Salvani asked.

"Someone," the youth said.

"Someone, hey?" Salvani walked forward, holding his rifle very much at the ready. "What sort of answer is that?"

The young man glanced at the rifle. "The only one you'll get."

"Oh?" Salvani tried to sound tough and skeptical but was nonplussed.

"Where's Maurice?" he demanded.

109

"Maurice? Oh." The youth flicked a finger this way, that way. "Yes. Him. He'll be back."

"And just when will that be?" Salvani said.

The youth shrugged. "Sometime."

"He said he'd wake me."

"So he didn't."

The answer was cool to the point of insolence and Salvani felt a prickle of anger. He took more rough steps forward and jabbed his rifle in the young man's chest. "What's going on here?" he growled. "Where's Maurice? And I won't ask you again, who are you?"

The voice was rough and the jab of the rifle rougher, but the youth was unperturbed. He casually pushed away the rifle. "Nothing is going on," he said. "Maurice will be back. And you can say I'm . . . Pierre. But what's your problem?"

"Problem!" Salvani scowled. "Maurice said he was taking us down to the road."

"If he said he'll do it, he will," Pierre said.

"But—" Salvani flushed. "But we've got to get to the road today!"

Pierre gave an indifferent shrug. "No one is stopping you."

"No?" Salvani stared balefully around at the colossal jumble of rock and scree and woods clinging to the mountainside. All downhill, Le Pic had said the night before, and maybe it was, but the valley which they were in, gouged from vast cliffs, seemed to end at a ridge. And who knew, beyond that ridge another might raise its forbidding, wrinkled bulk. Follow the stream, Salvani thought, but who knew? The stream might slip underground or plunge over a precipice . . . He muttered a horrifying oath. "How far is it?" he demanded. "To the road?"

Pierre waved his slim forefinger. "Eight, ten kilometers."

Salvani muttered another horrendous oath. Ten kilometers! He could walk that before breakfast, carrying Judah

110

and a sack of wheat, too, but here . . . For the first time he realized how savagely formidable mountains could be. "I'll wait," he said weakly, as if he had a choice, but feeling like a gorilla in a cage, the worse since the cage was vast and the bars invisible.

"Sure. Wait." Pierre gave a subtle, knowing smile, as if he knew exactly what Salvani was thinking. "But don't worry, *Italien*. Rest, let the child sleep."

"It's the kid I'm worried about," Salvani said, not altogether truthfully. "He might need a doctor."

For the first time Pierre lost his air of detached, sly amusement. "I know. But Maurice said he had no fever, so it was better to let him sleep. He said it's the best cure, sleep."

Maybe, Salvani thought. Maybe it was, unless it was the sleep from which you didn't ever wake. But . . . feeling untypically and maddeningly helpless he walked back to the cabin, and looked down again on Judah. He was still sleeping lightly, his forehead cool. So maybe Maurice was right at that.

There was bread, wine, and a hunk of roast meat on the table. Salvani stuck the bottle under his arm, scooped up the rest, went back to the door, and sat on the step. Pierre was standing as before, light, poised, one hand on his ax.

"That's good, *Italien*," he said, "eat."

"Yes." Salvani tore off a piece of meat with his broken teeth and wolfed it down. "Just tell me one thing," he said. "Who are you?"

"Ah." The sly smile reappeared on Pierre's face. "Ask no questions," he said, "and get told no lies," turned and, with an easy, practiced rhythm, swung his ax again.

The chunking of the ax crept into Judah's dreams, too. He was dreaming that he was in a room with very high walls. His father was with him, sitting on a suitcase full of diamonds. Someone was hammering on the door: *thud, thud, thud.* His father turned to Judah and put his finger to his lips and Judah knew that he must not make the slightest sound, not a whisper or a murmur as the pounding on the door went on, slow and frightening. *Thud, thud, thud,* and as the door shook, his father grew smaller, and smaller, until, still with his finger to his lips, he disappeared. "Papa!" Judah called. "Papa, come back!" And then he woke and cried aloud, "Papa."

In an instant the big soldier was looming over him, a dark face bristling with whiskers and his breath smelling of tobacco and wine, but, oddly, Judah wasn't terrified. The face was becoming familiar, associated with help, and what, through Judah's eyes, had been an ugly, ferocious, one-eyed visage was losing its terror, and even its ugliness.

"All right?" Salvani asked, fingers crossed, as it were.

"Yes." Judah blinked. "I was dreaming." He looked searchingly at Salvani. "It was a room. A funny room. There was . . . there was . . ." He frowned, the dream already going, like smoke in a breeze.

"Well, don't worry about the dream," Salvani said. "Let's see if you can get up. Can you do that?"

"*Course* I can," Judah said with surprising force and jumped out of the cot. "I'm not a baby."

"And your . . . your head." Salvani fumbled for words. "Does it feel all right? I mean, inside?"

"Inside?" Judah stared at Salvani incredulously. "I don't know what my head is like *inside.*"

He burst out laughing and Salvani laughed, too, out of relief, and threw a mock punch. "You're all right. I think you are. Come on, let's get you washed and fed."

He led the way out, but at the door Judah stopped and flicked behind Salvani's legs. "Who's that?" he said. "That man."

"Him?" Salvani looked at Pierre. "Chico, I wish I knew. You!" he called. "Pierre, or whatever your name is. Where do we get washed?"

Pierre dropped the ax and walked toward them. "In

112

the stream, over there." He peered around Salvani's bulk. "The kid, he's well?"

"Looks like it," Salvani said.

"So." Pierre straightened himself. "Maurice was right, hey? Maybe he's right on everything else."

"Maybe," Salvani said, taking Judah by the hand and leading him to the stream.

Cool and lucent it flowed in a series of miniature waterfalls over jade-green rocks. Salvani laid down his rifle and vigorously splashed his face, then lay back on a moss-strewn bank while Judah, at his urging, although with considerably less enthusiasm, cautiously dabbed his face. Not a bad place, Salvani thought, lighting a cigarette. Not a bad place at all. The air was pine-scented, pale butterflies fluttered across the glade, a woodpecker, green and lemon, flashed among the trees. Really a man could pass away the war here. In fact, millionaires *paid* to come to places like this; yes, you could build a cabin of your own, go hunting, catch rabbits, fish, and stuff like that; then remembering that Judah was kneeling by him and, Salvani knew without being told, was about to ask a question he had come to dread—and heard it.

"Will we go to Papa today?" Judah asked.

Salvani, dreams of a sylvan idyll gone, sat up and forced a bright smile. "Er, perhaps not *exactly* today," he said. "But soon. Really soon, now. Maybe tonight even. Tomorrow anyway. Definitely."

Judah looked at him solemnly. "Where is my papa?" he said.

That was another question Salvani had dreaded, for fear the answer would stick in his throat. But he gave a hollow laugh. "Didn't I tell you? He's in Italy. You know, Italy? Just where we're going. You'll like Italy, it's beautiful. Beautiful!"—thinking of the vermin-infested slum in which he lived but babbling to keep the thought of Signor Fleur away from Judah's mind. As he paused for breath,

Judah cut in, but with one of the odd erratic leaps of childhood, *he* changed the subject.

"Have you got any children?"

"Yes." Salvani was delighted. "Look." He fumbled in his tunic pocket and pulled out a battered wallet. "See?" he fished out a tiny, cracked photograph. "That's my wife, and those are my children. That's Antonio, the big one, and that is Lucia, my daughter. And this one here, that's Frederico. He's just about your age. You'd like him. And listen, you can meet him! Yes, maybe we'll all go on a trip. Maybe to the seaside!" Neither Salvani nor his family had ever seen the sea, nor, for that matter, had they ever been on a train, but, profligate, he promised that, too. "On a train!" He leaned back awaiting thanks and praise, but got neither.

"I've been to the sea," Judah said. "Lots of times. But not," he added disdainfully, "not on a train. We go by car. A big car. A big, big car! We've got a house by the sea. We've got servants. Have you got servants?"

Salvani spat out his cigarette end. "No," he said. "We've not got any servants. And we've not got a car. And we've not got a house by the sea, either." Jesus Christ, he thought. I could be home and dry and I'm stuck with a kid babbling about cars and servants. Suddenly the green hollow wasn't enchanting, the woods enticing, the stream murmuring sweetly. It looked like a trap—and to cap it all, to have a kid stuck on him who stood for wealth and privilege, the things he had spent his life struggling against. "Go and play," he growled.

"Play?" Judah looked around the glade, round-eyed, as if he expected swings and slides to appear. He put a confiding hand on Salvani's knee. "Will you play with me?"

"Me?" Salvani gave a despairing groan, then, looking at Judah's head, still blotched green with Jeanne's ointment, which seemed impervious to water, found the groan turning into a laugh. He raised his hands in surrender, not only to Judah but to whatever mysterious fate had brought him to where he was. "What?" he asked. "What should we play? Hide and seek?—no, not that"—that being a little too close for comfort. "What?"

"Sailing boats," Judah said.

"Boats?" Salvani wondered whether Judah *had* damaged his brain.

"On the stream!" Judah screwed up his face at Salvani's stupidity. He grabbed Salvani's hand and tugged with surprising vigor.

"Coming, coming!" Salvani heaved himself up and walked with Judah to the wood, where, with great deliberation, the child chose a number of twigs and sticks, and then introduced Salvani to the game of sticks.

And Salvani was enchanted by the simple race of two sticks down the stream to the finishing stone; exultant when he won, despondent when he lost, poring over each stick, suspecting Judah of dropping his stick before the count of three, deeply suspicious that he was losing every race because Judah had artfully chosen a swift current; happy with a simple, shared pleasure as the sun shone, the butterflies danced their airy minuets, and the birds played hide and seek through the trees, away from war, from murder, from the sickness of diseased minds; as, like a poisonous reptile, Palet was stirring in his lair in Chambéry.

10

In the high, pure valley, as remote from the world as if they were held in the palm of God's hand, Salvani and Judah, innocents, played their innocent game, while below them, on the plains and through the hills of all Europe, from Bayonne to the Volga and from the Baltic to the Mediterranean, the trains clanked with their sealed cargoes of suffering, and Levi, Aaron; Cohen, Leah; Rosenthal, Benjamin—aged thirteen, ten, and six years—were, with another four hundred Jews, stuffed into a gas chamber in Chelmnitz, Leah crying; and twenty kilometers away as the crow, or the vulture, flew, in the pleasant town of Chambéry, in a police cell, bloodstained and battered, lay Le Pic, his wife Jeanne, and the dying Chasseur, while up three flights of stairs, in a handsome room overlooking the valley of the river Isère, sunshine flooding in through elegant sash windows, a universe away from the cells and yet inextricably linked with them, and the trains, and the reeking chimneys of the ovens of the crematorium of Chelmnitz, where Cohen, Leah, tears stilled forever, was being thrown into a furnace, Palet, Agent de Milice, was staring sullenly across a table draped like a coffin with purple felt, but bearing, instead of a cross, a bottle of Pernod, two glasses, a carafe of water, and a riding crop bound with heavy brass wire, the property of the other man in the room, Palet's master, a superintendent of Milice, arrived that morning from Grenoble, and the master of all he surveyed, subject, of course, to his masters, the men in black uniforms with their grinning skulls, and their masters, Barbie in Lyons, Himmler in Berlin, the Führer himself . . .

"A *squad* of men!" the superintendent was saying incredulously. "And *transport!* To La Chambre for one Jew kid?"

"You know the orders," Palet said.

"Of course I know the orders!" The superintendent glowered across the table.

"Our duty," Palet said.

The superintendent slammed the table. "Are you telling *me* what my duty is? Just remember who you are talking to, Palet." He stood up, paunchy, a dab of mustache on a pasty face, his fingers heavy with rings, resembling the owner of some not very successful small business, which, in fact, he had been: a rural undertaker, embittered because the peasants stripped their dead of their rings, preventing him from stealing them—but now, fate having dealt him an ace, the ace of spades, able to flash all the rings he wanted; they coming from other bodies.

He snatched up his riding crop and strode down the room, slapping his thigh with the whip, a mannerism he had picked up from German SS officers, reverentially straightened a huge portrait of Marshal Pétain, and then, having imposed his presence on the room, went back to his chair behind the table.

Palet was sitting, unmoving, in his strange posture, as if he was deformed. The superintendent, who, in a vulgar way, was something of a dandy, looked at him with distaste. Despite his handsome face, the man was repulsive: his expensive suit was wrinkled, as if he had slept in it; his silk shirt was grimy, his fingernails dirty; he smelled of alcohol and stale food; and he had boils on his neck. But regardless of his own authority, Palet made the superintendent uneasy.

Creepy little swine, the superintendent thought, but the orders from Lyons *were* absolute; not one was to escape. *None.* On the other hand . . . in the town—who knew how

117

many Jews were skulking down there hidden by traitors: radicals, socialists, Communists, atheists—even Christians! And they needed rooting out, too, all of them, the enemies of the state, but, he dropped his whip, it would do no harm to tread carefully.

"Now look, Palet." He poured himself a drink and pushed the bottle across the table. "Really, about this Jew kid. You think he'll be in La Chambre—"

"I know he will be," Palet said.

"All right." The superintendent assumed a reasonable air. "But you can't be absolutely sure, can you?"

"The Italian's going home." Palet gulped his Pernod and poured himself another. "That's why he's going to La Chambre. To get on the Mont Cenis road." He drank again, some of the drink pouring down his chin and onto his shirt, not bothering to wipe it off. "And we know he's got a Jew with him."

The superintendent fiddled with his riding crop and glanced, rather furtively, at Palet. What was wrong with the man? He sat so awkwardly, as if his skin didn't fit him—even the way he held his glass was, somehow, wrong, clutching it with three fingers, like a parrot; and he couldn't even sit on a chair like a normal human being, which he prided himself on being. "But"—he shook himself from his reverie—"one kid . . . no. We've a lot to do here, clean this place up . . . First things first. That's all."

"That's all?" Palet raised his head ominously. "You mean I can't have a squad of men?"

"I didn't say it like that," the superintendent said. "I am saying that they can't be spared from here. Not just yet. Not on a wild-goose chase."

"It's not a wild-goose chase." Palet stood up and shrugged. "Still, if that's what you think."

"That's what I think," the superintendent said.

"All right." Palet rammed his hands into his pockets. "I'll put that in my report."

"Your—" The superintendent's jaw dropped. "No need for you to do that. I'll make out any reports that are necessary."

Palet nodded, slack-jawed. "You'll tell them about the Jew kid, will you? Word gets around, and I don't want to get blamed."

"Now, just a minute." The superintendent felt a quiver of alarm, such as, alone in a house at night, one might feel on hearing stealthy footsteps. "We're not talking *blame* here, not at all. Just a sensible use of resources."

Still slack-jawed, Palet nodded again. "They'll understand that, will they, in Lyons?"

The superintendent felt more than a quiver of alarm, he felt a real tremor—the footsteps louder! Coming up the stairs! Lyons! Long arms stretched from there. Long arms and long shadows . . . Beads of sweat trickled down the backs of his ears, but not without cunning himself, he smiled. "Sit down, have another drink. Help yourself. I'll tell you what I'll do. I'll ring Grenoble now, this minute, and get clearance." He placed his ringed hand on the telephone. "How's that? Does it suit you?"

His hand halfway to the bottle, Palet froze. That didn't suit him at all. Not that he had any objections to Grenoble knowing of his zeal, but the morning was ticking away and by the time the superintendent had got through to the commander—if he ever did and *if* the commander gave permission, which he very much doubted—then, by the time he had rounded up a squad of men, and got transport, and got to La Chambre, the Italian and the kid could be over the Mont Cenis Pass and beyond his covetous grasp forever. "Wait," he said.

"Wait!" The superintendent gave an exaggerated start of surprise. "But I thought that—"

"Never mind what you thought," Palet said with his usual mindless insolence. "There's something else."

"Aaah!" The superintendent leaned forward, alert, a

hyena catching a whiff of carrion. "And what might that be?"

Palet twisted and turned, as if he had to screw the words out. "Money."

"Money . . ." The superintendent licked the corner of his mouth with a furred, spotted tongue.

"Yes." Slowly and painfully, Palet said what he knew, or what he thought that he knew, muttering his story as the superintendent crouched lower over the table and his tongue crept from corner to corner of his prim mouth until Palet had finished.

"Half," he said.

"Half?" Palet pretended to consider, although he was thinking what a dolt the superintendent was, what an idiot! How could he know how many diamonds the kid had on him? He made a face. "It was my idea," he said.

"Yes, but I'm taking the responsibility," the superintendent said. "And you'll have the credit for picking up the Italian and the Jew. And for arresting those three downstairs."

Palet pouted discontent, but grudgingly assented.

"Good." The superintendent rubbed his hands together, the rings clicking. "You see, Palet, reasonable men can always come to an agreement. I found that out in business. You won't know about that, business, but you'll learn. Yes." Businesslike, he cleared away the bottle, the glasses, and the whip. "I'll write you a letter."

"Letter. What do I want a letter for?"

"Of accreditation." The superintendent rolled the word around his tongue. "For the authorities in La Chambre. Oh yes, accreditation will be needful. All good business practice. And!" He raised a finger, struck by inspiration. "Look, Palet, while you're there, you'd better pull in some people."

"People?" Palet asked.

The superintendent tutted, in his turn thinking that

120

Palet was a dolt. "Make it look good. *Good.*" His mask of righteous servant of the state slipped, showing the face of a cunning petty businessman—one step away from bankruptcy. "I can't send you and a squad of men to La Chambre because there might be a Jew kid there. We grab a few people."

Palet tugged at his collar where the spilled Pernod was making it stick to his neck. "What people?"

The superintendent looked at him through undertaker's eyes, which preferred the profitable dead to the living. "Does it matter?" he said.

Palet rounded up a squad of five men, venomous patriots in blue uniforms, and requisitioned a truck.

"Put your foot down," he said to the driver.

The driver looked at him sideways. "It's a dangerous road," he said.

"You do as I tell you," Palet said, "or you'll find out what danger is. Got that?"

The driver got it, sensing, as the superintendent had, the genuinely frightening quality of Palet, who slouched beside him, cursing every minor impediment on the road, a peasant with his cart, a stray goat, a German patrol point where they were casually waved through, and the debris of a retreating army: broken-down trucks, smashed crates of loot, a field gun in a ditch—as they swung south into the vast, gloomy gorge of the Maurienne, the river Arc boiling on their right, the huge sides of the gorge gouged and shattered by landslides and mountain torrents. At the head of one, where the torrent was a mere stream, sparkling in the sunshine, a wrathful Salvani was haranguing an obdurate Judah.

"You've had dozens of goes on that side," Salvani was saying. "The current's quicker there. No wonder you're winning—" bitterly. "You've *got* to let me try there. It isn't *fair.*"

But Judah wasn't listening. He stared past Salvani and raised his hand and pointed. "Uncle," he said, "there's a man."

Salvani swung around, cursing himself for leaving his pack and rifle on the far side of the stream, and peered into the sun, into the grove, and at Maurice.

Maurice stepped from the trees. "Caught you by surprise, *Italien*."

Salvani ducked his head sheepishly. "Ah . . ." he gargled. "Just playing a game—to keep the kid happy."

"Yes?" Maurice gave a skeptical smile. "I've been watching you for ten minutes."

"Hmmm, er, yes." Salvani coughed. "I was just, er . . . well, not paying too much attention . . ."

"That's when they get you," Maurice said, not needing to explain who *they* might be.

"Got the message." Salvani picked up his pack and slung his rifle over his shoulder and then, *they* very much on his mind, he asked with elaborate casualness, "Where might you have been all morning?"

Maurice stared at Salvani through flinty eyes. "Business," he said.

"Oh?" Salvani waved a hand at the bleak crags. "What sort of business might that be?"

"My business," Maurice said flatly.

"And you just sloped off and left us?"

Maurice frowned. "The boy was here, Pierre? Yes. So." He opened his hands. "Look, Italian, I've got animals up here."

"Animals."

"Yes." Maurice's frown deepened into a scowl. "You think you and the child are the only important things on earth? I've got my own life to live. Soon the winter comes— and the Germans—and where will you be? Home in Italy, hey?"

"I paid you." Salvani was defensive.

"Paid!" Maurice was contemptuous. "You think I've done this for a revolver? I did it because Le Pic asked me to."

"All right, all right—" Salvani felt a hand steal into his and looked down on a timorous Judah. "Keep your hair on. I wasn't doubting you—" thinking: Not much, I wasn't. "It's just, well, you know . . ."

"Yes." Maurice opened his hands. "Yes, I guess so. Not so easy for you, wandering around . . ."

And you can say that again, Salvani thought. "So," he said, "this town, La Chambre."

"Sure." Maurice nodded. "La Chambre. An hour or so. Nothing."

He took them back to the cabin, crammed Salvani's pack with bread, cheese, wine, cigarettes, brushing aside thanks, and with a brisk clap of his hands led the way from the cabin, and the glade, but, to Salvani's regret, not down the valley but up, threading their way through boulders bigger than houses, onto the lifeless edge of an arid ridge which fell away from a huge buttress of rock, itself a mere prop, to an ice-streaked fang gouging the sky, above even the buzzards.

But Salvani had no eyes for the drama of mountain scenery. He had reached the stage where up meant bad and down meant good, and the farther down they went, the better he felt, and the very idea of *level* had the allure of Paradise. And, over the ridge, down they went, and down again, to the first, determined scraggy junipers, the first dwarf pines, to their more majestic sisters, and to a stream, a serious stream that intended to become, as soon as maybe, a river, and whose banks, strewn with splintered trees and the gnawed bones of drowned animals, showed what it could do when the winter snows melted.

They stopped there, briefly, to snatch a mouthful of bread and to drink.

"No sailing sticks here," Salvani said, and to his un-

123

speakable delight, Judah raised his scratched, dappled face, smiling, and said that they could make a real boat and sail away . . .

But Maurice was up, brushing them forward over yet another splintered ridge, where Salvani heaved Judah onto his broad back as they climbed over its gaunt shoulders and down to another valley, and another stream, but one which, for all its latent strength, slid away to a wide valley where maize shimmered in the afternoon sun.

"Nearly there?" Salvani asked.

"Yes." Maurice looked over his shoulder. "Nearly there."

"Right." Salvani hitched Judah higher, following Maurice into a plantation of fir trees, breathing in its resinous odors, and out onto sweet pastures where cows grazed, as slow and tranquil as the passing of the seasons, and where, coming uphill from the peaceful meadows and the vale, running like a deer and soaked to the skin with sweat, waving them back into the cover of the firs, and stammering out a message, was Pierre.

"What—" Salvani began but was chopped off as Maurice rattled off questions in patois and was answered in the same incomprehensible talk, but he did not need to speak it to understand something serious had happened. The look on Maurice's face spoke louder than words, and when the words did come they confirmed his fears.

"*Italien,*" Maurice said, "there is big trouble. Yes—"As Salvani's heart, five minutes previously as light as a bubble, began to sink.

"Oh . . ." Salvani batted away a few flies from his face. "And what might that be?"

Maurice took a deep breath. "In La Chambre. There's a *rafle.*"

"A *rafle?*"

"A roundup!" Maurice hissed the words. "Milice and Germans. Looking for Jews—"

"Hold it!" Salvani grabbed Maurice by the arm and pulled him away a few meters. "Don't say that before the

124

kid," he said. "Now, are you saying we can't go into La Chambre?"

Maurice smacked the side of his head. "Did you hear me? There—" He pointed down the peaceful vale. "There, fifteen minutes' walk. Milice and Germans. Knocking on doors, you know?"

Salvani did know. He knew very well what knocking on doors meant, if the person knocking wore a uniform which wasn't a postman's, and he knew, only too well, what could happen when paramilitary thugs decided to have a day off, boozing, for free, in their bars—especially when the state connived and put behind them the full weight of its fist. "Yes," he said. "I do know. But what about cutting across the valley? Getting on the road the other side of La Chambre?"

"Italien—" Maurice sounded like a man coming to the end of his tether. "The Germans aren't only in La Chambre. They're in Modane and Lanslebourg, all the way to Mont Cenis. The road is *closed*."

"But—" In the cool shelter of the firs Salvani could not bring himself to face the disaster. "Over there—" He waved to the other side of the vale. "We could keep off the road—"

"We?" Maurice reached into his pouch and pulled out a bottle which wasn't full of water, and took a long swig. "We aren't going anywhere. You can go where you want to." Quite unexpectedly he handed the bottle to Salvani. "Have some brandy. It's good stuff."

Salvani liked a drink as well as the next man, but he knew that if ever there was a time not to drink it was then, but for politeness's sake, and to keep Maurice sweet, he took a sip. "I was hoping for more help than that," he said. "I mean, you're not just going to dump us here, are you?"

"Dump!" Maurice took another long pull on the bottle, eyeing Salvani malevolently. "You wanted to come here, I've brought you."

"But I didn't know the Germans would be here, did I?"

Salvani said, his voice rising with his temper. "All I want to do is to get to Italy. For Christ's sake, it's only fifty kilometers!"

"—— Italy," Maurice shouted. "And —— you."

"Stop it! Stop it, do you hear me?" Pierre lunged forward and grabbed Maurice's arm, and was thrown aside.

"Keep off!" Maurice sounded, and looked, dangerous, but as Salvani, rather more dangerous, was about to move in and calm things down—that is, give Maurice a tremendous bang on the ear—Judah burst into tears.

As for any child, time had little meaning for Judah. It was measured in brief bursts of pleasure, or pain, tedium, too; and the events of the past days were already happenings of some remote past. In a watchful way, he had trusted the big Italian soldier with his rough kindness, and without complaint—or very little—he had marched with him, pumping his small, scraped legs along, three of his steps to every one of the Italian's, a stoic in his small way, as brave as, if not braver than, Salvani.

But now, in the cool wood with the sun-splashed meadows below, and the promised road which was to lead to his father, there were three men shouting and swearing, pushing each other, red-faced and angry, with the smell of spilled alcohol overwhelming the odor of the tall trees. It was a sight frightening enough for an adult, terrifying for Judah because he knew in some way that the violence was related to him, to his existence, some failing of his own and one the more appalling because he did not know what the failure could possibly be—although he had heard that loose remark about men looking for Jews—and so from his innocence and terror, and because there was nothing else he could do, he cried, as, across Europe, millions equally terrified, and equally innocent, cried, too.

"Jesus!" Salvani scooped Judah up in a rough green-clad arm and glared at Maurice. "See what you've done?"

"What you've both done," Pierre said.

"What!" Salvani stared over Judah's head.

"*Both.*" Pierre jerked a contemptuous chin. "Cursing and pushing. No wonder the kid's scared. It's what drinking brandy does. Agh! Brandy at this time of the day."

"But I didn't have . . ." Salvani, patting Judah's head as a shrewd shopper might pat a melon, testing its firmness, began a feeble remonstrance, but let it slide. "Well, it doesn't matter what it is . . ." as he spoke, wondering what he was talking about yet turning his mind to a matter of sharper concern, "but if you won't take me to the border, I'll go on my own."

Pierre shook his head. "Do you know what the mountains are like? How can you get there?"

"I don't know," Salvani said. "And Christopher Columbus didn't know he was going to America, did he? But he got there." He lowered Judah and eased his rifle and pack over his shoulders. "Anyway, you've done what you said you'd do and I've got no complaints. We'll get going and try and keep off the main road. No hard feelings, it isn't your fault those pigs down there got here first. You've got your problems and I've got mine, so"—he spoke briskly, and with a certain satisfaction—"you can both —— off. Come on, *bambino.*"

He took Judah by the hand and was ready to step out, to cross the sparkling stream, to climb the hill opposite, and to head for those glittering and beckoning peaks he had headed for—how many lifetimes ago?—when Maurice threw down his bottle of brandy and said, "Don't be an idiot."

"Aaah . . ." Salvani let go of Judah's hand and turned, balling his fist, ready, at last, to release his feelings in the way most accessible to him; that is, to knock someone—it didn't need to be Maurice but he was available—comprehensibly into Kingdom Come. "Do you know what happened to the last man who called me that?" he asked, in a conversational tone.

"I can guess," Maurice said. "But I've got an idea, and beating my brains out won't help you to hear it. So what do you want to do—beat me up or hear me out?"

Oxen shouldered and oxen necked, and with all an ox's strength and slow, steady persistence, Salvani loomed over the small, obdurate Maurice. "I'll hear you out," he said slowly. "But make it good. You know what I mean?"

Maurice raised his hands in a very French gesture, but began to speak, and when he had finished, all thoughts Salvani had of knocking Maurice senseless had gone, and instead of feeling ox-like strength, he felt an ox-like stupidity.

"It's the best I can do," Maurice said.

"It's more than the best." Salvani put his hand on Maurice's shoulder. "What can I say?"

"Say thank you," Pierre said. He took Salvani by the arm. "You know he's taking a big chance—a big one—" He waved away Maurice's protest. "Remember that, soldier. Remember France."

"I'll remember," Salvani said. "Believe me. I'll remember."

"And you, little one." Pierre squatted by Judah. "Remember us, too, hey? When you are home, remember us. And here"—he tweaked Judah's cheek—"see, for you. Give me your hand. Come."

Judah, first looking for approval at Salvani, held out his scabbed left hand.

"There." Pierre pressed a slice of cake into the small palm and folded Judah's fingers over it. "From my mama. Ah!" He stood up, a little embarrassed, and held out his hand to Salvani. *"Bon voyage, Italien."*

"Bon voyage." Salvani shook hands warmly. "And thanks, you made us see sense," raising his hand in a Roman salute as Pierre left the shelter of trees and headed down the valley.

Salvani watched him go, lithe and light-footed. "Where is he going?" he asked.

128

"To La Chambre," Maurice said. "Into the lion's den." He picked up the pack and the rifle. "There, little one," he said to Judah. "All friends again now. Just a little farther to walk, and don't you worry. Don't worry at all," leading Salvani and Judah back up the valley to where the lifeless crags baked in the afternoon heat.

At the head of the valley they headed west, away from La Chambre, the valley hidden from them by the flanks of the mountains; creeping under the spine of the range, skirting snow fields, themselves mere fragile fingers of the ice above, until after four or five kilometers they began to descend and then:

"Mother of God!" Salvani mouthed, and other more secular oaths which he would not have cared to have his mother hear. "This is it? *This?*"

They were staring into a valley, a gigantic gorge plunging into a chokingly narrow slot with a road slashed through it, and a railway line and factories jammed along a river from which a coiling mist was beginning to rise.

"Yes," Maurice said. "It's the Maurienne valley. That's the river Arc down there."

"And we go down there?"

"Yes."

"And then go up there?" Salvani pointed across the gorge, to forest, rock, waterfall.

"There, yes."

Salvani sank to the ground. Earlier, when Maurice had proposed his plan, he had expected rough going; in fact, Maurice had hinted as much. But this! Salvani stared down again and, half laughing, but without humor, said, "I thought that we'd done the hard bit."

Maurice sat beside him. "It's not so bad."

"It isn't? You could have fooled me." Salvani looked again into the chasm. As much as the stupendous, and horrendous, gorge, it was the factories which astounded him. After what had seemed like ten thousand years that they'd been wandering among remote peaks, the harsh thumbprints of industry were a reminder that there was another world in existence—one maybe, in some ways, more promising, but, more probably, menacing.

He pulled out a cigarette. "Let's just go through this again. We go down and then climb that bloody great mountain over there. Right?"

"It's not a mountain." Maurice was faintly amused.

"You could have fooled me," Salvani said. "Still, we climb it, and then come to a minor road. Yes?"

"Yes."

"And that goes north."

"Yes," Maurice said. "Over the Col de la Madeleine."

"And that's a lonely road?"

"Oh yes, it's lonely."

"And that takes us to a major road."

"Right." Maurice lit a cigarette, too. "Forty kilometers, on a road. Even with the child it's an easy walk."

"Just forget the easy stuff," Salvani said. "This major road . . ."

"The N90." Maurice waved away a moth. "It goes to the Little St. Bernard Pass—fifty kilometers, no more. Then Italy."

"And what if that road is blocked, too?"

Maurice blew smoke from his nose. "What can I say? That's a chance you'll have to take. One thing is sure: that road"—he pointed down to the Mont Cenis road—"*is*. But it's up to you."

And that was it, Salvani thought. It was up to him—or down to him, more like. It was a gamble, but worth taking. Even if he was picked up then, he would have done his best—and it meant another day of freedom. But there was one more thing.

"That river. There's not many bridges, right?"

"Not many," Maurice admitted.

"So they'll be guarded, won't they?"

Maurice shrugged. "Probably."

"So how do we cross it?"

"Ah!" Maurice ground out his cigarette against a rock and stood up. "You'll have to get your feet wet. Come on, *Italien*. Time to go."

He stepped away and beckoned, leading the way into the shadow of a huge stand of pine trees, following a barely discernible trail—Salvani, clutching Judah, sliding and stumbling behind him, a cataract muttering as they descended into the gloom, as if, like sinners not contrite, they were being pulled down from the immaculate peaks, down and down again into a purgatorial abyss, the light failing and a new sound, at first faint, subtle, as if the wind was sighing in the treetops, except there was no wind, and as they plunged down, Maurice, wraith-like, beckoning, the sound grew louder and more ominous, as if down in the darkness and the mist, waiting for them, was some beast, uncoiling itself in its lair.

Struggling to keep his footing, and to hold on to Judah, who seemed to be finding the descent rather jolly, Salvani called to Maurice to ask what the noise was, but dancing surefootedly, Maurice didn't deign to answer as the sound grew louder, and then, coming at last from the trees, Salvani saw the source of the noise.

"Cross that?" he asked, staggered. "Cross it?"

"Yes." Maurice pointed his arm, straight out. "Cross it."

It's a joke, Salvani thought. A stupid, crackpot joke. He looked left and right. There were no factories to be seen, but almost at his feet, the river, shining a curious clayey-white, and a hundred meters wide, poured with frightening strength through rocky banks. He lowered Judah and strode to Maurice. "Get our feet wet," he shouted, raising his voice over the roar of the waters. "A —— seal couldn't get across there."

Maurice shook his head and backed into the mist, beckoning, guiding Salvani and Judah along a jagged bank, following the river as it curved a little, and the banks, even in that cleft, became more marshy than rocky, and the river widened, its waters swirling in a huge, sinister whirlpool as if gathering its strength before gushing through more bleak rocks, and there Maurice stopped, leaning against a boulder, and said, "Here."

"Here?" Salvani wanted to seize Maurice by the scruff of his neck and hurl him into the river but instead picked up a piece of driftwood, a bough almost as big as Maurice, and, with a bitter, fleeting memory of the game of sticks, heaved it into the river; immediately it was sucked under to reappear, almost vertical, before being swept away. "Wonderful," he said. "You saw that?"

Maurice grinned, took Salvani's hand, and ran it across the boulder. "Feel it, hey?"

Salvani frowned. "But it's not rock, it's—"

"Concrete!" Maurice laughed. "Here." He pulled Salvani down and Judah, the three of them crouching against the concrete block and hidden by the alder bushes and tall, dying foxgloves.

"You saw the factories," Maurice said, throwing his voice against the roar of the river. "They are hydroelectric, you understand? They make electricity from the water, yes?" leaning forward as Salvani, vaguely understanding, nodded and Judah began to pipe up, learnedly, about electricity.

"Yes, sure." Maurice patted Judah's head in a way that meant shut up. "So they make dams across the river—to make the engines go—yes!" a little irate as Judah piped up again. "Yes, *turbines*. Now, they started a dam here, but it was never finished. The war, you know . . . it changed many things . . ."

"Right, yes, lots of things." Salvani had no wish at all to go for a walk with Maurice down Memory Lane; certainly not now, at the bottom of a vast chasm, a child at his knees, Italy never seeming so far away—and a river, man-killing just to hear it, to cross. "But getting over!"

"Ah." Maurice clicked his fingers as if bringing himself back from the memories of yesteryear. "You're lucky."

"Yes?" Salvani peered through the mist at the river, which gurgled against the bank as if to say, "Come in. Come in. Come in and let me drown you." He licked his dry lips. "I've news for you," he said. "I can't swim."

"That's why you're lucky," Maurice said. "You can walk across the water."

11

"Walk, hey?" Salvani was bitter. "I'm not in the mood for jokes, and I'm not Jesus Christ."

"No joke, *Italien*." Maurice tapped Salvani's knee. "The dams I was speaking of? This is one that didn't get finished. This block here, and under the river—concrete! The concrete runs under the river to the other side. We walk across it—the water's only a meter deep!"

"Wonderful!" Salvani pointed to the river surging past. "One step and your legs will be knocked from under you. We wouldn't last a minute."

"Aah." Maurice put his finger against his nose. "But you will. Come and take a look."

Salvani nervously following, Maurice edged along the huge concrete block.

"See," Maurice said.

"Yes, I see," Salvani said, seeing, bolted into the concrete, a slender wire hawser which led into the water.

Maurice bent and tugged on the hawser, which lifted with surprising ease. "You hold it when you cross. It's all right. Really, I've done it plenty of times when the cops cracked down on—"

"Smuggling."

"No!" Maurice sounded hurt. "Trading, but—" He dismissed the fine economic distinction. "But this is where you cross." He frowned at Salvani, who was looking distinctly dubious. "I tell you I've done it."

Yes, Salvani thought, but not carrying a knapsack, a rifle, and a kid. He stepped away back to the comparative safety of the other side of the block. "Er . . ." He was deliberately casual. "I don't suppose that you'd—"

"No!" Maurice didn't need to hear the end of the sentence. "I brought you here, right? I could have left you outside La Chambre, yes? I've done more than I bargained for. You'll admit that, I've been more than fair . . ."

He's talking to persuade himself, not me, it occurred to Salvani as he scooped Judah up. Not that he blamed Maurice. If the Milice were having a roundup, then someone like Maurice would probably be among the first to get copped. "You've been fair," he said.

"I have, haven't I?" Maurice sounded like a man asking for absolution.

"Yes." Salvani absolved Maurice. After all, who would cross the scary river at dusk, or even in broad daylight, unless he had to: and who knew what might be waiting on the other dark bank: what men, what dogs . . . "And we'll find this track all right?"

"Yes." Maurice was anxious to please. "Cross, climb the bank, cross the railway line and the road, and you'll see a milestone. Just by it there is a trail—a foresters' path. Go up—"

"Not down?" Salvani asked.

Maurice slapped his thigh in exasperation. "*You* said no jokes. Go up and you come to a ridge. There are boulders —big ones—with two rocks on them sticking up like this—" He stuck his hands by the side of his head. "Like—"

"Like a rabbit!" Judah shouted.

"Yes." To Salvani's amusement Maurice sounded irritated again, an emotion which Judah did seem good at arousing. "Like a rabbit. Go around the rocks and you find a trail that takes you to the road over the Col de la Madeleine. Then"—he shrugged—"follow it."

"Right," Salvani said.

"Yes?" Maurice sounded anxious for approval.

"Sure." Salvani wrapped his greatcoat around Judah. "River, road, climb mountains, rabbit's ears, track, road. You've done a lot for us, truly, and thanks a lot. Say thank you, Judah."

"Thank you," Judah said. "Thank you very much, monsieur."

Maurice bent a little and peered at Judah, whose faintly blotched head was poking out of Salvani's lapels like a baby kangaroo from its pouch.

"Aah," he sighed, a man defeated by forces beyond his control. "I'll take you across."

"There's no obligation." Salvani spoke in a carefully neutral tone.

"No," Maurice said. "But I'll do it. Let's sit down. We'll wait a while, let it go darker . . ."

"Understood." Salvani agreed, although he felt a deeper lowering of his spirits at the thought of crossing the river in the dark.

"But you carry the child," Maurice said.

"Sure." Salvani took a cigarette from Maurice. "What will you do, when we've gone?"

"Go to my cabin maybe." Maurice waved his hand. "Maybe go to Le Pic. Keep out of the way until the racket dies down. They won't be too bothered with me, anyway. It's the politicals they'll be after, socialists, Communists . . ."

"Many around here?" Salvani was surprised.

"Some." Maurice stretched out his legs. "From the factories. But the peasants are poor, you know."

135

"Yes." Salvani thought of Le Pic and Jeanne in their hovel with the pictures of their dead and lost relatives on the walls—sitting and smoking and rocking Judah as the darkness came and the mist thickened into fog, blotting out the far bank and the stars, with the river filling the cleft with its roar, until Maurice flicked away his cigarette and stood up.

"Time to go, hey?" Salvani struggled to his feet.

"It's not so bad," Maurice said. "Trust me."

He took the rifle and pack while Salvani shook Judah awake. "Now listen, Judah," he said. "You've got to sit on my back and hang on to my collar tight. *Tight*. Very tight, as tight as you can, because we're—"

"Going to have a piggyback ride!" Judah said gleefully.

"Yes!" Salvani affected a jovial and totally false cheeriness. "A piggyback! Across the river."

"*That* river?" Judah's expression changed from one of gleeful anticipation to, Salvani thought, wholly justified anxiety.

"Yes. That little river . . . Isn't it nice, ha! ha! ha!" Salvani laughed hollowly, half choking as Judah seized his collar with an amazingly strong grip and they moved around the concrete block to Maurice, already holding the hawser, and to the river itself.

"Ready," Maurice cried.

"Ready," Salvani said, less ready than he had ever been for anything in his life.

"It's easy," Maurice called. "Really. Two minutes."

"Sure." Salvani grinned mirthlessly.

"Right." Maurice backed into the river. "Come on."

Salvani grasped the hawser with one hand, put the other behind his back to hold up Judah, and took a step forward.

The water plucked at his ankles, a mild childlike tug: come, come along. A little farther; just one step more, and just one more, and another, into the night and the darkness and the fog—and then you are mine. And for the first

136

time Salvani became aware that the river had a smell, a faintly sweet, sticky odor, like a graveyard, and he thought of the stream they had crossed that morning with its banks strewn with bones; and with that in mind, clutching the hawser as if his life depended on it, which in fact it did, and gripping Judah with a hand of iron, he moved out farther—and then one step farther, the current pushing at his calves, and then his knees, as he felt for his footing on the smashed slabs under the water.

He took another, sideways step, another, slipped on something oozy, and the river pounced and he felt his legs sliding away . . . "Jesus," he croaked, "Jesus Mary and Joseph," dragging himself back upright, soaked to the waist. He swayed on the hawser for a moment, wanting to go back, but moved on, more crab-like skidding steps, and there the river was pouring down with astonishing power, as if it really did have a will and purpose of its own, to drive his legs from under him, to wrench his fist from the hawser, and to suck him down into its depths.

He stopped again, sweat pouring from his hair, peering blindly into the fog, the graveyard smell stronger, and realized that for the first time in his journey he was not merely exhausted, or battered, or jumpy with nervous tension, but frightened, really frightened, terrified of the river and its horrifying power and mindless raving and of the fog and the darkness. He gasped for air, as if he were drowning already, and stretched out a leg and there was nothing, no foothold—and something wrapped itself around his ankle. He gave a weird cry, such as the first man may have made on seeing the sun go down for the first time, dragged himself back, and was unable to move farther, absolutely.

I'm scared stiff, he thought. Scared stiff. This is what it means—and this is how it all ends, trapped like a rat in a drainpipe, and, "What the . . . ." he bellowed, because something was banging on his head, something small but

137

hard, and banging with determination, and Judah's voice was shrieking in his ear.

"Come on, Uncle!" Judah cried, his shrill voice cutting across the roar of the river. *"Come on!"* banging Salvani's ear and kicking his sides as if he were a balky mule.

"All right!" Salvani bellowed back, shaking his head as if to shake off his terror, but even then he wasn't sure that he could move until a shape loomed from the fog and a lean hand took hold of his coat and pulled him across the terrible gap, holding him as he sidled along the hawser, goaded by Judah and coaxed by Maurice, until the river shallowed, a thicket of stringy willow whipped at them, another huge concrete block appeared, and they were on the far bank.

Salvani let Judah slide from his back, let out a huge breath, and stamped on the ground to make sure it was real. "Christ," he said. "Christ Almighty. There was that bit in the middle . . ."

"Yes." Maurice was nonchalant. "A hole. I didn't know. But the river—it wasn't there the last time—the hole, I mean. But it was easy, yes?" He stooped over Judah. "Did you like that?"

Salvani raised a fist. "Of all the stupid questions," he began, and was astounded to hear Judah say that he had and wanted to do it again.

Maurice smiled . . . "Not tonight, but your big soldier will do it for you lots of times."

"I'll never cross a river again as long as I live," Salvani said sincerely.

"Maybe." Maurice straightened his slight, wiry figure. "Silence." He crooked his fingers. "Come."

They clawed their way up a rocky bank and through a tangled wilderness of bushes and rank weeds, sodden leaves slopping against their faces, thorns hooking at their legs, the baffling fog hanging over them, until, free from the miniature jungle and on level ground, Maurice stopped and raised a finger.

Judah nodded, understanding only too well: not a cough or a sneeze, not a murmur or a whisper, or red eyes might glow in the night and yellow fangs be bared.

"Good." Maurice patted Judah on the cheek. "I'm going to see if the road is clear. Come when you hear this." He made a curious, haunting whistle, and was gone, a wraith in the fog.

Salvani dabbed Judah's face with the sleeve of his coat, hoping that the enemy knew as little about bird calls as he did, wet, depressed about his cowardice in the river, and thinking about the railway line and the road not thirty meters away, which led to Italy. A thought as rotten and corrupting as a fungal spore began to germinate at the back of his mind: Why not just slope off? Leave the kid with Maurice—he seemed a decent man—and nobody could say that he, Salvani, hadn't done his duty, his duty as a human being, that is . . . All that stuff about Jews and what might be happening to them was probably rubbish anyway—and who would hurt a kid? So . . . he, himself, could get over to the Rabbit's Ears or wherever . . . But better tell Judah that he was just going away for a moment and to wait for Maurice's whistle . . . And he almost did. Almost. He put his finger under Judah's chin and lifted his head and was about to say, Just stay still; in fact, he said, "Judah, listen to me—" when Judah, his eyes wide and watchful, placed a finger against Salvani's lips and, his small face pale against the ambivalent swirling fog and darkness, whispered "Shsssh, Uncle." And from the night came a fluting whistle.

Salvani stared down at Judah for a long moment and then, standing brusquely, swung the child over his shoulder.

A ghostly figure by a railway line, the tracks glistening, Maurice was waiting, beckoning them forward up another shrub-grown bank, and to the road.

On their knees in dripping foliage, they waited, listening. Below them the river gurgled, waterfalls sighed, but there was no sound of man: no grinding of engines, no clatter of jackboots, no raucous bellowing of orders, and no savage yammering of dogs.

"So." Maurice patted Salvani on the shoulder. "Across the road, the milestone. The trail."

"Yes." Salvani nodded.

"*Italien.*" Maurice sounded troubled. "You're Catholic?"

Catholic! Salvani rolled his eyes. A theological debate! Cold, wet, skulking in a horrendous chasm after the worst experience of his entire life, God alone knowing what lay ahead of him, and . . . "Yes," he said, "about as much as the Pope. For Christ's sake, why?"

Maurice patted Salvani again, like a man calming a horse. "It's just . . . well . . ." He fumbled around Salvani's neck. "Excuse me," he said. "I thought that I would like you to have it."

"Have it?" Salvani, not a man to like the too close proximity of other men, ran his hand down his throat. "Have what?"

"A little medal," Maurice said. "St. Christopher—you know, the patron saint of travelers—he carried wayfarers across a river. Now—" He chopped off any further debate. "Go," he said. "Go, *Italien.* Go, child"—raising a last, unseen hand, and vanishing in the night and fog.

One grinding, cursing hour later Salvani and Judah had climbed from the trees and the fog into a transformed world of moonlit clarity and were sitting by the Rabbit's Ears.

They rested for a while, and yet Salvani didn't feel exhausted or even particularly tired. Rather, he felt exhilarated, as if by climbing from the fog and the rank smells of the river he had escaped from a sinister trap, and, although he would have found it hard to put into words, a moral trap, too. Would he really, he wondered, have left Judah . . . would he? Probably not, he hoped, although he felt in his heart that merely thinking of dumping Judah had been an act of betrayal.

But he wasn't a man to worry too much about might-have-beens. In his steady, matter-of-fact way, what concerned him was the here and now, and that was sitting by the Rabbit's Ears and looking down on yet another valley but one which made him feel hopeful, for down there, among silvery pastures and inky woods, was the road Maurice had promised: clearly visible, white in the moonlight, twisting upward, lonely; and once on it, Salvani guessed, there would be as much chance of meeting a German soldier or a Milice as Mussolini.

He hunched forward, as solid as the rocks themselves. Maurice had said it was about forty kilometers to the next main road, the one running to the Little St. Bernard Pass. Obviously they couldn't get there before dawn, and in fact, he didn't want to. The night was the time to arrive, so they had, what . . . say twenty hours . . . On the other hand, he wanted to get as far as he could before morning—the question was, how far? He felt fine and Judah was sprightly enough, but the kid would need rest, a real one, before too long. So should they stay here in the eyrie, or push on . . .

He turned to Judah, who was snuggled against him like a cub. "How are you?"

Judah rubbed his head against Salvani's side. "All right," he said, yawning a little, and he was, more or less. His cuts and bruises were healing, and although he was tired, he was becoming used to that—it being something, such as his separation from his father, to be endured, knowing that it would end sooner or later. In the meantime, he was ready to accept his lot, to tramp on with the big Italian, treating him, actually, like a huge, amiable beast of burden to be climbed on or off as it suited him and, if necessary, to be kicked and beaten as when crossing the river.

In fact, Judah was finding the journey not unpleasant. Indeed, it had, at times, been enjoyable—playing sticks in

141

the stream—or exciting, as when crossing the river, and he looked forward to telling his father of his adventures. Of course, it had been frightening, too—terrifying at times, but he had spent a good deal of his brief existence in a state of fear, anyway. So, "All right," he said.

"Good." Salvani had made up his mind, anyway. He was going to get to the road and make as much distance as possible, certainly to reach the summit of the pass. After all, anything could happen in these mountains—more fog, storms, a blizzard. "Hoopla!" he said and bent his broad back to let Judah scramble up. "I'll carry you—to the road."

Salvani had thought that it would be an hour, at least, to the road, but it took not much more than twenty minutes—the trail they were on, apart from one minor hiccup when it snaked over a ridge, running across pastureland and over a brook to the road itself.

It wasn't much of a road, potholed, furrowed, but Salvani stood upon it with deep satisfaction: rough though it might be, it was a road, gravel-strewn and graded, and one he could follow without clawing his way up and down mountains and ravines—and without depending on guides who might or might not have their own ideas about where you ought to end up. Of course, the road might lead them slap-bang into a German patrol, but that was in the hands of the gods. In the meantime, he stood, legs apart, hands on hips, bearing his knapsack, rifle, Judah, and his conscience, lightly, a formidable figure, and feeling, for the first time since the crash, lucky. He slung Judah down and took a deep, satisfying breath.

"*Bambino,*" he said, "you know what we're going to do?"

Judah, about the height of Salvani's knee, peered upward. "No," he said with his usual frankness.

"Well." Salvani shrugged off his rifle and pack. "We're going to sit down and have a bite to eat, and have a little wine, and then I'm going to have a cigarette. Now—"

He pulled off his greatcoat, wrapped the dry, upper

part around Judah, rummaged in the knapsack, produced bread and, blessing Maurice, wine, fed Judah, snatched a mouthful of food himself, then, oblivious of his wet trousers, settled himself down.

Yes, he put a vast arm around Judah. Not so bad, not so bad at all—and so far so good: a poor man, used to counting days by a poor man's calendar, one day at a time, and if at the end of each day you had food and a cigarette, that day hadn't been so bad . . . and such a night, one of great glory, the sky strewn with stars, the moon, trailing one cloud like a bride's discarded veil, and the Milky Way, a glittering bow arcing against the blackness of the ultimate heavens, and—"Oh," he cried, and "Oh," again. "See! Did you see, Judah?" raising his arm.

"Shooting stars!" Judah cried. "And there's one. Look, Uncle!"

"Right!" Salvani laughed. "It's lucky to see them. Did you know that?"

"No"—Judah wriggled away from Salvani's protective arm—"But look, there's another one!"

"Aaah." Salvani looked up with awe as yet another star flashed across the sky, and another. "I've never seen so many. Never."

"We must be *very* lucky," Judah said.

"Very." Salvani beamed. "What a sight. Aaah, a millionaire couldn't buy such a sight—*ten* millionaires put together." He hoisted Judah onto his knee. "Do you like the stars?"

"Yes!" Judah nodded vigorously. "I've seen them. Papa had a big telescope. I've looked at the moon through it."

"The moon! Through a telescope! Aah . . . a telescope . . ." There was longing and humility in Salvani's voice. "What did it look like, the moon, through a telescope?"— wistfully.

"There were mountains," Judah said. "And volcanoes."

"Volcanoes?" Salvani stared at the placid moon and

143

frowned dubiously. "Are you sure? You mean like Vesuvius?"

"Yes," Judah said.

Salvani screwed up his eyes, peering at the moon. "There's no fire or smoke."

"No." Judah struck Salvani's knee. "They've all gone out, Papa says."

"Oh." Salvani was disappointed. "Still, they might come back, like Vesuvius. That goes out sometimes. It would be nice to see, though, wouldn't it, big fires on the moon? Did you see anything else?"

"Mars," Judah said and pointed, somewhat speculatively, at a star low in the sky.

"So that's Mars." Salvani gazed at the star with approval. "That's something I'd *really* like to see through a telescope. There are people on it, you know. Martians."

"No there aren't," Judah said.

"There are." Salvani was indignant. "They've built canals, all over the place. I read about them."

Judah shook his head vigorously. "There aren't any canals. Papa told me."

"Now listen." Salvani looked piercingly at Judah. "There *are* canals. This magazine I saw had *pictures* of them. They wouldn't print the pictures if there weren't any, would they?"

"They're not canals." Judah was as indignant as Salvani. "They're cracks. Papa told me."

"I don't care what your papa said. I'm telling you—" But what Salvani had to say wasn't told, and the mysteries of Mars were left unriddled, and all the wonders of the heavens were forgotten as something darker than the night came their way.

"Down!" Salvani flattened Judah and crouched, his rifle pointed. "Who's there?" he growled. "Come on, who is it? Answer or I'll blow your head off. I'm not kidding around here. Answer . . . well, I'll be dammed to hell and back!"

144

He stood up and scooped Judah to his feet as easily as a man picking daisies.

"I said shooting stars were lucky, didn't I. Look, just see what we've got here."

Judah's eyes opened to the size of saucers. "It's a—"

"A donkey! Now don't move." Salvani moved cautiously forward, but the caution was unnecessary, as the donkey seemed only too glad to have company. In a friendly way, it blew through its nose as Salvani grabbed its bridle, and, another pleasant surprise, the bridle led to a crude saddle.

"Well, well." Salvani rubbed the donkey's nose. "Where did you come from?" He looked around at the silent valley, the mountains, and the white road. "Run away, I suppose, or got lost . . ."

"Whose is it?" Judah put a tentative hand on the donkey's neck.

"Don't know," Salvani said, "and that's a fact. But whoever he is, he's a good man."

"How do you know?" Judah asked.

"Because"—Salvani grinned—"because he's going to lend us his donkey—" not adding that he intended to take the donkey before its owner appeared to claim it, possibly with the aid of a shotgun.

He slung the knapsack over the saddle and swung Judah onto the saddle. "All right? Comfortable?"

On his perch, which at that was not much higher than Salvani's head, Judah beamed. "Uncle," he asked, "what's its name?"

"Oh." Salvani thought for a moment, frowning in concentration. Then, "Stella," he said, "Stella Fortunata. *Lucky Star.* How's that? Is it a good name? Yes? Then let's go."

He grabbed the bridle and led the obedient donkey up the road for a few yards, then paused to make sure the saddle was secure and that Judah *was* comfortable and secure. Ahead of them the road snaked upward to some high pass, but there was nothing to it, Salvani thought. Nothing at all. But before he marched on, he glanced back.

There the road dipped into mist and darkness. La Chambre was down there in the dark with its Germans and Milice.

"Beat you," he said. "Beat you all ends up. Come on, Stella!"

"And come on, Stella," Judah cried as they moved on, triumphant in the wilderness.

12

The moon, unvexed by volcanoes, shone serenely and the stars followed her silent progress, as Salvani, Judah, and Stella Fortunata wended their way up the white road to the pass of the Madeleine, while behind them, in the darkness and the mist, in La Chambre, in the police station, in the basement, in a cell, with two of his men, Palet was crouched on a plank cot.

It was a typical police cell, the sort which could be found anywhere across Europe—or the world: a low-wattage lightbulb, a bucket stinking of human waste, the floor smeared with squashed cockroaches, damp walls scrawled with obscene drawings and scratched with messages from forgotten transgressors: foul, abusive, pious, blasphemous, defiant, sentimental, all untouched by indifferent policemen.

But as Palet sat on the cot, one shoulder unnaturally high, a cigarette smoldering between his fingers and thumb, the cell was no longer a small-town lockup in which, it was true, occasionally a prisoner might get beaten up by irate policemen yet where the light of Justice at least gleamed, but a dungeon in which, carried by the men in field gray, and black and silver, the New Order of Adolf

146

Hitler had arrived in the shape of Palet, his men, and a manacled prisoner with a battered face and broken teeth, who, in a pool of urine, was slumped in a corner.

"Where is he?" Palet was saying. "Where?"

The man shook his head, strings of blood and mucus swinging from his nose and mouth, and mumbled something through his splintered teeth.

"You'll have to speak up," Palet said, and cocked his head as the man mumbled again.

"No." Palet flicked his cigarette end into the bucket. "That won't do. 'Course you know him. He's your cousin, it says so here." He fished a crumpled document from his pocket. "This is a police file—see?" He waved the paper in front of the prisoner's unfocused eyes. "This is you, André Champson. You went to Spain and fought for the Communists in the Civil War—see? And this man Philipe Pleven, known as Maurice, is your cousin. He's a smuggler, a criminal—look!" He leaned forward and slashed the document across Champson's eyes. "A criminal. He knows Le Pic, who's an enemy of the state, and he's hiding a bandit and a Jew kid. That's an offense against the state. So where is he?"

Champson coughed out a clot of blood. "Don't know."

Palet flushed. "I said don't say that." He jerked his thumb and one of his men stepped forward and kicked Champson in the ribs. Champson toppled over and the man pulled him back by the hair.

"Montags," Champson dragged a word from the back of his throat.

"*Montags*? Montags!" Palet said. "What the —— are montags?" He burst out laughing, his men joining in, the three of them laughing heartily.

"Mo . . ." Champson tried to raise his head. "Mo . . ."

"Mountains!" One of Palet's men cried with an air of Newton discovering the Law of Gravity. "He means Pleven is up there, in the mountains."

He looked at Palet, waiting for recognition of his genius,

but failed to get it as Palet, the hyena-like laughter gone from his lips, spat. "That's no good. The mountains!"

He got off the cot, sank to his haunches, shoved Champson's head back, and stared at him, his handsome face an inch from Champson's disfigured features. "Where in the mountains? Where?"

But Champson was gone, his eyes rolling upward and his mouth agape. Palet cursed and snapped an order and one of his men threw a can of water into Champson's face. Champson came half back to consciousness but sagged away again.

"I'll get more water," the man said.

"No." Palet clicked his fingers and pointed at the bucket. "Use that."

"Good idea, boss," the man said, and with unfeigned admiration he picked up the bucket and hurled its contents of excrement and urine over Champson.

"Now." Palet minced forward. "Where?"

Through the mask of filth Champson opened the eyes of a human being. He gazed at Palet for a second and then murmured, "Albiez."

"Albiez." Palet sucked his teeth, then snapped another order. One of the men left the cell, his footsteps echoing. Palet sat back on the cot, lit a cigarette and blew smoke at Champson until the man reappeared. "Well?" he demanded.

The man shook his head. "No such place. Not around here."

Palet threw his cigarette at Champson and stood up. "Thought so. Well, you know what to do."

He left the cell and walked along a gloomy corridor. There were more cells and as he passed them he peered through the spy holes. Pierre was in one, smeared with blood, moaning, his wrists broken. In another was Pierre's brother, covered with vomit. In the last cell there were three criminals playing cards, drinking wine from a bribed

148

policeman, smoking, laughing, awaiting trial for robbery, assault, and attempted murder.

At the end of the corridor there was a barred door. A policeman opened it and Palet went through and up a flight of iron stairs to a room. A sergeant of the Gendarmerie was sitting behind a desk with a large ledger open before him.

"Champson," Palet said. "Dead. Suicide."

The sergeant looked up. "Suicide?"

"You heard me," Palet said. "Write it down."

The sergeant looked away and lowered his head, like a dog guilty of stealing food, and scratched away. "Time of death?" he muttered.

Palet looked at the clock on the wall. "An hour ago," he said.

Across the road from the police station was a café and, late though it was, it was open for business, and, even odder in a town which went to bed early and which was occupied by a foreign army, it was full, and Palet walked into a babble of noise, although that stopped abruptly as he entered: glasses halted halfway to lips, sentences cut off in the middle—but not one eye meeting his, only the café owner grinned and bowed obsequiously.

Palet stood motionless, savoring the moment, a moment of power, one as absolute as any king ever wielded—and over such men. Men, at least in that small town, of authority, influence, wealth—on speaking terms with senators and préfets; men who before the war would have brushed him aside on the street but who now cast down their eyes when he stared at them, recognizing a new power, backed not by money but by the hangman's noose and the executioner's ax.

The sense of power, like lust, engorging his throat, Palet slouched across the bar and pushed through a door which led into the hotel. Two German soldiers, automatic weapons on their knees, nodded him through into a back room.

In the room was a table with a dull, maroon cloth on it, a few chairs, a sofa, its cover worn shiny, a huge portrait of Adolf Hitler; and at the table, by a lamp with a green shade, a carafe of wine by his side, upright, dapper, scarred, was a captain of the German Army.

"Come in. Come in." The captain was polite, courteous even. "Have a glass of wine."

Palet took the glass, downed it in one gulp, and sat down crookedly, one arm sprawled across the table.

The captain pushed the carafe forward. "Noisy in the café?"

"Yes," Palet grunted, and poured out more wine for himself, ignoring the captain, and drank half a glassful. "They're having a party, sort of. They're glad you're here."

"Yes." The captain didn't sound surprised.

"You're better than the Italians," Palet went on, needlessly as far as the captain was concerned. "They're a dirty lot. Cowards. Anyway, now you're here we can really get to work. Crack down. Round up the Communists and that lot. Law and order."

"That's why we're here," the captain said. He stood up, every inch a German officer, and stepped to a bureau. Wounded somewhere, Palet thought, that's why he's on a soft touch like this. Not that he held that against the captain, being all for soft touches himself.

The captain came back to the table with a bottle of fine cognac and two small glasses. "Help yourself," he said, and took a cigarette from a gunmetal case.

Palet poured a large cognac into his wineglass and took out his cigarette case—gold—and flicked a light from his lighter, also gold.

The captain leaned back in his chair and blew a smoke ring and waited until it had drifted into shapelessness. "How did it go, over there?"

Palet shuffled his feet. "Got three Communists. And a lead. To a Jew."

"That's something." The captain blew another smoke ring. "Have you caught any Jews yet?"

"No." Palet scowled. "I've only been here a few hours."

"Of course." The captain tapped his glass thoughtfully. "They're cunning. Cunning as rats. In Poland . . . I could tell you a tale or two."

I'll bet you could, Palet thought enviously—Poland, what a place to be, crawling with Jews, all of them stuffed with gold and jewels. "Mustn't seem much," he said. "Here after Poland, and me looking for one Jewish kid."

"Not at all!" The captain crackled with authority. "All of them, they're all worth catching. Remember, little rats grow into big ones . . . and they breed . . . spread . . . You're to be complimented."

"Complimented?" Palet looked suspiciously at the captain.

"Certainly." The captain stubbed out his cigarette, jabbing it into the ashtray as if he was squashing an unpleasant insect. "Hunting down this one young rat. Excellent. Devotion to duty and to detail. An unpleasant duty but our duty nonetheless. It's why we're fighting this war. It's a crusade to purify Europe."

"Sure. Right." Palet had no interest in political harangues, or crusades. "I'll get on with it."

"Good." The captain sat upright, his back as stiff as a board. "By the way. You'll have help tomorrow."

"Help?" Palet halted by the door, his head thrust forward.

"Yes, two men from Lyons. Real experts. But don't worry, you'll have this Jew brat. You deserve him."

Palet made an indeterminate noise and clutched the door handle, but the captain hadn't finished. "If I might," he said. "Your jacket, it needs cleaning."

Palet looked at his sleeve. It was smeared with blood and excrement. "It's the job," he said.

He went upstairs to his commandeered room, one almost

151

identical to the room he had in Allevard, and Chambéry: gloomy, uncomfortable, a sickly picture of the Virgin Mary, a portrait of Pétain, a bare lightbulb, a bed. He locked the door, poured out a brandy, courtesy of the hotelier, took out his wallet, then stripped off his jacket and threw it in a corner. He had no intention of having it cleaned. He had other suits as expensive—as many as there were men his size in France.

A door banged below and from the bar came a few drunken goodbyes. Palet twisted his mouth disdainfully— the last of the customers, having celebrated the arrival of the German Army and the first arrests of their real ene- mies. They would have more cause to celebrate tomorrow; every arrest had a knock-on effect. After all, if you arrested someone it meant that they were guilty of something, and they had to know other people, so it stood to reason that they were guilty, too, and in their turn they knew other people . . . In fact, if you worked at it you could end up ar- resting the whole world. And why not, Palet thought, they were all pigs, all of them, including the German captain.

He grinned mirthlessly. He could have the kid! The Germans could have every traitor in La Chambre as long as he got hold of him, and he would, he felt it in his bones. It was just a question of getting hold of the right man. Le Pic had spouted quickly enough when he realized what would happen if he didn't, and the lad, Pierre, too. Of course, Champson hadn't, but Palet shrugged: maybe he didn't know anything anyway. But there was someone in the town who knew what hidey-holes the man known as Maurice had—it was just a case of sorting out the lies from the truth . . .

He sprawled on the bed. As he did so, there was a clatter of boots on the stairs and a knock on the door. For all his apparent awkwardness, he was back on his feet with the ease of an athlete and a revolver appeared in his hand like a conjuror's trick.

"Me, boss," a voice said.

Palet opened the door a crack, then let one of his men in.

"Didn't want to bother you, boss," the man said, "but we've got a good suspect. He's a cousin of this Maurice."

"They're all —— cousins," Palet said.

"Yes, well—" The man looked longingly at the bottle of brandy. "A cop has just come in, he's been away at a funeral—"

"Never mind where he's been." Palet laid his gun on the bed. "What's he got to say?"

"He says this cousin, Doriot, he was in a smuggling racket with Maurice."

"They're all smugglers." Palet sat on the bed and glowered at the Virgin Mary.

"Sure, but there's something else." The man looked at the bottle again. "Any chance of a drink, boss? I've been on my feet all day and—"

"Have one." Palet waved impatiently. "What's this something else?"

The man swigged from the bottle, wiped the top with an elaborate show of good manners, then smiled craftily. "He had Jews staying with him, up at his farm, when the Italians were here."

"What?" Palet raised his right hand, his fingers crooked. "Jews?"

"Yes"—the man took another drink—"Jew kids!"

"The —— !" With his disconcerting speed Palet was on his feet again, his revolver in his hand, but the man shook his head.

"They've gone, the Jews. Went with the Italians over Mont Cenis. But it's a good lead, isn't it?"

Palet nodded, a cousin of this Maurice, a fellow criminal and Jew helper . . . Not that Palet had any illusions about that; he would have been making a packet out of the Jews, gouging them, screwing the last centime out of their dirty pockets, so, if he, Palet, played his cards right, there would be plenty of loot . . .

"So what do we do, boss?" Palet's man leaned against the door, bottle in hand. "Go and pick him up?"

Palet sat back down, reached over to the bedside table, grabbed a map and opened it.

"Where does he live?"

The man leaned forward, squinting, and jabbed a finger down. "There."

Palet brooded over the map. One road wriggling a few kilometers up into the foothills to a hamlet. He glanced at his watch. "No," he said. "He might hear us driving up and make a break for it and in the dark we'd never get him. We'll nab him in the morning."

The man, swaying, was dubious. "But he'll see us coming then, won't he?"

Palet swayed backward and forward for a moment, the bedsprings squeaking, his revolver sliding down the holster, leaving an oily smear, and then cackled, a sound as unnatural as a toad bursting into laughter. "That's the idea," he said.

The moon sank, and the stars. The sun began to climb over the eastern horizon. Palet awakened and set to work to make his idea reality, and on the Col de la Madeleine Salvani woke, too, with a huge snort.

He rubbed his hand over his stubbly chin, yawned, grunted, and looked around. Judah was lying wrapped in Salvani's greatcoat, sound asleep; the donkey was nibbling at a fuzz of sparse moss—and was firmly tethered to an iron crucifix which marked the top of the pass.

Salvani patted the donkey's neck. "A good walk, hey?" he said, and it had been. Not that where they were was anything to write home about: a boulder-littered pass, a few crows cawing and fluttering, the crucifix . . . But there was a stream and it was flowing north, over the watershed.

Salvani led the donkey to the stream, let it drink, stripped and splashed himself vigorously, then climbed back to the crucifix, and bleak though the pass was, he felt cheerful. The feeling of luck was still strong—the shooting stars had meant something—they were going to make it home.

He tethered the donkey and walked to Judah. He was awake now, unmoving, peering from the cocoon of the greatcoat.

"Let's have you up." Salvani unbuttoned the coat. "We'll give you a nice wash and then have some breakfast and then you can have another ride on the donkey. Come on, now."

Judah let himself be washed, and fed, munching hard bread and cheese without complaining, if also without enthusiasm. "Uncle," he said.

Salvani braced himself for the inevitable question, and to give a lying answer, but Judah was not asking about his father. He pointed a finger and said, "Who's that man?"

"Oh," Salvani said, "that man," looking at the crucifix. "It's Jesus. You must have seen him before—well, his statue. It's everywhere."

Judah nodded but screwed up his eyes. "Why is he here?"

Salvani stirred uneasily. He had a vague respect for Jesus, although he had no belief whatever in miracles, did not believe that Jesus had risen from the dead, and like most of the men of his own class that he knew, he had a cordial dislike of the Church, which he saw as a vast, parasitic organization battening on the poor, but explaining that to Judah . . .

"Well . . ." He fumbled for words. "Jesus was a good man. A good *poor* man," emphasizing the poor, as he did not believe there was such a thing as a good *rich* man. "He went around doing . . . doing good things. For poor people. That's why there's a statue of him here. To cheer you up—" that remark, as he looked on the crucified figure, sounding so improbable that he almost burst out laughing.

"But why is he like that?" Judah asked. "All spread out?"

Salvani stifled a groan. "He was killed, that's how they used to do it a long time ago. A long, long time ago. Nobody does things like that these days." He swung his greatcoat and pack across the saddle. "Don't let it bother you. Come on, time to get moving."

But Judah hadn't finished his questions. The sight of the crucifix and the thought of Christians had stirred a memory. "What day is it?" he asked.

"What do you want to know that for?"

"Is it Saturday?"

"Well . . ." Salvani ran through the days—some days, too, he thought—and nights. "It might be. Why?"

"We can't go anywhere on Saturday," Judah said.

"What?" Salvani raised his eyebrows. "Why not?"

"Because it's Shabbat."

"What's Shabbat?" Salvani asked.

Judah sighed and adopted his vastly irritating air of talking to an obtuse person. "It's a special day. You say special prayers and stay inside—"

"Oh!" Salvani clicked his fingers. "Sunday!"

Judah shook his head vigorously. "No, Shabbat is on Saturday."

"Really?" Salvani was intrigued. "You have Sunday on Saturday! Do you go to church?"

"Synagogue," Judah corrected Salvani. "I *told* you, we don't go anywhere. You can't work on Shabbat and you can't light any fires—"

"No fires?" Salvani peered down quizzically. "How do you do the cooking?"

"It's all done on Friday."

"You know," Salvani was approving, "that's not a bad idea. Not bad at all," and it wasn't at that, he reflected.

Give everyone a real rest, the wife, too, although he was certain he'd seen Fleur knocking about on Saturdays—other Jews, too. Just like the rest of us, he thought. Break the rules when it suits you—but if you're not hurting anyone, why not . . . still, "Don't worry," he said. "I've just remembered, it's Sunday. Our Sunday, ha, ha! Up." He heaved Judah on to the donkey. "Here, let me do up that button." Fussing with clumsy kindness and grinning, thinking of telling his wife and kids about the journey. He smiled at Judah and Judah, proudly straddling the donkey, smiled back, and a thought began to form in Salvani's mind: When they got back to Italy, why hand the kid over to the authorities? Why not just take him home? Another mouth to feed wouldn't break them and it would be better than sticking the kid into some bleak institution—anyway, keep him until they traced his relatives. He took the bridle. "Ready?"

But Judah was not ready quite. He was frowning at the donkey's back. "There's a funny mark here."

Salvani glanced down. "Oh, that. See, when Jesus was alive, when he was wandering about doing . . . doing all those *good* things, he rode on a donkey and they say all donkeys have a cross on their backs because of it."

"A cross . . ." A shadow fell across Judah's face and he glanced timorously at the crucifix.

"I've told you it's all right," Salvani said. "You don't have to worry about crosses or crucifixes or anything else. Anyway"—his tough realism breaking through—"it's better than walking, isn't it? So let's go." He pulled on the bridle. "Come on, donkey."

"Stella," Judah cried. "Stella Fortunata!"

"And that's right." Salvani laughed. "You're a clever lad, yes you are." Shaking his head in admiration, laughing, Judah triumphant on the donkey, he led the way down the pass, following the living waters of the stream, leaving behind the bare, windswept summit, the boulders and rocks, and the iron crucifix, black against the sky.

Beyond the crucifix, across the river Arc, sweating as the sun began to exert its power, two clergymen were walking on a path which slanted upward across meadows as smooth as bowling greens and dappled with flowers to a wooden farmhouse with a wide veranda set against the hillside.

By the farmhouse a man was pitchforking hay into a small barn. As the clergymen toiled up the path he raised his hand to his eyes, waved a salute, and ambled to the house. A moment later he reappeared on the veranda with a woman.

The clergymen climbed the steps up to the veranda and the woman gave a curtsy. "Father," she said, somewhat flustered. "What brings you here? Not bad news, is it? Nothing's happened . . . I mean . . ."

"Wait." The man patted the woman on the shoulder. "Don't leave the Father out here. Come in. Please."

He gestured them into a room, large, airy, simply furnished, practical, with two children peering from behind a stove. "I'm afraid my wife assumes the worst," he said to the younger of the clergymen. "She has a brother, a prisoner of war in Germany, so . . ."

"Nothing like that, I assure you," the young clergyman said.

"That's a relief." The man smiled. "But you'll understand."

"Oh, yes." The clergyman smiled back. "I understand."

"Well." The man shrugged. "I don't know what else could bring you—"

"The children do their duty," the woman broke in. "Every Sunday at church, and preparing for Communion—they know the catechism—"

"The Father knows that," the man said. "But please, take a glass of wine before you tell us why you're here."

"Etienne." The older clergyman took off his shovel hat and mopped his face with a handkerchief. "Etienne—"

"A moment," the young clergyman said. "A glass of wine would be very welcome. Thank you."

"Glad to hear it." The man produced a bottle, glasses, poured. "Please sit."

"Etienne," the older priest began but was again smoothly interrupted by his colleague.

"In a moment." He sipped his wine and cocked his head, as if savoring the taste of the wine and enjoying the sunlight streaming through the windows and the subtle odors of hay and flowers mingled with the not unpleasant smell of animal manure.

"There's just you here?" he asked politely.

"Just us." The man gestured to his wife and children. "You're new here, Father."

"Oh yes, quite new." The young priest offered his glass for more wine and then paused. "What's that noise, underneath us?"

"A cow, Father. We keep them under the house."

"I thought they would be in the fields, eating grass."

Etienne filled the clergyman's glass. "It's in for milking. Easy to see you're not a countryman."

"You're right," the clergyman said. "I'm not a countryman and"—he reached into his pocket and brought something out—"and I'm not a priest, either."

Under the room, in its friendly, odorous stable, the cow lowed; in a splash of crimson and lemon, goldfinches fluted past the window; in the valley a church chimed, a light, silvery tinkle; a warm breeze stirred the dust in the sunbeams; and the man and woman stared in disbelief at the clergyman.

"Etienne," the elderly priest moaned. "I'm sorry— they've taken a hostage, I had to—"

"Shut up." Palet hit the priest with the heel of his hand, sending him sprawling.

The woman half screamed, stifling it with her hand, and dragged the children to her, but Etienne stood absolutely still, looking down the barrel of Palet's revolver. "Who are you?" he asked.

"Milice." Palet drank wine, his unwavering eyes fixed on Etienne.

"But what . . ." Etienne waved his hand helplessly. "What do you want?"

Palet put his glass down and leaned forward. "Your cousin Pleven. Philipe Pleven. Also known as Maurice."

"Maurice?" Etienne scowled. "Why this? Dressing up—guns—hitting the Father and"—his voice growled menacingly—"frightening the wits out of the wife and kids. All you had to do was ask. Everyone knows where Philipe lives."

"But he's not there," Palet said.

"Well." Etienne opened his hands. "Maybe he's in La Chambre—"

"Not there either," Palet said. "Try again."

"How the hell should I know?" Etienne was red-faced. "In the mountains maybe, he's got animals up there, or maybe hunting."

"That's no good either." Palet pushed his head forward. "Where's his hideout?"

"Hideout?" Etienne laughed, then stopped abruptly as he saw the expression on Palet's face. "There's lots of shelters up there."

"Which one?" Palet asked.

"I don't know. Honestly—" Etienne sounded baffled and afraid. "Father—" He turned to the priest, who was on all fours. "Tell him—"

"Outside," Palet said.

The woman wailed and put her hand to her throat. "Stop them," she appealed to the priest.

"It's all right," Etienne said. "Don't worry."

"Worry . . ." The woman's voice faded hopelessly away.

"Etienne," the priest hauled himself up, "I'm sorry but—"

"*Shut up!*" Palet smashed the table with his fist. "What

do you think this is? A —— debating society? You—" He jammed the pistol under Etienne's chin. "Out!"

"I'm going," Etienne said. "No need for this. Look—" He raised his hands and backed through the door. "You're frightening the kids, for Christ's sake."

But he said no more because Palet kicked him in the stomach, sending him flying down the veranda steps into the arms of Palet's Milice.

13

Under the appalled eyes of the priest and of his wife and children, Etienne was kicked down the path and thrown into the back of a van. And like an animal being taken to market, was driven to La Chambre and dragged down to the cells.

But for the time being Palet didn't join his prisoner. "You're wanted," the duty sergeant said. "The German captain." He hesitated. "Just passing on an order."

"Order," Palet said, staring balefully at the sergeant before turning and going up the stairs.

"Jesus, that's an ugly customer." The sergeant spoke out of the corner of his mouth to another gendarme who was lounging in a chair and browsing through a paper. "See the way he looked at me? Like a spider."

"No." The gendarme, older, grizzled, his pension in view, turned a page of the paper. "No, I didn't see anything. Anything at all."

Palet went up the stairs, gave a perfunctory knock on a door, and slouched into a room. There were three men in it, the captain and two men in plainclothes.

"Ah," the captain waved a well-manicured hand. "Palet, these are the gentlemen I mentioned last night. Herr Kellner and Monsieur Blanc. Herr Kellner is attending to the interests of the Reich and Monsieur Blanc is his liaison officer. They are from Lyons."

Palet sat down and squirmed in his chair. "Lyons," he muttered. "Yes."

"Yes." Kellner nodded significantly. "And you're from Chambéry?"

Palet grunted, which Kellner, knowing anyway, took for assent.

"The thing is—" Kellner took out a toothpick and began poking his black teeth. "We're wondering why you're here, do you see?"

Palet growled at the table. "I told the captain."

"Yes, and he's told us that you've already made, what? three arrests. Commendable."

"Communists," Palet said.

"Communists." Kellner grinned, knowingly. "But this Italian and the Jew kid." The grin vanished. "What's your game?"

"Game?" Palet gnawed at his thumb. "What game?"

Kellner stared at Palet through pale blue eyes as if calculating whether he was being impertinent. "Look, we don't have unlimited manpower. Not yet, anyway, so we have to balance our resources. Be businesslike! We can't just have freelances wandering about—there's no order in that, no method. So what's so important about this Italian and the Jew?"

Palet took his time answering. He pulled a cigarette from his elegant case, lit it, and blew smoke to the ceiling. "It's not just those two."

"Oh?" Kellner rolled the toothpick in his mouth. "What then?"

"I heard about this car crash, outside Allevard." Palet knocked cigarette ash over the table, and himself. "All right, what's a crash? But I heard there was a suitcase full

162

of clothes. I figured out that it was Jew stuff"—he lied—
"and then I heard about this soldier and the kid. The
soldier had robbed a café and assaulted a woman—"

"That was a police matter." Blanc spoke for the first
time.

"Yes." Palet pouted. "But there were Jews involved,
weren't there? And I was tipped off that there were Communists up there, so I went to investigate. Nothing wrong
in that, is there?"

"No one has said that there is," Kellner said. "Get on
with it."

"I am, aren't I?" Palet turned his head away like a sulky
pupil being reproved. "I got these Communists, see. In a
farm. They'd hidden the Italian and the Jew kid and
handed them over to a fellow called Maurice who was
bringing them here. This Maurice is from around here, so
he's got to know lots of Communists and traitors. Stands
to reason, doesn't it? Get him and we get them and the Jew
kid. I cleared it all with my boss in Chambéry. You can ask
him if you want." He stared at the men opposite, his eyes
opaque. "That's what we're here for, isn't it? Catching traitors and Jews."

There was a long moment's silence—long, that is, in a
world in which a moment could be measured by the time
it took to splinter fingers and break teeth, a world in which
moments could last for eternity.

"And have you?" Kellner said at last. "Have you caught
any Jews?"

"No," Palet said. "No, I haven't, but—" He smiled, a
smile which instead of illuminating his handsome face
made it ugly, like foul graffiti on a noble sculpture. "But
I've got a Jew hider. Downstairs. Now."

Outside, a voice rasped orders in German, boots clat-
tered, an engine coughed into life, a dog barked savagely.
Inside the room a butterfly, red and black, fluttered against
the windowpane . . .

"Well, well. Good. Very good!" Kellner grinned again,

like Palet's smile not an expression of human kindness, more like an animal baring its teeth. "Captain, perhaps we could . . . ?"

"Of course." The captain bellowed an order and a corporal in an immaculate white jacket appeared with a tray laden with bottles, glasses, poured out drinks . . .

"A Jew hider," Kellner said.

"Yes." Palet gulped his drink. "He's been keeping them up there in the mountains, where you thought I was wasting my time."

"Now—" Kellner opened his hands in a frank man-to-man appeal. "No one has said that. But we have to be *organized*. There can be no order without organization, and no law. And believe me, if you knew what efforts the Führer is making to clean Europe of this vermin . . . Still . . . what's the name of this Jew hider?"

"Doriot. Etienne Doriot." Palet doled the name out.

"So." Kellner stood up. "We'll go and interrogate him."

"You!" Palet jumped to his feet, banging the table in his ungainly way, but quick as a snake. "He's my prisoner."

"Yours!" Whatever friendliness there might have been in Kellner's voice vanished. "That man belongs to the state, to the Reich, and the Führer—and so do you! Is that clear?"

It couldn't have been clearer, and Palet knew it. One false step on his part and *he* could end up downstairs in the iron world where time ended. "I didn't mean," he mumbled, ". . . not mine . . . just that I . . ."

"Yes, of course." Palet having been taught his lesson, Kellner was willing to reward him, giving the obedient dog a tidbit. "You'll be given credit for the arrest—" He sat down again, waving Palet back into his chair, and lit a cigar. "Look, Palet. I think that you have a future! I really do. Tracking down those swine . . . excellent. But if you'll forgive me, you are still a little . . . *raw*. A little—ah!" He raised his finger, a man struck by exactly the right word. "A little *romantic!*" He puffed vigorously on his excellent cigar, a man warming to his theme. "We all go through it, the excitement of the chase, the joy of duty fulfilled. But there is more to it. Believe me. This prisoner yesterday, the one who died—"

"Committed suicide," Palet said.

"Yes—" Kellner waved that aside, a matter of no importance now that the man had met his end. "But what records do you have, hey? What notes of the interrogation?"

"Notes?" Palet was incredulous.

"Of course! What questions, what answers, what questions weren't answered! They tell a lot. And how to ask questions. That's very important. For instance, were you friendly? Did you offer him cigarettes, a drink?"

"Offer . . ." Palet stared at Kellner as if the man was insane. "A drink?" He laughed, a hideous magpie-like rattle, and waited for the others to share the joke but met serious faces.

"Listen," Blanc said. "You're talking to an expert."

"Expert . . ." Kellner modestly disclaimed the title. "Believe me. I've met *real* experts, all over Europe . . . but this man, how long did you have him downstairs?"

"A couple of hours," Palet said.

"There," Kellner waved his cigar. "You see! You could have had him for days—weeks . . . and what did you get from him?"

"I got Doriot," Palet lied.

"Yes." Kellner was slightly put out. "Anyway, let's go and see this Jew hider. We have cigarettes, Blanc?"

"Yes."

"And matches?"

"Oh yes, matches." Blanc patted his pocket and both men laughed, sharing a little private joke.

They made for the door, but Kellner, a bottle of brandy in his hand, turned and opened the window, gently brushing out the butterfly, then, "After you," he said to Palet.

165

Palet led the way downstairs. A gendarme was chatting affably with a thief, another was berating a small boy, the duty sergeant was laboriously scratching in a heavy ledger, and his grizzled comrade was still reading his newspaper. But as Palet, Kellner, and Blanc entered the room all talk stopped and did not recommence until they had gone down the iron stairs, and through the iron door, where sounds of ordinary human conversation ceased.

Doriot was in the cell where the evening before Champson had met his end. Kellner peeped for some time through the spy hole as if he was a naturalist observing a rare and fugitive species of animal life, before opening the door and moving into the cell.

Doriot was sitting on a bunk, his head between his knees, but as Kellner entered he sat upright, a hand protectively thrust forward.

"Now, now!" Kellner raised his hands. "No need to be afraid. Come in—" He waved Blanc and Palet in, a genial host greeting his guests. "I think you know Monsieur Palet?"

"Know him!" Doriot clutched his ribs. "You—"

"Ah." Kellner moved in front of Palet. "Yes. We know. Monsieur Palet exceeded his duty this morning and he has been reprimanded for it."

"Duty!" Doriot was incredulous. "What duty?"

"Arresting you." Kellner sat down on the bunk opposite Doriot and leaned forward confidentially. "Here, take a cigarette, and have a drink, it will make you feel better. Good. You see we're not bad chaps, but we have a job to do."

"Just a minute," Doriot said. "Who are you, and where are my wife and kids?"

"Oh, you'll find out who I am," Kellner said. "And your family, they're at your home, of course. Where else should they be? They know you are here helping us, and the sooner you do the sooner you can be back with them. In fact"—he glanced at his watch—"if you cooperate you can be home for supper. So let's begin."

He nodded at Blanc, who pulled out a notebook and pencil and with a meaningful nod showed them to Palet and began scribbling as Kellner started his questions: name, age, married of course, children; he droned through a series of humdrum questions, nodding approval at the humdrum answers . . . "Friends?"

Doriot shifted uneasily. "What do you want to know about them for?"

"Just answer the question," Kellner said patiently.

"I know lots of people." Doriot shrugged. "I've lived here all my life."

"But friends," Kellner said. "Close friends."

Doriot hesitated, his eyes flickering from Kellner to Blanc to Palet.

"I don't have close friends. We . . . I . . . keep people at a distance."

"All right." Kellner was understanding. "What about enemies?"

Doriot shook his head. "I don't understand. Why are you asking? Friends . . . enemies?"

"You leave that to us," Kellner said. "You have to trust us. Who are your enemies?"

"But"—Doriot clawed at the air—"I don't have any."

He fell silent, his eyes screwed in concentration—and acting, of that Palet was certain—acting and lying; not about being friendless; never having had a friend himself Palet found that utterly convincing—but a man without enemies, it was too ludicrous to think of; *every* man was every other man's enemy, every man's hand raised against his neighbor; every dog had its teeth bared at the world. He leaned against the filthy wall, crooking his fingers, conscious that while the German was droning on, time was ticking away and the Jew kid was wandering free, a fortune in diamonds!

167

"Enemies," Doriot said. "Is this what it's all about? Some-one paying off a grudge?"

"But you've got no enemies," Kellner said. "So who would want to pay a grudge off? So you've got no friends and no enemies. Let's talk about Jews."

"Oh." Doriot was noticeably less confident. "Them."

"Yes." Kellner was equable. "Tell me about them."

"They were just Jews." Doriot was thoughtful. "A couple of kids and a woman. An old man stayed sometimes. They've gone now. Went with the Italians." He licked his lips. "Could I have that drink now?"

"Of course." Kellner passed the bottle over.

"Well." Doriot drank and wiped his mouth. "The Jews. There was no law about it. The Italians said it was all right and it made a few francs. Anyway, lots of people put them up."

"We'll get around to them," Kellner said. "But how did you get some? I mean, you didn't walk about with a placard saying Accommodation for Jews, did you? Of course not. So how did you get them?"

It was dank in the cell but beads of sweat were gathering on Doriot's forehead. "I didn't *get* them. I . . . I was in a café and . . . and a Jew asked me if I'd put some kids up. He said it was healthy up in the hills, dry . . ."

"But why did he ask *you?*" Kellner sounded pleasantly curious. "You see what I'm getting at?"

"I don't know. Maybe he'd asked lots of people."

"Which café was this?"

"Er . . . the Maurienne."

"Who was with you?"

"I can't remember."

"Neighbors, family, these friends you don't have? And what were you doing? Playing billiards, cards?" The ques-tions continued, Kellner asking them in a quiet level voice which invited confidences. "Were you ever in a political party? Did you ever buy a socialist newspaper? Who else

168

sheltered Jews? Did you ever hear anyone attack Marshal Pétain? Support Great Britain?"

Blanc scribbled away and Palet twitched, jerked, fingering his boils, thinking that a good kicking would have got the information in five minutes, but as the questioning went on, a pattern appeared. Certain names were repeated, Doriot was caught in contradictions, and a picture of the district began to appear: who were patriots, who were traitors, those who were playing both cards; but none of it was of any interest to Palet and he began to slip into the vague but horrible imaginings which occupied most of his idle moments—until he was jerked into wakefulness.

"Let's talk about Philipe Pleven," Kellner said.

Blanc's pencil stopped its scribbling and Palet stopped his twitching as Kellner pushed his large face forward, a face from which every trace of geniality had gone.

"Pleven," Kellner said. "Your cousin, right?"

Doriot reached for the bottle, but that was no longer there. "Sort of. I mean, there's a lot of us . . . connected. Marriages . . ."

"Inbred," Kellner said.

"Not inbred," Doriot protested.

"*Inbred.*" Kellner made it sound as if Doriot was related to sheep or cows. "And this Pleven, known as Maurice—he's a Communist, isn't he?"

"No, not Philipe."

"But Champson was, wasn't he?" Kellner's voice was beginning to thicken. "Wasn't he? And he's your cousin and Pleven's. That's right, isn't it?"

"Maybe." Doriot shook his head. "But that's got nothing to do with me. I'm a good Catholic. Ask the priest—"

"*Scheiβ* on the priest!" Kellner glared at Doriot. "Where's Pleven. *Where is he?*"

"I don't know. I swear it. I told him—" He stared with hatred at Palet. "I told him I don't know, he rambles about."

169

"Don't say that!" Kellner's face was red with rage. *"Don't!"* He jumped to his feet, looming over Doriot, his fists balled. "You be careful," he said. "Be very, very careful." He breathed hard, a man fighting to keep control of himself. "I've been very patient with you. Very." He raised a finger. "I'll . . . I . . ." He swung on his heels and faced Blanc. "I'm going outside for a moment. Just for a moment. But when I come back . . ." He took a huge breath and strode from the cell, taking Palet with him.

Their footsteps clacked away and there was silence in the cell, the sort of silence that is found only in great caves, dungeons, or the grave. Doriot and Blanc sat facing each other. A cockroach scuttled from under the waste bucket. Blanc stamped at it and missed.

"Yes," he said, meaninglessly. He poked the pencil into his pocket as if work was suspended for the moment, went to the door, peered out, then took his seat again. He sighed and shrugged. "Doriot," he said quietly, almost whispering. "I know this—" He waved his notebook. "It's a lot of rubbish. But these Germans, they're obsessed with *lists*, everything cross-indexed, and if they get a name . . . talk about a dog with a bone. I'll tell you, I wouldn't like to get into their clutches."

"Theirs," Doriot said. "What about *him*, that pig, whatever he's called."

"Palet?" Blanc spat out the name. "What can I say about a man like that? And the Germans, Christ, how I hate them."

"You do, hate them?"

"Of course I do." Blanc handed over the brandy bottle. "I'm French."

"Then why are you working with them?"

"Someone has to." Blanc gave Doriot a cigarette. "I was a detective sergeant. I've been ordered to do this. I mean, I could have got out of it, but the way I see it, I'm a brake. You know, these Germans, they do terrible things.

170

Terrible. And the Gestapo . . ." He raised a finger to his lips, tiptoed to the door, and looked out. "All right, no one there. The Gestapo, and he's one, Kellner, what they do . . . my God, unspeakable. That's why I'd tell them what they ask."

"I have," Doriot said. "It's in your notebook."

"Oh." Blanc looked sour. "Yes, but they're going to need more. Communists. Socialists."

"Everyone knows them," Doriot said. "They didn't make any secret of it."

"Yes," Blanc said. "But there are lots who did keep it a secret."

"How do you know?" Doriot asked. "If they kept it a secret?"

Blanc tapped Doriot on the knee. "Don't be too clever. We know there are plenty of traitors: Communists, socialists, Gaullists, even priests! Against the state! Can you believe that."

Doriot, his face slightly flushed with the brandy, looked around the cell. "If this is the state, yes I can."

"No! This—you being here, it's an accident!"

"An accident!" Doriot laughed aloud.

"Don't, don't!" Blanc shook his head. "Doriot, you have contacts. Give us some names. Nobody will ever know. And we'll make it worth your while, believe me. All you have to do is—"

"Be an informer," Doriot said. "No thanks."

"Think again." Blanc was desperately sincere, a true friend urging the right course of action. "Think of your family!"

"Spy on my neighbors," Doriot said. "No."

"I hope that isn't your last word," Blanc said.

Doriot stared across the two feet of foul air which separated him from Blanc.

"You hope wrong, then."

"You're a fool," Blanc said.

"Maybe."

"They'll be coming back soon." Blanc pointed at the door. "Give me something."

"I've got nothing to give you," Doriot said.

"Give me some Jew lovers."

Doriot shook his head. "I don't know any."

"Then—" Blanc clenched his fist. "Give me this Maurice."

"I don't know where he is," Doriot said. "And I wouldn't tell you if I did."

"All right." Blanc stood up. "Take off your boots."

"What for?" Doriot frowned and, half consciously, drew his feet under the bunk.

"You're now a prisoner," Blanc said. "It's standard procedure."

Doriot hesitated for a moment and then took off his boots as Blanc poked his head through the door and shouted. A moment later Kellner and Palet appeared. Kellner strode forward and without any warning at all stamped on Doriot's bare toes, and as Doriot screamed Kellner snapped his fingers and Blanc handed over a box of matches, winking knowingly at Palet as if to say: Now you're going to see something; now you're going to learn something; now you're going to see an expert at work.

The experts got to work. Beyond the iron doors, a floor above them, the police went about their banal toil, and a floor above them the German captain, finishing a leisurely lunch brought in from the hotel, strolled to the window, a coffee in hand, the second movement of Liszt's First Piano Concerto playing on a commandeered gramophone, and looked down on the main promenade of La Chambre.

There were German troops on the street; conquerors but not behaving as such, the reverse, rather as if they were guests: four infantrymen sitting quietly outside a café, two more on the pavement, one offering a child a sweet while his companions chatted affably, with much use of sign

172

language, to the child's rather attractive, *chic*, mother—
and how *chic* French women were, the captain thought, so
well . . . *trimmed*, even in wartime. And on a traffic island,
dwarfing a neat gendarme, there was a huge German military policeman halting a German army truck to allow an
elderly man to cross the road, saluting him as he did so.

Eminently satisfactory, the captain reflected—correct-
ness, order, efficiency, *purification*—dabbing his lips with a
napkin and raising his eyes to the vista to the north of the
town: sweet pasture, cows grazing, dotted with farms, a
church or two with their delicate spires, a glimpse of a
sparkling stream, a gushing river, and a rough road beside
it winding upward until both were lost among the huge
shoulders of the mountains menacing the sweet vale.

"Charming," the captain murmured, dabbing his lips
again, and brushing a spot of wine from the ribbon of the
Iron Cross tucked across his gray uniform. "Charming,"
beating his free hand to the music as below him, in the
cockroach-infested cells, on the squirming body of Etienne
Doriot, farmer, husband, and father, good Catholic, guilty
of guilt by association, the standard-bearers of the Third
Reich and the New Order of Europe demonstrated their
skills before the admiring gaze of Palet.

14

Over the mountain, beyond the Col de la Madeleine, on
the same rough road the captain could see, but far from
his New Order, tramping along with the donkey still patiently bearing Judah, Salvani was thinking much the same
thing, although in different words.

Not bad, he was thinking. Not a bad trip at all. And the

day's journey had not been at that, marching along the pass, feeling well, even singing with Judah joining in, and now he was looking onto a wide cultivated vale. And somewhere at the bottom of the vale was the main road to Italy and the town of Moutiers.

But until he had found out a little more about what was happening down there, Salvani had no intention of going into Moutiers. In fact, he had no wish to go there at all, as he was certain that the Germans would be there, as in La Chambre, but he had thought what he could do about that. The main road ran southeast into Moutiers, then sharply northeast, and he guessed that they could cut across the V of the angle and miss the town altogether and then, dodging and ducking by night, make the forty-odd kilometers to the border, if not that night, then the next. There was the problem of food but he had a solution to that; it was strapped across his shoulders, and he knew enough about human nature to believe that one peep into its black muzzle would persuade most people to hand over a little bread and cheese.

In the meantime, he was content to stroll along, until he saw, not more than a kilometer off the road, a chalet, with a cow, and a man with a dog bounding at his heels striding purposefully away on some errand.

Salvani halted in the lee of a huge boulder and waited, stroking the donkey's nose, until the man was lost to sight. He glanced at the sun. Another couple of hours and dusk would start creeping in, and in rural France, apart from thieves, smugglers, and robbers, the villagers down below would be indoors for the night, so . . . time to lie up for a while. A hundred meters away the stream, almost a river now, slid smoothly over red rock. A grove of ash had colonized its banks and there was an elegant carpet of lush grass, a place good for hiding, good for resting, and good for the donkey.

"Right." He slapped his thigh. "We're going to rest, Judah, and the donkey."

"Stella!" Judah cried fiercely.

"Stella it is." Salvani led the donkey down to the stream and lifted Judah down. "How are you? Not sore?"

"Yes, I am," Judah said with disconcerting directness.

"Aah." Salvani tethered Stella to a tree and took her rough saddle off, thinking that there wasn't much he could do about soreness. "We'll just rest here a bit and then you'll feel better." He shoved a wedge of cheese into Judah's mouth. "Eating together." He waved at Stella, who was nibbling peacefully. "But I want you to sleep. Can you do that?"

"I don't want to sleep," Judah said. "I want to talk to Stella."

"Yes, but Stella wants to sleep. See."

Judah stared at Stella, who was undoubtedly blinking her eyes. "But she's chewing."

"Right, but donkeys do that," Salvani said. "Eat and sleep at the same time."

"Really?" Judah was round-eyed.

"Really." Salvani mentally crossed himself.

"Can I do it?" Judah asked.

"No, only donkeys. Now lie down." He spread his great-coat and Judah obediently lay on it, but not to sleep. "Uncle," he asked, "why didn't he write?"

"Write? Who?"

"Papa. A letter."

"Oh." Some of the brightness left the afternoon. "He probably has." Salvani sat by Judah. "But in wartime things get lost—" like us, he thought. "Anyway, we haven't been to a post office—but we will. We'll go to the first post office we see."

"Will we write to him?" To Salvani's exasperation, Judah sat upright.

"Yes. Yes. A nice long letter." Salvani pressed Judah back.

"And a postcard?" Judah wriggled under Salvani's arm.

"And a postcard. Now try and sleep, hey?"

"All right." Suddenly obliging, Judah lay down and closed his eyes. "I'm sleeping," he said. "Can you see me sleeping?"

"Yes," Salvani said. "I can see you sleeping."

"Is Stella sleeping?"

"Yes."

"And chewing?"

Salvani stifled a groan. "No. No, she's not chewing. She's sleeping. Now you sleep, too."

There was silence for a few seconds until, "I'm chewing, Uncle. I'm chewing and sleeping."

"Right." Salvani pulled out a cigarette and matches and waited for the next remark, but there was none, because in another of the amazing transportations of childhood Judah *had* fallen asleep.

Salvani breathed a profound sigh of relief, leaned against a tree, and lit his cigarette. Nothing more to do but wait; nothing to do but chance their luck. And he still felt lucky as Stella nibbled away, her velvet nose deep in the grass. Judah slept, the stream gurgled and splashed, and crows streamed in a black convoy across the violet sky, heading home as the dusk gathered and mist formed in the distant hollow of the mountains.

Time to go, and for all Salvani's feeling that luck was with them, a time to lick lips and wipe sweaty palms, to tug at one's collar and . . . and since there was nothing else for it, to brace broad shoulders and to set off with a steady stride down into the vale. And for all his nervous doubts, Salvani was right and his luck was holding. They passed the first scattered upland farms, a tiny hamlet, a church, but the landscape was swept clear of people. They came to another hamlet where dogs barked ferociously and a voice from a window shouted, "*Qui est là?*—Who's there," at Salvani's growl the window shutter being hastily pulled to.

The dusk deepened; the stars came out, one by one; the owls began to yip; and still Salvani, Judah, and Stella Fortunata descended into the valley, the donkey's delicate

176

hooves pattering behind Salvani's steady stride. Outside another hamlet they met a man who promptly ran away, which pleased Salvani; as he had suspected, only those with something to hide were roaming about at this time, when all good Frenchmen and women were having their supper.

Down they went, and down again, the road veering left into a huge defile, and the friendly stream suddenly departing with an ominous gurgle, as Salvani looked down and saw a road, a real road and not a mere mountain trail, and it was the road he wanted, the road to Italy and home, but between him, the child, and the donkey and the road was a river, a real river, but one with a bridge flung across it, and over the river and over the bridge was a sight which made Salvani, his overcoat beaded with mist, holding Stella's bridle with one hand and patting Judah with the other, very thoughtful indeed.

Salvani looked across the bridge; and over his shoulder, over the Col de la Madeleine, beyond the wind-scoured pass and the black crucifix, in La Chambre, Palet, too, was thoughtful, or as thoughtful as his narrow, cunning brain could be. He was sitting in the back room of the hotel with the German captain, Kellner, and Blanc. The table was littered with bottles and glasses, thick with cigar smoke, and the mood was one of hideous cheerfulness, as one stamp on his bare foot, and one flare of a match, had been sufficient to persuade Doriot that his best interest and that of his family, and of France, and of the New Order, lay in cooperating, and he had provided a list of undesirable elements over which Kellner was smacking his lips.

"You see," he said to Palet. "All these names? And we have an informer! Alive!"

Palet shrugged, crookedly, as if his shirt was sticking to his back. "He'll just feed you a pack of lies."

"No, no." A day of triumph behind him, Kellner sipped at a glass of fine claret. "Not him. I have a . . . a . . ."

"An instinct!" Blanc said. "An instinct plus experience."

"Maybe." Palet stared into his own drink, a tumblerful of the coarse brandy he preferred. "But we didn't get that Maurice, did we, or the Jew kid."

"Palet." Some of Kellner's humor leaked from him. "Don't let this Jew kid become a *mania*. There's other work to be done. Anyway, we know the Italian and the kid are holed up with this Maurice and we know where Maurice will be. Tomorrow you can go and pick them all up, and if we pick them up first, you'll have the credit for the arrest. Now cheer up, man, you look as if your mother has just died. Have a drink." As he raised his glass to his lips, there was a knock at the door. "Ah," he said, "supper," but instead of a waiter a gendarme shuffled into the room, saying that Palet was wanted on the telephone at the police station and that no, he didn't know why but that it was urgent.

Palet showed no signs of urgency. He twisted around and glared balefully at the gendarme, wondering what the message might be, and from whom, as if a trap was being set for him.

"Better go," Kellner said, in a tone of voice which meant *Get going*. "Might be news about your Jew kid, ha! ha! ha!" Laughing as Blanc joined in heartily, as if he had just heard the best joke in the world.

Palet stood up slowly, as if he had to break his joints to do so. "I'll be back," he said.

"Of course! And we'll be waiting!" Kellner laughed again and waved a dismissive hand.

In the police station the grizzled sergeant was waiting, and before Palet could snarl at him, he jabbed his thumb at the telephone.

"From your boss," he said, "in Chambéry. They've gone off the line but you're to ring back—right away."

Palet stared at the phone as if it was a personal enemy but picked it up only to get vague crackling noises. He tried again and got the same sounds mixed with curious distant echoing voices, as if people from another planet were trying to communicate with Earth. "Hello," Palet shouted. "Hello." Nothing happened and he held out the phone to the sergeant. "I can't get through," he said.

The sergeant shrugged, disclaiming responsibility for the French telephone system. "They said it was urgent."

Palet cursed, shifting from foot to foot, as awkward as a crow, and held the phone to his ear. *"Hello,"* he shouted, and unexpectedly, a clear voice cut across the weird background noises and said it was police headquarters Chambéry and yes, the superintendent of Milice did wish to speak to Palet and—with icy distinctness—that the superintendent was engaged but that Palet was to stay on the end of the line until called back—and that was an emphatic order.

Palet slammed the phone down. He was tempted to leave, giving the sergeant some excuse that he had been called out on a lead, but thought better of it. The voice at the end of the line had been sharp and behind that voice was another, his master in Chambéry, and although he was maddened by the thought of Kellner and Blanc sitting gorging themselves and hatching plots, probably against himself, he slumped into a battered chair, watching the fingers on the station clock jerk around, wiping his mouth on his sleeve, fingering his boils, and wondering just where the Jew kid and the Italian were, and what he would do to them when he caught them.

"Mother of God!" Salvani peered through the mist and strode forward, calling, because across the bridge, its hood up, was a truck, and lounging against it were men in Italian green and speaking Italian, who *were* Italian: soldiers—and not just any old ragbags of the army but Bersaglieri, crack infantry, armed to the teeth and ready, if necessary, to blast their way to the frontier and, what was more, as soon as the engine of the truck cooled down, more than willing to take Salvani and Judah with them.

"You're lucky." The sergeant of the Bersaglieri, arms folded, leaned against the parapet of the bridge.

"Lucky!" Salvani laughed. "I'm the luckiest man in the world."

"If the engine had boiled a kilometer farther on . . ."

"Right. Don't tell me." Salvani waved his hand, waving away that thought.

"And no one behind us either," the sergeant said. "At least as far as we know. Not that we know much. The whole thing is a complete cockup."

"You can say that again." Salvani puffed on a cigarette.

The sergeant did, in more colorful language, and looked across the bridge at the towering cliffs on the far side of the river. "And you really came over there?"

"That and more," Salvani said, with a sense of profound satisfaction.

"With the kid?"

"Yes." Salvani looked down on Judah, who in a fit of shyness and caution was hiding behind the tails of his greatcoat.

The sergeant flicked his cigarette end over the bridge, a fiery spark dwindling as it spiraled into the abyss. "How's that engine?" he called.

The driver gingerly put his hand on the engine. "Should be all right," he said.

"Should be." The sergeant muttered something uncomplimentary about the driver's mother, but, "Don't worry," he said to Salvani. "We'll get back all right. Another couple of hours and we'll all be home."

"Yes." Salvani felt a spasm of unease. "The Germans . . ."

The sergeant shrugged. "Don't know. We came through Albertville. There were Germans there but they just waved us through. A sort of truce, I suppose. Anyway, I guess no one wants to get shot just to stop us. Well—" He turned away. "Makes you sick," he added obscurely but sincerely as the driver said that they could go.

They ambled back to the truck. "You'd better go in the

180

back," the sergeant said. "Not room for us all in the cab. Take the kid, too. He'll feel better being with you. That all right?"

"It sure is. It's just fine. Fine, believe me," Salvani said, grinning with delight as he turned to Judah, but finding that it wasn't all right with him because, although assured that his days of walking were over and that they were going for a nice ride in a truck, Judah had realized that the next stage of the journey did not include Stella and had the donkey's reins in a cat's cradle around his arms, and his head.

"Come on now." Salvani tried to disentangle the reins. "We've got to go."

"No!" Judah dodged behind the donkey.

"We *have* to." Salvani grabbed at Judah. "We're going home and Stella's got to go home, too."

"No!" Judah's scream of rage echoed across the valley— and was abruptly cut short as one of the soldiers, as big as Salvani, picked up Judah by the scruff of the neck and threw him into Salvani's arms. "Get him on the truck," he growled, "or start walking. And shut him up."

Judah clung to Salvani, no longer the merciless abandoner of donkeys but the defender of little children.

"No need to hit him," Salvani said.

The soldier took a menacing step forward. "You want to make something of it?"

"Break it up." The sergeant, wrathful, stepped between them. "Get on the truck, quick. You want the —— Germans to come? And"—to Salvani—"keep that kid quiet."

There was no need for the last order. Judah was weeping, but weeping silent tears of shock and anguish as the truck roared into life and, juddering and shaking, moved on, Judah in Salvani's arms and Salvani himself moist-eyed as, for a hundred meters or so, Stella Fortunata pattered along after the truck until the donkey was lost in the mist and the night as mysteriously as it had appeared.

And there was no trouble, no trouble at all. Wheezing

181

and groaning, the truck lurched along. Moutiers was, if not sleeping, then drowsing. Two gendarmes on push-bikes watched them pass, a German army truck was parked by the cathedral, an armored car by a bridge, and then they were through the town, grinding along a twisting road, through a tunnel, another, a stretch of road littered with the debris of a fleeing army—abandoned trucks, a car or two, a smashed piano; at Aime, more an overgrown village than a town, heart-stopping moments at a road-block, Judah thrust down, the rough soldier throwing his coat over the child, flashlights shining and a hard voice from behind the flashlights challenging and answered by a harder voice from the sergeant, the ominous clatter of jackboots, until a calm superior voice said, "Let them pass."

Pass they did, the men laughing, cheerful and confident, Judah, still tearful, being comforted by Salvani, *his* heart bounding with relief, and the sense of a huge burden having been taken from his shoulders, luxuriating at being with his fellow countrymen, hearing his own language, and sensing freedom as the valley, tranquil in the moonlight, widened with every kilometer until they ground into another town with a glinting sign saying Bourg-St.-Maurice, customs 3 kilometers, and to huge cheers from the men and a triumphant honking of the horn, Italy 31 kilometers, and then all exuberance dying as they came to another roadblock and heard another voice, a peremptory one, one which meant business and the business being to shoot you dead, ordering everyone out. Now. Including Judah.

As the voice rasped out its order, in the police station of La Chambre the telephone rang. The sergeant answered it and beckoned Palet. "For you. Chambéry."

Palet grabbed the phone, grunted his name, and listened, and as he did so his face darkened with rage.

"I don't believe it," Palet spat. "I don't believe I'm hearing this."

"You'd better believe it," his superintendent said. "You asked for two days and that's what you've had. Back tomorrow. Prompt."

"But—" Palet grabbed at the telephone. "You don't understand. I've got—"

"Have you got the Jew kid?"

"No," Palet said. "Not here, but I've got a prisoner—"

"I don't care if you've got the Chief Rabbi!" The superintendent chuckled, enjoying his little joke. "You're to be here tomorrow with your men. Tomorrow morning—10 a.m. On the dot. With a full report."

Palet glared at the telephone, his eyes as black as obsidian and his mouth pulled into a rictus. "Kellner," he said. "Herr Kellner, of the Gestapo."

There was silence. At the other end of the line another reptile taking that in. "What about him?"

"He's here," Palet said. "He's complimented me on my work and he's told me I can go after the Jew kid."

"Did he!" With relish, a big lizard about to devour a smaller one, the superintendent laughed. "Well, give Herr Kellner my compliments—we know each other, actually—and tell him my orders come from Lyons, from Major Barbie's office directly, in fact. I'm sure that he'll understand. And *you*—" sharp teeth ready to crunch into Palet's skull—"back tomorrow—" the *or else* left unspoken as the line went dead.

Palet let the phone drop, kicked the station door open, and barged his way back to his room, where he crouched on the bed, pouring down brandy, sweating and cursing. Diamonds! handfuls of them, slipping from his grasp: flashing, dazzling, pure light, purer than the brightest star! His mouth filled with saliva, dribbling from the corner of his mouth—a few hours away and yet, with inconceivable terror at his disposal, he had been outwitted by a dirty Italian, a dirty Jew kid, and a few dirty traitors . . .

On the stairs there was the clatter of boots, laughter, an

183

obscenity, more laughter. Palet whipped out his pistol and jabbed it at the door, his handsome face contorted with rage, jabbing his pistol at phantoms, sweating, mumbling curses as in the night a church clock clanked ten, as if telling him that the hunt was over.

Give or take a quarter of an hour, in Bourg-St.-Maurice another church clock was clanking the same hour. But it was music to the large ears of Salvani as, a tearstained Judah in his arms, watched by two sullen gendarmes, he leaned against the truck as a sergeant major of the Italian Army Engineering Corps checked the soldiers' paybooks, the roadblock being Italian, and beyond it nothing but a few kilometers of mountain road to the Little St. Bernard Pass, and Italy.

BOOK
2

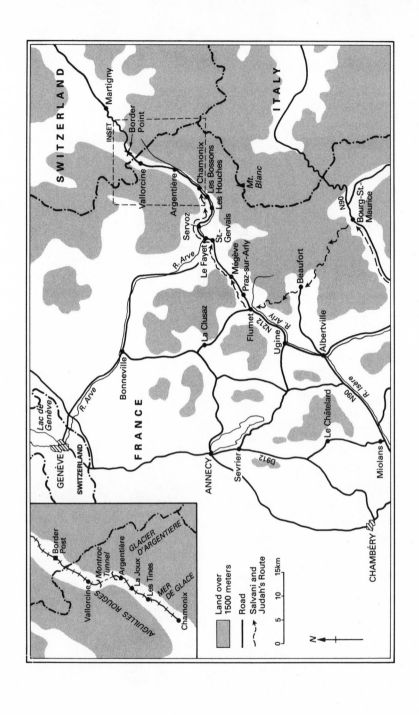

SWITZERLAND

ITALY

Martigny

Border
Point

INSET

Chamonix
Les Bossons
Vallorcine   Les Houches

Argentière

Mt.
Blanc

N90

Bourg-St.-
Maurice

Servoz

St.-
Gervais

R. Arve

Le Fayet

Megève
Praz-sur-Arly

Beaufort

La Clusaz

Flumet

N212

Albertville

R. Arly

Ugine

Bonneville

FRANCE

Lac de
Genève

R. Arve

N90

R. Isère

Le Châtelard

GENÈVE

SWITZERLAND

ANNECY

Sevrier

D912

Miolans

CHAMBÉRY

Border
Post

Montroc
Tunnel

Argentière   GLACIER
D'ARGENTIÈRE

Vallorcine   La Joux
Les Tines

AIGUILLES ROUGES

MER
DE GLACE

Chamonix

Land over
1500 meters

Road

Salvani and
Judah's Route

0   5   10   15km

N

15

In a commandeered hotel in Bourg-St.-Maurice, Salvani, Judah, and the soldiers wolfed down mutton stew and the best wine the hotel had to offer, offer free, that is.

Gorged, Salvani lit a cigar. "Excuse me," he said to no one in particular. He went out of the back of the hotel and relieved himself in the corner of a yard. There was a shed in the yard and as he returned he peered into it. There was something in the shed and he ran a speculative eye over it before going back inside.

The Bersaglieri were standing and stretching themselves—and stuffing their packs with looted wines, brandy, food, and tobacco.

"Ready to go, are we?" Salvani asked.

"More or less." The sergeant major of Engineers stood

up. "Come here, Corporal," he said. "I want a word with you."

"Yes?" Salvani followed the sergeant major into another room, feeling a prickle of unease as the sergeant of Bersaglieri followed him. At the door the sergeant major waved them through and called to one of his men. "Bruno, entertain the kid, you know? And the rest of the men."

"Sure!" Bruno gave a delighted smile as the sergeant major closed the door.

"Sit down." The sergeant major waved to a chair and produced a bottle of valuable burgundy and a box of expensive cigars.

"Ah—" He clicked his fingers and bellowed, "Luigi!"

Luigi entered, was ordered to bring glasses, darted out, and as he reappeared from the other room, there was a burst of applause. "Bruno," he said. "He's going to do Noah's Ark, with all the animals!" darting out again.

The sergeant major put his hands together and waved his fingers. "A shadow show. Bruno's good at it. He's a Sicilian," as if that explained Bruno's amazing skills.

"Glad to hear it," Salvani said, hunching forward, his own shadow looming menacingly on the wall. "So what's this about?"

The sergeant major fiddled with a cigar, glanced at the tall sergeant leaning against the window, and cleared his throat. "There's a problem."

"Oh?" Salvani kept his voice neutral. "And what might that be?"

The sergeant major pointed to the door. "He is," he said. "The *bambino*."

"Judah?" Salvani said. "Judah is a problem?"

There was another burst of applause from the next room and a scream of delight from Judah as a donkey, Stella Fortunata, trotted into the Ark. The sergeant major sighed. "I didn't tell you before—no point in spoiling your meal. But I did tell you that over there"—he jerked his head in the direction of Italy—"the Germans have taken over."

"Sure," Salvani nodded.

"Yes, well, they're on the pass, the Little St. Bernard."

"That's right. You told me." Salvani pushed a wineglass with a blunt finger. "What of it? We're allowed across, aren't we?"

"Yes, but . . ." The sergeant major proffered the wine bottle. "Look," he said. "I might as well spit it out. It's not just the German Army up there. It's the Gestapo. And . . . they're picking up civilians. Something to do with Jews. Don't ask me why."

"Are you saying . . ." Salvani stared at his wineglass as if it might contain the answer. "Are you saying I can't take the kid across?"

"That's about it," the sergeant major said.

"But—" Salvani half laughed. "A kid. Jesus, we can smuggle him over. No?"

The sergeant major was shaking his head. "The Germans up there—listen, I don't know what's the matter with them but they're going through everything with a fine-tooth comb. And there's another thing. They've got posters up. Anyone who even helps a foreigner gets the death penalty. Shot on sight."

More applause, laughter, an elephant boarding Bruno's Ark . . . "I'll dodge round," Salvani said. "Go over the mountains."

"Have you seen the mountains up there?" the sergeant major said. "And what happens if you do get over?"

More silence broken by more applause and laughter—giraffes. "I know," Salvani said. "There's a monastery up there, right? I'll hand the kid over to the monks. They'll look after him." He felt a deep sadness at the thought. Life in some dreary institution could never take the place of a home, a real home full of ragamuffin children, cheerfulness, bickerings, small joys, small sadnesses; life, anyway—but even that idea was dashed as the sergeant major with gruff sympathy said that he couldn't do that, either.

"It's sealed off. You couldn't get a mouse in. It's bad luck. If you'd got here a couple of days ago—"

"A couple!" Salvani exploded with rage. "That —— Balbo! I told him to lay off the booze. Christ, if he was alive I'd—"

"No good crying over spilled milk." The sergeant major was abrupt.

"Ah, you're right." Salvani poured himself wine and stared into the glass and the deep-red liquid. "I did my best, I did, you know."

"More than that," the sergeant major said. "But listen, the best thing you can do . . . well, there's a church down the road. Hand him over to the priest. He'll pass him on to nuns, somewhere. And"—he looked away, a man reluctantly doing a dirty job, but one which had to be done—"and you'd better get on with it. These lads"—he pointed to the silent sergeant—"they're going now, and I'm off at first light."

"Understood." Salvani heaved himself to his feet. "I'll get him, then."

The sergeant major opened up his hands. "It's hard to be a human being."

"Isn't it just." Salvani made for the door as Judah burst into the room.

"Uncle," he shouted, his face aglow. "Uncle." He tugged at Salvani's coat. "Come and see. Bruno's going to do a rhinoceros!"

"Yes," Salvani said.

"It's the *hardest*, Bruno says. The hardest in the world." Judah tugged again at Salvani's coat.

"In a minute." Salvani ruffled Judah's hair. "You go and watch now."

Judah stood on one foot and stared solemnly around the room—at the sergeant major, the tall sergeant, then, as

Salvani nodded encouragingly, he tiptoed back, into more heartfelt, warm applause.

Salvani waited until Judah, with painstaking earnestness, had slowly closed the door, then faced his comrades. "I can't do it," he said, flatly. "I just can't."

The sergeant major moved uneasily. "It's up to you. If you want to hand him over up at the pass . . ."

"I'm not doing that, either," Salvani said.

"Hey." For the first time the sergeant of the Bersaglieri spoke. "Don't think that we're going to get into a firefight up there. I'm as sorry for the kid as you are, but we're going home."

"Don't worry about that," Salvani said. "There won't be any fighting because I'm not going there either."

"Well—" The sergeant major frowned at Salvani. "If you're not going to take him to the pass and you're not going to hand him over to the priest here, just what the hell are you going to do?"

"What I'm going to do—" Salvani pulled out his Michelin map and spread it on the table. "I'm going to take him to Switzerland."

"Switzerland!" The sergeant major stared at Salvani as if he had grown an extra head.

"Yes." Salvani bent over the map. "It's neutral, so at least the Germans won't get their hands on him, and the Red Cross will look after him. Yes—" He raised his hand. "They might intern me, but they'll probably let me out. Anyway, I'll take that chance when I get there."

"Get there!" The sergeant major banged on the map. "Do you know what the mountains are like between here and Switzerland. Yes, I know you've crossed rough country, but Christ Almighty—you'll have to get over Mont Blanc!"

"No, I won't," Salvani said. "Because I'm going by road. Look." He put his finger on the map. "We're here, right? Bourg-St.-Maurice. You see this road?" He pointed to a line which wiggled its way northwest. "It goes through here—Beaufort—then this little place"—he stooped and peered—"Flumet. Then there's this road going to . . . La Clusaz and Bonneville. That's only what . . . ten, fifteen kilometers from the border. And I know that part of the world. I was there for a couple of weeks when I first came to France. It's just woods and hills, plenty of little roads, easy enough to dodge through . . ."

With deliberation the sergeant major walked around the table, poked his face forward, and smelled Salvani's breath. "How much drink have you had? Do you think that you can walk, what, a hundred and fifty kilometers without being picked up?"

"No," Salvani said, "because I'm not going to walk. Come on."

He went through the back door, the two men at his heels, strode to the shed in the corner of the yard, switched his flashlight on, and said, "Take a look at that."

The sergeant major poked his head into the shed and his eyes opened wide.

"Well now," he said. "Well, well. I never noticed that."

"Right." Salvani patted a saddle, but a saddle attached not to a donkey but to a machine, a huge, ungainly, but powerful-looking motorcycle with a sidecar. "It's a Gnome," Salvani said. "Handle that right and it would take you up Vesuvius."

"If it runs," the sergeant said.

Salvani rubbed his bristly chin. "We'll soon find out. Christ, on this we could be in Switzerland before dawn."

The sergeant major moved uneasily. "Take it easy. The place is full of Germans . . . roadblocks . . ."

"Ah." Salvani was dismissive. "We walked through those back roads today, with a donkey, and no one said boo." He squatted, opened the gas tank, and poked a straw into it. "Some fuel. So let's see if it goes."

He swung a leg over the saddle, flicked on the gas switch, and gripped the handlebars.

"Hold it," the sergeant said. "The wheels are padlocked."

"Doesn't matter," Salvani said. "I've got it in neutral. Cross your fingers—" not adding, as he wished to: And cross your hearts—as he stood up on the pedals, took a deep breath, and lashed down on the starter pedal. There was a faint wheeze, like air escaping from a balloon, then silence.

"That's nothing," Salvani said, loudly. "Nothing. The engine needs turning over, that's all."

He kicked again—and again, the engine wheezing and puffing, the other men's interest turning to skepticism, then derision, until, as the sergeant major raised his hand to dismiss the attempt, and as, indeed, Salvani, sweating and cursing, was himself about to give up, the engine belched a huge cloud of smoke and roared into triumphant life.

Salvani roared with the engine and raised a triumphant fist as the engine boomed with a tremendous throaty bellow and the motorbike shook and vibrated as if waiting only to release its power on an open road.

"Said it would!" Salvani bellowed, his voice lost as the deep growl of the engine echoed and reechoed off the walls of the shed. Salvani grinned at the two sergeants, raised his fist again, and switched off the engine.

"It works." The sergeant major coughed and wiped his eyes. "But—what!"

He swung around as the shed was flooded with yellow light and a man holding a lantern appeared at the door.

"The hotel owner," the sergeant major said.

"Ah!" Salvani nodded politely. "Just . . . er, just testing your bike, monsieur."

"Stealing it," the man said.

"No!" Salvani affected an air of injured innocence. "Not stealing. Well," his native honesty coming to the fore. "Er . . . well, I'm going to borrow it for a while. Just for a while. You'll get it back. I'll give you a receipt."

"A receipt." The man laughed, a bitter, resigned laugh.

"You take my wine, food, tobacco, and now this." He shook his head. "It was the pride of my life when I bought it. And you'll give me a receipt."

"Sorry," Salvani said. "I know it's hard."

"Hard." The man opened expressive arms.

"Aah." The ramrod sergeant of the Bersaglieri stepped forward and pushed the man aside. "Fortunes of war."

"War?" The man spat. "What has that got to do with fortune?" but got no answer.

The motorbike was unlocked and wheeled from the shed, the sidecar crammed with looted food, wine, brandy, water, tobacco, a spare can of gas, a gift from the Bersaglieri, and, furiously protesting, Judah.

"I want to stay with Bruno!" he yelled. "I want to see more animals!"

"Get in," Salvani said, Judah wriggling in his arms like an eel. "Get *in*." He placed his hand on Judah's head and shoved. "Bruno's going to bed."

Inexorably forced down, Judah made a last, desperate, and improbable bid for freedom: "*I* want to go to bed," as Salvani slammed the canopy over him. The canopy was made of rough green cellophane and Judah, his face and tiny hands pressed against it and his mouth still opening in protest, looked like a newt in an aquarium.

The soldiers, smiling, waving, making ludicrous, comforting faces, listened to Judah's muffled cries as the sergeant major took Salvani to one side.

"You're set on this?"

"Yes," Salvani said. "Set."

"All right." The sergeant major scraped the ground with his toe. "The first town you come to, Beaufort—it's only small but you're not going to blast your way through. It's got narrow streets. You'll have to zigzag."

"So I'll zigzag," Salvani said.

The sergeant major sighed. "Twenty minutes," he said, "half an hour at the most and you could be in Italy."

"*I'd* be," Salvani said. "Not him."

The sergeant major handed over a cigarette, the flare of the match lighting his hard, apparently brutal face. "You've got a good night for it."

"Yes." The streets of the town, and the huge crags around it, were light as day in the moonlight.

"You know you're crazy?"

Salvani grinned ruefully. "Maybe. But you know something? If I'm crazy and the Germans are sane, I'd rather *be* crazy."

The sergeant major cocked his head, listening to Judah's muffled cries. "I could have you arrested. As a deserter."

Salvani laughed out loud. "That *is* crazy."

"Maybe." The sergeant major sucked at his cigarette through a cupped hand. "But I'm going to tell you something that *is* crazy. I mean really crazy."

"What could be crazier than this?" Salvani looked around at the quiet town, the soldiers clustered around the motorbike, the sullen hotelkeeper.

"It's this." The sergeant major took hold of Salvani's lapel and pulled him close, whispering, as if what he had to say was so insane that he feared another human being hearing him. "Up there, on the pass, there's a customs post, right? And one of the officers, he's a decent man, you know? Well . . . he told me . . . listen, what can you say? I mean it is crazy—insane—but he told me that they're killing them."

"What are you talking about?" Salvani brushed the sergeant major's hand away. "Who's killing who?"

"The Germans," the sergeant major said. "They're killing the Jews."

"I can't believe that," Salvani said. "I just don't believe it. But listen. There's one thing you can do for me."

"Sure," the sergeant major said. "Let your family know about you."

"That, yes, but—" Salvani nodded at the hotelkeeper. "Keep him under wraps, hey."

"Will do," the sergeant major said. "Have to let him go tomorrow, though."

"That's fine," Salvani said. "We'll be in Switzerland by then."

The soldiers, amused but comforting, stepped back as Salvani and the sergeant major reached the Gnome, where Judah was still beating against the canopy, his mouth opening and closing.

"Thanks a lot, lads," Salvani said.

"That's all right." The sergeant of the Bersaglieri ducked his head a little sheepishly. "You know, you couldn't expect us to . . ."

"Not at all." Salvani shook hands with him and the sergeant major and one by one with all the other men.

"Best of luck," the men cried. "See you in Italy."

"Sure," Salvani answered, and, to the fabulous Bruno, "I'll see your show back home." Raising his hand in salute as he kicked the engine into life and, to a chorus of cheers, slowly, and a little uncertainly at first, drove up the main street to a sign saying Beaufort and turned left onto a narrow road which led northwest, away from Italy, away from home, but which, he silently prayed, would take him to the one land in Europe where the bayonets were sheathed, the machine guns silent, where, surrounded by stars, the lights shone undimmed, and where, although he did not know it, the sound of trains in the night was not an affront to human decency.

16

Palet lay on his bed in the seedy hotel in La Chambre. For him a bed was not a place of rest and repose but more like a sickbed, a place to lie sweating and twitching—and even when he slept he had nightmares.

Now he lay there in his suit, staring at the ceiling, gulping brandy and muttering curses and obscenities against the world. *Had* them, he thought. Had them in the palm of my hand, cursing and gulping, the brandy running unheeded down his chin.

He twitched on his rumpled bed. Kellner, the Frenchman, and the German captain sat dining, congratulating themselves on a good day's work; the priest knelt before an altar begging for forgiveness; Pierre, his broken wrists untended, lay moaning in his cell in a stupor of pain; Doriot, his broken foot roughly bandaged, sat in his farmhouse wracking his brains for more names he might scratch down with scorched fingers to hand over to Kellner, and waiting for Maurice to appear so that he might hand him over, too, desperate to escape another trip to the cells, and more desperate for his wife and children; Le Pic, his wife, and the Chasseur were in cells in Chambéry, the Chasseur already under sentence of death; and Maurice, himself, was in a hut in a remote valley, talking earnestly to another man, who was nodding solemnly as Maurice said that there would be just one or two of them at first, men and women they could trust absolutely, sworn brothers and sisters . . . two rough men in rough clothes in their high valley, almost as remote from the world as the moon, sparking another light in the darkness as Palet, pouring down glasses of brandy, mumbled and cursed as, like a vampire bat returning on black wings to its victim, the thought crossed and recrossed what was left of his corrupt consciousness: had them—had them in my hand—could have had them, could have; and now . . . where were they . . . in Italy . . . mumbling as he poured down the brandy, sweating and fingering his boils in the night.

In fact, not forty kilometers away, and an hour's twisting drive from Bourg-St.-Maurice, at the head of a pass, Salvani was squatting against a boulder, looking down on a valley, broad for the Savoie, and on the shingle roofs of Beaufort and on the menacing fangs of its ruined castle.

It was another splendrous night: the heavens spangled with stars, the moon's steady, tranquil light chequering meadows and forest, crag and mountain; and still though the night was, it was full of small sounds which only quietness allows one to hear: the drizzle of a distant waterfall, the branches of a tree creaking, the sighing of the forest, owls squeaking, and the never ending faint clatter as the mountains withered away, casting down their burden of shattered stone. But Salvani was as indifferent to the night as it was to him; what he was thinking was should he go on. He pulled savagely on the cigarette; it had been one thing, bravely and truthfully, saying he would make a tremendous dash through the night with Judah when they had been surrounded by comrades, but what the hell was in it for him? And who knew what was waiting down there in the narrow streets of Beaufort: police patrols, or, worse, the —— Germans with their machine pistols only too ready to blow you to pieces and ask questions afterward—and even if he got through, there was this Flumet place, and then another town, whereas . . . he looked over his shoulder . . . the Italians would still be at the hotel in Bourg-St.-Maurice—as easy as falling off a log just to swing the motorbike around and head back. They would be there in

an hour, among friends—drive up to Italy the next day
. . . and what the hell—he muttered a curse—what the hell
was he supposed to be: some kind of saint, wandering
around with a kid . . . "Go back," a voice whispered inside
his head. "That's it, go back, you've done your best; more
than your best; more than any man could reasonably be
asked to do. Go back . . ."

He flicked away his cigarette, strode back to the bike,
opened the canopy, and Judah looked up at him. "Are we
there yet, Uncle?" he asked, yawning and rubbing his eyes
with tiny fists.

"No," Salvani said.

"Oh." Judah popped his head up and peered around.
"Will it be long?" he asked and yawned again.

"No," Salvani said. "No. Not long. Just settle down now.
Try and sleep."

"I can't sleep," Judah protested, but halfheartedly, yawning again, his eyes closing, Bruno and his animals, it
seemed, forgotten.

"Well, just try." Salvani patted Judah on the head and
closed the canopy over him. "—— it," he said, swinging
over the saddle. "Just —— it," as he kicked the engine into
life and headed down the pass, to Beaufort.

And nothing happened. Nothing at all. No fiends in field
gray jumped out, spraying them with bullets; no police
called halt; not a dog barked or curtain twitched back.

Lying low, Salvani thought, edging at walking speed past
the church. Keeping out of it. What you don't know can't
hurt you—and who knew what shadows you might see in
the ghostly moonlight, what terrors, what horrors, what
hunched shapes . . . although, as he crossed the bridge,
and a silent river, he laughed. What would they have seen?
A broken-down Italian soldier on a motorbike with a Jewish child and—he laughed again, exultant, lightheaded as
they left the town, and a sign like a friendly stranger said
Flumet, 15 kilometers, as he changed into second gear, the

Gnome responding with a huge surge of power—going to Switzerland.

And that was all right; absolutely A1 all right. Boom through Flumet, and the Clusaz place, and they would be home and dry. In fact, he thought, if it was all as easy as this, he'd drop Judah at the border and come back. Come back tomorrow night! Christ, there would be nothing to it; yes indeed, shouting with joy and relief, as he steered through dark avenues of woods, the engine, pulsing with power, effortlessly taking its burden up, and up again, as if as eager to get to Switzerland as its passengers; on to a bare, scraped plateau, then coasting effortlessly downward, through another hamlet, a church with an onion dome perched on a steeple, pasture, the world tilting toward another huge cleft, and, set against a backdrop of colossal cliffs, Flumet slumbering not four kilometers away; and the engine gave a little cough.

It was a slight cough, muffled, like a mourner at a funeral, but as the road leveled, it coughed again, a throaty cough this time, ominously like a death rattle, and then, in a dying murmur, the motorbike stopped.

Salvani frowned down at the bike, as if he expected the Gnome to suddenly revive and growl on, but, save for a slight and mysterious slow tocking, like a death-watch beetle, nothing happened, and after a minute or so it was clear that, without something being done, nothing *was* going to happen.

Salvani swung off the saddle and stared at the Gnome, unable for the moment to grasp what had happened. One moment the bike had been booming along, eating up the miles, powerful, effortless—and now! The extent of the catastrophe sank in; if the bike wouldn't go, then they were in trouble, real trouble.

He swung off the saddle and tried to think. Gas, yes. He found a stick and poked it into the tank. Plenty, so what next? Pushing! That made machines go— Yes, he grinned with relief—a good push! He grabbed the handlebars and heaved. Silently the bike moved forward, slowly, then faster, and faster still, aided by an incline, Salvani's boots clattering beside it—but it remained silent and the slope leveled off, became an ascent, and gravity ceasing to work and Salvani breathless, it came to a halt again, still silent, but this time even the ghost had fled.

"Aiee." Salvani groaned with frustration. "What . . . what . . ." he muttered. "Think. Think now, Vito." He frowned in concentration, recalling vague memories of mechanics' talk: carburetors, and points, and there was something about valves, and plugs—or were they to do with wireless sets? But carburetors . . . He searched along the road until he found a twig, then crouched by the side of the bike. The trouble was, he didn't know where the carburetor was, or even what it looked like, but he peered into what seemed a hideous and complicated tangle of pipes and wires and prodded with the stick, feeling as he did a sense of utter futility.

A few bits of soil fell from the engine casing, leaves, and what looked like rust. Salvani prodded again, blew into the pipes, rubbed them with the cuff of his overcoat, and swung on the starter again. Nothing. The machine stood inert, mute and seemingly malign. Salvani got off the bike. *Basta!* he growled, and kicked the bike. *Basta!* It seemed incredible to him; there was the bike, the road, the mantle of the night and what—a mere hundred or so kilometers between him, Judah, and the border; three or four hours . . . and now! He clenched his fist, stuck in the middle of nowhere, friendless, guideless, and the hundred kilometers seeming a thousand—and for what, he cursed, a bit of dirt, a speck probably too small to see.

Still, better than the last time, he thought. Better than with the major. Nobody hurt at least, and who knew, might get the bike fixed tomorrow, somehow, move on tomorrow night. We'll see. But first things first.

He poked along the side of the road until he found what he had hoped for, a fairly level patch of land with a scrubby growth of bushes. Then he went back to the bike, opened the sidecar and lifted out Judah, who sighed, mumbled, and opened his eyes.

"Are we there?" He yawned.

"No, not yet." Salvani sat Judah down. "Just sit still for a minute." He patted Judah's head, then went back to the bike, ran it off the road onto the level stretch he had found, and rammed it as far into the bushes as he could. He grabbed a few boughs, broke them off, and made a clumsy form of camouflage around the bike, then stepped back. It looked all right in the darkness, and it might in daylight, too, but he guessed—hoped—that there wouldn't be much traffic along the road anyway. He threw another branch over the bike, spat, went back to Judah, and scooped him up with one arm.

"All right, little one," he said. "Just going for a walk. Come on, now." Judah lolling on his shoulder, he left the road, climbed up through the trees, onto a sweet-smelling pasture, and came to a shed with hay stacked in a corner.

"This will do," he said, talking to keep up his spirits. "Slept in worse," scooping out a hollow in the hay for Judah—and thinking of the last shed they had slept in, battered and bloody, with two dead men in a ravine . . .

He took a swig of brandy and lit a cigarette and sat for a while, listening to the night: owls, the whirr of a nightjar, the melancholy clank of a bell as, somewhere, a goat was disturbed . . . and a beautiful night, one to make a man dream of glories beyond words with the moon and the Milky Way trailing across the heavens in all their starry splendor.

Salvani finished his brandy, stubbed out his cigarette, and stood and stretched himself.

"What a dump," he said. "What a —— dump." Then burrowed into the hay himself.

* * *

Salvani woke with a mouthful of moldy hay. He spat, grunted, rolled over, and, like a bear coming from hibernation, heaved himself on to all fours, and saw a man looking at him.

"Ah!" As Salvani reached for his rifle, the man held up his hand. "No need for that."

"I'll decide that," Salvani said.

"Of course." The man shrugged, unperturbed. "Might I ask what you are doing here—and him," raising eyebrows as Judah, too, came from the hay, if not like a bear then like a bear cub, loudly proclaiming that he was thirsty, until he saw the man, when, like any wise cub, he fell silent and slipped behind Salvani.

"Never mind us," Salvani said. "What are you doing here?"

The man sat down on a chunk of wood and pulled out a pipe. "I'm a painter."

"Painter?" Salvani glanced at the shed. "You paint these?"

The man, tall for a Frenchman, a tanned face, blue eyes, smiled faintly.

"I might do better if I did. No, I paint pictures, landscapes."

"Oh!" Salvani stood up, straw sticking to him, looming over the man. "What are you doing wandering about up here?"

"Painting," the man said mildly. "There's a view . . ."

"And you find us and just sit smoking your pipe?"

"What should I do?" The man poked at his pipe. "Don't worry, I've not been to the police. By the way, you wouldn't own a motorbike, would you? It's all right—" He held up a hand. "It wasn't very well hidden, but it is now." He looked steadily over his pipe. "So what's *your* game?"

"Why should I tell you?" Salvani tried to look menacing, and succeeded, not that the man looked menaced.

203

"No reason," he said. "Except that if you don't tell me, you won't get any help. And in case it had escaped your attention, you look as if you need it."

There was no arguing with that, and although Salvani groaned at the thought of telling his tale again, he did so, taking the man out of Judah's hearing and muttering into his ear, the man nodding gravely, until Salvani mentioned Switzerland.

"Switz—" His jaw dropped. "But, man, that's—"

"Crazy. Yes. I've been told that before." Salvani bit his thumb. "But what would you do, hey?"

The man leaned back and looked at Judah sitting patiently in the hay, the morning light bestowing on him a benign nimbus. "I don't know," he said. "I'm just glad it didn't happen to me."

"And I'm *sorry* it happened to me," Salvani said. "But it has."

"Fate," the man said.

"Yes, Fate." But Salvani had other things on his mind than the mysterious workings of the Universe. "Are you going to help us or—"

"Or are you going to break my neck?" The man shrugged. "Yes, I thought you might consider that. But I'll help. You know I came here to escape the war. I was a painter in Paris . . . You think you can escape, but you can't really . . ." He stood up and dusted off his trousers. "First things first."

"Sure," Salvani said. "But what is the first thing?"

"That's the easy bit." The man smiled again. "I start painting. What could be more natural? People know I'm painting this view, and if any snoopers see me, they're not going to suspect anything, are they? Such as a crazy Italian and a child hiding in here."

"The motorbike—"

"Later." The man knocked out his pipe. "I know a man in Flumet . . . but we'll see. Let's keep up a routine."

He walked to a corner of the shed, picked up a curious collection of rods, shook them, and transformed them into an easel. *"Voilà!"* he addressed Judah. "Magic, hey?" and was visibly disconcerted when Judah firmly announced that it wasn't.

"I've seen it before," Judah said. "Lots of times!"

Salvani grinned like a doting parent. "He's been around," he said proudly. "He's seen lots of things!" He beamed at Judah and patted his head. "Why, he's seen Mars. Through a telescope!"

"Has he?" The man picked up a folder and took out a canvas with a half-finished picture on it. "Have you ever done any painting, child?"

"Yes!" Judah shouted. "At school. Big paintings. Bigger than that," adding recklessly, "A lot bigger! I got gold stars for them!"

"Hmm," said the man, whose name was Patrice, looking at Judah with less enthusiasm than a few moments earlier. "But look—" He took out a large sketchbook. "Do you like these pictures? They're watercolor sketches."

"I know!" Judah said. "Mine were better than those. A lot better!"

Patrice might, or might not, have muttered under his breath as he turned to pick up his easel, but certainly, when he turned, his smile looked as if it were there by an effort of will. But he said to Salvani, "It could be a long day for the child. This might keep him amused." He handed over a new sketchbook, a box of watercolors, and a brush. "You have water, food? Right. I'll be at the top of the meadow."

He walked across the field and set up his easel and a bright parasol. Clever, Salvani thought. No one would imagine that, a hundred meters or so from where the artist was, two refugees were hiding. And a stroke of real luck to have met the man . . . Get the bike fixed—yes, the bitter disappointment of the previous night gone with the morning mists, he clapped his hands together and fed Judah and himself.

"Now," he said, vigorously brushing crumbs off Judah. "Are you going to paint?"

"Is this Italy?" Judah asked.

"Not quite," Salvani said. "No, but we're *nearly* there."

"You said that yesterday," Judah said. "And"—adding with what seemed to Salvani needless accuracy—"the day before that, *and* the day before—"

"Yes." Salvani chopped Judah off in midflow. "These things take time. Now let's see some of this painting you're so good at."

"All right," Judah consented, as if doing Salvani a favor, and sat in a corner, tongue sticking out, deeply concentrating and himself a study in concentration.

Salvani lit a cigarette, sat, stretched his legs out, content to let a few hours slip away, feeling lucky again. "What is it?" as Judah pulled at his sleeve within two minutes.

"Finished!" Judah said proudly.

"Finished!" Salvani stared down. "You've only just started!"

"Well, I've done it," Judah said. "I'm a very quick painter. Look."

He held up his work, a *mélange* of watery colors running into each other and with a circle in the middle with lines radiating from it, like a huge spider.

"And that's . . . ?" Salvani said.

"It's you!" Judah snatched the painting back impatiently and pointed to a pencil scribble. "See?"

Salvani peered at the scribble. "What is it?"

Judah sighed. "It's your *name*." He put his finger on the page. "Look, 'Uncle by Judah.' "

"But they're not letters. And you're moving your finger the wrong way. Didn't you get taught how to write?"

"Of course!" Judah was indignant. "I was the best writer—"

"Sure." Salvani waved aside another revelation of Judah's amazing abilities. "But that . . . Look." He took the pencil and wrote the words.

"No!" Judah grabbed the pencil back. "You've written *Italian*. This is Hebrew. It's our language."

"But I thought that you spoke Italian," Salvani said. "And French."

"Yes." Judah nodded. "But we speak Hebrew at home."

"Yes?" Salvani stared at the words again, wondering if he was having his leg comprehensively pulled. "And you read it *backward?*"

"It's forward for us," Judah said.

"I suppose it is if you say so." Salvani rubbed his chin.

"I do." Judah was firm. "Now you paint something."

Salvani grinned. "I couldn't paint the back door."

"Draw, then," Judah said.

"All right." Salvani took the sketchbook and pencil. "What shall I draw?"

Judah thought for a moment. "A rhinoceros. Draw two of them."

"I couldn't draw *one* of them," Salvani said.

"I'll bet Bruno could," Judah said. "I'll bet he could draw anything! He was clever."

"Was he?" Salvani resisted the temptation to say that if Bruno was so clever *he* could take Judah to Switzerland. "Well, I can't draw a rhinoceros."

"Then"—Judah screwed his eyes in concentration—"draw a cow."

"A cow." Salvani gripped the pencil with fierce determination, drew, and finally, with becoming modesty, although secret pride, held it up for Judah to admire and was bitterly piqued when Judah made a face and said the picture was awful.

Salvani held the drawing away and squinted at it. "It's not. Not awful."

"It is." Judah was scornful. "Its legs bend the wrong way!"

Salvani peered again. Now Judah had mentioned it,

there was something odd about his otherwise rather jolly cow gamboling across a field dotted with flowers—an artistic flourish Salvani had vastly admired. "Are you sure?"

" 'Course, there's cows outside—" Judah dashed to the door.

"No!" Salvani threw himself at Judah, but that was unnecessary. Judah stopped as if he had run into a plate-glass window: an invisible barrier—one invisible to the rest of the world, that is, but only too visible to him; a dividing line between one world and another and, perhaps literally, between this world and the next.

"Sorry, Uncle." Judah turned, one hand to his mouth. "I nearly forgot. Sorry."

"Aaah," Salvani sweated with relief. "But you didn't, that's the main thing. You were good. Really good. But just remember, won't you? Never forget. *Nowhere* without me. So . . . it's all right, really. Yes. Now do another picture, hey? *You* do a rhinoceros," hoping that would take longer than a portrait.

Judah set to work and Salvani leaned back and gazed at him. Wonderful, he thought. Writing backward, going to church on Saturday, having a secret language . . . all that going on around him, in France and Italy, and he had never known—wonderful and interesting. He abandoned his own artistic efforts and relaxed, looking fondly on his child prodigy, sipping wine, occasionally peering through the slats at the artist painting under his bright umbrella— a serene morning, pure fleecy clouds drifting slowly, the quiet hum of insects, birds flashing across the meadow, butterflies, Judah producing one unlikely animal after another, and then, above the drone of the insects, another drone.

Salvani peered through his gap. A personnel carrier was growling up the road and the men on it were dressed in field gray. Salvani stood, hardly breathing, as Patrice turned from his easel and, shading his eyes, looked down on the road and the carrier—as any man would have done.

But nothing happened. The carrier ground on toward Beaufort and the world returned to its tranquility, except that, after a few minutes, Patrice dismantled his easel, packed his paints and canvas, and strolled back to the shed.

"You saw that?" he said. "Nothing to worry about. I suppose the Germans are just moving troops into Beaufort. But listen, I have to go now."

"Yes?" Salvani frowned.

"The light has changed—" Patrice caught Salvani's suspicious glance. "Don't worry, it's how you paint a landscape, the shadows change . . . I go to Flumet to have lunch. It's a routine. Best to keep it."

"But you'll be back?"

"I'll be back. At dusk, and with a friend to look at your motorbike."

"That will be all right? You wandering about?"

Patrice smiled. "Artists, you know? We're all crazy, wandering about in the moonlight and absentminded, forgetting things. I'll leave my painting behind."

Salvani grinned back. "Crazy like me, hey? But . . . talking of craziness: Do you think we'll make it? Get through?"

Patrice shrugged. "I think maybe. Yes. It's just crazy enough to work. We'll see. My friend will advise you."

"And . . ." Salvani picked his words carefully. "This friend of yours . . . he . . ."

Patrice took out his pipe and polished it on his sleeve. "He won't betray you. Did you ever hear of a man called van Gogh? No? He was a painter, too. He lived in Provence for a while. People there thought *he* was crazy, but he had a good friend. The postman. And people around here think *I'm* a little mad, and my friend is the postman, too. Strange, hey? Not that I'm a van Gogh," he added, a little wistfully. "I don't know why I'm telling you this, but"— briskly putting away his pipe—"my friend is trustworthy. Absolutely. You'll have to get through the afternoon somehow—"

"No problem," Salvani said.

"Good." Patrice stooped over Judah. "Did you do some pictures?"

"Lots!" Judah proudly demonstrated his work. "This is an elephant, this is a rhinoceros, this is Uncle—" pointing helpfully at Salvani. "This—" he stared down—"I'm not sure what this is exactly, but this is—"

Patrice said, "But you've finished the whole book!"

"Yes," Judah said proudly. "I'm quick! I was the quickest painter in school. Can I have another book?"

Patrice looked at the sketchbook rather piqued, then turned to Salvani. "These . . . they're not easily come by now . . ."

"He can use the other side of the pages." Salvani choked back a guffaw. "And do some drawings for him. He can color them in."

"Good idea." Before the dazzled eyes of Salvani and reducing even Judah to silence, Patrice did a series of lightning sketches, villages, people, a cow with its legs the right way around.

"Amazing." Salvani shook his head with sincere admiration. "Just amazing."

"Nothing," Patrice said, but showing his pleasure just the same. "Just a knack. So I'll be off."

"And back."

"And back." Patrice held out his hand. "And back, soldier."

"I'm not a soldier," Salvani said. "They made me wear this uniform, but I'm not a soldier. And don't want to be one, either."

"Glad to hear it." Patrice shook hands. "And I will be back," striding across the sweet meadow, down to the road, and to Flumet.

Under a ruined castle and by a sparkling river, in the Gendarmerie, a phone buzzed, *buzz buzz*, like a bluebottle.

A gendarme, his mind on lunch, stared at the phone and

was tempted to ignore it, especially as his lunch was being prepared for him by an attractive widow, and in fact ambled to the door—but the buzzing continued, and things being what they were . . . he cursed and picked up the phone.

"Beaufort," he grunted. "Yes. Just a minute." He fumbled for a pencil and scratched a few notes, frowning. "Right . . . no . . . see what we can do."

He hooked the phone back, tapped his chin with the pencil for a moment or two, then went back into a small room where another, older gendarme, his hands in his pockets, was standing staring through a window. "What do you want," he said over his shoulder.

"It's a bit funny," the first gendarme said.

"Funny?" The older man peered closer through the window. "Everything's funny these days."

"No." The younger man held out his notes. "It's a call from Bourg-St.-Maurice."

"What do they want?" the other gendarme said, as if the police in Bourg were importunate, poverty-stricken relatives.

"It's about a stolen motorbike—"

"For Christ's sake!" The older man turned around. "A stolen bike! Do they know what's going on? Tell them to stuff it."

"Er . . . there's more to it." The younger gendarme repeated the message, as he spoke the older man looking at him incredulously.

"Is this a —— joke?" he said.

"No." The younger man shook his head. "The owner of the bike was positive." He looked at his crumpled notes and named a name.

"I know him," the older man said. "He's got a hotel. He's given us some good tips. But is he *sure*? An Italian and a kid coming *this* way?"

"That's what they said."

211

"But what the . . ." The older man took the notes. "What were they doing coming here? Why not over the Little St. Bernard?"

"Search me." The younger man shrugged. "But what do we do?"

The older man clenched his fist, crushing the notes. "Do this—" He threw the notes into a wastepaper basket. "Some poor sod and a refugee kid pinched a bike and took a wrong turn. Forget it."

The younger man shifted uneasily. "I took the call . . ."

"*I* took it," the other man said. "Let them be. Tell Bourg to report to Moutiers."

"They can't," the younger man said. "The lines are down. The Italians wrecked them."

"Yes, well . . ." The older man turned back to the window, craning his neck a little to look sideways. A hundred meters or so to the left, a narrow street widened by a church. Steps led up to the church doors. The personnel carrier Salvani had seen earlier was parked by the steps, German soldiers stood around casually, peering about them like tourists, and on the steps was a tall German lieutenant.

The lieutenant, one hand on his hip, turned around with an easy, arrogant grace, the very image of a conqueror, waved to his sergeant, who, jackbooted, swaggered up the church steps.

The older gendarme felt a prickle of unease. Down there were the new masters, and who knew what they were capable of? And the poor devil on the motorbike *was* Italian, an enemy, phone calls were logged, everyone knew that the Germans were fanatical about carrying out orders to the letter. He swallowed, hard, went to the wastepaper basket, and retrieved the notes. "I'll tell the boss."

The boss was told and took the message seriously; that is, he informed his new master, the elegant German lieutenant, of the presence of an Italian soldier with a child and a stolen motorbike, and, to show his zeal, set his men to

212

work; that is, they, cursing, asked around the town whether anyone had heard a motorbike the previous night—with no result, the town having, it seemed, been struck stone-deaf at dusk, and himself, in person, phoning the district police headquarters at Albertville, and speaking to an irritable commissaire.

"So," the Beaufort inspector was equally irritable, as he wanted his lunch, too. "So I thought that I'd let you know. The man is Italian—armed to the teeth. A real brute, by all accounts—a savage. And where's he going? There's only two roads out of here, to Albertville and to Flumet—"

"Have you let Flumet know?"

"No." The inspector grimaced with exasperation. "The line isn't working, and to send a man—it would take all day, and I've got enough on my plate here with the Germans."

"Now just calm down." The commissaire's voice died away and then crackled back into life, mysteriously magnified. "*Calm down.* There's hordes of Italians wandering about and refugees and Christ knows what. You just get on with your job."

"That's what I'm doing," the inspector said. "Informing you."

There was a long, calculating silence, broken by joviality. "And so you have, and quite right, too. Look, it's difficult for all of us just now, but do your best. You mentioned the Germans. How are they?"

"Good, I suppose," the inspector said. "Very correct, polite, civil."

"Not like the Italians, then, ha, ha! Well, work with them. Remember, though, we're policemen. Our job is *crime.* I think you'll find the Germans are good at that. Very law-abiding. Law and Order, that's the thing."

"Yes." In Beaufort—castle, river, glades, hanging woods, church with rare, painted marbling—the inspector tapped the table. "Commissaire, they're asking for lists of names—"

"Traitors."

The inspector cleared his throat. "Commissaire, these lists, they're neighbors—"

"Enemies of the state!" The commissaire's voice was strident, the voice of a man attempting to deny the undeniable, lest, if he should not, the last thing on earth he might hear would be the swish of the blade of the guillotine. "Full instructions will reach you. But *cooperation*. Do you understand?"

The inspector, thinking of the tall German lieutenant and his burly sergeant, and hearing, too, the *clunk* as the diagonal blade was released, understood perfectly. "Full cooperation. And you'll let Flumet know—about this Italian."

"Yes!" The commissaire barked, but although the inspector had a feeling that there, in Albertville, his superior wanted to, was about to, say something more, some half-strangled apology, a peremptory voice broke in, speaking French with a German accent—ordering them to clear the line, "in the interest of the German Army."

The line went, not dead, but full of an ominous buzzing. The inspector hooked back the telephone and went for a gloomy lunch with the mayor, and to prepare his list of enemies of the state—a short one, he promised himself, while twenty kilometers to the west the commissaire rapped out his orders and went for *his* lunch, a more cheerful one, since he had already struck up a cordial relationship with the German commandant with whom he was eating. But at the door of his office, where he was already patting his stomach in anticipation, his inspector deferentially asked for a moment.

"This Italian, sir, and the child."

"Yes." The commissaire could be jovial when it suited him. "A lot of fuss about nothing, but put up a show."

The inspector nodded agreement. "Of course, but while we're at it, I thought—" He tapped a large-scale map on the wall and made a few suggestions.

214

"Good, good." The commissaire patted the inspector on the shoulder. "I'll leave it up to you entirely. Just get on with it. Make a show."

The inspector got on with it. He had once been involved in a very nasty case concerning a man and a child, and the memory of it had never left him, so he took the matter seriously, the fact that the child was Jewish being of no consequence as far as he was concerned. He sent for his sergeant and gave him detailed instructions.

The sergeant frowned. "But if he was going through Flumet he'd have gone through last night," he objected.

"And maybe he didn't," the inspector snapped and went out for *his* lunch.

The sergeant was a conscientious man and so, after battling with disconnected phone lines—stoically enduring incredulity bordering on abuse from indignant auditors— he carried out his instructions to the letter. Also, he was a family man, and as long as children didn't misbehave, he was fond of them in a detached sort of way, and although he didn't believe that there was a monster of an Italian roaring around the countryside on a giant Gnome bike, the touch about the child had a ring of truth; somewhere in the district there might just be a child in trouble.

And so, when he had carried out his orders to the letter, he went a step further. He went to the detectives' office and left a message there, and he went to the office of the CRS, the riot police, and told them, and the highway police, and finally went downstairs to a gloomy room in the basement. There was no one in but he scrawled a message and left it on a tacky desk. Then, his duty done and more, and with a clear mind and conscience, he left, banging the door behind him. A scrap of cardboard fell to the floor and he picked it up and dutifully pinned it back. Written on the card, crudely, in block letters was one word. MILICE.

17

The sun dipped and a cool wind sighed down from the icy peaks; men finished their lunches and began to think of their suppers. Darkness drew near, owls opened their eyes, bats stirred their wings. In Thrace, Aaron Goldman was torn to pieces by dogs for striking a Gestapo officer. In Amsterdam, Jacob Rosenthal and his wife, Naomi, were assured by a polite German officer that they, and their four children, were going on a first-class train to a new life in the East, and that, of course, they could take their belongings. In Warsaw, three thousand Jews were being selected to travel west to a new life, life for them all meaning death as the darkness gathered.

The first stars came out. Judah, sleeping among his paintings, awoke, but, as if aware that the growing darkness meant more than the mere setting of the sun, sat quietly in his corner. More stars shone, appearing one by one as if awaiting their turn. The moon moved among the stars, icy peaks glittered, the phantom owls beat across the pastures, and still Judah sat, motionless in his corner, and Salvani sat in his, only the red glow of his cigarette showing that he was there at all, both of them waiting, at the mercy of others, of Patrice, of the sheltering darkness, and of inconceivable decisions made far away by beings as alien to humanity as any nightmare creatures spawned by some horror in remotest space.

Then, as the moon shone its full, implacable face, Patrice came, but he came alone.

"Where's your friend? The mechanic?" Salvani asked, his voice thick with suspicion.

"Not coming. But it's not what you think, *Italien*." Patrice took Salvani by the elbow and led him aside. "They know about you and the child and the motorbike."

"Oh?" Salvani moved Patrice's hand and stepped back, one pace. "That's not actually amazing, is it? The owner must have told the cops and maybe someone saw us in the town back there—Beaufort. But so what? For all they know, we might be in Switzerland by now."

"It's a bit more than that." Patrice shook his head. "They're putting a special watch on the roads."

"What?" Salvani took another step back. "For us? And one bike? That's a bit heavy, isn't it?"

Patrice shrugged. "Maybe the police are just showing the Germans they're alert . . . or the hotelkeeper, in Bourg-St.-Maurice, my friend says that he's pals with the police—an informer, you know?"

"Aren't they all?" Salvani said bitterly. "But listen, Mister Artist. How come you know all this?"

"Ah . . ." The moonlight revealed Patrice's faint smile. "My friend, I told you, he's the postman. His wife operates the switchboard for the telephone. All the calls go through her. By tomorrow the whole district will know, about you, I mean, and there's maybe one or two won't mind handing you over."

"Yes." Salvani swung his head, balked, like an animal in a maze with deceptive exits, all being sealed one by one. He squared his shoulders. "Well." He went back into the shed and began collecting his belongings.

"What are you doing?" Patrice asked.

"Moving on." Salvani slung his rifle.

"Through the night? Without a guide? Do you think you can do that?"

"Don't know." Salvani turned, dark in the night. "But I'm going to try. I've got a map and there's that star, the North Star, that shows the way."

"But the police?"

"They'll be looking for a man, a kid, and a motorbike.

On the road. We'll be a man, a kid, no bike, and off the road."

Patrice ran his fingers down his cheek. "Why are you doing this? Really, why?"

"Mister," Salvani said. "I don't know myself any more. But if you want to help, just shut up and show us how to get through this Flumet place, point the way to the border and we'll start walking."

"I'll do that," Patrice said. "But I think that I can do better."

"What better?"

"*Italien.*" Patrice raised a delicate hand. "I'm going to take you to a magician."

Judah was aroused, warned to be silent, absolutely and totally. Patrice picked up his canvas, Salvani his knapsack— a magical night in which to go to meet a magician: silvered fields across which flickered ghostly moths, a black wood with creaking boughs, a stream gurgling, a serpentine road uncoiling through the woods, a mist rising from a chasm, a river muttering ominously; across the chasm a dog yammering ferociously, answered by another. And as Salvani was beginning to wonder just what sort of spells the magician might cast, Patrice stopped, turned, and held up slim fingers to his lips, then pointed. "Flumet," he mouthed.

Salvani peered through the trees. Clear in the moonlight a line of houses teetered on the edge of the chasm, a stubby church tower poked above them, and thrown in one bold arch across the ravine was a bridge.

Patrice pulled at Salvani's sleeve and the three of them sank to the ground.

"Not far, hey?" Patrice whispered.

No, Salvani thought. Not far at all. What's a hundred meters or so across a bridge to the shelter of houses and the lair of a magician? But between them and him was the bridge, bright, shadowless, bare, and beyond the bridge, against the dark wall of a house, a flame spurted, went

218

out, and a dot of light glowed, red, like the eye of some malignant animal.

"Police," Patrice whispered.

"Jesus," Salvani cursed to himself. A bare bridge, a cop with a pistol as big as a dog's hind leg, lurking in a corner . . . A cat couldn't get across . . . He pointed his finger down into the chasm.

Patrice shook his head and put his lips to Salvani's ear. "Three hundred meters sheer—and the river . . ." He looked at his watch. "Now listen carefully. Five minutes—" He held up his hand. "Five minutes I cross. Wait until you hear a noise. A noise, hey? Then *you* cross. *Vite. Vite*—quick—you understand? And take off your boots. You understand why? Silence? Yes. Then *run*."

"Boots . . ." With deep reluctance Salvani began to undo his bootlaces. Boots on, a man might feel he had a last line of defense; boots off . . . "Run where?"

Patrice looked at his watch again and stood up. "Just run."

"And the noise?"

Patrice bent down, mischief in his voice. "A motorcycle"—patting Salvani as he walked away.

Salvani picked up his knapsack and, with equal ease, Judah, his boots, the laces tied together, swinging from his mouth, and watched as Patrice started across the bridge.

One step, and from behind the red eye, an acrid voice challenged: *"Qui va?"*

"C'est moi, c'est moi." Patrice held his hands high in mock surrender, his canvas in his right hand. "Only me, Patrice, the artist," his voice carrying clearly through the night.

In the dark wall the red eye blinked and a gendarme stepped forward, one hand on his holster, stepping forward across the bridge. *"You,"* the gendarme packing into that one shouted word humorous disdain. "Ah, you artists. Come on, then," with the weary condescension of a man who did a *proper* job.

219

"Thank you." Patrice dropped his hands and walked forward, half laughing as if to agree that yes, he was a mere buffoon, joining the gendarme, two figures as black as silhouettes, going back across the bridge, half-heard scraps of banter, not all pleasant, drifting back to Salvani: "You should be in a loony bin . . . could get shot for this . . ."

On tiptoe, literally, with his big toes sticking through holes in his unwashed socks, Judah clinging to his neck, Salvani stood poised among the trees, waiting as, maddeningly, at the far end of the bridge, the gendarme halted, leaning against the parapet, lighting another cigarette, clearly ready enough to break the boredom of his watch by talking—even to an artist.

Come on, come on, Salvani said to himself—then from behind the houses there was the roar of a motorcycle, a cry from the gendarme and the clatter of boots as he ran into the town, Patrice on his heels, and, taking one breath, Salvani ran across the bridge, thinking as he ran, Jesus, if Mussolini saw anyone run this fast, he'd give them a gold medal.

Ten, thirty, seventy meters, a police whistle shrilled somewhere—ninety meters, a hundred, and ten more, and another ten—and a shadow jumped from a doorway and seized Salvani—half ducking to avoid a swing of Salvani's huge fist, and saying, "Come. Come quick, *vite!*"

To the accompaniment of the usual barking and howling of dogs, the shadow pulled Salvani into a narrow entry, and as the police whistle shrilled again and a voice bellowed a protest, they scrambled up a flight of wooden steps, crossed a curious creaky catwalk overhanging the chasm, and went through a door which swung behind with a *clack* that Salvani thought was the most satisfying sound he had ever heard in his life.

"Wait," the shadow said. "Stand still."

A match flared and a candle burned with a steady flame, and another, lighting dimly a room small and cluttered with objects: oversized furniture, gaudy vases purple and poisonous green with chipped gilt lips, and stuffed animals—a one-eyed polecat bared yellow teeth at a moldering badger, which stared, cross-eyed, at an owl, its silent wings forever still, clutching a lark in its claws. Pictures, too, in heavy frames: Napoleon defeating someone, and yet another foe, on a huge horse, waving a sword . . . A crucifix . . . And amid them all, shadows flickering as a draft caught the candles—short, stocky, balding, in a vest, suspenders, blue trousers, a man who looked the most improbable magician Salvani could imagine, especially when suddenly he grinned, showing toothless gums.

"*Voilà!*" he said. "We fooled them. Sit. Please." He turned away and opened a cupboard as, Judah on his knee, Salvani took a chair and, feeling more of a man, jammed his feet into his boots and looked appreciatively at the table, where the man had placed a bottle and three glasses.

"We wait," the man said, raising a finger.

Wait for what? Salvani wondered, but sitting waiting, Judah clutching his collar as the candles wavered and the shadows flickered, the animals coming into an eerie half-life, and a clock rasped *tick, tock, tock, tick,* until the man stood up abruptly, his head cocked, and as Salvani was sliding Judah off his knee and reaching surreptitiously for his rifle, there was a brief double rap on the door and, laughing, Patrice came into the room.

"So," he said. "You've met the magician."

"Sort of," Salvani stuck out his hand. "I almost banged you with it, on the bridge."

"Yes." The postman took Salvani's hand. "I thought I was going for a trip—into the river—*phwwwt!*"

"Still—" Patrice smiled. "No—don't thank me, thank . . . Jacques. *Jacques*, you understand?"

"I understand," Salvani said, understanding only too well. "And I've never seen either of you in my life."

"Yes." Patrice looked across the table. "I think you know that already. But it worked, didn't it? We have a friend

221

who has a motorcycle and"—he put his forefinger and thumb almost together—"that much gas. He started his bike, the cop—well, he was on guard for that—ran—I chivvied him a little—you ran . . . and here we are."

"And your friend?" Salvani said.

"Why," Patrice tapped the bottle, "he was just trying his bike, seeing if it was working still!"

"At this time of night?"

"There's no law against it. Clever, though, no? The art of magic—you make them look the way *you* want. But it wasn't my idea. Thank the magician."

He waved at Jacques and, suddenly, Judah squealed, "Are you really a magician?"

Jacques stared gloomily at Judah. "Watch." He produced a pack of cards from somewhere, nowhere, flicked out four kings and an ace, and flipped them face down. "Where is the ace?" he asked.

"That's *easy!*" Judah, as ready as ever to demonstrate his modesty, wriggled forward and poked a confident finger down. "Oh," his face changing as Jacques turned the card over and showed the stern face of a king.

"It's that one, then," Judah said, a shade less confidently. And "Oh," again and again, and once more, and, baffled but determined as he stared at four kings: "Then it's *that*—" his eyes popping as the last card was flipped over and a jack winked at him.

"Neat," Salvani said. "You could make money doing that."

"Maybe." Jacques swept the cards together. "If you want to cheat. But I don't like doing that. Do you?"

"No, I don't," Salvani said.

"I'm glad to hear it." Jacques leaned forward, opened his hand, closed it, and from Judah's ear produced, to his amazement, a franc coin. "It's all tricks, you know."

"I guess so." Salvani jiggled Judah on his knee, faintly jealous at the awed way in which Judah was staring at Jacques. "But we need another trick. Hey? Real magic."

222

"*Real* magic. Aaah . . . For that, you need to talk to him." Jacques nodded at Patrice. "A little canvas, a brush, paint . . . and *voilà!* A work of art. But perhaps we can do some magic. Yes!" He waved his fingers in front of Judah's eyes. "Perhaps we can make you invisible!"

Judah's eyes opened wider than any owl's. To be invisible! He saw himself unseen, unguessed at, running around playing pranks, frightening people, eating whatever he wished. "Do it," he shouted. "Make me invisible, now!"

"Not just this minute," Jacques said. "And don't shout, *ever*. But soon. If it suits—" He pointed at Salvani.

"Oh, it suits me," Salvani said. "If you gave us wings as well, it would be just perfect."

"Maybe we can help there, too," Jacques said.

"Wings!" With the treachery of childhood Judah abandoned Salvani completely and stood next to Jacques, open-eyed. "Fly!"

"Almost," Jacques said. He gestured to Patrice. "You explain."

"Yes." Patrice leaned forward. "But do you want to eat? Wash?"

"No." Salvani was decisive. "Let's hear the tale first, if you don't mind. Come here, Judah," brooking no protests as he gathered Judah to him.

"There is a tale at that." Patrice took out his pipe and polished it on his sleeve. "*Italien*, your idea of going north, through La Clusaz—well, it's up to you. But you know the roads are being watched?"

"Yes." Salvani shrugged a little impatiently. "We've been through that."

"Not really." Patrice made a spill from a twist of paper and lit his pipe from a candle. "Now please understand me . . ." He blew out a thin trickle of smoke. "Italians aren't that popular in Savoie, you know that?"

"Yes." Salvani knew that, and understood it, too. Invading armies weren't likely to be popular.

"Right." Patrice peered into the bowl of his pipe. "But there's more to it than that."

"Oh?" Salvani moved Judah from one knee to the other, his movement making the candles flicker, and the shadows. "What might that be?"

Patrice put his pipe, dead now, on the table. "You know the Ovra?"

"Sure." Salvani knew the Ovra, the Italian secret police, as vicious as the Gestapo, if without the Gestapo's venomous efficiency. "Pigs."

"Aren't they all!" Patrice didn't need to explain who the *all* were: the Ovra, the Gestapo, the Milice, the SS, all those who, strutting and all-powerful, above the Law, gloated in their power to oppress the powerless. "But"—Patrice glanced across at Jacques and forced his words out, a man bringing embarrassing news—"in the north the Ovra shot some mayors. Executed them . . . for not cooperating."

"What!" The candles flickered and swayed. The polecat showed its fangs, the owl, long dead, gripping the lark, long dead too, stared down, wide-eyed; Napoleon rode, in triumph, over a battlefield littered with corpses. "But"—Salvani looked down on Judah dreaming of invisibility and flying. "But people have helped us, all this way. There was—"

"Don't tell us!" Jacques snapped the words out.

"No," Patrice agreed. "But you understand why maybe going up through La Clusaz isn't such a good idea. So"—he lit his pipe yet again—"we've got another thought."

"I'd like to hear it," Salvani said.

"All right." The faint dry smile showed on Patrice's face. "Let me tell you a story. You like a story?"

"Surely," Salvani said, and he did, preferably one with wicked rich landlords and noble bandits and a beautiful girl. And Judah liked a story too, that enticing word penetrating the mistiness of his drowsiness and causing him to murmur, "A story?"

"Should he hear it?" Salvani asked.

"Yes," Patrice said. "There's no harm in it. The story"—he paused as Jacques poured out wine—"it's by an Englishman called Chesterton and . . ."

It was a murder mystery, which pleased Salvani, although the detective was a priest, which didn't please him, they, in his experience, being better at creating mysteries than at solving them, but the story was a good one. A man had been murdered in a house in London. A dozen people had been watching the house, back, front, and sides, and every one of them swore that no person had gone into or left the house all day.

"Not one person," Patrice said. "And all the witnesses were honest. But the victim was murdered, there was no one hiding in the house, and there was no tunnel. Impossible, hey?" He leaned forward, his clever face alert. "How was it done?"

It wasn't, Salvani knew, really the time to be answering riddles, but he was interested—absorbed. His fists were clenched and he started to sweat with the effort of concentration, trying to think—trying, until, to Jacques's open respect, Patrice's amused admiration, and Salvani's deep irritation, Judah whispered, "I know! The man got away in a balloon. Up the chimney!"

"Well, that's really good," Patrice said. "Really clever."

"It certainly is," Jacques agreed. "I would never have thought of that, not in a thousand years. And what about you? *Italien?* What's your answer?"

Salvani, his head as empty as a sieve, forced a smile. "The same! Yes, I was going to say that. A balloon."

"I said it!" Judah was indignant. "I said it first!"

"Of course you did." Salvani's smile turned into a hang-dog leer. "I mean, I almost thought of it. *Almost.* But"—hastily—"you thought of it first."

"And *said* it first." Judah was remorseless.

"*And* said it first. Yes." Salvani patted Judah on the head,

225

resisting the temptation to bat him on the ear, but, pride overcoming pique, said fondly, "He's clever, isn't he?"

Not needing reassurances on that score, Judah said firmly that he *was*, that he was the cleverest boy in his school, the cleverest boy in Modena—"And I was right, wasn't I?"

"Yes," Patrice said. "Absolutely right. But it's time you were in bed, I think. Jacques?"

Jacques stood up and called through a door and a woman came in, stout, bustling, efficient, and with an air of command that even Judah recognized and obeyed.

"My wife," Jacques said.

"Madame." Salvani bowed awkwardly and clutching Judah with a rough, affectionate grasp followed the woman up a flight of steps into a room with a bed—with crisp white sheets. "He's not been in a bed since . . . I don't know when," he said, looking longingly at it himself. "And we've not had our clothes off for . . ."

"I'll look after him," the woman said. "And wash your clothes. Go down now. They want to talk to you."

"Yes." Salvani stood in the doorway. "I don't know how to thank you."

"Don't," the woman said. "Go." As firm and commanding with Salvani as with Judah, who, his shirt half over his tousled head, was already informing her what amazing deeds he would do when he was invisible.

Salvani bumped his way back downstairs, to the dead animals and the living men. "A relief, you know?" he said. "Have someone else to look after the kid for a bit . . . We're all right in here, I suppose?"

"As safe as anyone can be," Patrice said.

"Yes." Salvani wiped his mouth. "But about getting out of here: you're not really going to put us in a balloon and stick us up the chimney, are you?"

"No." Patrice laughed, and Jacques with him. "That wasn't really the answer to the story. But you know that, of course."

"Er ..." Salvani coughed, covering up his embarrassment. "Er ... um ... sort of. So what was the answer? How do you make people invisible?"

Patrice thought for a moment, fingering his pipe. "Jacques, perhaps you could explain?"

Jacques, stocky, scrubby, leaned forward. "*Italien*, I'm a postman. Right?"

"Right." Salvani leaned forward, too, dwarfing Jacques.

Jacques opened a drawer and took out a map. "Now, the mail moves around. It comes in and goes out, of course, and it goes east—east, *Italien*, you see, to Mégève and St.-Gervais, that's twenty-one kilometers—and sometimes I go with it. You understand?"

Salvani nodded. "So?"

Jacques looked steadily at Salvani. "St.-Gervais is as far as I go. But the head postman there ... he's a friend. We do ... a little trading."

Smuggling again, Salvani thought, and almost burst out laughing. The entire district seemed to do nothing else. "Fine," he said, "trading. I'm all for it. And?"

Jacques hesitated and glanced at Patrice, who gave a quick nod, as if to say, Go ahead. "My friend in St.-Gervais can sometimes get me a pass, see. A pass to go on, out of my district. To go on a little farther. You understand?"

"I understand," Salvani said, thinking, What a racket. "A little farther to where?"

"Ah!" Jacques stabbed his finger on the map. "To another friend here. In Chamonix, seventeen kilometers farther on. And Chamonix to the Swiss border is eighteen kilometers."

"Eighteen?" Salvani slapped his hand on the table. "Jesus Maria, I could *hop* that far!" He clutched his glass, his hand trembling, the wine glowing in the candlelight. "And you can do it? Get us to this Chamonix?"

"It's possible," Jacques said in his stolid, matter-of-fact way.

"And from Chamonix to the border?"

227

"It's a valley," said Patrice. "Wild. Mont Blanc on the south, mountains on the north. A village or two, woods, rocks, a river. There's a railway line, but no rides for you, understand?"

"Rides!" Salvani brushed that possibility aside. "Monsieur," he said to Jacques. "You get me there and I'll do the rest. Yes"—exultant, tracing the route from Flumet to Chamonix on the map—forty, fifty kilometers, at most—and then his common sense butting in. "But how do we get to Chamonix?"

"That's the question." Patrice poured more wine. "Jacques?"

"We thought about it," Jacques said, as stolid and practical as Salvani himself. "*Italien*, we don't have a post-office van where we could stick you in the back—the gas shortage, you know? Sometimes a truck comes through and we put the mail on it, but that's no good for you. But—" He fished out a cigarette and lit it from the candle. "But there is a bus comes out now and then from Albertville. I go on that. With special mail."

"A bus means people," Salvani said.

"Yes." Patrice's clear voice came from the shadows. "People. But, *Italien*, you remember the story. A murderer went into a house, and came out, and no one saw him?"

"I remember. This is when you tell me how to make myself invisible, right?"

"Not I, *Italien*," Patrice said. "No, our magician here. Show him, Jacques."

"Sure." Jacques stood up. He left the room and reappeared holding something, waved his hand, said, "Abracadabra!" and Salvani's jaw dropped.

"But that's—" He frowned. "That's only a—"

"Yes." Patrice laughed. "In the story no one saw him because he was . . . ?"

"Well, I'll be damned," Salvani said.

"Saved," Patrice murmured mildly.

"And Judah?"

Jacques solemnly held up another object.

"And I'll be—saved again." Salvani shook his head. "And it will work?"

"Maybe," Patrice began but stopped as Jacques's wife came in, bearing a tray.

"Soup," she said. "The child has eaten and he's sound asleep. Eat," in a voice that meant no arguments.

"And think, *Italien*," Patrice added.

They ate in silence, Salvani methodically spooning down broth, and tearing at good bread, and thinking. Once he laid his spoon down to speak, but Patrice shook his head.

"Tomorrow," he said. "Sleep on it," as if he knew what Salvani *was* thinking.

The meal over, Jacques and his wife at his heels, Salvani fumbled his way up the stairs. Halfway up, Jacques tugged at his coattail. "Look," he whispered.

There was a narrow shuttered window, shoulder high. Jacques opened the shutter a crack and Salvani peered through.

It was as if Jacques was truly a magician. Salvani looked out onto a moonlit night: mountain and meadow, pasture and wood, all transformed, transmuted, altered unutterably by the moon's serene, unchanging light. And below Salvani, below his feet, the chasm of the Arly dropped in its sickening, slashed descent to the muttering river, and across the river was the bridge.

Jacques pointed, jabbing his finger under Salvani's arm. On the bridge, pacing slowly, yawning away at his watch, was the gendarme. Jacques grinned, a delighted, mischievous grin which on his commonplace features did indeed make him look like a wizard, and tapped his forehead in the universal gesture signifying idiocy.

Salvani grinned back but was, abruptly, shoved on by the woman, up the creaking steps to the bedroom.

Very much the mistress, the woman said, "Water by the bed, a towel, a nightshirt. No noise. You understand?"

"Understood." Salvani sucked his teeth. "Madame, monsieur." He edged cautiously into the bedroom. "After these shootings, the Ovra, after what they did . . . and I'm an Italian. What can I say. Why are you helping me?"

Candle in her hand, the woman peered around Salvani and cast a practiced eye over Judah. "It's not for you, *Italien*. It's for the infant."

Jacques winked at Salvani and, prodded by his wife, went back down the stairs. Salvani closed the door and carefully eased his burdens down. Through warped shutters, narrow shafts of moonlight picked out objects, the bed, the bowl of water, another stuffed animal, a fox, its ears pricked, one delicate paw lifted, beaded eyes glinting, bared teeth gleaming, and Judah, clean, polished almost, sleeping with a thumb in his mouth.

With slow, infinite care Salvani shrugged off his clothes, laved his face and torso, dragged on a nightshirt, long enough but bursting across his shoulders—Patrice's, he guessed—sat cautiously on a wicker chair, gazed on Judah, and listened, in the quietness, to his light, steady breathing.

Well, damn me, he thought, damn me. I thought I was defending you, child, but you were defending me. He leaned forward, massive elbows on massive knees. A mouse scuttered across the skirting board, stopped, then darted on, behind the fox.

"What do you think of that, Signora Fox?" he whispered. "I'll bet you caught lots of mice in your time, hey? But I'll bet you never got caught *by* one."

He lifted up Jacques's gifts. "Look, Signora Fox. See them? They make you invisible. Yes. A murderer walked free under the noses of a dozen people, wearing these. A real magic cloak, hey? And you know who it was? You know what that clever English writer thought of? The man no one ever sees?" He patted the fox on the nose. "Right, you poor old devil. It was a postman. And maybe we'll get through Chamonix, invisible, too. Maybe."

He turned and tucked the sheets around Judah's neck and, dragging his greatcoat over him as he lay down on the floorboards, looking at the postman's uniform, and the postman's big bag in which Judah would be spirited away with him, he yawned again, his jaws cracking like a flake of granite falling away from a cliff, and he thought, vaguely, in that last moment before sleep comes and turns the toil of the day into the phantoms of the night, as magically as the moon turns day into clear, enchanted night: Yes, maybe. He sleeping the sleep of the just, and Judah the sleep of the innocent, as the other creatures of the night crept out from their dark, filthy dens.

18

Salvani awoke with a grunt of surprise at seeing above him a ceiling instead of a sky, and grunted again at seeing a fox; moth-eaten, dusty and dingy, a very different creature from the delicate animal he had seen last in a glittering moonbeam.

He heaved himself up, looked at Judah soundly sleeping, padded to the window, and peered through a knothole in the shutter onto a small square. A woman on her knees was scrubbing a doorstep; a small dog, wagging its tail, was staring at an indifferent cat lounging on a wall; a child with a satchel, late for school perhaps, ran across the square, shouting something.

Nice, Salvani thought enviously, nice and normal, thinking of what lay ahead for himself. He dressed quickly and, boots in hand, went to the door. He gazed at the postman's uniform, borrowed, he supposed, as it looked big enough for him, then, his face somber, went cautiously down the creaking stairs and found Patrice.

"*Italien!*" Patrice waved to a chair. "Jacques is out and Madame is downstairs with a customer. Where is the child?"

"Sleeping." Salvani sat down. "But he'll stay quiet even if he wakes. He's learned to lie low."

"Aah, the lessons we learn." Patrice shook his head. "Drink? There's a sort of homemade coffee, fruit juice, wine . . ."

"Wine," Salvani said emphatically. He leaned forward, cupping his chin in his hands.

"You look serious," Patrice said.

"I am." Salvani looked around gloomily at the animals. "Last night, getting in here safely, anything would have sounded good, but now this idea, the postman's uniform . . . Chamonix, is it going to work?"

"As to that," Patrice said, "why not ask Madame? It's her plan."

Salvani turned and saw Madame, spruce, severe in the doorway, and his jaw dropped. In his own rough, decent world it was taken for granted that although women ruled the home, and if you came back on payday a little tipsy your wife might bang your ears with the frying pan, that was *all* that they did—but to do more, to plan a scheme such as this, and organize it—he looked at Madame with a new and different respect. "Well," he asked. "Will it?"

"*Italien,*" Madame looked Salvani squarely in the face. "*You* have to go. The child we could keep, but what sort of life would he have here, locked away, maybe for years, until this filthy war is over, listening to the children playing on the square . . . caged."

"No cage," Salvani said. "When I go, he goes. But . . ."

"But what?" Madame leaned forward, alert. "It's a dangerous time for you, but there's something else, hey?"

232

There was something else; and what was haunting Salvani was the knowledge that if he was caught wearing a postman's uniform instead of his own he would stop being a soldier and become a spy and then would rapidly become truly invisible, twelve rifles of a German firing squad being able to create a spell more potent than was ever conjured up by the greatest magician who had waved his wand . . . but as he looked at Madame and Patrice, and thinking of Jacques, and realizing that they, too, were risking going into the land of shades and ghosts, he decided to keep that fear to himself and merely made a vague gargling noise and muttered that there was nothing, no, well, grateful, truly . . .

"So." Madame clapped her hands together in a business-like way. "*Italien*, you may use this room. No one can see in. But the child must be silent. I'm sorry, but one neighbor with a grudge . . ."

"Understood," Salvani said, grimly. "We've got them in Italy, too."

"Good. I'll bring him down and you can eat together." Madame nodded curtly and left the room.

"You've decided, then?" Patrice asked.

"She decided me."

"An able woman," Patrice said. "And forceful."

"She sure is." Salvani picked up a fork and scored random lines on the tablecloth. "You're all taking a big chance. If I do get picked up . . . a postman's uniform, they know I've been around here, and Jacques a postman . . ."

Patrice prodded at his pipe. "We have a story for that."

"Oh?" Salvani put down the fork. "What might that be?"

"These postmen, they're all friendly, they help each other."

Salvani helped himself to more wine, thinking that he'd bet the postmen did—help each other—smuggling—and that they were probably all cousins, too.

"So?"

"So." Patrice smiled. "There's a town a few kilometers west of here, Fontaines d'Ugine. You *could* have found your way to it. The postman there, he's a big chap like you, and when you get on the bus to Chamonix, Madame will phone him and he'll go to the police and say his uniform was stolen off the line. Madame's idea, too. Clever, hey?"

"Yes," Salvani agreed, a little ruefully, his last exit blocked off. "Why are they doing it? Helping."

"It's a question," Patrice said. "Maybe they're just good. They're Catholics, devout . . . and Madame is sorry for the child. They had one of their own."

"Had?"

"Yes. A boy. You know the bridge we crossed last night. Their child walked on the parapet. He'd been told a thousand times, of course, but you know what children are . . . a dare . . . a slip . . ."

"Mother of God!" Salvani, the proud father of a whole brood, could grasp the dimensions of that disaster. "And the only child . . ." He had no words for that, none at all. "And you, why are you helping?"

Patrice stood up. "I'm going to have a drink. I don't normally at this time, but . . ." He went to the cupboard and took out a bottle of cognac and two glasses. "You?"

Salvani shook his head. "Too strong for me in the morning."

Patrice shrugged and poured himself a small drink. "I come from Paris. I had friends there, artists. I had dinner once with Picasso."

"Really?" Salvani raised his eyebrows, although for all he knew or cared, Picasso was a performing dog.

"Yes." A little of Patrice's humor glinted for a moment, as if he knew very well that Salvani had no idea what he was talking about. "But one of my friends was . . . a girl."

You were in love! Salvani thought, liking a good romance as much as a tale of bandits; and his heart warmed to Patrice. "Is she still there?" he asked as delicately as he knew how. "In Paris?"

"No," Patrice said. "She's not in Paris. You know they call Paris *la ville de lumière*? The City of Light?"

234

"No," Salvani said. "I didn't know that."

"Well." Patrice put his finger on the fork marks Salvani had made on the tablecloth. "There is a suburb of Paris called Drancy. There's a big stadium there, and a mainline railway station. And the Germans and the police rounded up all the Jews—did I say my friend was a Jew? No? Well, she was, and she was taken to Drancy, too, and all her family, and put in the stadium with all the other Jews and—"

"Patrice." Salvani moved uneasily in his chair. "You don't have to go through this—" not knowing what was coming but fearing it just the same.

"I'll tell you." Patrice's voice was thick. "They took them to the stadium and then—" He ran his finger along the fork marks. "Then they put them on a train."

Salvani moved again, restless, anxious. "A train where?"

Patrice hesitated, then slipped his hand into his pocket and took out a slip of paper. "A man gave me this. A railway man. He could have been shot for that. It's a secret. A German state secret. See." He spread the paper open, and Salvani craned forward and read.

27th March		
Bourget-Drancy	Dep.	17.00
Compiègne	Arr.	18.40
	Dep.	19.40
Laon	Arr.	21.05
	Dep.	21.23
Reims	Arr.	22.25
28th March	Dep.	9.10
Neuberg (frontier)	Arr.	13.59
30th March		
Auschwitz (terminus)	Arr.	5.33

"Your friends went on that train?" Salvani asked.

"Yes."

Salvani squinted down. "Where's Auschwitz?"

235

"Poland," Patrice said.

"Poland . . ." Salvani rubbed his chin. "That's a long journey."

"The longest on earth." Patrice stood up suddenly, and put the paper away, and bustled about the room collecting his painting equipment. "Because no one ever returns. No one. Do you understand that?"

"No," Salvani said. "I don't. Why is that?"

"Because"—Patrice had his back to Salvani—"because they're killed. The Germans, they're killing the Jews. All. But I have to go and paint."

"Paint?" Salvani was aghast at the thought.

"The routine, *Italien*, remember?" Salvani had a glimpse of a tortured face as Patrice made for the door. "You asked me why *I* am helping. Now you know."

The morning ticked away. Judah was read to by Madame from children's books bought, Salvani guessed, for the dead child. Jacques returned from his morning round, staggering Judah, and Salvani too, with more magic, and Patrice returned, serious-faced, and after lunch, and after Judah, without a word of protest, had been whisked away for a nap by Madame, telling Salvani that the motorbike had gone.

Salvani flushed. "I thought that you'd hidden it."

"I did," Patrice said. "But there was an oil slick on the road. The bike must have been leaking. One of the police spotted it. I saw them up there. Still"—he looked over his pipe, his eyes shrewd—"it solves your problem, *Italien*, hey? No dash through the night on the bike. Now they're looking for a man and child on foot, roaming around. Not for a postman on a bus. And"—he glanced again at Salvani—"the weather is changing. Not good for the two of you to be walking to La Clusaz."

"But"—Salvani made a last grab for his own choice, a last snatch at his hope that he need not change uniforms—"it will be bad weather in Chamonix, too, won't it?"

"It certainly will be," Patrice agreed, "but you'll only have to walk eighteen kilometers, and it will be mist, rain, good for hiding—good for you. And remember, *Italien*, they won't be looking for you there."

A clinching argument, and Salvani, in a brooding way, accepted it, still brooding, though, as Jacques and Patrice, apologizing, went to the café across the square, saying that they went there every day, himself longing to stretch out his legs in a bar and share in cheerful banter over a glass of wine and a game of cards, and brooding still as Madame reappeared, a skein of wool in her capable hands, and sat by the window, her knitting needles flickering and clicking, and as Salvani wondered how she could sit so composed by the abyss which had engulfed her child, she, stiff in black and starched in white, said to him, who was more used to being told by women *not* to, "Drink, *Italien*. Have some brandy." A finger, as dextrous as any magician's, gathered up a strand of wool and slipped it over a needle. "You've had a hard time."

Yes and more to come, Salvani thought.

Madame nodded, clicking away. "*Italien*," she said, "you have a family?"

A family! Salvani launched into a description of his wife and children, paragons of beauty and virtue, proudly showing his smudged, precious photograph.

"You miss them?" Madame admired the snapshot.

"Miss them!" Salvani struck his broad chest. "Madame," he said, melodramatically but with perfect truth, "there is a hole here, an aching hole."

"Yes." Madame, herself with an aching heart which would never be healed, bowed her head. "And now you're going to Switzerland."

Salvani stared into his glass, one which seemed to encompass all time and all space, and, not a man given to introspection, nonetheless wondering what had brought them together: Patrice, masking his tragedy with irony; Jacques, his stubby fingers belying his conjuror's skills; Madame, her stiff rectitude belying her cleverness—all of them carrying their own burdens without complaint and reaching out helping hands; and Judah, maddening and adorable, and himself, a rough, barging fellow . . . Well, he thought vaguely, drinking more brandy, it was the war; it was madmen obsessed with power, lunatics drawing on vast maps, their hands smearing away borders and frontiers, and men and women and children . . . "It's the way the cards fall," he said. "That's all there is to it." Not having more to say, and not having to, as a clatter on the stairs told of the return of Patrice and Jacques.

Judah was brought down again, demanding magic, pop-eyed as it was produced, asking for a shadow show and, much to Salvani's amusement, showing scorn at Jacques's attempt to do a rabbit, proclaiming, to Jacques's irritation, that Bruno could do a whole Noah's Ark, the afternoon fading as other shadows gathered and mist uncoiled from the gorge, a little bell tingling now and then and Madame bustling down the stairs to deal with a customer, the rattle of bolts as the shop was closed and its doors locked, soup, Judah demanding to be made invisible and having that request granted as Madame swept him, with much agonized rollings of his eyes, to bed.

"He can sleep with me, tonight," Madame said, closing the door.

"He's a lad and a half," Salvani said.

"Yes," Jacques agreed with more than a note of wistfulness. "Have some more—" stopping as Salvani jumped. "Only rain," he said. "Rain on the windows."

"Sorry." Salvani grinned diffidently. "A bit on edge, you know?" He took some wine from Jacques. "This weather—does it mean snow, in Chamonix?"

"No," Jacques said. "On the mountains, of course, but not the way you're going. Rain, yes, snow flurries maybe, but nothing you can't cope with."

Salvani dipped his bread into his wine. "I was asking for the child's sake."

"Sure." Jacques shrugged. "It's all for the child. Er, *Italien*—" He tapped on the table and the rain tapped on the window, as if there was someone, or thing, wanting to be let in.

"Yes?" Salvani said.

Jacques gestured to Patrice, the wave of his hand chasing shadows across the room, giving the animals a momentary, disconcerting life.

Patrice took up Jacques's silent invitation. "The bus—when it comes—you can't tell how long it takes to get to Chamonix. It could be a couple of hours, it could be five. There's no timetable. You understand."

"I understand," Salvani said. "So?"

"So . . ." Patrice paused, picking his words. "So we've been thinking, in the sack, it could be hard for the child."

"He's been through worse," Salvani said, an edge to his voice. "I've thought about that, too. If he was an ordinary kid I wouldn't even try it, but Judah, he's been taught in a hard school."

"Yes." Patrice held up his hand. "But one wriggle, one cry . . . and who knows who might be on the bus . . ."

Salvani jutted his chin forward. "Are you backing out?"

Patrice lowered his hand. "It's just that we have an idea. To make us all safer."

"All?" Salvani frowned.

"Yes, all." Madame appeared, her corsets creaking slightly as she sat next to her husband. "Not us here, we know what we're doing. But there are others helping. So—" She seemed uncharacteristically indecisive. "We're thinking that when you go we should give the child a sleeping draught."

It took a moment for that to sink in, but when it did Salvani flushed a deeper red than the wine. "Drug him? Stick drugs into him?"

"It's not what it sounds like," said Patrice.

"No?" Salvani glowered across the table. It wasn't that he was unfamiliar with drugging children. Italy had been awash with *soothing* medicines which mothers cheerfully poured by the gallon into children with toothache or earache or who simply wouldn't go to sleep. But the truth was that although he still had no real idea of what would happen to Judah if he fell into the hands of the Germans, he had a profound intuition that outside the shelter of his own strong arms there was a nightmarish darkness where monsters posing as men lurked, waiting to do unspeakable things to those who wandered, or were lured, into that darkness—and into oblivion: and drugging Judah, that lively, patient, enduring, clever, funny, and endlessly maddening child, came close to shoving him into that darkness, if only for a few hours and for his own good. "I don't like it," he said. "It's . . ." He scraped his fingers across his forehead. "It's like . . ."

"I know," Patrice said. "But you'd give the child an anesthetic before an operation, wouldn't you?"

"Yes." Some of the rage in Salvani ebbed away.

"And you've carried him when he's been asleep?"

"Too true." Salvani grinned ruefully. "Over bloody great mountains—excuse me for swearing, Madame."

"I've heard worse." Madame, stiff in her black dress, corsets, rectitude, and sorrow looked Salvani full in the face. "We'll leave it for you to decide. But remember us, and the others."

"I'll do that." Salvani met Madame's eyes. "But if we are caught I won't talk—what?" Swinging around as Patrice made a muffled exclamation. "You think I would?"

"Italien." Patrice sighed. "The Germans are here now, the Gestapo, and the Milice. I've seen them at work. You'd talk—don't take this personally," as Salvani scowled. "If you were in a cell with the child and a man came in with a blowtorch—"

"I don't believe that," Salvani said. "I just don't believe that could happen."

240

"That's the problem." Patrice shook his head. "None of us did. Well—" He drained his glass. "Think about it, that's all we ask."

"All right," Salvani said. "I'll think about it."

"Think hard." Jacques, solid and stubby in his suspenders and vest, stood up. "Bedtime."

"Bed?" Salvani raised his eyebrows.

"Yes," Jacques said. "We're getting up very early."

"Because?"

"We're moving you!"

"So another person will know about us." Salvani was beginning to think that, far from their journey to Chamonix being a secret, the whole of Savoie knew about it.

"Yes." Jacques stuck his thumbs in his suspenders and smiled. "But he won't tell. He's good at keeping secrets."

"If you say so." Salvani stood up, too. "But—" A thought struck him. "If you're moving us, it means . . ."

"Yes," Jacques said. "The bus is coming. Tomorrow, from Albertville."

Salvani crept up to his room and sat on the chair. There were vague scuffling sounds from the walls, rodents, he supposed, remote knockings and crackings, creaks and groans, as the house settled down for the night.

The rain pattered on the windows, by the door the postman's uniform swayed in a draft, looking horribly like a hanged man. Salvani shuddered and dropped it into a corner. Then, for a moment, he peered through the crack in the shutter.

The square was running with water. Beyond it the roofs of the houses shone in the rain, but beyond them was nothing but swirling mist and darkness. Salvani muttered a curse before going to bed and sleep taking him, in the end, as the rain fell.

The rain fell steadily: on the plunging waters of the Atlantic, on the islands where free people lived, sleeping without fear of a knock on the door; on the darkness of Europe,

241

where all Law ended; on Paris, that City of Light, where a train, its boiler sizzling, was being shunted, ready to take another thousand human beings to their deaths; sweeping south, drenching quiet fields and woods and villages, and falling on the ulcers of Nazi Germany's rotting empire, on the prison fortress of Lyons, where Major Barbie of the SS was feeding his ferocious dog tidbits and wondering whether to torture a young woman suspect before or after dinner, and on Chambéry, where two moral defectives, imbeciles, as alert and poisonous as scorpions, were facing each other across a table, one of them, paunchy, pasty-faced, wearing a new ring, sipping coffee, a gift from his Gestapo masters, and berating the other man.

"Now, now," he was saying. "Don't look so sour, Palet. I know that you're upset about being brought back from La Chambre, but really . . . one Italian and a Jew kid!"

"I could have got them." Palet squirmed in his chair. "A couple of days more—one! It wasn't much to ask."

"Not to you." The superintendent raised a finger. "But suppose everyone was to ask for one more day to chase hares! Think! There would be thousands of days gone. In fact, all over Europe, millions! We're an *organization*, a big one—" He stood up and patted his stomach with both hands as if to demonstrate what bigness was. "But the bigger the organization, the more care we have to take over details. Think of it this way. We're a huge *machine* and you're just a tiny cog in it. But if even the tiniest cog doesn't work properly the whole machine can go wrong. Do you take my point?"

Palet dragged his sleeve across his mouth. "A tiny cog?"

The superintendent tutted. "Why do you take things so personally? *I'm* a cog, admittedly an important one, but we're all part of the great machine! And let me give you some advice. If you want to become a bigger cog you need to alter your attitude. Learn some manners, the social graces, try and be more . . . more cultured. You met Herr

242

Kellner in La Chambre. Now, there is a truly cultured man, one you can learn from. In fact, we can all learn from them, the Germans; so cultured, polite, and *efficient*. In the Riviera—Nice, Cannes, Monte Carlo—they had a rat hunt there last week, nothing like it ever! Not a Jew left, you can guarantee it. Wonderful—but that's not why you're here."

"Oh?" Palet wiped his mouth again. "Why am I here?"

"Why don't you get a handkerchief," the superintendent said. "It's what I'm talking about—culture! It's not as if you can't have anything you want. But . . . yes." He smirked. "I'm moving you."

Palet raised his handsome face. "Annecy? That was crawling with Jews when the Italians were there. There'll be lots of them hanging around in the villages."

"Palet—" The superintendent raised a plump hand, admiring as he did so his new ring, late the engagement ring of Hannah Dolloz, eighteen, at that moment drenched in the sports stadium of Drancy, waiting for the next train to Auschwitz and the gas chamber. "Palet, don't make suggestions. It's already decided where you're going."

"All right," Palet said. "Where is it?"

"There." The superintendent shoved a file across the table with his riding crop and looked at Palet through sly, malicious eyes.

Palet opened the file. "There!" he spat the word out. "That dump!"

"It's not a dump at all," the superintendent said. "It's an important town. Small, yes, but important. But"—he rapped the table with his whip—"I can send you somewhere else—if you wish."

There was no need for him to spell out the hidden meaning behind those words and Palet knew it. At best it could mean some filthy hole on the Spanish frontier where there were no Jews to catch, and not even any money to be made from smuggling since the Spaniards had nothing to offer and no money to buy—and at worst, the blood-splattered cells of the New Order were open to all.

"All right." Palet clawed at the file as if he was strangling a kitten. "When do I go?"

"Go when you like—as long as you're there by tomorrow." Tittering at his little joke, the superintendent waved Palet out into the night.

Palet slouched to his room and sat in his habitual hunched posture on the edge of his bed, drinking his raw brandy. He wasn't in fact displeased with his assignment. Where he was going, as long as there was no Gestapo officer like Kellner to throw his weight around, he would have virtually a free hand—lots of pickings, human and cash—and although he still felt a baulked savage bitterness at the thought of the Italian and the Jew slipping through his fingers, there were bound to be others . . .

He swallowed his drink, went to the door, and bellowed for one of his uniformed men downstairs.

"Boss?" A hulking half-drunken brute appeared.

"We're leaving tomorrow." Palet handed over a travel warrant. "Get a car. Pick me up at ten."

"Sure, boss." The Milice peered at the warrant through groggy eyes. "Should I get gas?"

"Of course you get gas, you half-wit. You think that we're going to push the car? Get plenty, too."

"I'll do that." The Milice stuffed the warrant in his pocket. "Er, boss, where are we going?"

Palet bared his teeth in what might have been a venomous grin or a snarl. "Albertville," he said, sitting drinking and sweating as the evening darkness deepened, the mist swirled, the rain slashed at the window, and snow drifted onto the huge implacable mountains.

19

J acques woke Salvani. "Time, *Italien*," he said, a candle in
his hand.

"Right." Not feeling right at all, Salvani heaved himself
onto the edge of the bed, rubbing his face, as Jacques
put the candle down and left the room, pointing at the
postman's uniform.

Salvani stood up, paced forward, and put his hand on
the uniform—a bit frayed and shabby, very like his own,
in fact. Uniforms, he thought, not much difference in any
of them; put them on and you become something else, a
number, that was all, a number in a huge mob; and if you
wore green, like his own, you went off to kill other men in
gray, and they went off to kill men in khaki, and if you
dressed men in sky-blue and pink they'd go off and kill
men dressed in purple and orange. But this . . . once he
put that on, he wouldn't even be a number. Patrice hadn't
known the half of it when he said wearing it would make
him invisible; he would become, literally, a nobody, a non-
person, a nothing. No Geneva Convention for him, no Red
Cross to look after him—only a firing squad waiting for
him, if he got that far and some fanatical Nazi didn't shoot
him out of hand—thinking those thoughts but, even as he
thought them, knowing that he was crossing a true divide,
more than leaving Bourg-St.-Maurice, and more than
crossing the real watershed outside Beaufort, as if a force
greater than himself was moving his arms and legs, putting
the uniform on, even tugging the tunic down to make it fit
properly. "Right," he muttered. "Vito Salvani, postman.

Vito Salvani, first-class mug. Vito Salvani, the biggest idiot in the entire world." Collecting his own clothes and rifle and going down the stairs.

Patrice and Jacques were there, sitting at the table, and Madame, a drowsy Judah in her arms.

"Ah!" Patrice, an artist to the last, raised his hands. "A postman to the life," as Jacques matter-of-factly said, "Shave," and Madame, "Eat."

Salvani scraped his chin with a savage-looking cutthroat razor, ate, wolfing down ham, eggs, cheese, bread; with a soldier's eye to the future, stuffing himself while the food was available, as Madame coaxed Judah into taking a kind of gruel.

"And now?" Salvani put down his knife and fork.

"Now we go." Jacques picked up a leather satchel. "Real mail," he said. "For Mégève and St.-Gervais, food and drink, a map of the Vale of Chamonix. And—" He gave an almost imperceptible nod to Madame, who scooped Judah in her capable arms and took him from the room, saying firmly, "Wash."

"And?" Salvani asked.

"And this." Jacques reached under the table and produced a sack marked, in formidably official lettering, *Poste Française*. In the service of the government. Only to be opened by an authorized servant of the state. "Patrice did the lettering," Jacques said. "They don't really mean anything, but the Germans—Patrice says that they can be very correct."

"With papers." Patrice was sharp. "Not human beings."

"*You* know," Jacques said. "Before you get on the bus I'll clip the sack with a seal. That doesn't mean anything either, but it all helps."

"Yes," Salvani said, thinking that he was going to need all the help he could possibly get.

"And there is this." Jacques handed over a card. "It's a pass. A copy of an old one of mine. If you're challenged along the way, just wave it. Don't let anyone look at it too closely, hey?"

"It looks good." Salvani brooded over the card.

"Patrice did that, too," Jacques said. "Last night."

"You did?" Salvani looked at Patrice with admiration.

"Nothing." Patrice dismissed the compliment, although sounding pleased, and adding, with a touch of his dry humor, "Art has its uses sometimes."

"Yes, sure." Salvani had turned his attention back to the sack. "The child will be able to breathe? I mean, maybe all day in there . . ."

"He'll breathe," Jacques said. "Madame has poked lots of holes down the seams. Anyway, it's been tested. The peasants carry live animals in them, piglets and hens—especially on All Souls when they go and see relatives for a meal."

"All Souls." Salvani was reflective. "That's the Feast of the Dead."

"Remembrance." Jacques stood up brusquely. "Time to go. Put your uniform in here—" He put the sack on the table. "There's room for that and the child."

Salvani folded his uniform and packed it away as Madame came back with Judah, looking proud of himself in a smart raincoat, hat, and rubber boots.

"They belonged to—" Madame looked down. "Better that they're used."

"Sure." Salvani was awkward to the point of being mute, but stammered out a few gruff words, until Jacques cut him off.

"Here." He handed Salvani a postman's greatcoat and shrugged his own on. "We go now—ah! But not with that!" as he saw Salvani, from force of habit, pick up his rifle.

"Leave it." Patrice took the rifle. "I've a feeling it might come in useful."

"Maybe." Salvani stuck out his hand and took Patrice's. "Thanks. You know?"

"I know." Patrice clapped Salvani on the shoulder and bent and patted Judah on his smart new hat.

"And thank you, Madame." Salvani held out his hand again but instead of taking it Madame pressed a bottle into it. "For the little one," she said. "It's up to you. Now go." Pushing him as Jacques opened the door and led the way out.

It was dark, and still raining. Not a night for sentries to be guarding bridges, or anything else, Salvani thought, as, holding Judah by the hand, he followed Jacques along the little catwalk, down a few precarious steps, and into a narrow alley. There Jacques stopped.

"*Italien,*" he muttered, "we have to go along the street, not far, but *walk* quietly. And the child, he has to keep quiet. *Absolutely.* Understand?"

Salvani patted Jacques on the shoulder, turned, and picked up Judah. "Silence," he whispered and placed his finger on Judah's lips and felt a cold, tiny finger placed on his own.

They edged out onto the street, narrow, steep, heavy-gabled buildings crowding in; past a baker's, a blank, shuttered house, a butcher's, a café, nothing moving but themselves and the rain, spattering against their faces, and then Jacques pulled Salvani into another slot of an alley and put his mouth close to Salvani's ear.

"There. See the building?"

Salvani saw it, a gray bulk looming through the spinning raindrops.

"Go up the steps. The door is open and there's someone waiting for you inside." Jacques tucked the sack under Salvani's arm. "I'll see you before the bus comes. Now go."

Go! Salvani stared at the building. Ahead of him the street widened—not much, but through his eyes the space looked as vast and as bare as a prairie. For a moment he hesitated, but a dog, sounding as if it was the original hound from hell, began barking. Jacques nudged him, so he went, his back itching and his scalp crawling, crossing

248

the street in long strides, expecting a harsh challenge, the crack of a pistol, striding, striding again, his face wet with rain and sweat, up the steps, shoving open a huge door, heaving his way inside and feeling a cool, strong hand gripping his wrist, guiding him down an aisle to where, over a vast carved wooden altar, a red Mass lamp swayed in some fugitive-draft, and hearing a firm voice say, "Sanctuary."

"You're a priest!" Salvani said.

"And a motorcyclist." The priest laughed. "But this way."

He led Salvani and Judah around the altar into a small room, windowless, a table, two battered easy chairs, a candle glowing in a corner.

"You'll be safe here, and comfortable." The priest waved at the chairs. "The room's virtually soundproof."

"It's good of you." Salvani lowered Judah.

"Nothing." The priest, tall and looking taller in his black cassock, a hard, grooved face, dismissed the thanks. "You wait here until the bus comes. It stops just outside. But I want to talk to you. Will the child be all right in here for a little while?"

"Sure." Salvani took off Judah's coat and hat. "You'll be fine, won't you?"

Round-eyed, Judah stared at the priest, then tugged Salvani to him. Salvani listened, then stood upright. "Of course, you can speak now. What do you want to say?"

Judah turned his head to the priest. "I've got a new coat," he said, "and a new hat and shoes!"

"And very nice they are, too," the priest said. "Where did you get them from?"

Salvani raised his hand to stop Judah answering, but Judah was more than a step ahead of him.

"Found them," he said. "In a shed. On the mountain."

"You were on the mountains?" the priest asked.

"Yes." Judah was clearly refreshed by rest, food, care, a hot bath. "A wolf came! And a bear! A big one."

"And what did you do?"

Judah slid off the chair. "I shouted at them! I shouted, *Ayin hara, ayin hara*. And they ran away."

"*Ayin hara?*" The priest frowned. "What does that mean?"

Judah stared incredulously at the priest. "Don't you know that? It means Go away, go away, evil spirits. You say it and they go away, the evil spirits. I've been saying it for days and days!"

"You have?" Salvani was astonished. "I didn't hear you."

"No!" Judah stamped his foot. "I was saying it in here—" He tapped his head. "All the time. That's why the bad men didn't catch us. Because I was saying *Ayin hara*."

The priest nodded and, somber-faced, ruffled Judah's hair. "It's a good saying. Keep on saying it. But—" He turned to Salvani. "That word?"

"Right." Salvani nodded. "Just sit here, Judah. I'm only next door."

He raised his finger to his lips, then joined the priest in the church, the two of them sitting in a pew before the vast altar.

The priest seemed to be in no particular hurry to have his word. He sat, long legs outstretched ending in a pair of hefty boots, whistling almost soundlessly.

"Er." Salvani coughed, the sound echoing in the darkness above. "You wanted to speak to me . . . ?"

The priest shook his grim, carved head. "I thought that you might want to talk to me."

"Me?" Salvani tugged at his collar. "What about?"

The priest turned around, an arm over the back of the pew. "You're Italian, yes? And a Catholic?"

"Ah." Knowing what was coming, Salvani shifted his bulk. "Well, sort of."

"Hmm." The priest turned his head away, staring at the altar and the dim red lamp. "I thought that you might want to confess."

"Confess." Salvani moved again. "You know, Father . . ."

"You've a perilous journey ahead of you," the priest said.

You can say that again, Salvani thought, and I've got a perilous journey behind me, too. "Look . . . all this." He gestured at the altar. "I mean, it's all right, but you're in the army—you knock about, do wrong things, and I'm sorry for them. I am . . . but I can't go through the whole business, confessing, anymore. And I'm sorry about that, too. No offense."

"But you are sorry for your sins."

"Yes, I am," Salvani said.

"That will do."

"It will?" Salvani knew more than enough about his Church to be disbelieving.

"Well." The priest gave an unexpected smile. "Maybe not officially, but I'm not going to press you on the words. Just be truly sorry and try not to commit any more sins."

"I'll do that. Promise," Salvani said. "But, Father, I want to ask you something."

"Yes?"

"I'm doing the right thing, aren't I?" Salvani wiped his mouth on the sleeve of his tunic. "Taking the child."

The priest took his time answering, clicking the toes of his boots together. "Yes," he said, finally. "When Jacques first came to me I wasn't so sure. We could hide the child and maybe find another way of getting him across the border—no"—raising his finger—"I don't know how. It's all new to us, this . . . this *evil*. But with your child . . . there's something strange going on. This tight patrolling . . . Is there something special about him, do you know?"

Salvani shook his head. "Not that I know of. Just another kid. His father was a nice fellow. That's all."

"Well, take him. You've a good chance. With any luck, you'll be over the border before midnight."

The priest made to stand up, but Salvani took his arm. "I've another question." He pulled out the bottle.

"I know about that," the priest said. "I'm just a country

251

clergyman. Normally I might ask my bishop about a thing like that, doping a healthy child. But times aren't normal, are they? No, I think that it's right to do it to save a life. We've two paintings here—" He looked up and Salvani followed his gaze.

A gray light was slowly filtering in through windows high in the wall, and Salvani could make out, vaguely, two enormous paintings, on either side of the altar.

"They're appropriate to you," the priest said. "I've been thinking about them ever since Jacques told me about you and the child. The one on the left"—he pointed a long finger—"that's the Flight into Egypt. When Jesus was born, King Herod thought that he would grow up to be a worldly king and take his throne, so he tried to find him and kill him. Joseph and Mary fled with the baby. That's what the picture is, the Flight into Egypt."

Salvani moved his arms and legs uncomfortably, profoundly embarrassed by the mere thought that he might be compared to the parents of Christ. "What's the other one?" he asked, anxious to shift the emphasis from himself.

"That?" The priest turned his eagle head. "When Herod couldn't find Jesus, he killed all the children of Israel under the age of two. He thought that way he could make sure that Christ would be killed. But you know this, yes? Of course. All the babies killed in order that not one should escape. It's called the Massacre of the Innocents." The priest stood up and stretched shoulders not much less broad than Salvani's. "Patrice, the painter? He's going to clean the pictures for me. He says that there is a new massacre of the innocents taking place. I don't know that I believe him. The Church authorities have said nothing. But Patrice, he's a man you can believe. Anyway, give the child the sleeping draught. You can do it with a good conscience."

"Right." Salvani stood up, and stretched, too.

"You're a hefty man," the priest said.

"You're not so small yourself." Salvani nodded an acknowledgment.

"So, so. I thought of sending you to Chamonix as a priest. A clergyman and a child—but—" The priest smiled, his fierce face transformed. "You could have been pestered for blessings, advice . . . so best a postman. Be surly, a man with a grievance. Doing a job you don't want to do. Now go and sit with the . . . innocent."

The sickly dawn, a pallid light, filtered through lowering cloud and rain, struggled across a sodden Europe, a dawn not bringing the cheerful hope of a new day but the hopeless vacuity of despair to millions, and terror to millions more, although others woke with relish at the prospect of the new day's tasks: the rulers of the extermination camps of Poland, the members of the death squads who roamed Russia looking for Jews to kill, other murderers and torturers, and Palet.

Palet rarely slept properly, and never peacefully, more like an animal, twitching at every noise, waking at intervals from nightmares, twitching and sweating.

But during his wakefulness he had thought of his assignment to Albertville and the more he had thought of it the more pleasant it had become. A small town but an important one in its way; sure to be some Jews waiting to be winkled out, plenty of opportunities for blackmail, too— he knew those small towns, didn't he just, and, above all, it would be a place where he could exercise his very own form of terror in which a stare across an expensive restaurant could be as satisfying as a session in a police cell.

He swung up from the bed and opened the shutters on the window. A creeping pallor in the sky and spattering rain. He shouted downstairs for coffee, not washing or shaving. The coffee came as he was dressing himself in the clothes he had worn the previous day, and the day before that.

He finished dressing, sucked down some coffee, stuck his pistol in his holster, and picked up the file on Albertville, an occasional wolfish grin of satisfaction flashing across his bitter, handsome face as he read some juicy tidbit of slanderous gossip—all valuable, priceless in fact, since the lives of men and women could depend on what use he made of them.

He finished the file, drank his coffee, unlocked his door, threw the rest of his clothes into a suitcase, then wandered back to the window. Under the scribbled sky a few people were moving on the streets: workmen, shoppers, a policeman or two, a German patrol, an old, bent woman hobbling with painful slowness into a church.

Palet took out his pistol and pointed it at the woman, grinning as he peered down the gun sights. There was a bang on the door and a hoarse voice called, "Boss?"

"Come in." Palet swung around and as the door opened he shoved his gun forward. "You're dead!" he growled.

"Jesus!" The man in the doorway started back. "Gave me a shock there."

Palet holstered his pistol. "We'll give some real shocks where we're going. Got transport?"

"Yes, a car. A big Renault. They want it back, though."

"Doesn't matter. We'll get a better one in Albertville." Palet slung an English-made white raincoat around his shoulders and put on his hat. "Bring my bag."

The car was waiting outside the hotel, a police driver at the wheel, a Milice sitting by him who jumped out hurriedly when Palet appeared, stubbing out a cigarette.

"Get in," Palet snarled, climbing into the back with the other Milice. He wound down the window, spat throatily onto the pavement, wound the window back, and lit a cigarette. "Get going," he said.

The big car hissed through the rain. None of the men spoke. Once Palet saw the driver looking at him through the rearview mirror. He stared back and the man dropped his eyes. At a road junction they were stopped by a German checkpoint. A hulking *Feldgendarme* glanced at Palet's pass, saluted, and waved them on, politely wishing them a good day. Palet grunted but his eyes were on the road to his right. A road which he had taken before and which led to La Chambre. He twisted his lips, the loss of the Italian and the Jew kid still rankling and festering, and with a rare insight, he realized that it would rankle the rest of his life, like an incurable ulcer.

An hour later they reached Albertville. The driver pulled up outside a building, large for the size of the town itself. "This is it," he said.

Palet slid from the car and pulled open the driver's door. "Who were you staring at?" he said.

"Staring?"

"In the mirror."

"I was looking at the road behind us." The driver sounded confident to the point of indifference, but beads of sweat were showing on his hairline.

"Yes?" Palet pushed his face forward. "Well, stare at me again and you won't be driving a car any longer. You might find yourself taking a walk with me in the woods."

"Sorry." The driver licked his lips.

"—— your sorries." Palet slammed the door, and the oozing ulcer stanched for a while, his Milice at his heels like two dogs, he swaggered into the police station.

A conscientious sergeant, too hardened by life to be intimidated by anyone, took Palet's announcement that he had arrived without surprise, wrote down his name and time of arrival, shuffled from the office, and returned with a beefy inspector of police.

"Ah, Palet!" The inspector shook hands without noticeable warmth. "I knew you were coming, although, to be frank, I don't know why."

"That *is* why." Palet withdrew his damp hand and wiped it, openly, on his coat.

"Excuse me?" The inspector frowned.

"Because you don't know why. We're specialists, see?"

"Er, yes." The inspector glanced at the sergeant, whose face remained as expressionless as the door of a cell. "Well, you'll find me willing to cooperate. I've booked accommodation for you and your men in a hotel—"

"What sort of hotel?" Palet asked.

"Oh, a good one, believe me. Excellent. I can recommend it—" The inspector, a man of weight and authority in his own right, was beginning to sound, and to feel, like a tourist tout; but there was something about Palet, his awkward crooked stance, the flatness of his voice, his deadlooking eyes, even his grimy silk shirt spotted with food stains and specks of blood, which made him deeply uneasy, as if—understanding more than he knew—the criminals had taken power.

"Ah, yes." He stood upright, puffing out his chest a little. "Anyway, it is a good hotel. German officers are staying there. And I have an office for you downstairs—"

"—— that," Palet said. "Not downstairs. Find somewhere better *upstairs*. And let's see this hotel, have a drink."

"Yes, yes, of course." The inspector swiveled. "Sergeant, find Monsieur Palet another office."

The sergeant dropped his pen and said, in a voice as flat as Palet's, "There aren't any more offices vacant."

"Then *move* someone!" The inspector turned back and with a smile as false as a dentist's said, "Your hotel. Of course. Now. And a drink? Yes . . . why not . . . My umbrella?" He snapped his fingers. "Well, ha ha, it doesn't matter, only a few meters, and what's a little rain"—jabbering in an unreasonable near panic as he ushered Palet and his men into the street, pretty even in the rain with flower boxes, even with a German armored car parked by a sign saying Mairie, and into a handsome hotel with skiing mementos on its walls, ordering drinks and, still jabbering, saying, "Yes, I'm sure that we'll all get on well together. You doing your job and I mine . . ."

256

But Palet wasn't listening. "What's that?" he demanded, staring through the window.

"That?" The inspector joined him, craning his neck. "Oh,"—surprised. "It's a bus."

"I can see that," Palet said in his grating voice. "What's it doing?"

The inspector peered again at the bus, a ramshackle vehicle which looked as if it had been built before the First World War, and probably had been. "It's going on a run," he said. "Occasionally they get one going."

Palet stared through the window as if even the movement of a vehicle unauthorized by him was an insult. A few people were climbing onto the bus carrying packages and parcels, nodded on by a gendarme.

"They're all checked," the inspector said. "The passengers. They all need passes. You know"—he shrugged—"people do have to travel, even in these days. Sick relatives, elderly parents . . ."

"Where do they get the gas?" Palet said.

"Ah!" The inspector nodded. "Good question. That's an official bus. It carries the mail. Bulky items and so on. So it does get a ration of gas now and again—when there's any to spare, that is. You know, Monsieur Palet, the affairs of the state must be continued, just like us, the police, we have to carry on—"

But Palet, turning away to his drink, had lost interest, although for reference, as it were, he asked, over his glass, "Where's it going to, that bus?"

"That?" The inspector looked at the ceiling, concentrating. "I think I can tell you that. Yes, I'm certain. It's going to Chamonix. But if you want the details I can send someone to check."

"No." Palet gulped some brandy. "Leave it. I'm not going there, to Chamonix."

In another part of the town, by the railway station, in a seedy café, the bus driver with a three days' growth of whiskers on his chin was eating rabbit stew and looking up as a big postman stood over him.

"Just wondering what time you were going," the postman said.

The driver belched. "Why? You want to come?"

"No." The man shook his head. "Just in case anyone comes into the office with mail. You know what they're like, the word gets around that there's a bus going and they all decide to send something."

The driver belched again. "About an hour, say two o'clock, two-thirty at the latest. Got to be in Chamonix before dark. That's if the —— bus makes it." He speared a lump of rabbit, chewed it noisily, and spat out a piece of gristle. "But"—he looked up through calculating, covetous eyes and rubbed his fingers together—"if you've anything you want taking."

"Ah." The postman gave a rueful grin. "Not this trip, but"—he sat down, looked over his shoulder, and said in a confidential voice—"there might be a little something on the return trip, eh?" He leaned forward closer. "It will be worth your while. Right, got to go. Have a drink on me."

He left the café, walked through the rain to the post office, and picked up the phone. "State business," he said. "Poste française. Yes, Flumet."

20

In Flumet, Madame put down the phone, put on a black hat and coat, picked up a basket, left the house of the magician, and walked to the church.

The priest was there, reading a breviary. He raised his harsh head, then returned to his devotions as Madame walked down the aisle and into the small room behind the altar.

"Madame!" Salvani, growling on all fours, backing away from a dominant Judah, tried to turn his growl into a cough, and shoved himself to his feet.

"I should have knocked," Madame said, dryly.

"Just a game we were playing, wolves and bears . . ." Salvani looked more sheepish than wolfish. "Judah has some magic words. Say them."

Judah, treacherous, was already holding Madame's hand. "*Ayin hara,*" he said, adding, helpfully, that it was to drive away evil spirits. "Are we going back now? I want to do magic with Jacques."

"Not just now," Madame said. "We're going to have some food, see?" She opened the basket. "You, too, *Italien.*"

"Now." Madame wiped Judah's nose. "Sit there for a moment while we talk." Somewhat like a magician herself, she produced another item from her bag, a children's picture book.

"Look at this," she said. "I'll read it to you in a minute. It's a good book and there are wolves in it."

She tapped Salvani on the elbow and they moved into a corner. "The bus," she said. "It's coming, from Albertville."

"It is?" For all his stubborn courage, Salvani's heart sank a little. He wanted, really, for the bus not to come ever, so that he could go back to the magician's house, drink, chat, play cards—although not against Jacques—and while Madame took care of Judah, to sleep, and to wake up to find the war over. "What time?" he asked hoarsely.

Madame shrugged. "Ninety minutes, two hours. But it is coming. So we have to think."

"Think?"

"Yes." Madame looked steadily at Salvani. "The sleeping draught. You've decided?"

Salvani spread out his hands. "The priest says it's all right, so . . ."

"Very well." In absolute contrast to Salvani's vague moral

259

anxieties, Madame was businesslike. "We'll have to guess when to give him it. It has to last, you know." She paused, her mind working. "We'll give it an hour, get him to the toilet, then the draught."

"The toilet. 'Course. He'll be in the sack for hours. I hadn't thought of that."

"You've thought of enough, I think," Madame said. "Sit down. Rest. I'll take over."

And she did. As Salvani slumped in an easy chair, Madame read the story to Judah. The priest came in more than once, looking meaningfully at Salvani, he knowing that the priest wanted him to formally confess but having no intention of doing so, preferring to study the map of the Vale of Chamonix; not that it told him much—a road, a railway line, a river, two or three villages . . . and then the frontier—a fence he would try to jump when he got there; and as the minutes ticked away, at the back of his mind was the thought of the bus inexorably drawing nearer. He was not an imaginative man but he had a picture of the bus: an ugly, snub-nosed brute, belching smoke, grinding through a narrow, choking, rainswept ravine, creeping closer, like some ancient creature, creeping—

"*Italien*. Time," Madame said, a drowsy Judah on her lap. "I'll do it."

"Ah, that." Salvani took a deep breath. "Has he been to the . . . ?"

"Yes." Madame stroked Judah's forehead. "He's a good boy."

"He is that." Salvani rubbed his face vigorously and took a step or two forward, looking into Judah's face. "Are you sure?" he said. "I mean, he's half asleep now."

"Yes," Madame said, "and in an hour he'd wake up, inside—you know?"

Salvani didn't want to think of that, Judah waking up inside a bag, in the dark, unable to move . . .

"So." Madame held out her hand and reluctantly Salvani passed over the bottle. Madame, as deft as ever, shook it

260

vigorously, and reached inside her bag, producing a cup, a child's cup, with fairies and elves dancing around it, and, as Salvani watched queasily, filled it with a sticky brown liquid and held it to Judah's lips. "Little one," she said, bouncing Judah a little, "here now, drink this."

Judah half opened languid eyes and opened his mouth, but as the cup was raised to his lips, he wrinkled his nose with distaste, pulled his head back, and suddenly, and rather shockingly, his eyes flicked wide open. "What is it?" he said.

"It's a drink," Madame said. "It's good for you. Come on, now."

As tentatively as a deer at a water hole, Judah cautiously tasted the drink, then shook his head violently. "No," he said.

"I'll give you something nice afterward," Madame said. "Plums."

"I don't want it." Judah began to wriggle.

"It's medicine," Madame said, holding the cup away.

"I'm not sick." Judah's face was set in a stubborn expression Salvani knew well.

"No, it's to stop you from *being* sick." Madame kept a plump arm around Judah. "All the children have to drink it."

Judah shook his head again. "I'm not all the children and I'm never sick. I'm *not*. Am I, Uncle?"

"No." Salvani stepped forward and sank to his knees, his face close to Judah's. "No, you're not. You're a strong boy."

"We've walked a lot, haven't we?" Judah smiled, his eyes wide, dark pools of delight. "Over all the mountains and across all the rivers."

"We have," Salvani said. "And you chased all the wolves away! But you've got to take the medicine."

"Have I?"

"Yes," Salvani said. "You do. You really do. Please. For me."

Judah stared at Salvani through the unfathomable eyes

261

of childhood, stared and stared again. "All right," he said. Madame raised the cup, but, almost roughly, Salvani took it from her.

"Here," he said, raising the cup with its dancing fairies to Judah's lips. "Drink it all, all down, yes—" feeling a deep racking guilt as Judah drank, draining the cup.

"Good boy," he said, cursing the world as Madame dabbed Judah's lips with a napkin and fed him a plum, coated with what Salvani knew to be a rarity, sugar, rocking the child, singing a song, herself close to tears.

On his knees, Salvani, from a world in which sentiment was not despised, was near to tears himself, but then he heard a click behind him and saw the priest in the doorway.

"We've done it," Salvani said thickly. "See?"

"Yes," the priest said, seeing a woman holding a child in her lap, and a man on his knees, but seeing more than that, too. "How is he?"

"Going," Madame mouthed.

The priest joined them, the man, woman, and child, watching as Judah's eyelids drooped over eyes as dark—and as bright—as mountain tarns, opened, drooped again. He murmured something about wolves and, possibly, bears, something else faintly in a language none of the others knew, and as his eyes closed, and a tiny trickle of saliva ran from the corner of his mouth, "Papa?" and then he was gone.

"Jesus Christ Almighty," Salvani said. "Is this what we've come to?"

"It seems so," the priest said. "But *you've* done nothing wrong." He raised his hand. "I shouldn't do this but—" He placed his thumb on Judah's forehead and made the sign of the cross. "Does no harm." He stood up. "Brother, I want to show you something. Would you care to?"

Salvani didn't care to, he wanted to hover over Judah, but he followed the priest into the church.

"I just wanted to show you this," the priest said. In a

niche was a statue of the Virgin Mary—crude enough, plaster, simpering, splashed gaudily pink, red, blue, with five candles burning before it.

"Pure beeswax," the priest said. "They burn sweetly." He pointed. "Madame, Jacques, Patrice, Judah, yes, him! And yours. They burn for twenty-four hours. While you're going up the Vale of Chamonix they'll be burning. Only lights, you know, but lights in the darkness. Go back now."

Salvani did, but as he did he looked up at the pictures the priest had mentioned that morning. They were visible now, the Massacre of the Innocents and the Flight into Egypt.

The bus, as ugly as Salvani had imagined, ground out of Albertville; gears squealing, smoke billowing from its exhaust, rain slashing on the windshield where an inefficient wiper jerked and whined; and, after stopping three times to pick up a passenger or two, lurched into the small town of Ugine.

A couple of passengers got out, a couple more got in, a gendarme went through the bus demanding passes, at the last moment a postman handed a mail bag to the driver, had a receipt signed, and stood back in the rain as the bus lurched forward and swung right into the valley of the Arly, the ancient engine spluttering and the vehicle moving as if it was being pushed rather than driven, butting its way through a pine-covered gorge, not going at much more than a fast walking pace but not stopping either, rusty and worn out, but creeping inexorably forward like the last dinosaur searching for a last mate, into St.-Nicholas-la-Chapelle, merely one elegant church, its steeple wreathed in mist, and, with its engine reverberating in the narrow street, into Flumet, where Jacques in his uniform, standing on the church steps, ducked inside and into the small room behind the altar.

"It's here," he said. "Oh." Looking at Madame and Judah, Salvani and the priest, but most of all at the sack, lined with Salvani's tunic and trousers, gaping open.

"Now?" Salvani's voice was rough.

"Yes." Madame stood up, Judah in her arms.

"You've got a minute or two," Jacques said. "The driver won't go until I've seen him, but . . ."

"Understood." Salvani stooped over Judah. The child was deeply asleep and breathing so lightly that Salvani, in a fit of panic, thought for a moment that he wasn't breathing at all. "Do it," he said.

Madame lowered Judah into the sack, tucking the arms of the frayed tunic around his neck, and as she did so Salvani remembered queasily what Jacques had said about the peasants carrying hens and piglets, live in sacks on All Souls Night—knowing what happened to the little piglets.

"Right." Jacques sealed the sack. "Wait for a bang on that door. Then just stroll out. We'll be outside. *Bonne chance.*"

They shook hands, hastily, and Madame kissed Salvani on the cheek. *"Adieu,"* she said, and then the two of them were gone, leaving Salvani and the priest alone.

"Sorry, Father," Salvani said. "I just can't any longer, you know, confess the way you want me to."

"It will come to you again, remember the candles burning for you." The priest raised his hand in a benediction as there was a knock at the door.

"That's us." The priest nodded and, as Salvani picked up the sack, swung the door open.

The bus was not thirty meters away, disconsolate faces peering vacantly through the bleared windows. One or two passengers were standing at the bus door making farewells, but, Salvani's heart beat faster, in front of the bus facing Patrice, who was gesticulating and laughing, was a gendarme, and also, what made his heart *jump*, across the road, by the bridge, was a motorcycle with a sidecar, and on the

264

motorcycle, a rain cape glistening in the rain, and a steel helmet, was a German soldier, and in the sidecar another, with a machine pistol.

"All right." The priest stood in the door, the bus driver sounded his horn, and Patrice, shouting something—laughing—lurched in front of the bus, the gendarme jumped after him, Madame appeared, blocking one side of the pavement, and the priest, his arm on Salvani's shoulder, shielding his other side, walked casually to the bus and pressed him up the steps, saying, "My best regards to Father Martin." Then stepping forward and, with authority, retrieving Patrice, drunk, from the clutches of the gendarme and hauling him into the church as Salvani, without a second glance from the driver, settled into a seat, the street emptying, except that, as the bus driver crashed the ancient gears and the bus gave a shuddering leap forward, from the corner of his eye Salvani saw the German soldier kick his motorbike into life and swing into the road, waving the bus on, although heading in the same direction.

The bus made another lurch forward, the driver turning the air inside the bus as blue with his language as the exhaust was turning the atmosphere outside, then settled into a heavy jerking rhythm. Salvani slouched in his seat, one arm sprawled protectively over the sack, his face set in a sour, brooding expression which said, as plainly as any words, don't talk to me or else! but keeping an eye on the road. But no Germans passed on the motorbike, and they didn't pass either at a hamlet called Praz-sur-Arly where the bus stopped, briefly; but just outside the next town, Mégève, it roared past them and as the bus stopped outside a café it was waiting there, too, pointing at the bus, the two men seeming impervious to the rain, and as menacing as a loaded shotgun.

"Mégève!" the driver shouted. *"Wait!"*—snarling at a bent old woman with a bag as a man in plainclothes, a uniformed gendarme, and a postman came out of the café.

The driver stretched out a leg and kicked the bus door open, making more than one attempt.

The plainclothesman, for all his plainclothes having *police* written all over him, put his foot on the doorstep.

"For Sweet Jesus' sake!" The driver banged the wheel. "They've all *been* checked, three times! Come on, I've got to get into Chamonix before dark, and at this rate it'll be morning before I get there."

The plainclothesman hesitated, swung himself up, glanced along the bus, and hesitated again.

"Come on!" The driver growled again, and another voice broke in, the postman complaining. Caught between the two, and with the alluring prospect of a café, the man turned away, but not without a parting shot.

"Full check at St.-Gervais," he shouted. "Better have your passes in order."

There was a shuffle of passengers, some on, some off; the postman swung up and casually dropped three satchels in Salvani's lap. "St.-Gervais, Chamonix and Les Houches. Hand them over, will you?" Jumping away as the driver, pounding the wheel like a mahout kicking a reluctant elephant, dragged the door shut and, almost with an effort of will, forced the bus to start, muttering oaths and imprecations as it juddered forward, and as Salvani breathed a sigh of relief, swinging onto the road, although the sigh was cut short as he realized that the German soldiers on their motorbike had swung around, too, pointing in the same direction.

And why was that? Salvani's mouth went dry. Jesus Maria, he had thought that on the bus he would be safe, at least until Chamonix; but now—two venomous Germans tailing the bus, gulping exhaust fumes in the rain; what reason could they have if not to—to what he didn't want to think about; and what had that viper of a cop said in Mégève—a full check at St.-Gervais!

The bus hit a huge pothole and swerved, jouncing the passengers. The post parcels bounced off Salvani's knee.

"Flumet. Just a village, rather pleasant—"

"You—" Palet struck the map with his fist. "It's a cross-roads. You can see that, can't you?"

"But he could be in the hills," the inspector said. "In a hut, we're looking—and this weather—"

"—— the weather! He's trying to break out. He's trying to get to Switzerland!" Palet stared at the inspector, but not seeing him. He was seeing an Italian soldier, a dirty, cowardly, ape-like figure shambling across a mountain, towing a Jew kid, a pasty-faced whining rat—a blob of filth, but one worth millions, millions! And somehow, *somehow* the Italian, the scum of the earth, had managed to stay free: slipped through the net at La Chambre, Moutiers, Bourg-St.-Maurice; and now he had doubled back—and on a motorbike! It was unbelievable—inconceivable! He struck the map with a curious mechanical motion and spittle dribbled from the corner of his mouth.

Mother of God—the inspector stepped away—he's going to have a fit, he thought. He's an epileptic. "Monsieur," he said. "Monsieur Palet."

Palet's eyes suddenly refocused and he wiped his mouth with his sleeve. "Car!" he said.

"Car!" The inspector clutched at the word with relief. "Ah! Monsieur Palet, a *car*. We've not had authorization yet. No!" as something inhuman showed in Palet's face. "Why bother with bureaucracy. Ha ha! Take mine. Here—" He thrust keys in Palet's hand. "Come along, I'll take you to it. Yes—" leading the way, hurrying down the stairs and outside, standing bareheaded in the rain with only one wish, to get Palet and his gorillas as far from him as possible. "Yes—first right, Flumet in less than an hour—" and, as Alphonse, leering at his terror, drove off, wiping his face clear of more than rain.

Waved through the roadblock at Ugine, and cursed on by Palet, Alphonse taking risks along the Arly gorge in the rain, Palet arrived in Flumet in under an hour, the car skidding to a halt in a bow wave of water outside the church.

Palet jumped out and glared at the deserted, shuttered street, running with water. "Where the —— is everyone?" he shouted. "And where's the —— gendarme?"

The two Milice climbed out of the car and joined him, peering aimlessly around.

"Don't know, boss," Alphonse said. "I saw a café just down the street. It looked open."

"Café!" Palet spat out the word. "What do you think this is, a day's outing?"

Alphonse shrugged sheepishly. "Just thought there'd be someone there, might know where the cop is."

"He'll wish he was on Devil's Island when I get him." Palet wiped rain from his face, hesitated for a moment, then went up the steps to the church and shoved the doors open. "Anyone in here?" he shouted, his grating voice echoing around the walls and the altar, and the paintings of the Massacre of the Innocents and the Flight into Egypt. He pounded his fist on the huge door and went back to his men. "You," he said to the silent Milice. "Search that place. Every corner."

"The church?" The man was uneasy.

"Yes, the —— church, and get on with it. You"—to Alphonse—"you come with me."

They sloshed down the street and barged into the café. It was merely a narrow, low-ceilinged room, a bar with an unshaven man behind it, two men in overalls playing billiards on a small table, and, in a corner, comfortably settled, his tunic unbuttoned, a coffee and a bottle before him, a gendarme—all of them looking up with alarm as the door bell clanged.

"Messieurs!" the barman affected a jovial welcome, as if two long-cherished friends had appeared, but fell silent as Palet sidled to the gendarme.

"You," Palet said. "Get up."

The gendarme pouted a little, asserting, unwisely, his authority. "Who are you?" he demanded.

"What do you think," Palet said. "The —— Boy Scouts. *Up!*"

The gendarme pushed himself upright and fumbled with his buttons. "What can I do for you?"

"Do?" Palet turned his face away, but with an eerily unnatural movement. "There—" jabbing a finger at a door marked *Salle privée*—private room.

"Monsieur!" The café owner moved along the bar. "A moment—" falling into silence as Palet banged open the door to a shriek from a semiclad woman stooped over a bowl of water.

"Out." Palet, a leering Alphonse eagerly looking over his shoulder, jerked his thumb. "Get out."

The woman, clutching a dress to her shoulders, backed from the room as Alphonse, gripping the gendarme's arm, pulled him into the room, slamming the door shut behind him.

"Monsieur!" The gendarme shrugged himself free from Alphonse's grip. "Barging in here, it isn't right."

"Right?" Palet struck at the gendarme's chest, shoving him backward. "Right!" he shoved again. "I say what's right here. Do you get that?" shoving again. "Why weren't you on that bridge?"

Shoved again, the gendarme was shoved a step too far for his pride. "Where are your credentials?"

"Here!" Palet pulled his pistol out and jammed it under the gendarme's chin. "I'm Palet, special agent, Milice. Any more questions? Right—" as the gendarme shook a white face. "Now, why weren't you watching the bridge?"

"Just taking a break." The gendarme raised his chin. "Just for a few minutes. And I've got a friend across the street. She's watching the bridge for me. Anyone comes near, she'd be over for me in seconds."

Palet slowly lowered his pistol, fixing the gendarme with

273

his eyes like a snake with a frog. "Who've you seen? To-day?"

"No one—I mean, no one I don't know by sight," the gendarme added hastily as the gun was raised again.

"And who's passed through?" Palet demanded.

"Through?" The gendarme wrinkled his brows in thought. "A couple of German army trucks, a cart, couple of cyclists—I know them both, and, oh yes, the bus."

"What —— bus?" Palet said.

"From Albertville. Going through to Chamonix."

"*That* bus . . . I saw the —— thing leave," Palet muttered. He lifted his head and the gendarme, not needing a shove this time, backed away voluntarily. "Who got on?" Palet said. "Who?"

The gendarme swallowed. "Three or four people. But listen, I knew them all, and those who got off, and they all had passes—"

"And on the bus? *On* it!"

"Er." The gendarme licked dry lips. "A lot of people— it's the bus. I mean, it doesn't go often, so when it does—"

"Who!" Palet's hand, still holding the pistol, was twitching uncontrollably.

"I'm thinking," the gendarme stammered, thinking Christ Almighty, the man's crazy. "Yes, er, there were some old women, a couple of old geezers sitting together, a family, er, er, a blind man, nuns, and . . . and . . ." his voice ran down . . . "and a man and a boy."

"A man and a boy," Palet said in a deadly monotone.

"But they had passes," the gendarme said. "From Ugine to Chamonix, listen, they weren't Italian. This fellow, he spoke French, and the boy—"

"They *speak* French!" Palet bellowed and then, with another horrifying shift, relapsed into his flat, expressionless voice, as if a corpse was speaking through his lips. "Could they have got to Ugine from here? On the other side of the river?"

"Yes. Yes, easily, there's a back road," the gendarme gabbled. "They could have gone that way, at night, but they had passes, and civilian clothes and—"

"Where's the bus now?" Palet asked in his dead, flat voice.

"Er." The gendarme felt on the brink of collapse and he realized that what he had always thought a mere writer's fiction was absolutely true: his knees were actually knocking together. "The bus now, er, look, sir, say—say—it should be"—gabbling—"Praz—no, Mégève, er ah! yes, say St.-Gervais. Yes, thereabouts—"

Palet wasn't listening. "Phone. *Phone!*" with another sickening shift of his voice.

"Not here. No. Across the street. One minute. I'll take you." Stumbling over his feet, the gendarme lurched to the door, Alphonse shoving him in the back and Palet, reptilian, on their heels.

The billiards players had gone from the café and the barman, his head averted, was polishing glasses, unseeing and unhearing as the three representatives of the French Republic kicked their way through the door, although as they left he raised eyes suffused with new hatred.

"Here, here." The gendarme splashed across the street, gesturing to Palet. "Just up here."

Palet and Alphonse followed him up a slight incline to a square and a house, part dwelling, part shop, which bore a sign saying *Poste francaise,* and another on the door which said, uncompromisingly, *Fermé.* Closed.

Palet jerked his head at Alphonse, who battered on the door and battered again, but as Alphonse raised his foot to lash at the door, it swung open and, completely undaunted by the sight of the men, a pillar of rectitude in black, Madame appeared, demanding to know whether they could read.

"Madame." The gendarme saluted. "Excuse us but—" the *but* left unexplained as Palet shoved him aside.

"Milice." He stepped forward, as if the word was, as it had been in the past, an "open sesame," but stopped as Madame, not yielding an inch, stared over his shoulder at the gendarme.

"What is it, Louis?" she asked.

As if drawing strength from Madame, the gendarme drew himself upright. "Police business, madame. The telephone . . . this gentleman . . ."

Madame looked at Palet as if he was an indigent begging at her door, although with less charity, and Palet, standing in the rain, for all the warrant card in his pocket and the gun in his holster and the ape-like Alphonse at his shoulder, felt his untrammeled power leaking away under her gaze.

"Urgent," he said. "Madame—" the word choking him as he said it. "An affair of state."

Madame stood unmoving and to Palet's fury looked again at the gendarme, who nodded.

"Better let us in," he said.

"Of course. Police business." Madame, even then taking her time, stood back and let the men enter. "In there—" She pointed to a small booth. "What number do you want?"

"Police," Palet snarled. "St.-Gervais. Priority!"

Unhurriedly Madame went behind the counter into a cubicle and dialed a false number. She waited a minute, then, equally unhurriedly, went back into the post office. "The line is dead," she announced.

"Dead!" Palet gave her a glare which had frightened hard men but which had as much effect on Madame as a dandelion seed.

"It happens a lot," she said. "Especially when it rains."

Palet clutched the telephone until his knuckles were white. "How long? How long before you can get through?"

Madame shrugged. "I'll try again if you want."

Palet edged from foot to foot, then slammed the phone down. "You," he shouted at the gendarme. "Stay here and keep trying. You got that?"

"Yes, certainly. Absolutely. Er, monsieur—" as Palet made for the door. "In case—someone asks—where are you going?"

"St.-Gervais," Palet spat as he went out into the rain.

"What's the panic?" Madame asked.

The gendarme undid his collar and wiped his face. "That—"

"Pig," Madame said.

"Well, pig." The gendarme coughed a little. "He's a servant of the state, you know."

"He's still a pig," Madame said. "So?"

"It's that Italian, and the kid. You know, the one we've been looking for?"

"I thought he was in the hills," Madame said.

"He thinks he's on the bus." The gendarme rubbed his chin thoughtfully. "There *was* a fellow with a kid. They'd got passes, but you never know, they could have stolen them and the clothes. Funny things happen."

"Yes, they do." Madame looked thoughtfully at the gendarme. "Why don't you go upstairs, Louis? Jacques and Patrice are there. Get dry and have a drink. I'll keep trying the call for you."

"That's very nice of you. Very nice, indeed. Yes. But you'll keep trying?"

"Oh yes, I'll keep trying." Madame listened to the gendarme clump upstairs and then went into her cubicle, dialed a number, and after a short wait said, "St.-Gervais?"

In the post office at St.-Gervais a man said into the telephone, "Yes? Oh, madame. The bus? Just gone, pity. It was late going out anyway—trouble."

"Oh," Madame said. "What was that?"

"Police, Germans, plainclothesmen—the lot. Someone on the bus they wanted."

"Really." Madame's voice showed just the right amount of interest. "Did they get them?"

"Yes, two—just a minute."

277

There was a mild clatter as the receiver was put down, background voices, a man shouting, laughter, a typewriter clacking. Madame, her face impassive, touched a cross on her neck, then the man came back on the phone.

"It was a man and a woman. Jews, they think. Don't know what they were doing here. Might have been trying to get a train up to Geneva."

"I see. Did our mail go through?"

"Oh yes, no trouble there. Listen, madame, did you want anything on the bus?"

"No, just a message to someone I know. It's all right. I'll ring Chamonix."

Salvani crouched in his seat, staring fixedly through a rain-smeared window as the bus, which seemed to grow uglier with every passing kilometer, swung down a road in a huge circular sweep, down again, and again, the driver muttering and cursing over his wheel.

Salvani pulled out a cigarette and lit it, trying not to let his fingers tremble. Christ, he thought, much more of this and it's a heart attack for me. When the police had darted onto the bus in St.-Gervais he had been absolutely one hundred and ten percent certain that they were coming for him—knowing that the crackpot scheme wouldn't work, cursing the magician Jacques, the artist Patrice, the priest, Madame; but the cops had pounced on that couple: poor sods, a middle-aged man and woman, the man sobbing and the woman as white as a sheet as they were dragged from the bus and—Salvani had watched grim-faced—without reason their legs kicked from under them, and then dragged through the puddles—to a police van, with more kicks to help them on their way.

That hadn't been the end of it, either: a venomous-looking swine had gone through the passes of the rest of the passengers, and *gone* through them, even harassing a woman who looked about ninety and nuns—but hardly sparing a glance at Salvani, the magic cloak of a uniform in fact making him all but invisible . . . He furtively felt the sack, wondering if he had detected a slight stirring of limbs, and hoping to Christ he had.

"Le Fayet," the driver roared as the bus came to another halt in a small straggly village. A woman got off, and a man who had wanted Salvani to move, he muttering a curse and deliberately kicking Salvani's foot as he passed. Another lurching start, another creeping journey of a few kilometers, a short tunnel, and another stop.

"Servoz." The driver shouted the name as if it was an insult. Salvani clutched his knee, groaning with exasperation as, slowly, the bus crept on again. He leaned over the sack, rubbed the window with his sleeve, and peered through. It was still raining, harder in fact, a steady downfall from dark hanging clouds, but he was conscious of a change in the landscape—vast, pine-forested slopes slashed by twisting waterfalls and rock slides, themselves the mere flanks of gigantic mountains, guessed at rather than seen, although, as the clouds swirled, there were glimpses of snow fields, the snow yellowish and, seen through Salvani's unromantic eyes, more like old lard than like the pristine purity he had looked upon an age ago.

"Les Houches. *Les Houches!*" Salvani suddenly realized that the driver was roaring at him and that a sharp-featured woman was standing over him as impatient as the driver. "Post," she snapped. "*Post!*"

"Ah!" Salvani fumbled with the pouches he had been given.

"*Tsa!*" The woman snatched a pouch, rifled through its contents, snatching letters and throwing the pouch back. "Well?" she said.

"Well? Oh, yes." Salvani took out his crumpled receipt book; the woman scribbled on it and handed it back.

Salvani shoved it back into his pocket but the woman, as beaky and alert as a heron, hadn't finished.

"Aren't you going to read it?"

"Sure." Salvani glanced at the receipt and grunted. "All right."

But the woman still hadn't finished with him. "What's that?" She jabbed a finger at the sack.

"New," Salvani barked.

"I've never seen one like that," she began, but the bus driver had endured enough. He pounded his horn and crashed the gears and the woman climbed back down the steps, saying, audibly, "Imbecile," and looking with malevolently curious eyes at Salvani as the bus juddered on yet again—and after a mere four more kilometers stopped again.

"Les Bossons," the driver bawled.

Close to nervous exhaustion, Salvani stared through the window again, at a world which looked as if, on the sixth day of creation, God had caught His world with His elbow and sent the elements crashing down together: rocks, trees, water . . . Salvani stared bleakly at the introduction to the valley of Chamonix as the bus crested a rise; houses, cafés, a hotel appeared, a small church, a row of ornate buildings, a square—and as the bus gave a last wheeze and squeal of its uncertain brakes, the driver stood up, kicked the door open, and, as if he had spent his last energies, too, said, mildly, "Chamonix."

"And you didn't hold them?" Palet crouched over a desk in the police station at St.-Gervais, his shadow over the face of a detective in the French Sûreté.

"Why should we?" The detective, a cigarette dangling from his lips, stared at Palet, unintimidated.

"The phone call from Flumet, that's why," Palet said.

"Didn't get one." The detective blew smoke casually across the desk. "But they didn't get off here. We got those Jews, leastways one of your men did. You can see him if you like. He's downstairs with them." He jabbed downward with his thumb, significantly. "But no man and kid got off. See—" He shoved a list across to Palet. "There, man and son, going through to Chamonix. And we really checked that bus, because of the tip about the Jews."

"——!" Palet shook his head as if he was shaking flies away. "Where will it be now, the bus?"

The detective looked up at a wall clock. "Hard to say. If it hasn't broken down it'll be in Chamonix, more or less, maybe Les Houches, Bossons . . ."

"Ring Chamonix." Palet was on his way to the door. "Tell them to seal that bus off. They're to hold everyone— *everyone*. Got that? Tell them I'm on my way. Do it *now*!"

The detective looked through the window with cold eyes as Palet's car pulled up outside. "André," he called across the room, "we've had calls from Albertville today, haven't we?"

" 'Course."

"And they come through Flumet, don't they?"

"That's right." André turned back to his newspaper.

The detective stood up. Palet was climbing into the car, his two thugs scowling through the windows. "And —— you, too," he said.

"What?" André raised his eyebrows.

"Nothing," the detective said. "Nothing at all—no, not you—" speaking into the telephone. "Right, Chamonix police. What? No, no priority, no priority at all."

281

22

In the rainswept square of Chamonix the passengers, most of them elderly, hobbled off the bus mumbling complaints as a gendarme, swathed in a glistening cape, demanded their passes, he as impatient and irritable as they. Salvani waited, and waited again until an old man, half blind, argued with the gendarme, fumbling for his pass; then stood up, giving way to three nuns but barging aside a man and his son, and heaving his sack—and Judah—lumbered down the steps, the gendarme, his eyes rolling with exasperation, saying to the old man yes, times had changed and it was nothing to do with him but that if the old man—and yes, he was sure that he had valiantly risked his life in Verdun in the First World War—didn't show his pass he would spend the night in a police cell—nodding the nuns through and, after a glance at Salvani, and with a grimace which, from one uniform to another, said, *The damned public!* nodding him away, too.

Salvani grimaced back in sympathy and behind the vast headdresses of the nuns looked around the square with its signs written in more optimistic times: Hotel Majestic, the resort of Princes; Hotel les Alpes; Savoy-Hotel; Carlton—the promises of luxury mocking him; and across the bleak square, in the foyer of a hotel, a lounging German officer, a glass in one hand, a cigar in the other, laughing, sharing a joke with a paunchy civilian.

Salvani took a deep breath and strode forward, hoping to Christ that he was doing the right thing, heaving the sack over his shoulder, and bumped into a figure as swathed as the gendarme, who, recoiling from Salvani's bulk, said, *"Poste Flumet?"* took him by the arm and pulled him across the square behind another dinosaur of a bus, into an alley, stopped and said, "Sweet Jesus, I didn't know about this or—"

"Or what!" Salvani ripped the seals off the sack, tearing the stitching apart with fingers like grab irons, and heaved Judah up—still breathing.

"What's that!" The man stared, amazed.

"It's a bleeding ostrich," Salvani said. "What does it look like?" He rummaged in the bag for Judah's rainclothes.

"Christ," the man said. "Nobody told me you'd got a kid!"

"Well, I have. Here, hold him while I get these clothes around him." Salvani shoved Judah at the man, who promptly shoved Judah back.

"Put him back in," he said. "Quick, man. Listen—" He strode to the mouth of the alley, peered around, and hurried back. "Madame—at Flumet—phoned through. The Milice are coming here after you."

"What!" Salvani cried. "After me?"

"Yes. They're on their way now."

Salvani's face went dark with anger. "How do they know? I mean—"

"No idea." The man was abrupt. "All I know is that you've got to get out of here. The place could be swarming with cops any minute. Put the kid back in the bag and I'll point the way out."

"You're not coming with me?" Salvani shoved his head forward.

"No, I'm not." The man backed away as if Salvani was going to seize him and force him to be a guide. "Hurry up," his voice trembling with fright.

Salvani took a deep breath, the one which, with him, usually preceded an explosion of rage, but then let his breath out. "Right." He shoved Judah back in the sack. "What do I do?"

The man beckoned Salvani to the end of the alley and peered out. "See?"

Salvani stared over his shoulder at the square with the ancient bus looking as if it was collapsing on its wheels.

"There's the Mairie," the man said, "across the square. The Germans have taken it over. See?"

His heart in his boots, Salvani saw the usual armored car, a vast swastika hanging from a balcony, two sentries on the doorway.

"On the corner, that's the rue des Moulins. You've got to get there and just walk up it. It turns into the rue Joseph Vallot but it's the same street."

"Like this?" Salvani plucked at his overcoat. "Just walk up?"

"It might still be all right." The postman sounded like a man on the very edge of his nerves. "You're coming from the post office and there's a hospital up there, on the left. Anyone sees you, they'll think you're going there."

"And then?"

"Then"—the man pulled his hood even farther down over his face, as if trying to make himself invisible—"keep going. If you're stopped, say you're going to Praz, they might believe you, and there's a path on your right. That takes you to the river, and there's a walk along it. Cut up through the bushes and you're on a railway line. Then . . ."

Then I'm on my own, Salvani thought, but didn't say it. "The border?"

"What can I say?" There was anger and fear in the man's voice. "You'll see it when you see it. Look."

Salvani looked. It was appreciably darker, a sodden dusk coming in. Two workmen walked across the square, a gendarme going into the town hall, stopping to talk to the sentries, who dwarfed him, laughing . . . Salvani hesitated like a runner waiting for the starting gun. "Thanks anyway," he said.

"No thanks. We've never seen each other." The man shoved Salvani in the back. "Go!"

284

Feeling like a man going to the gallows, Salvani stepped forward and walked across the square, the sack over his shoulder. It wasn't much more than three hundred meters across the open space—two hundred paces; but as he walked, the distance seemed to be growing greater, the small friendly square as naked as an ice field. You're a postman, Salvani said to himself. Remember, you're a postman, nobody sees you, you're invisible, feeling as inconspicuous as a walrus. He pursed his lips and tried to whistle, as postmen were supposed to do, and realized he was whistling, in a squeaky way, the marching song of the Italian Socialist Party—stopped whistling—felt sure that Judah was awake, was certain that a sentry at the Mairie was watching him—and felt an almost overwhelming desire to start running. Jesus, he thought, going across the bridge at Flumet, I was running like ten hares, now I'm creeping like a —— tortoise—but moving on, step by step, walking heedlessly through a sluice of running water, and into the rue des Moulins, away from the Argus eyes of the sentries.

The street was narrow, giving at least an illusion of security, and he lengthened his stride, a man doing a job and anxious to have it done with and get indoors; along the street; shops, stores, small hotels, more shops, one with a sign saying "Welcome to our German Brothers," and hearing a shout.

Salvani turned his head. Across the street, in a doorway, was a gendarme, his cape buttoned. Salvani raised his hand in acknowledgment, pointed vigorously forward, and received a casual wave of a baton in return. Jesus Christ, Salvani thought, and all the angels—doubling his prayers as he saw a sign which said *Hospital*, and a huge German truck parked by it, really believing that the game was finally up and his journey ended.

But the truck was his salvation. It blocked him from the view of the gendarme for a crucial few yards past the hospital, and then the road kinked a little to the right, a few more long strides took him beyond the town, the street turning into a country road lined with trees and bushes, a few more raking steps and he saw, across the road, a lane.

Salvani stopped, lowered the sack, and stooped, as if to tie a bootlace. He looked around, no one in sight, stood up, strolled casually across the road and darted down the lane, into the trees and into the gathering night. And as he did so, Palet's car skidded into the square.

Palet was out of the car before it had stopped, stumbling as he landed, skinning a hand and smearing his elegant English raincoat, but charging into the police station and seeing a police inspector waiting for him, his hands raised in apology.

"Palet?" the inspector asked. "Yes. Well, sorry. Too late. We got your message from St.-Gervais this minute and . . ." He shrugged.

"This minute? *This minute!*" Palet raised his handsome head and stared at the ceiling. "I left that —— message in St.-Gervais thirty minutes ago."

"I can't help that." The inspector was stony. "All our calls are logged. If you want to see it."

"—— your log," Palet shouted. "Where are the passengers?"

"Monsieur." The inspector, stony before, was now appropriately glacial. "Where do you think? In the town. But I can assure you that everyone who got off that bus was checked by a reliable man"—he broke off and frowned as the door opened and Palet's men shambled in—"and I'd very much like to know what this is all about."

"You do? I'll tell you what it's all about." Palet leaned forward. "There's a man, an Italian. He's wanted for theft and assault *and* he's got a Jew kid with him. You understand that, don't you? A Jew kid, and you know the orders about Jews, don't you? I mean, you do know them?"

"But"—the inspector's icy manner was beginning to split—"I don't understand. An Italian and a Jewish child— here? I mean, a criminal . . . with a child. Why?"

286

"Because"—the murderous rage in Palet's voice shocked the inspector—"because you're not eighteen kilometers from the —— Swiss border, that's —— well why! And they were on the bus! So they're here!"

"Monsieur, monsieur." Like other men before him, the inspector was beginning to feel the authority he prized leak away. "I didn't know. I really didn't! Who"—he shouted louder than he had ever shouted before in his station— "who checked the bus in?"

"Charles," a detective leaning against a wall looking balefully at Palet's gorillas said. "But he's off duty now."

"Well, where is he?" the inspector said. "At home?"

"No." The officer spoke reluctantly, but spoke nonetheless. "He went to the café with the driver."

"Get him," Palet said. "Now."

"Of course." The inspector, longing to have one of his men crash a baton on Palet's head, snapped his fingers at the officer.

"Might as well go yourselves," the officer said. "It's only two minutes. Save time," grinning sardonically as the inspector dragged a coat on and grinning more as he watched his boss, Palet, and the gorillas splash through the rain.

"Are they in the café, Charles and the driver?" another officer poking at a typewriter in the corner of the room asked.

The detective stopped grinning. "Yes," he said. "Worse luck."

They were there, the driver mellowed by wine, a cheese omelette on the table, the gendarme mellowed, too, huddled over a table in the café, which was large but agreeably rough, more like a workingman's drive-in than a restaurant in a chic skiing resort, both looking up suspiciously as the inspector and Palet and his animals came in.

The gendarme, aggrieved at working after his shift was over, listened to the inspector and shook his head.

"Everyone," he said. "Absolutely everyone had a pass."

"Good enough for me." The inspector winked at the gendarme. "But this . . . this gentleman wants to be absolutely sure."

Palet elbowed the inspector aside. "A man and a kid." He bent over the table, his crooked hands resting on their knuckles. "Did they get off the bus here?"

"Sure," the gendarme said.

"They did?" Palet jerked his hand, sending a carafe of wine flying, his men snuffling at his shoulders, the café owner and his wife backing away into the shadows. "You're sure?"

"Sure I'm sure," the gendarme said. "Not that they needed them."

"Not need them?" Palet whispered, leaning closer, a hand, heedless, in the pool of wine. "What the —— does that mean?"

"Because I know them."

"You know them . . ." Palet raised a hand stained red. "You know them . . ."

"Well, I ought to." The gendarme looked at the inspector. "It was Jean-Pierre." He turned back to Palet. "He's married to my sister—the poor sod." He burst out laughing, the driver chortling with him, both stopping abruptly as they saw the expression on Palet's face.

"You think this is a joke?" Palet said. "You'll get something to make you laugh. I'll take you somewhere and tell you some jokes that will make you laugh your —— heads off—"

"Now, now." The inspector put a placatory hand on Palet's shoulder. "They're not laughing at you. You've been on a wild-goose chase, but we can't win every time, you know, hey!" He started back as Palet slashed his hand away. "No need for that."

"Isn't there?" His dogs bared their teeth as Palet stared at the inspector with his dead eyes. "I—I." He clawed at the air—unable to believe that he had been wrong, and

288

feeling as if he had not merely been wrong but tricked, fooled, and made to look a fool, charging in and out of police stations, cursing, threatening, sending messages which mysteriously failed to arrive, leaving behind him— he was certain of it—a line of sniggering policemen—to end up here, muddied and wet, with the driver and the gendarme laughing in his face—he wanted actually to find the man and the child who *had* been on the bus and kill *them*, drag them into a gutter and shoot them—

"Boss. *Boss.*" Alphonse spoke in his ear.

"Yes." He dropped his hand, already in the eerie recesses of his mind working out a plausible reason to explain why he had been in Chamonix, but as he turned to go, the inspector spoke.

"Come along, monsieur, I'll find you rooms for the night and we can go through the checks tomorrow, hey?"

"What checks?" Palet said.

The inspector raised his shoulders. "Where the bus stopped—who got on, who got off."

"Wait," Palet said, "you"—he stared balefully at the driver—"who was on the bus?"

"Monsieur!" The bus driver didn't bother disguising *his* irritation. "How should I know? It's bad enough keeping that bus moving without worrying about the passengers. That's up to the cops."

"Flumet," Palet said, and with a rare insight, and a fleet- ing memory of Herr Kellner questioning Doriot in the cell in La Chambre, Palet sat down and beckoned the café owner for more wine. "Have a drink." He poured the wine himself, pushing the glass toward the driver. "Flumet," he repeated. "Who got on there? Just try and think. Flumet."

The driver took hold of his wine. "Just people. Old Vil- leneuve, I know him anyway, a couple of others, an old woman who couldn't make the steps . . . and the postman."

"Postman?"

"Yes . . ." The driver looked into his glass. "He was new,

289

seemed to be anyway—he didn't know what to do at Les Houches. But he didn't have a kid with him. Just a mail-bag." He swigged some wine. "Come to think of it . . ." He screwed his face up, concentrating. "It was a big bag. Not seen one of those before."

"How big a bag?"

"About so—" The driver held out his hand hip high. "He was a big ugly sod, at that. Swarthy, you know. But why don't you ask him yourself? I saw him after we'd pulled in when I was doing my returns."

"Saw him where?" Palet asked.

"Going to the rue des Moulins."

"With the sack?"

"Yes, I thought he was delivering at the hospital."

"Does the street go to the hospital?" Palet asked the inspector.

"It does," the inspector said, thoughtfully, "but there's no postal deliveries at this time of night. And—"

"And what?" Palet dropped his mask of a reasonable man, and the reptile showed its voracious teeth.

"And"—the inspector was already jamming his cap on—"and it's the road to the frontier."

The men, four now since, to his disgust, the gendarme was roped back on duty, left the café, charging through the door and up the street back toward the police station, but at the corner of the square the inspector crossed the street.

Palet grabbed his arm. "Where are you going?" he demanded.

The inspector shook his arm free. "The Mairie, to report it."

"Report!" Palet said. "Who to?"

"The Commandant."

"The Germans!" Palet was enraged.

"This man's Italian, isn't he?" the inspector said. "A soldier. Of course the Germans have to know."

"But he can't be more than a couple of kilometers off!" Palet swung his head around. "You," he barked at his men, "get the car and get up that road. Take him—" He pointed to the gendarme.

"Jesus, boss!" the gendarme appealed to the inspector.

"Do it," the inspector snapped. "If you don't pick him up, get to Les Tines." He turned to Palet. "The road and railway come together there. Jump to it!"

Followed by a scowling Palet, he strode into the Mairie, where a corporal grudgingly admitted them to the Commandant, a stout, monocled army major who maddened Palet by asking if he had fallen off a bicycle, but who listened attentively to the inspector.

"Of course," he said. "We must get this man, a savage! A real human beast!"

"And the Jew kid," Palet butted in.

"And of course the Yid," the major said. "What do you suggest?" he asked the inspector. "You know the area."

"This." The inspector moved to the wall and the usual large-scale map. "You'd better see this, too," he said curtly to Palet. "This is the valley of Chamonix. Mont Blanc on the south, the Aiguilles Rouges on the north. There's no way across them without a guide, and in weather like this a guide wouldn't even try. But here's the river Arve, the road, and the railway; they run together, more or less, up the valley to these villages, Les Tines, La Joux, Argentière, and then Vallorcine—the border."

"Yes." The major removed his monocle, revealing a milky eye, replaced it, and peered at the map. "There are tunnels, aren't there, on the railway? There, at Montroc? And the road is near. We can block them easily enough."

"Right," the inspector said. "And then I thought tomorrow your men could sweep down the valley and I'll get my men and we'll sweep up, flush him out—what are you doing!" He made a face as Palet elbowed him aside.

"Tomorrow!" Palet snarled. "Tomorrow! He's on his

way tonight! Out there." He held up his hand and waved it in the air like a monkey clutching at a fruit on a bough. "And you're standing here driveling about tomorrow."

"Now look here, monsieur," the inspector bristled. "I want this man as much as you do, but how many officers do you think I have? And do you know what it's like out there? It's a wilderness, and on a night like this! We'd be looking for a needle in a haystack, and let me tell you, if this man is half the savage you say he is—"

"What's that?" Palet cocked his head. "If?"

"Yes, *if*." The inspector's temper was mounting. "*If*, then I'm more concerned about the people in the villages up there. And any men I *can* spare I'm going to send up to *them*."

"Are you, now?" Palet slid a crooked hand inside his jacket, pulled out his wallet, and flipped it open. "You see this, do you?"

"I see it," the inspector said stoutly. "And I'll give you all my cooperation, do everything in my power. But you don't even know for sure this is the man you're after. *And* you can't be certain that he *has* this kid. Be reasonable, man."

"Reasonable?" Palet's tongue poked out of the corner of his mouth. "I'll show you who's —— reasonable. When this is over, you'll find out what reason is, believe me. That man *is* the Italian, and he's got a Jew kid, and he's going to Switzerland and he's going tonight, up the railway line. Now do I get some men?"

"No," the inspector said, "because it's ridiculous. Tomorrow you can have every man in the district, but not tonight. But what I will do is take men up the valley now, myself, and drop them off in the villages, and if you want to go up the line, no one is stopping you. But it's a complete waste of your time."

"All right." Palet nodded slowly. "They'll be interested to hear this in Lyons. Yes." He turned to the major. "Will you let me have some men?"

The major took out his monocle again, polished it with maddening slowness, replaced it, and stared at Palet. "No," he said, "I will not. I agree entirely with the inspector."

"But—" Palet raised his card.

"And you can put that away," the major said disdainfully. "Remember who you are talking to, an officer of the German Army."

"He's got a Jew kid," Palet said. "And the orders, from the top—"

"I'm aware of the orders," the major said. "And no Yid is going to cross the border here. But use your common sense, man. This Italian could be anywhere, in the woods, in some hut, he might even have doubled back to St.-Gervais."

"No"—Palet began shaking his head—"he's going to the frontier. He's going there now." He had an image of the Italian, no longer the man of his past imaginings, a shambling animal with the brain of an ape, but a huge, towering shape like a figure from a fairy tale, a giant with supernatural powers, striding over mountains one moment and the next, invisible, slipping through cordons of guards, and now, phantasmal, going through the night, with the Jew kid, not eighteen kilometers from the border. "La Chambre," he muttered, swinging his head. "Bourg . . . Flumet . . ." Spittle bubbling on his lips.

The major stared at the inspector, who shrugged, bewildered, then gave Palet a slight push on the shoulder. "Monsieur," he barked. "Monsieur!"

"What?" Palet looked up.

"Here." The major poured out a cognac. "Take this."

Palet took it with a red-stained hand, raised his handsome, mud-splattered face, tossed the brandy down, and wiped the saliva from his mouth with the sleeve of his beautiful, filthy raincoat. "He's going to the border, now," he said, in an oddly quiet voice. "I would. Where did you send my men?"

The inspector coughed nervously, Palet's new voice being more sinister than his cursing. "Les Tines. That's six kilometers."

"And how long since the bus driver saw him walking off?"

"About—" The inspector looked at his watch. "About forty-five minutes."

"He can't have got there yet," Palet said. "Not dragging the Jew. Get your men."

"My men aren't going wandering around in the night—" the inspector said doggedly.

"They can do what they —— well want," Palet said, in the same terrible, quiet voice, as if he was a ventriloquist's dummy. "Get me to Les Tines. And, Major, will you send a foot patrol along the line—just as far as Les Tines—" And as the major hesitated, he added, "There is a Yid"— he used the major's own elegant expression. "Six kilometers. For my report to Herr Kellner."

"Herr Kellner?" The major gave a sudden ingratiating smile. "A German?"

"Gestapo," Palet said absently, as if it was of no consequence.

The major hesitated fractionally, brushing imaginary dust off his immaculate uniform, the world-conquering field gray, subject to no authority but its own, and the Führer's, impregnable and impermeable, but at the word Gestapo, it not seeming so impregnable after all. "Yes," he said. "I am ready to do that. A foot patrol. Now," thinking that an hour in the rain would do no harm to his men, and would do good to him. "I didn't realize that the Gestapo was directly interested . . . Had you only said . . ." barking orders at a lieutenant as the inspector, unnerved by the major's swerve of attitude, waited at the door for Palet, who, dirty, mud-spattered, his fine features sticking out of the white collar of his coat as incongruously as a prince's head from a toad's skin, was saying, in a disinterested voice, that he would, of course, tell Herr Kellner that the major had been most cooperative, the major thanking him effusively, and as Palet and the inspector backed into the night, assuring Palet that the road and the tunnel at Montroc would be sealed tighter—than an obscenity.

The forces of the New Order, and of Law and Order, moved efficiently into gear. Eighteen kilometers up the valley, in the black gorge of Vallorcine, four men were rousted from a cozy cabin where they had been playing cards with two French customs officers—and congratulating themselves on having the easiest posting in the German Army—and, cursing, were sent out into the bleak night: two on a desolate stretch of road, two in the railway tunnel of Montroc, where they promptly tossed up to see who would take first guard while the other snoozed in a railwayman's shack, while in Chamonix another squad of four men, cursing, too, had been dragged from the back room of a café where they had been enjoying wine, music, and the caresses of ladies who had been assuring them that they were infinitely superior to the filthy Italians, who never washed and, more to the point, had no money, and were trudging up the railway line as Palet, the inspector, and three gendarmes, crammed into a police car, arrived at Les Tines station, where they found Palet's car parked and inside it the two Milice and the gendarme, smoking and sharing a bottle of brandy in a cheerful little world of their own—abruptly shattered as Palet wrenched open the car door.

"But we *did*, boss," Alphonse, blenching from Palet's invective, stuttered. "We drove all the way up there"—waving vaguely at the road—"like you said, then came back here to watch the railway line. We've checked the stations, but there's not a sign of him. I mean, what more could we do?"

A pulse began pounding in Palet's forehead, a steady throbbing like a slow, muffled drumbeat in a funeral march. Oblivious to the rain, he turned his head askew, like a man hearing a solemn procession wending slowly far away.

"Boss?" Alphonse said. "Boss?"

"You," Palet said to the gendarme, his head still cocked, still listening to the distant drums, "walk down the line to Chamonix. There's a German patrol coming up."

"Germans." The gendarme shifted uneasily and glanced at his inspector, who looked away. "They hear me coming and they'll shoot. You know Germans . . ."

"You want *me* to shoot you?" Palet flicked a hand and a pistol was sticking in the gendarme's stomach. "Is that what you want?"

The gendarme gave a strange whinny. "No—right, I'm going, look!" backing to the station, scrambling down the track and, after a safe few dozen meters, promptly diving into the bushes.

Palet stood for a moment, his jaw slack, until the inspector called his name. He walked to the car, holding his pistol casually by his side. "What do you want?" he said.

"I want to get going," the inspector said. "Monsieur—" He fawned a little. "You remember? To let the villages know . . . and, monsieur, excuse me, shouldn't you put your gun away?"

"Gun?" Palet looked down with surprise. "Oh." He holstered it and leaned forward. "Where's the next station?"

"La Joux. Another two kilometers. Then there's Argentière, another two—but get in your car, man, you'll get pneumonia."

"I never get ill," Palet said. "Never. I make other people get ill, though," and burst out laughing.

"All right," the inspector said uncertainly. "We'll be off, then. See you up the valley."

He drove off with his men, shaking his head. Palet watched the car go, then got into his own car. "La Joux," he said.

At La Joux, Palet dropped off the silent Milice with

horrible threats as to what would happen to him if he didn't do his duty—threats the more horrible since the Milice knew perfectly well that Palet was capable of carrying them out—then went on to Argentière, where he and Alphonse got out of the car and walked around the deserted station.

"No one here, boss," Alphonse said helpfully.

"There is now," Palet said. "You wait here."

Alphonse rolled his eyes. "On my own?"

"All on your own," Palet said. "You see anyone, shoot, but not the kid. Understand that. I want him alive."

"But"—Alphonse said hopefully—"shouldn't I be with you? I mean, we're getting a bit strung out, aren't we."

"Would you sooner be strung *up*?" Palet asked.

"Boss!" Alphonse made a feeble effort to make that remark seem like a joke, knowing that it wasn't. "I just mean . . ." He made a final bid to avoid the terror of being left alone in the wilderness and the night, with a gigantic, homicidal Italian roaming around loose—his own forte being roaming around himself, beating up defenseless civilians. "Just, well, he could be anywhere, couldn't he?"

"No!" Palet stood on the platform, as intent as a spider. The line ran north and south, barely visible for more than a hundred meters or so in each direction. A bitter, gusting wind was blowing up the valley from Chamonix but Palet was hardly aware of it. He faced the wind, his head cocked in a sinister manner, as if his neck was broken, listening. There was the steady gush of the river, the sound of falling water from innumerable streams and waterfalls, and the woods were beginning to sigh as the wind ruffled their boughs. "He's here," he said. "He's down the line. I'll get you, Italian!" he yelled. "And the Jew bastard! Do you hear me? *Get you!*"

He swung on his heel and walked to the car, Alphonse following him. "Where will you be, boss?" Alphonse asked.

"Up at that Vallorcine place," Palet said. "Make sure

everywhere is guarded. I wouldn't trust those gendarmes to catch a —— rabbit." He opened the car door and laughed his weird laugh, like a dying man's last convulsive rattle. "Be funny, wouldn't it—if he jumped out of the dark and strangled you?" He stopped laughing. "And if he does get past you, you'll wish you had been. Strangled at birth—" slamming the car door shut with the clunk of an executioner's ax.

23

Not much more than a hundred meters from the station, Salvani was crouching in a thicket, with his strength and the wind at his back, having covered the eight kilometers at a lumbering trot, even with Judah slung over his shoulder like a bag of potatoes.

And lucky again, he thought. Two minutes earlier and he would have walked straight into trouble. But unlucky, too; somehow the cops had got on his trail. Maybe the postman in Chamonix had turned informer, or the gendarme had spotted him going past the hospital . . . Not that it mattered now. What did matter was that the line was being guarded—and even more alarming, they knew just who they were looking for. And who the devil was that man who had shouted down the track? He had sounded crazy, a real madman . . . and what to do now?

Judah stirred in the bag and Salvani patted his head, his own face wrinkled in thought. If the line was being watched, then the road would be, too. The obvious thing was to get off both, but what then? He would be plunging about in some wilderness and as likely as not fall off some cliff and break both their necks, or, even worse, he might slip and break a leg and lie, helpless, in some godforsaken gully, the two of them dying of exposure . . .

He peered through the bushes. The cop or soldier was walking up and down the platform of the station, but then he stopped, there was a crash of breaking glass, and the man disappeared.

"Well, well." Salvani clicked his teeth. The man had done what any guard with an ounce of sense would do—broken into a shelter, and if he had done so, there was a chance that the guard—if there was one—at the next station was doing the same. It was worth taking a chance on. He was going to break for the border that night, anyway—the stubborn strength of will and body which had brought him this far, a mere seven kilometers from Switzerland, driving him on as relentlessly as the wind.

"Judah." He peered into the sack. "Be quiet now. Very quiet."

Judah poked out his small face, pale even in the darkness. "I want to get out," he whispered. "I *have* to get out."

"Two minutes," Salvani muttered. "Two." He heaved up the sack and edged from the bushes. No sign of the guard, no crunch of boots on gravel, no roar of motorcars—the only sounds those of the restless wilderness as he shoved his way through bushes and shrubs, past the station, back onto the railway line, walked on fifty or sixty meters more, then pulled Judah from the sack.

Judah slipped from his grip, bolted into a clump of grass, and reappeared, wide-eyed. "I nearly—" he began.

"Yes." Salvani grinned. "But you didn't." He jammed the long-dead child's hat on Judah's head and buttoned up the long-dead child's coat, as he did so feeling cold hands on his cheeks.

"Uncle," Judah said. "Are we nearly there?"

"Yes." Salvani wrapped a scarf around Judah's neck, shielding him from the bitter wind and gusting rain with his broad back. "Nearly somewhere nice and warm with nice people—and lights, all the lights shining. You'll like that, won't you?"

"Ye . . . es." Judah tugged his hat down. "And will Papa be there—where the lights shine?"

On his knees, Salvani held Judah by the shoulders, his rough hands almost enveloping the child. "Yes," he said, "he'll be there."

"Promise?" Judah said.

Salvani turned his face away, the icy rain striking his unyielding face. "Promise," he said, rummaging in the bag for his own uniform, that shield, he devoutly hoped, against the bullets of a firing squad. But as he bent to unlace his boots, gunshots cracked, and leaving the uniform, he grabbed Judah, lunging away with every ounce of his awkward power, leaving behind, too, Alphonse, who, cowering in the station, had heard the sound of his private nightmare, the Italian, lurching at the door, and in a panic had blasted away, charging blindly out of his corner, shooting and cursing, until he saw a broken bough, swept by the wind, clattering along the platform.

Vomiting with fear, Alphonse, the terror of the Jews and all their conspirators, spewed onto the railway line. North of him, Salvani and Judah, a simple man and a child, under the scudding moon and inky clouds, and vast, insensate mountains, ran toward the land of lights as, behind them, the raw, jagged edge of the killing machine of Nazi Germany, the army patrol, a huge Alsatian dog snarling before it, was coming up from Chamonix through the valley, where nervous gendarmes were jumping at every shadow, and villagers, sitting with shotguns across their shaking knees, waited for the terrifying Italian monster to crash through their doors intent on mangling them—and ahead of the man and the child, a mere three kilometers away, lounging by a glowing stove in the stationmaster's office at Vallorcine, were the inspector from Chamonix, a French customs official, a languid German lieutenant, and Palet, he prowling about the room, peering through the window, going to the door, back to the window . . .

"Monsieur," the inspector said. "Why not sit down? We've done all we can."

"All?" Palet peered through the window.

"Yes. If the man is trying for Switzerland he has to come this way and the road is guarded, the railway line, and the tunnel outside Montroc. I tell you he's trapped."

"Trapped?" Palet wiped his mouth and smeared his hand over his raincoat. "What about him going over the mountains, hey? What about that?"

The inspector choked back his exasperation and grimaced at the customs officer.

"The mountains . . ." The officer, bored, having said the same thing twice, opened his hands to demonstrate the absurdity of the idea.

"Smugglers cross them," Palet said.

The officer shrugged. "They know every inch of the terrain, but on a night like this even they wouldn't try to cross. Believe me, your man can't possibly get over."

Palet stopped his pacing. "This man"—he nodded, his head jerking up and down as if operated by clockwork—"he's *crossed* mountains. Mountains and rivers. Yes, yes," he mumbled. "And gone through cordons. Yes! He's like"— he twisted his head, listening again to the distant funeral march—"like an invisible man!"

The three other men covertly exchanged glances, but Palet, with antennae as sensitive to slights as a cockroach to light, saw them.

"You don't believe me. But I *know* him."

"Know him!" The inspector was indignant. "You've met him?"

"Not met him." Palet leaned forward. "But I dream about him, lots of times. I'm going to stop that, him coming into my dreams. It's not right. They're my dreams, aren't they?"

The inspector moved uneasily. "Be calm," he said. "He may be a murdering pervert but he's only a man."

"Is he?" Palet swung his head for a moment or two, then put on his hat, went to the door, and grabbed the handle.

The inspector stood up. "Where are you going?"

"Back to Argentière," Palet said. "He's out there somewhere . . . wandering . . ."

"If you want to—" The inspector shrugged. "But better take a man with you, there's a German patrol out there. They're likely to shoot first and ask questions afterward— excuse me for saying so." He nodded at the lieutenant.

"Quite all right." The lieutenant stirred himself, slightly, from his languor. "It's what they're for. I'll let you have a man."

"You wouldn't have one that spoke French?" The inspector spoke more in hope than expectation, but was surprised by the answer.

"They all do, more or less. We're an Alsace regiment. Mülhausen, everyone there speaks some French. The border, you know." The lieutenant went out with Palet, barked a command or two, and returned to the stove, stretching out long jackbooted legs. "Bitter out there. Sleet, some snow. Your man must be keen on his work."

The inspector crouched forward confidentially. "Mad," he said, pointing significantly at his temple. "Absolutely nuts."

"Oh?" The lieutenant drew his legs back and sat upright, casual and languid no longer. "I wouldn't say that, monsieur, I wouldn't say that at all. He's after a Yid, isn't he?"

A dour corporal beside him, Palet crashed his car into gear and drove off through the silent houses of Vallorcine, the corporal, for all his dourness, wincing as Palet slid the car through a wild defile and swung around appalling curves, the car slithering within centimeters of the rocks, and sighing with relief as Palet, brakes squealing like a stuck pig, jammed the car to a halt at the station of Argentière.

302

"Boss?" an anxious voice called. "Is that you, boss?"

"No, it's the king of the —— fairies." Palet strode along the platform. "Have you seen anything?"

"Not a thing, boss." Alphonse shivered. "I've been out here since you left. And"—lying stoutly—"I've been down the line, and nothing. Nothing at all. And I'd have seen them, believe me."

"Would you, now?" Palet looked around. The clouds had broken before the wind, and the moon, as cold as a serpent's eye, illumined a phantasmagoria of vast blue-shadowed snow fields, icy peaks jabbing at the sky; huge shards of rock, as black as jet, slashed across the snow, and blacker forests of pine and larch tossed their heads restlessly, as might a herd of animals aware of wolves howling around them.

"Would you," Palet said again, prowling down the platform. "And would you have heard them? Hey!" He turned, himself, in his white raincoat and shadowed features, like a creature of the night, a figure from a dream, or a nightmare, on the bare, windswept platform, his head tilted.

"Boss." Alphonse backed away as Palet minced toward him. "I just—Christ, watch out!"

He ducked away into the shadows of the station as the German corporal swung up his rifle.

"*Da!*" the Corporal shouted. "*Da—là!*"

Palet swung around, dropping to one knee, his pistol out. Up the line, something moved along the track, something dark and large. "Got you!" Palet screamed. "Got you," blasting away with the pistol, aimlessly and futilely, the shape, Palet's worst dreams come true, leaping and writhing until a venomous crack from the corporal's rifle brought it down.

"Yes!" Palet stumbled forward up the track, his mouth dribbling, his pistol held out erect, his throat engorged, firing shot after shot, until, as the hammer of his gun clicked on an empty chamber, he came to the shape, kicking and stamping and cursing until he was pulled back.

"It's just a sack," the corporal said. "Look." He bent down and picked up the shape. "A postman's bag." He held it up. "Blown by the wind."

But he was talking *to* the wind. Palet snatched the sack and prowled back to the platform and Alphonse.

"You see?" Palet said calmly. "You see? It's the postman's sack and an Italian uniform. It's the Italian. He went past you. And the Jew kid."

"Boss." Alphonse held out his hands. "You can't see everything. You know?"

"Can't?" Palet slashed the pistol across Alphonse's face. "You didn't see that, either, did you?"

Alphonse staggered back, clutching his face, blood spurting through his fingers as the German soldier looked on indifferently.

"Start walking," Palet said to Alphonse. "Up the line. Get going!" He raised his hand again.

"Going! Going!" Alphonse jabbered. He wiped his bloody cheek and dropped off the platform onto the track. "Where will I meet you, boss?"

Palet stared down, longing to kick Alphonse in the face, but his rage for the moment blown over, controlling himself. "Montroc," he said. "The next station."

Alphonse shambled away and Palet watched for a second, then raised his eyes to where, beyond Montroc, a wall of cliff, black and silver in the fleeting moonlight, barred the end of the valley and the way to Switzerland. "Montroc," he said again and, the silent soldier at his heels, went to the car.

Salvani was looking at the cliffs, too, but on the far side of Montroc station, which he had passed through without any difficulty, dodging across a meadow and through a copse and onto the line again. But now he was pondering his problem.

To the right there was a road, but from his map Salvani

knew that it didn't go very far and, anyway, led to a remote frozen wasteland. There was a road to his left, also, but that ran into Vallorcine, the cops, and a firing squad. Behind him were more cops and the weird figure he had heard cursing into the night, and before him . . . He stared at the cliff again. The moon shone, went out, gleamed again as inky, ragged clouds scurried across it. Hailstones slashed across his back in a blast of wind strong enough to make him stagger a step forward, and almost taking Judah sailing with the clouds, until Salvani grabbed his collar.

No way over the cliffs in weather like this, Salvani thought, and looked again at his problem.

The railway line, his friendly guide from Chamonix, ran forward, heading to the border, but, now turning treacherous, led into a tunnel.

Salvani stared at the tunnel, and like a monstrous eye the tunnel stared back, as if challenging Salvani to enter, to go in out of the rain and the sleet, to take a step, and another, a few more, a hundred, and then to find out what might be lurking in the darkness . . . and Salvani knew what would be there—a guard, of that he was certain, but there was a chance that the guard would have ducked into a shelter . . . Sleet, as sharp as needles, slashed across his neck; Judah whimpered and Salvani picked him up with his strong right arm and slowly walked toward the tunnel, as if impelled not merely by the wind and fear but by some more indifferent force which moved poor wretches on the frayed and tattered hem of creation with the same detachment as it moved the farthest stars in the uttermost vacant silence of the heavens.

"Uncle." Judah tugged at Salvani's collar. "Uncle, are we going in there?"

"Yes." Salvani clutched Judah tighter. "But don't be afraid. We're going to the lights. And when you see lights, run. Do you understand? Run."

"Run to Papa?"

"Yes. Run to the lights and Papa." Staking his life, Salvani took a few more steps, said, *"Ayin hara,"* and entered the tunnel.

The tunnel was full of eerie sounds; water trickling down the walls, dripping from the roof, curious small clickings and clatterings, strange muted echoes, as if men were whispering furtively in the darkness . . . Step by step they went forward, the tunnel being longer than Salvani had guessed, and darker, like a coal mine. Maybe it curved, he thought—and then it was bright, brighter than he had thought possible. A huge light shone, dazzling him; a harsh voice shouted *"Halt! Halt!"* and Judah, seeing light, wriggled from Salvani's arms like an eel and ran forward, shouting "Papa! Papa!"

"Was? was?" The light dipped onto Judah as he clutched the soldier's legs, then swung up again, pinioning Salvani. *"Was ist das Papa?"*—What is this Papa? as Judah, squealing "Uncle," was hauled off his feet. *"Was ist das Papa?"* the voice demanded.

Helpless with Judah in the enemy's grasp, Salvani raised his hands. *"Kein Deutsch,"* he said, using the only German he knew.

"French?" the voice said in a deep guttural accent. "You speak French?"

"Yes," Salvani said.

"Hands up!" The light glared in Salvani's eyes. "Hands higher. No tricks."

"No tricks," Salvani said, wondering how best to jump the man, since he was holding a rifle, Judah, and a light, and presumably had only two arms—but then he was jabbed in the chest by a bayonet. Smart, Salvani thought vaguely. The light was lashed to the rifle muzzle.

"Uncle!" Judah squawked, sounding half strangled.

"Don't hurt the child," Salvani said. "Let me have him, hey?"

"I'll let you have a —— bullet," the soldier growled, but his voice, still harsh, sounded puzzled. "What's this uncle stuff?"

"I . . ." Salvani was almost listless. "I've been looking after him."

"Yes?" The man was skeptical, but his voice still had a note of something like uncertainty. "I thought—well, get moving. Carry the kid, but one false move—understand?" He half threw Judah forward.

"Yes, I understand," Salvani said. He took a shocked Judah in his arms and tramped along the tunnel, the clump of the German's boots echoing behind him, until he saw an arc of pallid light. The moon, he thought. Light at the end of the tunnel, that's what they say; all I need now is a train to come belting in . . . Made a big mistake; should have jumped the German while he was distracted by Judah. Should never have entered the tunnel; should never have done a lot of things . . . Should have stayed at home . . .

"Halt!" the voice rasped. "Against the wall."

Salvani halted and backed against the side of the tunnel. It was surprisingly light here, the moonlight slanting through the arch, and for the first time Salvani saw his captor, a burly man like himself, jackboots, a greatcoat buttoned to the neck, his face a black mask under a steel helmet, the very image of a superman, and the rifle, a savage bayonet . . .

"So what now?" he asked.

The soldier's bayonet waved slightly and Salvani felt a flicker of hope. Do that again, he thought, just a bit more, and I'll jump you—at least give Judah a chance to run—although to where he couldn't think.

"The kid," the soldier said.

"What about him?" Salvani asked.

"Why did he shout Papa?"

"He thought you were his father," Salvani said. "It was the light . . ."

"What's light got to do with it?" The soldier sounded more than puzzled, baffled almost. "And this uncle stuff?"

"I've been looking after him," Salvani said, wearily. "I

307

told him that when he saw the lights he'd meet his father. In Switzerland. That's all."

"He's well dressed. Warm clothes."

"Stole them." Salvani lied to the last.

"And is that right, you're taking him over the border?"

"Trying to," Salvani said. "Might have made it, too, if you hadn't shown up." A flake of rock was sticking into his back and he moved his shoulders. This must be what it's like, standing before a firing squad, he thought—looking at oblivion and worrying about a scratch; and I'm having a rehearsal.

"I don't get this . . ." The soldier hesitated. "They said that you were . . ."

"What?" Salvani asked.

The soldier shook his masked head, his bayonet, unwavering now, pressed forward.

"Let the child go," Salvani said. "Let him."

"Don't be ridiculous," the soldier said.

"Look at him." Salvani held out Judah, who suddenly thrust out his hand, two fingers jabbing forward, and shouted, *"Ayin hara!"* then turned and clutched Salvani around the neck.

"Ayin hara?" The soldier took a step back. "What does that mean?"

"It's a spell," Salvani said. "In his language. It's to drive away evil spirits."

The soldier was silent for a long moment. The wind blew cold through the tunnel with its mysterious sounds and sinister echoes, then "It works," he said.

"What?" Salvani could not believe what he was hearing.

"Come on." The soldier, his voice still harsh, lowered his rifle, stepped from the arch, looked cautiously around, then beckoned Salvani to follow him. "Lucky for you," he said, "there's two of us. We tossed a coin who should stand guard first. The other guard's kipping in a shed up there, and he's a real Nazi bastard."

"You mean . . ." Salvani was incredulous.

"I mean get going." The soldier, still faceless under his helmet, spat. "I was in Poland and saw what happened to kids. We're not all—*ach!*" He broke off and spat. "You can't make it down the line. It goes straight into Vallorcine and that's sewn up tight. But listen, when we got sent up here, a French customs man showed me something. There's a way around. A smugglers' trail."

"A trail?" Salvani stared down the railway line, which ran through a mere slot blasted through vertical crags.

"Yes." The soldier was hurried, turning his head to the tunnel, listening. "About seven hundred meters on your right you'll see a concrete pillar painted red and white. It shows you're near the frontier. There's a huge boulder next to it—a big one—and behind it there's a sort of gap. Get through it and you can work your way up the cliffs. I'll tell you straight, I wouldn't fancy trying it in *daylight*, but it takes you around Vallorcine and over the border." He turned again and stared into the tunnel.

"What can I say?" Salvani shifted Judah to his left arm and held out his right hand.

"Don't say anything." The soldier ignored the proffered hand. "Don't ever say anything about this to anyone at any time. If you get picked up, say you got over the top. Now beat it. *Schnell. Vite.*"

He made a mock jab with his bayonet and without another word strode into the tunnel, Salvani staring after him, for all the bitter cold, sweating, and for all his steady nerves, shivering, both at his luck and at his escape, but also with a sense of sick futility that his life, and Judah's, had depended on the flip of a coin, but then, shaking off all thoughts but that of survival, he lumbered down the railway line, as, behind him, Palet and the German corporal were entering the tunnel.

24

There had been no guard at Montroc: no German soldier in jackboots, no gendarme longing for a cozy back room in a café; only the deserted station, its gutters running with rain, and its silence broken by Palet's curses as he prowled up and down the platform.

"The guard!" He spat and dribbled. He swung around, glaring at the corporal. "Where's the —— guard!"

The corporal, hard as a rock, callous, indifferent to non-German life, steeped to the elbows in the blood of Polish and Russian men, women, and children, Jews and Gentiles alike, and regarding Palet as only a little above Slavs in the human species, resentful at being under his command but obedient to his own orders, finally broke his silence.

"What's the point in having one here? The road, it doesn't go anywhere but up there"—he jerked his thumb to a vast snow field surrounded by peaks as black and rotten as a rabid dog's teeth—"and the tunnel is guarded, so . . ."

"The tunnel . . ." Palet muttered. He thought of a black hole, like a sewer, where rats hid and scurried . . .

"It's guarded," the corporal said.

"Guarded? This man—" Palet had a vision of Salvani, a monstrous ape, literally an ape, with bloody eyes and yellow fangs, scuttling down the tunnel, strangling the sentries, breaking their necks with hairy hands . . . and with the Jew kid, dragging millions of francs with him. "You don't know this man." He pushed his face against the corporal's.

The corporal put his hand on Palet's chest and shoved him away, thinking, Try to hit me as you did that mug in Argentière and I'll blow your head off. "He's a Wop with a Yid. He's holed up somewhere around here. Call the men and beat the place out."

"No, no, no." Palet shook his head, more of a convulsive jerking than that of a reasonable man disagreeing. "He's not stopping here. He's—" He raised his head. The shredded clouds had gone, torn into rags by the wind, stars as bright and sharp as any diamonds pricked the night beyond the cold moon. "He's going to break out to the border."

"All right." The corporal tugged his collar tighter. "Let's go there," swinging on his heel and making for the car.

"No." Palet had his pistol out, refilling the chamber with cartridges. "This way. The tunnel."

The corporal stared at Palet with murderous disgust but, *Befehl ist Befehl*—orders are orders—and, maybe, just maybe, the filthy Frenchman was right, and it would be something to have caught the Wop and more especially the Yid. There could be a promotion in that, leave, anyway, and at least it would give him something to brag about back home. "Right," he said, following Palet up the track, to the tunnel, but wise in the ways of trigger-happy sentries on dark nights, he yelled, *"Deutsche Soldaten! Deutsche Soldaten hier,"* and went on yelling it, his rifle cocked, his voice echoing down the tunnel, until a harsh voice ordered "Halt!"

"Nothing?" Palet said.

"Nothing," the guard said woodenly.

"Nothing at all? You're sure of that? Sure?"

"Not a thing."

Palet raised his hands and wandered from the tunnel, muttering obscenities, but the corporal stepped in his shoes, as it were, standing in front of the guard.

"Where's Hoffman?" he demanded.

"Corporal"—the guard spoke from the corner of his mouth—"in a shed. For Christ's sakes, what's the point in us both being out here? We're taking turns, that's all."

The corporal stared hard into the sentry's face. "You sure—no one's come through?"

"Well, you couldn't actually miss them, could you?" the guard said. "In fact, I wish they had come through. We could all get back to our beds."

"Right." The corporal called to Palet, trying without much success to be ingratiating. "Should we get the car? Drive back, cover the road?"

"No."

"No!" The corporal was astonished. "Not go back?"

Palet shook his head. "We're going on." He stared around at the black gorge and whispered to the corporal, "He's here."

"Here?" The corporal started, and unslung his rifle.

"He's crossed over," Palet said.

"Not through the tunnel, unless he's invisible," the corporal said. "And not over it, unless he can fly—what are you laughing for?"

"Maybe he can." Palet gave a strange whinnying laugh, a hand on the bolt of his rifle.

"Take it easy. Let's just calm down here. Flying . . ."

"Flying?" Palet stopped laughing. "Of course he can't fly. He's a man. Just a man. But he's cunning . . ." His voice faded away as he peered around the gorge again. "Cunning and quick—like this!" He drew his pistol with the speed of a snake and shot into the night. "See! *Quick.* Come on—it's as near this way to Vallorcine as going back."

The pistol shot echoed off the cliff as Palet slouched forward, his pistol swinging, the corporal keeping a safe distance at his rear, and four hundred meters above them, on a ledge slippery with sleet, clutching Judah with one hand and a gnarled bush with the other, Salvani stared down.

312

Christ, Salvani thought, looking at the man in the flapping white raincoat, you're the lunatic in the station! Still after me, like a bloodhound! Came through the tunnel—but the guard had kept his mouth shut, at that. Something, really something, and his luck holding out. Yes.

Gripping the bush with a hand of iron, and Judah too, he poked out a foot and found another ledge, wide as a tabletop and safe as houses, and stepped onto it, swinging Judah with him, thinking, Lucky again, it never occurring to him that if he had been dealt a lucky card or two it might be because of his own enduring, and simple, goodness.

"Right, Judah," he grunted. "Right, come on, little one," finding another broad ledge, and secure behind a jutting edge of rock, steps which might have been chopped out by humans; heaving himself and the child up those to a recess almost deep enough to be a cave.

"Here." He stopped and pummeled Judah. "Got to get you warm, hey? Now come on, that's a good boy. Let's move on a bit. Just a bit more."

Judah's collar in his grip, they did move on a bit, and a bit more, the moon steady now, lighting their way, but dangerously at times, as when Salvani mistook a shadow for a ledge and found himself teetering on the brink of seven hundred meters of sheer rock, and treacherously beautiful, too—a haze, delicate as lace, turning into an ice-cold veil of water, drenching Salvani, but he saving Judah from the worst, swinging him over his shoulder—blessing Madame for giving the child waterproof clothing.

"*Avanti, avanti*"—On, on—Salvani shook himself like a huge dog and moved on, step by slanting step, slicing his hand on a razor-sharp shard but not caring because under his elbow, as it were, but a thousand meters of blanched rock below, across a railway line, glistening in the moonshine, and across a gleaming road, was a small town.

"It's Vallorcine." Salvani paused and automatically rubbed Judah's ears and nose. And it could only *be* Vallorcine, the last town in France, the last town in the darkness,

313

the last town of the torture chambers, and the last town where the New Order ruled, and the last town where dogs tore people apart, mother was dragged from child, father from mother, husband from wife, and all from the realm of humanity.

"Right!" Salvani gave Judah a last, brisk rubbing. "Three kilometers. Three," holding up three fingers, thinking, That's not far, a walk with the wife to the cinema, a stroll in the park with the kids, nothing, even if you're climbing up a mountain like a mountain goat, turning an awkward corner—and coming to a buttress.

It jutted out from the mountain, pinnacled and wrinkled, leprous white, split with shadows, every meter of it seeming to say "Come along and try me—and fall off!" and the trail ended.

Salvani groaned, from the depth of his very being, as if his rib cage was breaking like the beams of a very old house. Was this it? he wondered. Had his luck finally run out— the dealer giving him, on the brink of triumph, a blank card—or had the sentry been playing some vicious joke on him . . . But surely not. Surely.

He looked again at the pillar of rock—withered, mummified. One of the shadows looked deeper than the others, as if the buttress had sagged away from the mountain. If . . . and a big if, Salvani thought, *if* there was a route dodging the buttress, that had to be it—some sort of chimney— and once in it he was confident he could get up. The trouble being that to get to it meant taking a huge stride, almost a jump, into the shadows and maybe into a void; meant making an act of faith; but if smugglers had used the trail they must have got up somehow . . . He wiped his forehead, to go on or go back? Go back or go on? And he made up his mind.

"Judah." He crouched down. "Listen, chick. I'm going to jump into that shadow there, see. It's the way up the mountain. But listen—if I slip—you know, if I fall—"

"Fall!" Judah's eyes opened wide, terrified.

"Ha ha!" Salvani forced a croaking laugh. "I'm not going to, of course not. But just in case, just in case, that's all—you go *back*. It won't be hard except for the waterfall, but just be brave there and you'll be all right, and—" And what, he wondered. "And run to the tunnel and see the nice man there. But go back, you understand. Don't stay here. Promise?"

Judah stared at Salvani, then looked down the mountainside and said with maddening irrelevance, "But we've just come up!"

"I know!" Salvani choked back fear, dismay, the horrible thought that he was making the wrong decision. "But go back if I fall—" Then, knowing that if he waited any longer he would go back, too, stepped into the void, and, the smugglers knowing their business, found a spacious ledge.

From then on, it was easy. Salvani reached back and swung Judah up, and the rest of the chimney was no more difficult than climbing a stepladder, and they were free from prying eyes in Vallorcine, the smugglers having worked that out, too—and after a couple of hundred meters, like chimney sweeps of old times, they popped out at the top, and as flakes of snow, as delicate as apple blossom, touched their faces, they saw beneath them the railway line, the road, and, seeming almost within the grasp of a long arm, lights as steady as beacons on a rock-bound shore.

"And there it is!" Salvani stood triumphant on the mountaintop, clutching Judah's hand, the snow touching them, above the corrupt evils of the moral darkness of that other world, looking at light and lights and raising his fist in victory.

"See?" He held Judah up at the full stretch of his arms. "See, Judah, see the lights?"

Judah nodded but said, slowly, "We saw lights before, in the tunnel, but it wasn't Papa."

"No." Some of the elation drained from Salvani. "No, it wasn't. But he was a good man, and over there, in the lights, there's *lots* of good men. Lots. No bad men and—and"—thinking why spoil matters now?—"and we'll find your papa. Yes. So let's get there."

But, even with the Swiss border post tantalizingly near, getting to it was not as easy as Salvani had optimistically hoped. The trail climbed upward and away from the post, that being the smugglers' intention, and the snowflakes, so delicate and few, became thicker and more plentiful, sticking, not caressing, and the moon was back to its fugitive tricks, now shining, now not . . .

It was time to go down, but that was not so easy. The mountainside was seamed with gullies, but none of them looked passable, mere cracks flowing with water. Then they came to one that looked more promising, wider than the others, gushing with water but with broken sides and, a hundred meters or so down it, what might be bushes, which, after a cursing slither, proved to be just those, scrubby bushes clinging to a veneer of soil as tenaciously as Salvani and Judah clung to them, making their way down into the first pines and larches, sliding from tree to tree—the trees bigger as the slope gradually leveled—Salvani thinking of the last time he had plunged through a wood and come to a river—and finding as they came to the last trees another river, but not an evil one, not a man-killer, swift enough but shallow, wadable—across it the road and not one kilometer away the lights of a Swiss customs post, and not five hundred meters up the road, a red-and-white striped barrier.

Salvani ducked, dragging Judah with him and clamping his hand over Judah's mouth—and peered at the barrier. It was merely a pole across the road, but there were men standing by it, men in greatcoats and jackboots with steel helmets shining in the moonlight, and there was another man with them, distinctive in a white raincoat.

316

"Christ Almighty." Salvani scowled. "It's the loony. Again." The madman who had screamed at him down the track and fired at shadows outside the tunnel. "Christ," he said again, backing farther into the tree—his teeth bared and his hands clutching the air—looking, in fact, remarkably like the wild man of the woods who had haunted Palet's dreams. He backed away again, thinking: I'd like to get hold of you, wouldn't I just. It would be a long time before you walked around again; and thinking, too, that if they went back into the woods they could somehow slide along the edge of the river—dodging any German patrol hanging about in the woods, and cursing himself for not having followed the trail a little farther because then they would have crossed the border and—

And—he stared again at the barrier, and the men, one stamping his feet, another slapping his arms around his chest, another holding a ferocious dog on a lead, the lunatic in white . . . "Mary, Mother of God, and all the saints in heaven," he said, standing, picking up Judah, and laughing. "They're on the other side," he said. "The other side! We've crossed the border. We've done it! By Christ, we have!"

Laughing again, flushed with an innocent victory, he picked up Judah and strode from the shadows of the trees, plunged, hip deep, across the river, onto the road and into the moonlight, striding away from the hooked cross, like a poisonous spider, of the swastika and to the Red Cross of Switzerland, as behind him, in the land of darkness, the huge police dog strained at its leash, barking and snarling at his shadow, and Judah's, too.

"Da, da!" The dog handler pointed down the road.

"Was ist?" The languid lieutenant, alert, snapped a cigarette away.

"Der Kriegsgefangene," the dog handler shouted. *"Und der Yid."*

317

"Wo?" The lieutenant stuck his eager head forward.

"Dort! Unten am Weg—" The dog handler pointed down the road. *"Da: sehen sie?"*

"What?" Palet rushed to the barrier, shoving through the excited troops. "What is it?"

"Your man," the lieutenant shouted. "There, see? The man and the Yid."

"Ah! Ah!" Palet panted, like a man in ecstasy. "Where? Ahhh . . ." Seeing, striding up the road, silhouetted against the lights of the Swiss border post, the black shape of a man, hand in hand with a child. "Give me, give me!" he wrenched a rifle from a soldier and swung it to his shoulder, leaning on the pole, steadying himself and, as the hulk of the man who had invaded the deepest, most private recesses of his mind walked to the lights, getting him in his sights and thinking two shots would do, one for the man, one for the Jew kid, taking a breath—and having the rifle barrel knocked up by the lieutenant.

"You . . ." Palet brought the rifle down and stared at it as if it was some strange object which had fallen into his hands from outer space. "You—" He turned on the lieutenant, his face twitching.

"Are you crazy?" the lieutenant snapped. "Firing into neutral territory?"

"But"—bubbles of saliva formed on Palet's lips—"but he's there. Him and the Jew . . ."

"There's nothing we can do about it." The lieutenant handed the rifle to one of his men. "No interference with Swiss neutrality. Look." He patted Palet on the shoulder, man to man. "I know how you feel. One vermin has scuttled away. But don't worry, man. When it suits us we'll go in there and wipe them out. They're in a trap, anyway."

"No!" Palet stared over the lieutenant's shoulder, at the road, and the lights, and at the man and child nearing them. "You don't understand. The Jew kid—he's worth millions. Millions!"

"Oh?" The lieutenant dropped his friendly, reasonable, man-to-man attitude. "Is that what you're after? Money?"

"Millions, yes," Palet sprayed spittle over the officer. "And him, the Wop . . ."

The lieutenant pulled out a white handkerchief and wiped off Palet's spittle. "We're concerned with honor," he said, his voice cold. "With cleansing the race. With *purity*. But perhaps you can't understand that. Sergeant!" He swung away. "Normal duties," walking stiffly to his car and thinking what unutterable swine he had to deal with.

"So that's that." The inspector of police appeared at Palet's shoulder. "Pity, but there it is. We did the best we could. All cooperation. You'll remember that, won't you? Bit of a magician, that man. No disgrace, not catching him and the kid. Yes, well—" He placed his hand around his eyes, focusing down the moonlit road. "Going in now. All over. Er—" He glanced sideways at Palet, who was standing, hands on the pole, his mouth twitching. "You coming back to Vallorcine? Have a drink . . . Nothing to be done here . . . Well, suit yourself."

Cars started, coughing and wheezing—the French car, that is—doors slammed, men saluted, said good night. Palet stood, unmoving, as the snow began to whirl and dance and Salvani and Judah reached the Swiss frontier post, and under the lights were challenged, answered, and by an officer in immaculate white and blue ushered into a sparkling office where another officer, as spotless as the highest of his mountains, and as frigid, lost his composure as Salvani and Judah entered, like wraiths.

"What?" he said, a cigarette falling from his lips, spotting his spotlessness, as he saw, before his desk, a hulking blood-stained man and a tiny blood-smeared child. "What the devil!"

"Refugees." Salvani blinked in the light. "Refugees, sir. We've come"—he made a vague gesture and pulled Judah to him—"for sanctuary."

"Come!" The officer stared at Judah. "The child—his face!"

"Oh!" Salvani looked at Judah. "Oh, that. Sorry—" he said, not knowing why he was apologetic. "The blood. It must have come from this." He held out his slashed hand. "Sorry. But he's all right. Needs a wash and a good rest. Food. Sir, may we sit down?"

The officer tapped the table with a silver fountain pen. "The child." He looked at the first officer. "Wash him. Hot milk, soup."

"Thank you." Salvani, feeling oafish and filthy in the dazzling cleanliness of the room, gave a clumsy bow. "But look, sir, if I can do it? We've been through a lot and, well, tell the truth, I could do with a scrub-down, dry my clothes—"

"In a moment." The officer raised a manicured finger. "Take the child," he said to his colleague.

The officer put his hand on Judah in a paternal manner. "Come on, sonny," he said.

"Uncle!" Judah shoved away the officer.

"Uncle?" The senior officer lifted his head.

"I'll explain," Salvani said, hastily. "Go with the nice man, Judah. Go on. It'll do you good and I'll be here, just next door. Go on now."

Judah looked up solemnly, at Salvani, and at the two officers in turn, then beckoned Salvani, who stooped, listened to a whisper, then shook his head emphatically.

"No," he said, "these aren't the bad men. These are the good men. Now go and get dried before you catch your death of cold."

The officer took Judah by the hand and led him from the room as the senior officer tapped his silver pen, one end and then the other.

"Well," he asked as the door closed. "Uncle?" pointing to a hard wooden chair.

"It's like this." Salvani sank in the chair. "Any chance of a drink for me?"

320

"Yes." The officer was agreeable. "Hot milk or—" He reached into a drawer and took out a bottle of cognac, a glass, and cigarettes.

"I think the cognac," Salvani said. "Thanks very much." He took a mouthful, warmed to the marrow by it. "If I could get washed—"

"*Uncle*," the officer said. "Explain."

"Won't it wait," Salvani asked. "A minute or two."

"No," the officer said in a clipped voice.

"Well." Salvani shrugged. If the officer didn't mind blood all over his crisp office, it was all right with him; and he felt fine, the cognac warming him, hardly noticing his saturated trousers. "It's like this—" He told his story—artfully—leaving out what he thought that the Swiss had no need to know. "And that's that," he ended.

The tapping stopped and the officer stood up and went to the window, staring out to the other, dark border. "So that's what it was all about," he said, "the activity across there."

"I guess so," Salvani said. "Do you mind—" He gestured at the bottle.

"Help yourself." The officer turned around. "Your papers?"

Salvani shoved his hand into his inside pocket and pulled out his paybook. "See," he said.

"Yes." The officer took it. "Come with me," he said. "Bring your drink."

"Right!" Salvani said cheerily, stepping behind the officer, past a washroom, to another door.

"You'll have to wait in here for a little while," the officer said. "Just a formality, you know, while I write out your details."

"Sure." Salvani beamed. "Write on all you want," still beaming as the door clicked in his face, but the beam, or some of it, slipping as a key turned in a lock.

The customs officer dropped the key in his pocket, listened for a moment, went back into his room, stood at the window and stared again into the night, then picked up a telephone. "Yes," he said. "Martigny. Customs."

Salvani squatted in his room. There was no chair and, he realized, no window either, and the door, now he came to look at it, was stout. In fact, the room looked uncommonly like a prison cell; but he brushed that unpleasant thought aside. Just a storeroom, he guessed, and they probably had to stick him somewhere while they did their paperwork. In the meantime, he had drink, a whole bottleful, cigarettes, and—and again he felt a fierce pride: they'd made it! Him and a kid you could put in a pocket—beat the lot of them; the whole of France and the whole of Germany, too. Of course, he was interned, but that was better than some God-rotting German prisoner-of-war camp—*firing squad*—he reminded himself—and there was his family.

Well, he'd made that choice when he'd stolen the motorbike, and the wife and kids would be all right, fine, really—plenty of brothers and uncles to look after them. Probably be relieved to hear he was in Switzerland, and anyway, the Switzers—once some big shot heard his story, someone in the Red Cross, he'd be sent back home. No doubt about it, none whatever.

"Yes." He raised his glass in salute to Vito Salvani the brave—and Judah the brave, too—then cocked his head, listening.

A vehicle had pulled up outside, a truck by the sound of the engine. Doors slammed, there was the clatter of boots and a shouted order. For a moment Salvani felt a flutter of fear, then he relaxed. Just a vehicle to take him and Judah away into safety.

Got to get used to it, he thought. Get used to relaxing. Get used to feeling safe—raising his glass again as the door opened.

"Ah!" He scrambled to his feet, slightly lightheaded. "Ready, are we? Paperwork done?" Cheerfully following the junior officer back to the office and grinning at the senior man. "Where's Judah?" he asked.

"Eating," the man said, "while his clothes dry. We've talked to him."

"Good." Salvani raised the bottle. "Do you mind?"

"Not at all." The man waved to Salvani to sit. "Your story checks out. He doesn't say much, but—"

"Right." Salvani nodded. "He's learned to keep his mouth shut. A good little kid, though, isn't he?"

"Seems so," the man agreed. "You didn't tell us everything, though, either. For instance—" He raised his hand from a blotter.

Salvani stared down, baffled for a moment, then grinned. "Well, I'll be damned. He's still got those, hey? You know"—he shook his head—"he showed me those, well, a long time ago. Funny what kids hang on to, isn't it?"

"It is," the officer said. He picked up the blotter and poured the pebbles Salvani had last seen in the cave of Le Pic into a stout envelope. "Especially when they're diamonds."

"What!" Salvani raised his hand in disbelief. "They're diamonds!"

"Yes. Uncut, of course, and unpolished. But it's all right." The officer stuck the flap of the envelope down and stamped it with a heavy seal. "He won't be charged with smuggling. Probably get most of the value."

Half dazed but glowing with pleasure, Salvani smiled. "He'll be fine, then. At least he'll live well."

"I should think so." The officer strolled to a huge safe and stuck the envelope in it. "He'd be all right, anyway. There's the Red Cross, families that look after refugee children, and there's a Jewish Aid organization. Yes, he'll be fine. But you come along with me for a moment, will you?"

"Sure." Still grinning with delight, Salvani followed the officer through a side door into the customs shed—a long low counter for use in better times, a few sealed crates, boxes, and a third officer, who stood up casually and followed them through another door, out into the night, into a flurry of snow and onto the road.

"Here!" Salvani stopped dead. "What's this?"

Instantly his arms were pinioned, by experts, brawny policemen. "No good struggling," the officer said. "We'll club you if we have to."

"But—" Salvani felt himself being propelled forward, his arms twisted in elbow-breaking locks. "But I—look— Jesus! I'm a refugee!"

"No, you're not," the officer said. "You're an Italian soldier. A deserter. The border is closed to all combatants. Orders. I rang my boss in Martigny. He'll let the child in, but not you!"

"Not—" Salvani tried to dig his heels in, but arms as strong as his own forced him forward and two huge fists grabbed his collar.

"Come on," the officer said. "Come on. Walk like a man."

Palet stood at the French barrier, venomously balked. Unable to believe that his prey had slipped through his fingers, he stared balefully at the lights as if his glare could penetrate the building and destroy the Italian and the Jew kid. The wind blew bitterly through the mountain gap but he was unaware of it, listening to those distant muffled drums, which sounded now as if they were beating for his own funeral.

Finally he turned to go, to return to the darkness and the monsters who lurked there, monsters waiting to pounce on *him*—but as he turned, muttering obscenities, he took a last, bitter look, peered through a snow squall and cursed aloud, a malevolent cry of triumph, and darted into the sentries' hut.

"The dog," he shouted—screamed. "Bring it out!"

"What is it?" The German dog handler, his snarling brute bristling by his side, joined him at the barrier.

"There!" Palet jabbed a finger. "The Italian—" Saliva spurted from his mouth. "They're bringing him back! See! See? When the —— Swiss turn back, let the dog loose. You got that?"

"Got it," the dog handler said, as excited as Palet. "It'll get him. Yes. Heinie, Heinie." He rattled the dog's chain, the dog drawing back its muzzle, showing terrifying fangs, growling deep in its throat, and at another rattle of the chain thrusting forward, barking ferociously.

"Hear that? Do you?" Salvani tried to dig in his heels but was yanked forward, his toecaps scraping the ground. "That dog," he said desperately, "it's going to tear me to pieces."

"Yes," the officer said evenly. "They train them to do that."

"And that man"—step by step, his elbows and shoulder blades cracking, Salvani was forced forward—"that man in the white coat, he's crazy, a lunatic!"

"Milice, probably," the officer said. "I've been watching him for an hour. Halt!"

The guards stopped. There was a yellow line painted across the road. The officer put his toe on it. "This is the end of Swiss territory," he said. "The other side, from here to the barrier, is no man's land."

Salvani stared down, unable to believe that this was the end of his journey, that the travail of hundreds of kilometers should end here, that a scuffed strip of paint a few centimeters wide should separate him from security and . . . He looked up; not two hundred meters away, the man in the white coat stood waiting, and a soldier, and a huge dog, both men worse than the slavering brute.

"This should do it." The officer took out Salvani's paybook.

"Are you really—listen, let me try for the woods," Salvani made a last desperate plea.

"Shut up," the officer said. Then: "Now!"

He ripped up the paybook and threw the leaves into the

air as Salvani was shoved forward across the line and then, amazingly, inexplicably, was hauled back.

The officer watched the pages of the paybook flutter away in the wind and the snow. "That should attend to the formalities," he said.

"I don't—" The grip on Salvani's arms relaxed, a large hand patted him on the back, one of the guards laughed. "I don't understand!" Salvani said. "What's—why . . . ?" His knees almost giving away.

"It's simple, really," the officer said. "Sorry about the pantomime, but we had to do it. An Italian combatant came and was turned back. Then a French civilian, a post-man, came for political asylum." He dusted snow off Salvani's shoulder. "This is a postman's uniform, isn't it? So come on."

At the barrier, Palet, his mouth agape, like the dog, couldn't believe what he was seeing. The men were turning, walking back . . . "You!" he screamed. "You! That man is a . . ." He ducked under a barrier, his pistol out, screaming meaningless curses and blasphemies blown away by the wind, but stopping dead as the Swiss officer and the guards swung on their heels, guns pointing.

"This man is on Swiss territory," the officer called. "And under Swiss protection. One step more and we shoot to kill. Back—get back." His gun steady as Palet, whimpering, let his arm fall, watching with dead eyes as the men, Salvani safely in their midst, turned and walked up the road, the officer saying, "Funny, really, it was the dog that saved you. Those savages always overstep the mark"—chuckling with quiet satisfaction as they strolled to the customs post and to Judah, waving at them from the light.

FINIS

FIC   50621
CAR   Carter, Peter

           The hunted

$17.00

		DATE DUE		